Cursed

Brent Miller

Other books by Brent Miller
The Z Virus: Outbreak

Riva,
Thanks for the support and for
being a great friend!. I hope you
enjoy!. Brianna

Prologue

Garrick watched with despair as the moon rose into the sky, once again sealing his fate. Though he hated what he was going to become, he'd nearly given up fighting it. He knew he would never win, and all it caused was more agony. So he followed his friends to the woods – all of them walking in a group – repeatedly scanning the area, assessing his surroundings with each new step. Garrick hadn't seen anyone for a mile, but he wanted to be sure that there were no people anywhere he would feasibly travel. One thing he always knew he could trust was Aldric's desire to keep them as far away from people as possible. It was vital to protect the public, of course, but themselves as well. Still, he couldn't fight his instincts of confirming there was no one Aldric missed. To Aldric, it was about the pack, and Garrick couldn't shake the feeling that collateral damage may be an acceptable price of keeping them alive.

"Here," Aldric growled. The pack all spread out, giving themselves space as the moon climbed toward its zenith. Garrick watched as the silvery orb pushed its way higher in the sky. As a child, he'd always looked upon that same sight with joy and wonder. The beauty of the full moon shining, illuminating the night sky, had filled him with a sense of mysticism. It wasn't until recently that his perceptions had been shattered. All he could see now was grey. Gloom and darkness. As if the moon itself had lost its shine.

Aldric was the first to change, as always. He was the largest and most powerful of the pack, and Garrick could only assume that helped expedite the process. Whatever beast lurked under Aldric's skin was strong, so pushing its way to the surface was simple. Of course, it was bound to help that he did nothing to try to stop it. His teeth grew sharper, and his hair longer. His nails sharpened into claws as he cracked his neck, breaking the bones to allow them to reform according to his new shape. A slight pain was visible on his face – it seemed to be impossible to avoid that. His entire body was breaking down and being built back up. Even the strongest man would hurt. The pain was to be expected, but what was unsettling to Garrick was the pleasure. Aldric liked what was happening.

Cailean and Brooke seemed to be one as their bodies started to twitch. They both fell to their knees violently, trying to fight the convulsions that came with the horrifying expansion of bone and muscle. Garrick couldn't tell what made their transformations so much more violent than Aldric's. Maybe it was just time and experience. They fought back the screams of agony, probably more concerned about appearances than anything else. Cailean wanted to look strong, and Brooke just didn't want to look weak.

Cailean bit his lip, and Garrick watched as the teeth grew sharper and punctured the skin. As the wound started to bleed, his mouth elongated to allow for the new teeth, slowly forming a snout. Cailean's arms bulged, muscles shaping themselves around his already chiseled physique. With a loud snap, Cailean's legs twisted out of their sockets, and he dropped to the ground, unable to support himself on broken knees. His hands spasmed as he curled them into fists, probably digging claws deep into his palms.

Brooke finally released her pent-up scream as she dropped to the ground. She threw her palms out to catch herself, refusing to collapse. When her palm hit the ground, though, there was no semblance of humanity. A light coating of fur had covered her hands, and her fingers shrunk back as the hand itself grew into a paw. Her legs reshaped along with her arms. Her toes stretched, allowing her to stand again – her toes and front paws on the floor.

Hayden gave a short half smile to Garrick. She watched as he turned away and slammed a fist into a tree. The wood cracked, and Garrick almost feared it would fall over. She knew how much he hated it, and he could feel that she at least didn't get the same sick pleasure that Aldric did. But she didn't fight it; she never did. Not like him.

She screamed. She'd always had the lowest pain tolerance of any of them. Whether she wanted to or not, she couldn't handle the transformation like the others could. Watching the agony on her face just made the entire process worse for Garrick. He hated seeing her like that almost as much as he hated the monsters they all became. After the change, though, she was one of the more powerful wolves, only bested by Aldric and Cailean. Garrick wondered if that was part of what made the change so hard on her.

Hayden's eyes lightened. All the light that the moon had lost had been stolen by her eyes, which shone a lighter, more brilliant blue than he'd ever seen. She dropped to all fours as her back broke. Garrick could see the curvature change as it started to reform, and it elongated, protruding from her body. Though the process was fast, he was able to not only distinctively see the bone, but to watch as muscle, flesh, and finally fur surrounded her new tail. Her face twisted as it grew and stretched, and her ears grew to a point as fur coated them.

Garrick felt the beast pushing its way to the surface. He fought it with all the might he could muster, but he could practically feel claws scratching at his insides. It felt as if the beast threatened to tear him apart, taking his body by force. He saw his pack, three of them roaming around him; waiting for him to give up.

He could see miles away, picking up the slightest movements through the trees. And he could actually smell the town, although they were far enough out to be confident none of them would go there in the night. They'd be scared off by the lights and sounds, even of a sleeping town. Still, he could smell gasoline as cars drove, and if he tried, he could even hear the voices of people wandering the streets. They lived in a world he'd taken for granted – but would give anything to get back. The city taunted him with the life he'd lost, the smells and sounds of a world he used to call home.

"I know it's hard, Garrick," Chase said, placing a hand on Garrick's shoulder and pulling him out of his self-pity. He was the only one who shared Garrick's hatred of the monsters that hid beneath the surface. "We just have to trust Aldric." Garrick had trouble with the concept of blind trust. On nights when the moon was full, he lived in constant fear of harming the innocent. How could he wipe those fears away and simply trust someone who didn't seem to care?

Chase removed his hand from Garrick's shoulder quickly as he clenched his teeth and fists. Garrick watched as his jaw expanded, but Chase didn't make a sound. He wasn't the strongest of them all, but he was the best at biting back the pain. He wouldn't let it show – that was a victory that he always tried to keep over the wolf. Even so, Garrick could see it in his eyes. Chase's hands began to bleed as his fingernails grew, but he refused to open his fists.

Garrick felt his own canines forcing their way out, and tears formed in his eyes. Not from the pain, but from his defeat. It was only a matter of time. Before the change started, he was able to hold on to the admittedly delusional idea that he could stop it. As soon as his body started to transform, though, he knew there was no going back.

He dropped to the ground, falling to his hands and knees. Hayden inched closer to him, and she snuggled her body closer to his. She could sense his pain, both physical and emotional. Of course, as bones were ripped out of their sockets and muscles and tendons were torn, anyone could pick up on it. As his calcaneal tendon snapped, an earsplitting sound, almost like a gunshot, reverberated through the woods. He could see sadness on Hayden's face, but she just nuzzled her head against him.

Garrick's shirt was torn, and he watched as the three lines – the scar that had ruined his life – were slowly covered by hair. He saw the muscles in his arms expand and felt them as they tore and reformed.

His shoulders dislocated, and he dropped to the ground, unable to hold himself up any longer. He still had some illusion that he could keep it out, but no matter how much he fought, it never stopped anything. It just made the change – and the pain that came with it – last longer.

He could tsee Hayden's pleading eyes, begging him to just let go. Aldric had disapproval in his gaze. Cailean was already gone, and Brooke was sniffing for prey. Chase stood tall at Garrick's other side, as if attempting to give Garrick the strength he clearly lacked.

Garrick was getting dizzy. He felt himself growing weaker. He knew he couldn't fight much longer, and he knew that even if he did, it wouldn't matter. He tried to move, but his muscles couldn't produce the force required. Any shred of control he had over his body started to fade, and he started to become a passenger. Garrick was almost able to struggle back onto his hands and knees before he fell to the ground again as every bone in his legs shattered.

He looked up and saw Chase. The only reason he was recognizable was the fact that he was still standing in the same place, not far from Garrick. He stood on all fours, about four feet tall from the top of his pointed ears to the bottom of his paws. His tail hung limply behind him, and his neck, which had stretched slightly in the change, was coated in fur, as was most of his snout. The rest of his body had a thin layer of fur, but mostly was just the darkened skin of the wolf.

Garrick blinked, and his vision quickly faded. He knew he didn't have control anymore. He looked up at the sky, feeling his face elongate quickly, and howled.

Chapter 1

Two Years ago

Garrick sat in his usual seat in the back of the classroom, staring solely at the clock. His head wasn't in the lecture – not in the slightest. He was lost somewhere deep in the recesses of his mind, daydreaming up stories of himself as a hero, rescuing a damsel in distress.

In his head, he was revered. People knew him – and they respected him. He could do things no one else could. Sometimes he could fly, other times he had superhuman strength, and others still he just knew how to fight. In every daydream, though, he stood up to any challenge that presented itself. There was no rival too intimidating for him; No foe he couldn't take down.

But as the bell rang to dismiss them from class, he was pulled away from that. He was pulled into anonymity – the monotonous, daily life of a high school sophomore. He was average here. He wasn't particularly smart, not athletic, and definitely not brave. Out here, he was no hero.

Garrick shook his head lightly, forcing him back into a world that he didn't feel was home. He waited a moment as the rest of the class stood and started heading to the door. He wasn't particularly in a rush, so why fight the crowd? When the room cleared up, he begrudgingly stood and followed the other students. As he walked, he kept his head down and his backpack slung over his right shoulder.

"Hey!" A freshman stood just down the hall, reaching for a backpack which was being held much higher in the air than he could possibly reach. Of course, the perpetrator was none other than Cailean Phoenix. The stereotypical jock – big, strong, and a complete jerk. He towered over the poor kid, laughing as the freshman jumped up and down in a futile attempt to retrieve his belongings.

This scene was too familiar – nearly a daily occurrence in the halls. In his head, Garrick had fought this fight before. He had stood up to Cailean and pushed him back. He had taken the bag back, given it to whichever kid Cailean was tormenting that day, and then ducked under Cailean's punch. In his head, Garrick had hit Cailean once, knocking him to the floor. But this wasn't his head. Out here, that fight was hopeless. All he could do was stand aside.

"Garrick Elliott," Tyler said, tapping on Garrick's shoulder, "Hello?"

"What?" Garrick asked, startled back to the real world and away from his thoughts. Tyler knew Garrick well enough to know what was running through his mind. They'd been friends since they were in elementary school, and Garrick had always been the same. He was a dreamer, always locked in his imagination. Over the years, Tyler had gotten his friend's attention that same way countless times.

"Look, there's nothing you can do, man. He's like twice your size." Exaggerating was an understatement for what Tyler was doing. Cailean wasn't taller than Garrick, who stood around 5 feet 9 inches. Even taking into account musculature, Cailean wasn't significantly larger. He wasn't as bulked up as half of the other kids surrounding him. The problem was simply that Garrick had no muscle supporting his thin frame, and Cailean was nearly the opposite. As much as Garrick hated to admit it, any attempt to fight would just leave him broken like a twig.

"I know," Garrick said. "I just wish that I could –"

"Trust me," Tyler said. "I know. But you can't try to be a hero. Just remember that guys like him live for high school – it's the best four years of their lives."

"Yeah, yeah, yeah, I know. My life is only getting better." Garrick had heard the speech too many times. He'd heard it from his mom, from Tyler, and even from a teacher on one occasion.

"Who cares about that part?" Tyler laughed. "I find it much more satisfying that his is only getting worse. The devolution from high school jock to college drop-out is delightful."

Garrick felt the corners of his mouth twitching upward. It didn't matter whether Tyler was right, or even that his best friend always had a knack for cheering him up. Garrick was just picturing a thirty-year-old Cailean with a bulging gut watching high school football. There was a sick sense of vindication to be had there. Of course, that was assuming Cailean continued to stick to his stereotype and aged poorly.

Cailean had already gotten bored of messing with the kid, and he'd dropped the bag, letting its contents fall to the floor. He pushed past Garrick and Tyler, knocking his shoulder into Garrick's and throwing him off balance. Tyler turned around and clenched his hands into fists. The transformation in his eyes was instantaneous. Nothing Cailean did could bother him unless it was done to his friend. Garrick held his arm out in front of Tyler. His friend had calmed him down earlier, and it was his turn to return the favor. Tyler was always talking Garrick down about stepping in for other people, but when it came to his friends, Tyler's temper would overtake his logic. He wasn't one tolerate his friends getting pushed around.

"Let's just go, man," Garrick said. Tyler nodded, lowering his hands and hitting his fists against his legs. Garrick could see the anger start to wash out of Tyler's eyes. It wasn't that he was so quick to get over it, it was just that he was good at staying optimistic.

"Yeah. Okay."

Garrick and Tyler headed to the main gate of the school. They worked their way through a crowd of students who were anxious to get home until they finally found Tyler's mother's car. Since Tyler was old enough to drive, his mother had probably decided it was just easier to avoid driving during the day than deal with the traffic around school twice daily. Of course, giving him the car also inherently meant giving him permission to always give Garrick a ride home. Garrick opened the passenger door as Tyler clicked the unlock button on the key.

"That is quite feasibly your new record," Tyler said as he opened his own door. It had become a challenge in Garrick's mind to open the door as quickly as possible after hearing the locks disengage. He had never told Tyler about it, but it wasn't a difficult game to notice.

"I don't know," Garrick said with a smile. "Last Tuesday was pretty fast."

"We should start documenting your results. Bring the scientific method into this."

"We'd be skipping the majority of the steps of the scientific method."

"Garrick Elliott, more than occasionally, jokes are better if you don't think about them."

"Maybe that's why I don't have a good sense of humor."

"You are indeed a thinker," Tyler said. Garrick laughed. As quickly as Cailean could ruin his mood, Tyler could repair it. Tyler turned on the car and began to drive home. It was a little red car, at least ten years old, and it wasn't in the best condition. The door handles got stuck sometimes, and the buttons for the automatic windows had been jammed for months. Once, Tyler had been forced to ask another student for a jump before the car would start. But it was still a car, and – being in high school – being able to drive alone was cool enough for Garrick.

"Hey Tyler," Garrick quietly spoke up, breaking the brief silence, as they headed back to Garrick's house. Watching the trees go by, he could feel a somberness creep over him again. Something about forests always filled him with a strange sensation. A longing for something he couldn't explain. Maybe it was the mystery, or the vast expanse of trees that made him feel small.

"Yeah?"

"Do you really think that's true? That our lives are just going to get better?"

"Hey, I said yours. I never mentioned me." Garrick sighed quietly, and he knew his disappointment was present on his face. He didn't look at Tyler, not wanting his friend to see that he was annoyed. He was trying to be serious, and Tyler was joking around. He could clearly sense the change, though, because Tyler's joking smile faded as he said, "Of course it will. High school is just a stepping stone. It's just a trial you're forced to endure that makes you appreciate the rest of life more."

"I don't mean high school, though."

"Then what do you mean?"

"I don't know. It's just... I feel like I'm missing something. Don't you ever feel like you were meant for something more? Like... I don't know, like there has to be something to life more than this. I feel like there's something big, and it's right here, within my reach, but I just can't see what it is."

Garrick was staring out the window, up at the clouds in the blue sky. Trees flew past the window as Garrick tried to form his ideas into words. He couldn't think of what to say, but he could feel it. He knew that this couldn't be all that life had for him. He could feel it burning in his veins – there was some bigger purpose for his life than he was able to see.

"I know what you're saying," Tyler said.

"Yeah? So you get it?"

"Yeah, I can relate. There has to be more to life than this microscopic point on the map we call home – and these people who are so arrogant without any real reason. Somewhere we belong, more than this penitentiary of a town."

"Yeah," Garrick said, somewhat deflated. He shifted his focus from the sky to the trees. Even in the middle of the day, he couldn't see far into the woods. They'd always had a mystical feel to him, and as he looked deep into the trees, he almost expected an answer. It was as if he was trying to stare through them. As if they would open up and reveal his purpose. "That's exactly what I mean."

Present
Morning of the Full Moon

The alarm clock rang, startling Garrick out of that terrible and recurring nightmare. He sat up in his bed, breathing heavily and sweating bullets. As he stood, he rubbed his eyes, trying to clear the blurriness from his vision before walking to the bathroom. Splashing water on his face, he tried to forget what he'd seen through closed eyes.

"Come on, Garrick, snap out of it," he said.

His eyes looked significantly bluer with the water he'd splashed at them. Typically, they were dark green, but that changed with the presence of water. His brown hair was matted with sweat, so he ran it under water as well. When he turned his gaze downward, his eyes drifted toward his left arm and he instinctively brushed his other hand over the scar. He almost let his mind wander but caught himself before he fell too deep into thought. He couldn't be late for school again. He brushed his teeth and quickly dressed.

"Garrick, are you up honey?" his mother called from the next room. He smiled. She had told him, repeatedly, that she was going to start waking up to make sure he was able to get to school, but she could never get herself up early enough.

He couldn't blame her. She always had to work so late. It just brought a smile to his face that she made such an effort. With the smile, though, there was also a twinge of guilt. She wouldn't have to feel the need to get up if he could just get out of bed on time.

Garrick never understood how nightmares made it harder to wake up. Logically, it would make it easier, because he wouldn't want to be in bed. Maybe it was just the fact that the dream ruined any chance he had of getting good sleep. It felt like he hadn't in a year, but he knew it was always just worse around the time of the full moon. The nightmares wouldn't stop, but they wouldn't be as intense for the next few weeks.

He leaned against the doorway to his room and waited for his mom to walk out of hers. "I was just about to leave," he told her.

"Without saying goodbye?" she asked.

"You need your sleep," he said, pulling her in for a hug. She didn't respond because he was right. "I'm not going to be late," he added as an afterthought.

"Oh no?" she asked, jokingly suspicious. "Does school just start half an hour later for you than everyone else?"

"Very funny," he said. Timeliness was always so important to her, but she was never the type to yell or even get appropriately angry at her son. He'd seen her mad before, but it was always related to work. When it came to Garrick, this was the closest she got.

"I love you, Mom," he said as he broke the hug. She smiled.

"I love you too. Now get to school."

As Garrick headed toward the front door, he heard his mom's close as she went back to her room. He heard her flop down onto the bed. He opened the front door and stepped out onto the porch. Making sure to lock the door behind him, he walked to her car. They only had the one, but since his mom worked night shifts, it wasn't terribly difficult to share a vehicle. The cool, autumn breeze blew through what was left of the leaves, and he allowed himself a second to breathe before getting in the car. He felt the restorative power of the wind blow away the fog in his mind.

As Garrick opened the door to his car, Hayden walked up his driveway. She stood by the passenger door and leaned her arms on the top of the vehicle, propping her head down on top of them.

Her dirty blonde hair fell long past her shoulders. The natural waviness always made it look like she put in so much effort, but she never had to. She looked stunning as she rested her head on her arms and looked at him with those bright blue eyes gazing deeply into his soul.

"Well, you weren't about to leave me, were you, Garrick?"

"What are you doing here?" he asked. Since he typically met her at her door, he was surprised to see her. Still, not a second after he asked, his mind started racing with the ways his statement could be misinterpreted, so he felt the need to add, "That isn't what I meant."

"Calm down," she said. Normally, someone giving that command is absolutely no help to anyone, but her smile actually had a way of calming him – one that he couldn't entirely explain. He unlocked the other door, and she dropped into her seat. He couldn't understand how she could make something as mundane as getting into a vehicle look so elegant and graceful. He sat down next to her. "I'm just messing with you."

Garrick smiled, rolling his eyes. He didn't understand how he could constantly be nervous around her, even after so much time. As confused as he was, she clearly enjoyed that she still had that power over him. She'd told him before that it was cute when he got so nervous. Being called cute didn't do much to appease those nerves, but he accepted that he had to pick his battles.

He looked out the window, glancing quickly at the trees to his right. Hayden was staring in that direction. Probably not focusing on anything in general, just thinking about that night. But he wasn't going to – he couldn't allow himself to. Not for one second longer than necessary.

Garrick watched the clock, waiting for the dull experience of English class to come to a close. He was equally dreading and anticipating the ending of class. With the change so close, it became an hourly task for him to prepare himself for that earsplitting ring. There wasn't much he could do to dull the pain. He'd tried earplugs, but he couldn't have someone notice. Even plugging his ears would look strange, aside from not being nearly enough to be effective. All he could do was accept that it was going to hurt.

He watched as the seconds ticked by, counting down in his head. By this point, he had completely tuned out anything that the teacher was saying. All of his attention was on the clock. When there were five seconds to noon, he bit his lip. The bell rang, and he bit harder, drawing a drop of blood. It was his attempt to distract himself from the ringing. Pain was one thing that pulled his human side out and hid the other side. While it did manage to shift his focus slightly, the bell was still deafening.

As the bell faded away, Garrick stood, throwing his bag over his shoulder. He walked down the hall toward the lunchroom. He had his top lip over the bottom one and was trying to put pressure on the bite with his tongue. It didn't really hurt – he'd done it to himself enough times that he'd gotten over it. Anyway, it was nothing compared to the ringing that was slowly fading from his ears. However, he didn't want to come up with some excuse for a bleeding lip if anyone questioned him on it.

So many conversations droned on over the dull ringing that still resounded in his ears. It was surreal – being able to hear so many different things and actually comprehend any single conversation that he wanted. Out of all of the jumbled words from all of the students talking, he could pick out any of them to hear. He wasn't used to having so much control over his own senses.

Distracted, he almost walked right into Hayden when she approached him. He stopped, and she gently tugged him to the side of the hallway. She pushed him against the wall and gazed at him. People passed them, but he felt frozen in time looking into her eyes. The world kept moving, but he had a break from it.

After a moment of looking him up and down, Hayden sighed.

"Garrick, it doesn't have to be like this," she said. She was the only one that knew about his method of blocking out the bells. She had her own. Not her own, really, she shared it with the rest of them. But to Garrick, it was giving up, and he still wasn't ready for that.

"How was class?" He asked, changing the subject. She stepped closer to him and wrapped her arms around his shoulders. He wasn't sure if she intentionally ignored the question or if something just came over her and she wanted affection. On those days, it really could have been either. She looked up into his eyes and leaned forward, kissing him.

He could hear her breathing change ever so slightly, and he could almost even hear her heart beating faster. She pushed her tongue on to his lip, licking the blood off of it and running her tongue across the small holes he'd left in his lip. He gently pulled away and leaned his forehead on hers. She leaned forward again, but he didn't move toward her. He pushed her back, but she just looked annoyed and tried leaning toward him again.

"Hayden," he whispered. She didn't say anything. His lip wasn't bleeding any more. In fact, he could feel that the marks had closed up as he ran his tongue across his lip. Even though he'd experienced it before, the rapid healing was still shocking to him. His ears had healed without him even noticing, and the ringing was completely gone.

"Hayden," he said again. That finally snapped her out of her trance. One of the many negative aspects of her, along with most of the others, being so accepting of the change was the canine qualities which presented themselves.

"What?" she asked, "Oh, it was fine."

"You were doing it again."

"Well, you need to stop hurting yourself!" she whispered angrily. Hayden was clearly embarrassed that she'd reacted like that. She paused for a second before asking, "What do you expect me to do?"

"Sorry," he told her. He stood and leaned his back against the wall. She breathed heavily, trying to hide her anger, before she dropped her head and leaned against his shoulder. As she did, she let out a resigned sigh.

"No," she said, "I know it's hard to deal with. It took me a while too."

"It took you less than a year."

"Yeah, well, you know. People are different. I shouldn't get mad at you, it's just…"

"I know," he said, "It's okay." He could feel it too. Around the full moon, everything was different. It didn't matter how many times he experienced the change, he still couldn't get used to the few days before and after. It was like there was another personality fighting for dominance.

He turned around and wrapped his arms around her waist, pulling her close to him. He kissed her. "I love you," he said.

"I know," she said with a small smirk.

"Get to class," he told her, letting her go. He watched her walk until she turned a corner, then waited for the hallway to clear out. Not ready to proceed with his day, he dropped his bag to the floor and leaned his back against the wall, sliding down until he was seated against it. He buried his face in his hands.

Garrick had spent more time in his head than he could possibly remember over the course of his life. He'd always daydreamed or focused on his own thoughts, rather than anything around him. It had been his way of escaping the world. Recently, though, he would give anything to quiet his thoughts – to simply ignore everything happening in his head and focus on the real world. But he couldn't, especially not on that day.

He shook his head; even slammed the palms of his hands against his forehead, but the blaring noises that surrounded him wouldn't quiet.

He took a deep breath. *Calm down,* he thought. *Focus on your breathing.* Everything amplified as he started to panic. He could hear people's conversations as they took their seats in classes, and the chairs sliding along the floor. His own thoughts were even louder, racing through his mind, but he couldn't attach words to any of them. The world started to feel heavy, and he realized he wasn't breathing at all. Panic flooded over his body, though his brain knew there was a simple solution. The light making its way through his fingers grew brighter, and the noises started to blend together into a deafening screech. The lack of oxygen to his brain was starting to take its toll, but he couldn't force himself to open his mouth.

Finally, Garrick gasped in a deep breath. He wasn't sure if he'd finally convinced his body to act on his thoughts or if he'd fainted and just breathed afterward. His heart pounded, and his ears still rang with the cacophony of voices surrounding him. After a few more deep breaths, most of the voices quieted, leaving only a ringing in his ears that accompanied sudden silence.

He waited a few minutes, trying to calm himself down, before he finally stood up and walked to the lunchroom. He could constantly feel it, clawing to get out, fighting him for control. The others just gave up so close to the moon, they just let it take over. They were normal enough; no one would question them unless they were really close, and the only people close enough to notice behavioral changes were the other wolves. Garrick knew, as he sat by Tyler with his lunch tray, that he didn't have that luxury.

Garrick silently sat in the seat next to Tyler. The chairs in their lunchroom were all mismatched, probably because the school couldn't afford anything better. Random chairs were higher than others, and some tables had benches instead of any chairs at all. Garrick always enjoyed finding the chairs which were raised a little higher because it put him right about Tyler's height. Of course, even when Garrick tried to use the seats to his advantage, Tyler's perfect posture didn't help Garrick appear any taller.

As Garrick sat down, Tyler looked at him with a smile. His brown hair moved as much as it could when Tyler turned his head, but there wasn't much of it. Tyler was always joking about letting it grow out because singers had long hair. He looked at Garrick with hazel eyes. Garrick had always thought it was interesting how Tyler's eyes would appear different colors, but now they seemed consistent compared to his own. Now, the fact that one word could describe the color of his eyes made them more special. It made them human eyes.

"Hey," Tyler said, "Took you long enough."

"Yeah. I ran into Hayden in the hallway."

"Of course you did," Tyler laughed, "You two have been together for nearly two years, and anyone who just met you would think you're in the honeymoon phase."

"And you, my friend, have said that same thing daily since I met her."

"Not exactly the same thing. I like to vary my verbiage. Keep you guessing."

Garrick rolled his eyes with a laugh. He glanced down at his food for the first time since he'd sat down, and suddenly felt like he hadn't eaten for days. He picked up the sandwich and took a bite, making sure to remind himself not to devour it too quickly.

"Seriously though," Tyler said, "I'm really happy for you."

Garrick smiled, but he didn't know what to say. He'd run out of fake compliments for Tyler's girlfriend months ago, and he wasn't in the mood for concocting more. The two of them had dated on and off for two years, which was longer than he and Hayden had been together. But Garrick had never liked Kayla. He had never seen anyone hurt his friend so bad. Just thinking about it, Garrick could feel his heart rate rising. He wanted to lie to his friend, to say that he was happy for him too, but that was the human side of him. And it was quickly losing control as his thoughts grew darker.

"Hey," Chase said, coming up from behind and grabbing Garrick's shoulder. He pressed his fingers against the pressure point on Garrick's shoulder, and Garrick bit down on the pain. Chase had clearly sensed Garrick's loss of control in one way or another, and Garrick was thankful that he was there to tear him from his thoughts. He wasn't sure how he'd explain his irrational anger to Tyler. Chase sat next to them, and he and Tyler exchanged friendly greetings. Garrick steadied his breathing, trying not to think about anything that could be slightly bothersome. Chase emptied his lunch from his bag, and Tyler was sufficiently distracted from any reaction Garrick might have had.

"How?" Tyler asked. He sounded playful, but Garrick knew there was a hint of seriousness in his question.

"What?" Chase asked.

"You literally brought half of a fried chicken and pizza to school for lunch," Tyler said. Chase typically was able to hide his lycanthropy just as well as Garrick, or better, but one thing he didn't hide was the ravenous hunger that typically came on the day of the transformation. It wasn't hard to explain away, given that he was a teenage male, but it was still too risky in Garrick's eyes. Garrick would rather just eat mountains of food in the comfort of his own home.

"Yeah," Chase said with a shrug.

"How do you possibly eat so much food and still look like that?" He asked.

"I work out," Chase joked.

Tyler laughed and shook his head. "As do I, but I still have to eat healthily. I'm not bitter or anything."

"Hey, I don't eat unhealthily," Garrick defended. Tyler looked at the chips in front of him. "They're baked! They're good for me."

"Whatever you say," Tyler laughed as he took a bite of his broccoli. Tyler had always been stronger than Garrick was, and he had the physique to match, but Garrick never really thought about how much work he must have put into it. He'd just assumed Tyler liked rice and broccoli. Garrick could eat whatever he wanted, and he basically couldn't put on weight. Becoming a wolf tore every muscle in the body apart, and every time they reformed, they were stronger. He knew his friend was only joking, but it still gave him a slight twinge of guilt. It really wasn't fair that he was able to have something that Tyler worked so hard for without putting in any effort.

Garrick looked down at the sandwich that sat in front of him, one bite taken out from the corner. He was disgusted with himself and he had completely lost his appetite. But his stomach didn't agree with the notion that his brain had about not eating, and he had to take another bite to try to ease the hunger pangs.

Garrick was one of those teenagers who never outgrew peanut butter and jelly. That was what he ate on most days of the month. But on this day, he had a sandwich packed with every type of lunch meat in existence, and it was practically spilling out of the bread. He had learned a few tricks to keep the beast from tearing at his brain throughout the day, and meat was one of them. He wasn't sure if it was the protein or the fact that the meat appeased the carnivorous beast underneath his skin. Chase was actually the one who pointed that out to him. Every full moon, he brought a feast of chicken, steak, or whatever other animal he felt like eating that day. Garrick was thoroughly convinced the pizza was just because he liked it, even though it was loaded with extra pepperonis.

Another technique Garrick had learned was pain. As much as Hayden hated it, biting his lip was usually the best way for him to keep his ears from becoming too hypersensitive. He had experienced the ear-splitting ringing of the bells during the first few months, and he didn't want to go back to that. Everyone else had their own way of handling it, though. If they didn't fight the wolf, it wouldn't push back so hard and the side-effects would be less drastic. Still, Garrick refused to give in to the idea that he'd become a monster, even if he knew it was inevitable.

Garrick finished the rest of his sandwich in silence. He nodded along and smiled as Chase and Tyler handled the actual talking part of the conversation.

"What about you, Garrick Elliott?" Tyler asked.

"What?" Garrick asked as his heart skipped a beat.

"Nothing. I just wanted to prove to Chase that you were enraptured by the concept of rational thought once again," Tyler said with a smile. "He still isn't quite aware of the extent of your musing capabilities. What's going on in that alluring head of yours?"

Sick things, Garrick thought.

"I forgot," Garrick said. He tried to joke to cover up the fact that he was being discouraged by his mind once again, "I'm too stuck on the fact that you think I'm 'alluring.'"

"No, just your head," Tyler corrected. "The rest of you has a completely separate level of charm."

"I am literally disgusted by how adorable you two are," Chase laughed.

Garrick smiled. It was a compliment, although it didn't really seem like one.

The smile only lasted a few seconds, though. Under the table, and undetectable from where Tyler sat across from them, Chase elbowed Garrick hard in the ribs. Garrick bit back the pain from the unexpected hit. A few seconds later, the bell rang, and he heard it about as well as anyone else would. He knew Chase had more experience with their curse than he did, but he was still continually impressed with how well his friend was able to handle the small things. He stood up and grabbed his bag, and he and Tyler exchanged their convoluted handshake. He patted Chase's shoulder and then headed off to class.

After getting through a few more classes and dropping Hayden off at home, Garrick sat on his bed, leaning against a massive stack of pillows. He listened to music, trying to calm his nerves. The earphones were set on the lowest volume, and they rested on the mattress in front of him.

Music had always helped him calm his nerves, but he'd had to find new ways to listen to it around the full moon. When he was going to change for the second time, he'd tried listening to music. He had set the volume to near the maximum, like he used to listen to it, and put in the earphones. The second the music started – not even at a particularly loud point in the song – he'd blown out his eardrums. It would have deafened a normal person, but Garrick just had to deal with the intense pain until his ears healed themselves a few minutes later. Nonetheless, it wasn't an experience he felt the desire to repeat.

Hayden strolled into his room, dropping her bag on the floor next to his door. He was supposed to be packing. She put her hands on her waist and looked at him disapprovingly. He wanted to feel bad, but he was lost in admiring her. She wore the same shorts and wrinkled tee shirt that she always wore around that time of the month. Garrick fetched his own loose shirt and a pair of stained and torn jeans. None of them bothered looking too nice on that night, and most of them just had a single outfit they always wore, like Hayden and Garrick.

"How did you get in here?" Garrick asked as he pulled his shirt over his head. He put on the new shirt and quickly changed his pants.

"Your mom," Hayden said, nodding her head toward the hall. She was clearly annoyed. She always was. He waited until the last possible second to get everything ready, and she chastised him for it every month, but he never changed.

He knew he was being stubborn, but he felt like doing things the same way as everyone else was giving in. Even holding on to the minor details, like not getting ready until the moment he absolutely had to, gave him the slightest sense of victory.

"You really…" She started, but trailed off. She knew that he wasn't going to take the advice, and he was glad he didn't have to hear it again.

"I'm sorry," he said. He really was. While he didn't feel ready to start packing early and accept what was going to happen, he truly wished he didn't have to disappoint her. He knew she understood what he meant, and he could see in her face that she wasn't upset. She kept telling him they all went through similar things when they'd learned about what was happening. They'd come to terms a lot more quickly, but Garrick took pride in his obstinance.

After he finished packing the bag, he walked toward the door, and she stopped him. She kissed him, and he dropped the bag to the floor, wrapping his arms around her. Usually, a kiss would be the most wonderful thing in the world. Every kiss still sent butterflies fluttering around in his stomach, and it made him sure she wasn't upset with him. Now, though, he was just concerned it was a sign that the wolf was starting to take over.

"No," he said, weakly. He repeated it with more force, pushing her back.

"Garrick," she said, stepping closer to him again. He grabbed her arms and shoved her against the wall. He couldn't explain what he was feeling – he didn't know himself. There was a mixture of so many emotions, and everything was starting to blur together. He kissed her passionately, and she kissed back. He pulled his head back a bit, breathing heavily and biting his tongue to try to force his human side forward. He stepped back and let her go, trying to steady his breathing and his beating heart.

Even in a human state, Garrick would have had trouble turning down Hayden's clear advances. He refused, though, to take advantage of her in that altered state. Any time he was with Hayden, he wanted it to be her, not the wolf.

"It's okay to let it go," she said.

"No," Garrick told her, "It isn't."

"I'm sorry," Garrick said, "About earlier."

"Don't be," Hayden told him, "It was my fault."

They left it at that. It was always better to separate
things that happened during the moon, or the day of it. A different part of them was waking up, and their control was questionable at best. They'd had to learn not to take thoughts or
actions too personally on those days. Garrick always wanted
to talk through every problem. He'd always been afraid that
the small ones would grow. Anyway, one fight could be all it
took for someone like Hayden to realize she was way out of
his league. They'd been dating long enough that he was
slightly more confident, but every slight disagreement still left
him a little unsettled. It was like he was distant from a part of
himself. When he fought with her, it became two-thirds of
himself that he simply couldn't connect with.

Aldric stopped them in a clearing and they all spread
out a bit. Garrick and Hayden went a few feet away, behind a
small group of trees. They placed their bags near the trunk of
one of the trees. They were slightly early that night, so they
had a few extra minutes to kill. He unzipped the bag and
pulled out a water bottle. As he sat and leaned back against
the tree, he took a drink. He could feel it growing stronger in
him by the second. He tried focusing his breathing, but he
knew it wouldn't have any effect. It hadn't on a single occasion since his first transformation, not when it was this close.

Hayden took her shirt off, carefully folding it and placing it in her pack. He closed his eyes, trying not to picture her.
Anything that increased his heart rate only sped the process
up. Regardless of his efforts, his heartbeat increased rapidly,
pounding fast, and he tried his pointless breathing exercises
again.

He heard her softly walk toward him, and she sat next
to him, placing an arm around his shoulder. He knew she was
going to tell him that it was time, but he didn't need to hear it.
He could feel it clawing at him. He nodded, without opening
his eyes, still trying to fight it back. She nudged his head
closer, and he rested it on her breast. He heard her heartbeat,
slow and steady. Somehow, that was the one thing which

could keep him calm. He felt her hand on his chin, and he opened his eyes, turning his head toward her.

Her eyes shone a brilliant blue as she gazed deep into his. They were always blue, but they only held that perfect shine on these nights. He leaned in and kissed her softly.

"I love you," she said.

"I love you too," he told her. He meant it with every fiber of his being. She stood and walked away, stopping a few feet from him. He could feel his eyes starting to fill with tears. He could see her fighting back a scream, but she finally gave in. She screamed, dropping to the ground. He watched, unable to turn away, as her body transformed.

He took a deep breath, trying to hold back the wolf inside his own body. He wanted to at least wait until he knew she was too far gone to be able to remember seeing his pain.

He took his clothes off and folded them, placing them in his pack. Hayden, now a four-foot tall beast, walked over to him. Her arms had become two front legs, and her legs had bent back in a way that would have looked awkward on any human. She had light brown fur covering most of her body, but he could see the exposed skin on her snout had stretched and darkened. Even in this form, she was absolutely beautiful. A different kind of beauty, of course. It almost made him feel like what they were couldn't be as unnatural as he felt it was.

He knelt and extended his hand to her. She sniffed it cautiously, and then licked the back of his hand. He motioned for her to step back as he lowered his hand. When she inched her way backward, he didn't know if she understood him or if she was just trying to give him space for what she knew was coming.

As claws grew from Garrick's hand, he traced over the scar on his arm again. It was an instinct now, and sometimes he didn't even notice that he was doing it. A remnant of his subconscious always felt the need to remind himself what had changed him. He took one last deep breath before he pitched forward with a scream of pain.

Even though he knew it was useless, he tried to hold on to some of his humanity. He tried to keep the wolf back, but he couldn't. He felt as its power rushed forward and tore his body apart, causing him just as much pain as it always did. When he lost consciousness, all that was left was the wolf.

Chapter 2

Twenty-three months ago

Garrick sat in the back seat of Tyler's car. He wondered if his eyes could wear out from constant motion. He willed himself to stop, realizing he probably looked ridiculous. Rolling his eyes was a decent sarcastic gesture when used in response to a single comment, but it was definitely not a way to react to every sentence he heard coming from the front seat. In his mind, there was just no clearer way to make his exasperation known. Of course, it didn't affect the conversation, and they probably weren't paying any attention to him whatsoever.

"I can't believe you don't understand why I'm upset," Tyler said, his voice rising.

"I understand, Tyler," Kayla responded, annoyed. "I just don't think you have a right to be!"

Garrick felt increasingly awkward. They seemed to have completely forgotten he was in the car. It felt like he was at his friend's house hearing their parents scold them. He just sat silently in the back seat, willing his home to approach faster than it possibly could. He fumbled around his bag for his mp3 player – just trying to find any way to drown them out – still trying to make as little noise as he could. If they actually had forgotten about him, he'd definitely prefer it. It would be far less awkward if he didn't draw attention to himself.

"Really?" Tyler objected, "No right? Wow."

"All I did was eat lunch with another friend. A girl, at that."

"No, you left me by myself waiting for you the whole time. You didn't even text me and let me know."

The fight was ridiculous to Garrick. Maybe Tyler had a reason to be angry, maybe not. Although Garrick knew he'd support his friend if it ever came down to it, if he could avoid input, it would be preferable. He didn't feel that he had any authority to judge their situation, especially when he'd never been in a relationship. He didn't hold any frame of reference. This was actually the most functional relationship he had ever seen. He'd never met his dad, and he hadn't had a lot of friends aside from Tyler, so he didn't see a lot of parents. Still, though, he just thought that if two people really cared about each other, they would be able to avoid such trivial arguments between each other.

"My phone was dying. I didn't think it was a big deal. I knew I'd see you later."

"You could have found me and let me know," Tyler groaned, "or invited me."

"You don't like her."

"I love you," he countered. "It would have been worth it."

Her response was just an exasperated sigh. Garrick wondered if this was just what a relationship entailed. People always joked about old couples bickering. Maybe two people couldn't be romantically involved without falling into that trap. If that was all he could hope for in a relationship, though, he didn't feel like he was missing out on much.

"I'm just tired of always giving you 100 percent," he said. "I drop everything if you call. I'll reorganize my day according to your whim. It's just completely one-sided. You can't even be bothered to send me a text message telling me you're going to be busy during lunch?"

Garrick's attempts to avoid eavesdropping were being overwhelmed by his curiosity. It wasn't his business, and he was trying not to let himself get involved at all, even in his mind. Given that he was failing at that, he wanted to at least stay unbiased. As a friend, he saw it as his duty to inform his friend if he was wrong. He could tell Tyler that he was being a little over the top later, if he thought it would help. However, he was actually convinced that Tyler was right on this one. There had been many occasions where Garrick and Tyler were in the middle of something, and Tyler would just get up and leave. He'd spend an hour talking to Kayla, and then just pretend it didn't happen. A few times Tyler had cancelled plans or moved them around with Garrick so he could spend time with her.

Garrick tried not to hold it against Tyler too much. As good of a friend as he was to Garrick, he was also trying to be a good boyfriend. It only made sense that the balance would be difficult to find. Garrick refused to be some needy best friend who would explode if he couldn't spend time with Tyler. The part that really bothered Garrick was that he didn't believe she deserved Tyler at all. He just wished his friend had the good sense to find a girl who appreciated his actions.

"Whatever," she said, sarcasm dripping from her tongue. "I'm so sorry. Next time, I'll text you every detail."

Tyler pulled over at Garrick's house. Garrick barely said goodbye before he practically dove out of the car. There wasn't much he wanted more in that moment than to just get away from the whole situation. He walked to his door as quickly as possible, but his phone had already vibrated before he made it. He turned back and saw Tyler wave goodbye. Kayla looked out the window, clearly very annoyed.

The text just said, "*Sorry.*" Tyler had typed it as soon as the car stopped. The two drove off, and she was already looking back at him, hopefully forming a sincere apology.

"Garrick!" His mom called from down the street. Startled at first, he froze and wondered why she was outside. It only took him a second to accept it, though, and he sighed deeply. All Garrick wanted to do was lock himself in his room, hide away, and listen to music. For whatever reason, though, his mom clearly had plans for some sort of social interaction. He dropped his bag against the door and turned to face her.

"Yeah?" he asked, masking the annoyance in his voice with a smile. He wasn't angry at her, so he didn't want her to be upset, he just wished he didn't have to talk to anyone at that moment. After school and the emotionally draining argument on the ride home, he was just exhausted.

"Come help us out," she said. A moving van was parked across the street a few houses down, and his mom was standing on the gate, motioning for him to follow. New neighbors. "I want you to meet this girl."

Garrick let out an exasperated laugh. His mom was always trying to set him up with girls. She seemed to think he wouldn't be happy if he wasn't with someone. Deep down, he was still toying with the opposite idea – that a relationship would only make things worse. Maybe it was worth a shot, though. After all, she was a new girl. Maybe she wouldn't know how much of a loser he was. He just had to act cool for a few brief moments.

"Hey," he heard from the truck as he approached. The new girl's mom was in the truck, leaning with her elbows on the back of a couch, her face red as she took a few deep breaths. Clearly, they had been at this for a while. Offering his help, he lifted one side, and she the other. His arms were shaking, but he tried not to display that. As hard as he tried, though, it was clear he was having more trouble than she was, and she was already exhausted. Walking backward, he stepped off the truck, but tripped – dropping his side of the couch on his toe.

"Sorry," he said, biting back the pain to try to appear more masculine than he was.

"Smooth," a feminine voice chimed in. The comment was obviously meant to be a joke at his expense, but he had trouble being offended when her voice was so sweet and kind, as if she were incapable of saying something rude. Suddenly, his desire to impress her deepened while his ability to vanished. So much for thinking he could trick her into thinking he was somewhat cool. Now his only hope was that the new girl liked weirdoes, which wasn't likely.

He turned to face her as he tried to fabricate a clever response. Drawing a blank, he just looked her in the eyes and smiled weakly. She wasn't a 'new girl,' she'd just moved. On the bright side, he hadn't messed anything up. Garrick hadn't had a chance with her irrespective of how many couches he moved.

"Hayden Faye," she said, reaching out her hand. Although he'd mostly given up on impressing her, he still tried to maintain a firm handshake. She beat him there, too, though. A young man only a few years older than them, probably her brother, walked by carrying a box labeled 'books' and Garrick could only assume it was another heavy box. Although he didn't know him, he was grateful to Hayden's brother because if he hadn't been there, Garrick probably would have been stuck embarrassingly struggling with that box.

"I'm Caleb," he nodded, unable to shake hands.

"I'm Garrick," Garrick responded to both of them, trying to hide how awkward he suddenly felt. As Caleb walked away, he turned his attention to Hayden. "I've seen you around school. You're Cailean's friend, right?"

"I'm Brooke's friend," she corrected, suspiciously quickly. She let go of his hand and moved to the other side of the couch. An entire conversation was spoken with her mother in one brief smile. Her mom accepted the help gratefully,

probably eager to take a break from the heavy lifting. She
wandered off to help Garrick's mom move some boxes, so
Garrick was left alone with Hayden.

"Thanks for the help," she said as they lifted the couch.
She made it look easy – effortlessly hoisting up her end of the
couch. Garrick struggled to maintain his balance as he tried to
lift and keep up with her. He was able to stabilize himself
enough that he didn't lose his footing. What he did lose was
any hope at all of impressing the girl who stood in front of him.

Present
30 days until the full moon

Garrick felt crushed leaves beneath him as he stirred.
Groggily, he opened his eyes and allowed the assault of light
to rush into his tired eyes. Through the trees above him, he
could see bits of sunlight. In an attempt to get a better sense
of where he was, he looked around the area. While he had
grown to know these woods fairly well, it still took his mind a
few moments to fight its way out of the haze of the previous
night. After the moment he transformed, he couldn't draw up
a single memory. The others got flashes, but he still didn't.
He assumed it was because of how hard he fought to keep himself and his wolf separate. Maybe the wolf was returning the
favor and keeping its memories for itself.

He looked around a bit more from the spot where he
was lying. To his left was what was left of a deer carcass. His
breath caught in his throat for a minute. He had seen this a
few times before, but it didn't make it easier. The sight alone
wasn't necessarily difficult for him to process, it was more an
issue with the thoughts it provoked. Occasionally, the wolves
would find some kind of animal and eat it in the forest. At
least this time they had eaten it, and not just killed it for sport.
That made him feel better about it, but he still felt odd knowing

he was digesting raw deer meat. Completely psychosomatically, he felt nauseous. He knew the meat couldn't actually damage him – he would just heal too quickly – but he felt like this was something that should make him sick.

He looked away. To his right, he saw Hayden. She was lying on her stomach, her head resting on her arms. Her hair covered most of her face. He watched her breathe for a moment. In stark contrast to the dried blood on her arms and, he assumed, mouth – she looked so beautiful and peaceful.

After a moment, he realized she wasn't likely to be the only one covered in blood. As much as he didn't want to think about it, it started to become the one, pervasive thought in his mind. He dug his elbows into the ground and lifted himself up, working his way to his feet. Garrick sat up, then placed his feet on the ground as he tried to gain the balance to stand. He drowsily walked back to his bag. Opening and digging through it, he managed to retrieve his jeans and a bottle of water. Though his throat was bone dry, he had to choose a discomfort to remedy first – and he slid on his pants. All the others were much more comfortable with their bodies than Garrick was. As he took a long drink from the bottle, he wondered if the wolf never took it upon itself to drink or if the change just took all of the hydration out of him. Maybe he was demonizing the wolf, but he wouldn't be surprised if it decided not to waste time finding water because it knew it would just be Garrick's problem. He stopped himself, careful not to drink the entire bottle. After retrieving a washcloth from his bag, he used the rest of the water to dampen the cloth and clean his mouth and arms. Then he put his shirt back on.

He picked his bag up before retrieving Hayden's. He took them back to where she was sleeping and set them both down. He pulled out his jacket from the bag and laid it across Hayden. Although he hadn't worn it the night before, he always made sure to pack it for that specific reason. She stirred a bit, but didn't wake up. Then he grabbed the cloth and gently rubbed the blood off her, trying not to put enough pressure to wake her. When he was confident she wouldn't wake up to see her arms bloody, he sat against a tree and watched her sleep for a few minutes.

I should probably go find the others, he thought – but he didn't act on it. He had to intentionally repeat the thought another half dozen times before he was able to force himself to turn away. He didn't feel quite as heavy as he had when he'd awoken, so he didn't have much trouble standing when he stopped looking at her. His eyes drifted, scanning the area around them. A trail of blood spread out across the forest ground. If they'd all attacked the deer together, that trail would likely lead him to the others.

Garrick followed the trail. He lost it a few times, but didn't have much difficulty picking it back up. While his senses were always better than they'd been before the transformation, they weren't particularly useful at that moment. It was as if the wolf had been satisfied for a while and was peacefully sleeping in the recesses of his mind. However, he didn't need any of that to keep tracking the others. Along with the blood, there were broken twigs, and the ground looked much more disturbed than other areas. Dirt around it was softer, as it had been shaken about by multiple large beasts. The trail led him to a small clearing. It wasn't the same one they'd been at earlier. He thought he'd been walking for a while, actually. They didn't usually travel so far, though, and his sense of direction was still taking its time to wake up.

He expected to find three people sleeping at the end of the trail, but that wasn't what lay in front of him. The first thing he noticed was a tent torn to shreds. The pieces blew in a slight breeze. Following the blood, he saw two people, probably hikers, torn apart. Their bodies were covered in scratches, and missing small chunks of meat. It was as if they were attacked by an animal that decided they weren't worth eating.

A scream caught in his lungs, and all that came out was a quiet gasp. His body refused to react. All he wanted to do was yell, scream, or cry, but he couldn't make a sound. He just froze. His knees buckled under him as he lost all strength to stand. Garrick dropped to his knees, staring at the grotesque picture in front of him. He pleaded with himself to look away, but no muscle would respond to his commands. He'd lost any control of his body. He couldn't even close his eyes. All he could do was stare in shock.

He wanted to vomit, but even that required more movement than he could muster. He repeated to himself all the things he wished he could believe. *It was an animal. We never come out this far.* As hard as he tried to fight it, he knew that it wasn't a wild animal attack. They could have hidden or run from an animal. Werewolves, though, they couldn't escape.

"Garrick?"

The voice was only vaguely familiar, pulling on his mind from the edge of reality. He was lost, and wherever this voice was, it was somewhere far from him. Somewhere in another world.

"Garrick?"

He heard her again. Hayden's voice was barely recognizable, but he could feel her growing closer. Maybe she was just pulling him back to Earth, but that was somewhere he didn't want to be. He didn't want to have to think about what he was seeing. He just wanted to block out everything.

"Where are you?" This time, she was near. He wanted to respond, but he was frozen. He was finally able to move his mouth, but no sound could come out. The world around him still didn't seem real, and her voice was the only fragment of reality in it. He wanted to latch on to it – to beg her to keep talking.

She found him and walked up to him. She hadn't bothered dressing before she came to find him. For her, being with him was always the priority. All she had on was the jacket he'd set atop her, and she hadn't even taken the time to button it before searching for him. Her hair was still a mess, and there were leaves in her hair. He could still see a few spots of blood he'd missed on her arms. At least she'd wiped her mouth, probably on the washcloth Garrick had left, and her face looked as perfect as ever.

"What's wrong?" she asked. He didn't answer. He couldn't. He didn't have to. She followed his gaze, and the scene spoke more volumes than Garrick ever could have. "Oh. Oh my."

She dropped to her knees next to him and put a hand on his shoulder. The touch was enough to snap him back. His mind knew she was trying to help – and it wanted to accept her comfort – but his body reacted from fear. He shrugged his shoulder and shook her hand away, but she just put it back. She reached around him and turned him toward her, forcing him to look away from the devastation that had held his attention since he'd seen it. She pulled him close and he buried his head in her chest.

The image was seared in his mind, and he couldn't get rid of it; it remained even in the darkness behind his closed eyes. He tried to fight back the tears, but he felt so weak. He still had no control over his body, but the emotion finally took over as the initial shock died. Tears started pouring from his eyes. She rubbed his head with one hand and held him tight with the other. He could feel himself shaking. They had killed human beings.

She whispered things to him, but he couldn't make out exactly what she was saying. After a few times, he realized that she was just repeating, "It's okay." How? How was it okay?

She planted a kiss on his head, and then went back to stroking his hair. Her steady heartbeat was a soothing lullaby, and it helped calm him, but he still felt sick. He felt weak as she held him in her arms, comforting him. Part of him couldn't help but feel that the roles should be reversed. He should be the strong one. He should be comforting her, assuring her that life would move on. Instead, he was crying into her breast. He was broken.

That was when an even more disconcerting thought occurred to him. They had killed. How was Hayden so calm about it?

"Garrick, are you okay?" Hayden sent that text on Saturday at 10:04 am.

"Gar?" At 11.

"We need to talk about this sometime." Saturday at 9:07 pm.

"Hey, man. Do you want to talk about it?" Chase on Saturday and 9:18 pm

"Please, answer me." Hayden. Sunday at 9:32 am.

"Garrick Elliott! Let's hang out today?" Tyler on Sunday at 12:14 pm.

"Buddy, Hayden is freaking out. I know it's rough, but you should really let her know you're alright. Alive, at least." Chase on Sunday at 2:57 pm

"Are you alright? I know it was tough to see that." Brooke on Sunday at 3:22 pm.

"Garrick. Are you okay? You're scaring me. If you don't answer, I'm coming over." Hayden on Sunday night at 10:15 pm.

He hadn't been intentionally ignoring them. He'd just spent the majority of Saturday sitting on his bed, staring at the wall. He was still in shock. He couldn't remember what had happened on Friday night, and he was scared to find out. At least he could convince himself that he hadn't done it. What if the memories came back? Then he'd know if it was him. He didn't want to face that. He just didn't want to process it.

His mom worked Saturday, so he didn't have anyone in the house to force him to move. He just let the time pass. He didn't eat. He didn't have a television on or any music playing. He just sat in silence as the hours kept passing by. Everything felt too heavy to move, and any time he formulated a decent thought, it seemed to slip from his mind. All he wanted to do was sleep, but even that evaded him.

Sunday, he'd tried to move around the house a bit more. He played some music because he knew his mom would get worried. Hiding in his room, he'd left on some background noise so she'd think he was busy. He'd made her dinner, trying to take his mind off of that campsite.

Nothing worked.

He picked up the phone. *"I just need to get some sleep. I'll see you tomorrow."* He finally replied to Hayden. Deep down, he knew he should apologize to Tyler. He was the only one who didn't have a clue about what had happened, and Garrick wouldn't have a way to answer the questions he knew he'd have to face. However, he was only able to draw up the energy, both mentally and physically, to send one response, and he had to choose the person who'd show up on his doorstep.

*"I love yo*u," she said.

"I love you too," he told her. He dropped the phone and collapsed in bed, begging his body to – for the first time that weekend – allow him to sleep.

The trees towered above him. They seemed to go on forever as he looked ahead of him and only saw the empty woods. The symphony of birds singing in the trees and small animals scurrying about in the foliage filled his ears. Patches of sunlight fell on the ground, creating patterns in the leaves. Garrick had never felt more at peace – and more at home. All of the weight he'd felt over the past few days was gone, and he felt safe. Something was wrong, though. Cautiously, he looked down at his hands, examining them carefully. It almost felt like he wasn't himself. He took a few paces forward, examining the forest, looking for something. He didn't have any idea what he was expecting to find.

That wasn't true. A single thought ran into his mind, and he knew exactly what was off – and exactly what he was trying to find. The campsite. He was trying to find it. Maybe if he saw it again, he'd get some kind of closure. Maybe he'd see how things actually happened. Maybe he and Hayden were happily eating a deer while the others furiously killed innocent people. He wasn't sure that would make it better, but at least he'd know he didn't kill anyone.

He stopped. He didn't want to see it. What if he was wrong?

Garrick heard a sound coming from a few yards away. It sounded like a low growl from a beast hidden in the trees. How was that possible? It was broad daylight. It couldn't be a wolf. Yet, against all logic, he knew it was. He could sense it.

Cautiously, he stepped back, instinctively terrified of the creature as it emerged from the shadows in front of him. Its eyes were blue, but the color wasn't as pure and deep as Hayden's were. They were paler, a lighter shade of blue. It stalked toward him. This wolf didn't walk like Hayden, either. It was more powerful, not as gracious. It walked with authority, which just filled Garrick with fear. Garrick turned and ran – the adrenaline coursing through his veins stopping any negative thoughts or bad feelings from slowing him down. As he ran, he allowed all his burdens to fade, dropping them as dead weight that would only get him caught.

The wolf took pursuit. Garrick placed his hand on a tree branch and vaulted over the trunk of a fallen tree. The wolf leapt and cleared it with ease. It was gaining on him. The forest around him looked darker for some reason, as if the sun refused to shine through the canopy. It didn't make much sense, because as he looked around, it seemed that a majority of the trees had fallen. Garrick ran toward another tree, one of the few which still stood tall. He jumped up, driving his foot into the trunk and pushing down. Launching himself upward with the second step, he managed to catch a relatively high-hanging branch. Knowing what the wolf was capable of, he didn't let himself stop to breathe. He climbed, hiding within the branches and leaves. He was ten feet off the ground, but the wolf was running after him fervently. He didn't spare him-self a second to look at it – he just had to get as high as he could. Garrick pushed upward, one branch to another, climb-ing for safety. As powerful as that wolf was, it wouldn't be able to climb. He saw the top of the canopy, and the sun was just starting to peek through at him. Garrick reached up, grab-bing one last branch to hoist himself upward.

He felt an impact at his ribs. The wind was knocked out of him, and his hand slipped from the branch. The wolf had apparently jumped to him. He tumbled from the branch and fell toward the ground, still looking upward. The wolf had its paws on him, and it stared down at him as he fell. If the fall didn't kill him, the beast would.

The alarm woke him from his nightmare again. He was panting heavily as he shot up in bed. After allowing him-self a moment to catch his breath, he ran through the typical steps of getting over his dreams. He wandered to the bathroom and splashed water on himself, verbally reassuring himself it was just a dream. Still, it felt as though the running and the adrenaline in the dream gave him exactly what he needed to function again. Of course, that also could have been his rude awakening.

Garrick still couldn't get the campsite off his mind, but at least he felt like his body was responding to his commands again. He got ready for school, taking his time. Before he'd been scratched, Garrick had been the type of person who needed a dozen alarms to actually wake up. Since he'd been scratched, though, the first one was enough. He'd never gotten around to pushing back the time of the alarm, though, so he was always up early. He'd grown to love having time in the morning to actually get ready for the day. Before he left, he snuck into his mom's room and kissed her on the forehead. She stirred a bit and he said, "I love you, Mom," but she didn't wake up as he headed off to school.

The car ride with Hayden was silent the entire way. He parked at the school and they both sat in the car awkwardly. They both knew there was so much to say, but neither was willing to start it. Of course, Hayden had tried. She was just waiting for Garrick to be ready. After a few minutes, she looked convinced that he wouldn't, so she reached for her handle. He placed his hand gently on hers and pulled it back. If he didn't talk then, it would only get more difficult to start the conversation. He took a deep breath but didn't follow it through with anything. He was still formulating the words, and he didn't want to say anything he didn't mean.

"I'm okay," he finally offered. That was his brilliant line, what he had taken all weekend to concoct. He meant it, though. Of course, he wasn't happy, but he really did believe he was okay. He looked her directly in the eyes. "I'm sorry for this weekend. It's just hard for me to grasp it."

"I know," she sighed. "I just wish you hadn't shut me out."

"I'm sorry. I shouldn't have. I was just confused."

"Why?"

"You were so calm."

"You needed me to be."

"It's just that none of you even seemed to react," he added. He spoke slowly, careful with his words. The last thing he wanted was to sound accusatory, but he knew he wouldn't be able to move on if he didn't tell her how he felt – and if he didn't ask the question that had been burning in his mind. "It's happened before, hasn't it?"

"Garrick…"

"Please, Hayden. I have to know."

"Don't make me answer that."

He let go of her and looked down. He sighed, and they both just sat there for a moment. Garrick started to feel like it would be better to just drop it. His head would always be swimming with thoughts, but that was a clear enough answer in his head. He opened his door and got out of the car, then closed the door and leaned against it – holding his head in his hands.

He heard her door close and her footsteps as she walked around the back of the car to stand next to him. She was quiet for a bit longer, but he could feel her presence. He could feel the tension as she tried to force herself to say something difficult.

"Yes."

Garrick didn't respond. It wasn't a surprising answer by any means – it was just the one he'd wished wasn't true.

"Three times before. People camping at the wrong time."

"Why are we still going out there? I thought we were supposed to be protecting people," he responded angrily. He felt his voice raise, so he had to lower it back down as students walked around them. He breathed deeply, fighting back the anger.

"I don't know, Garrick. You know we can only remember flashes."

"I can't," he said. After a few minutes, he asked her the question he'd been dreading. If he was honest with himself, it was probably the fear of the answer that had kept him so debilitated through the weekend. "Was it me?"

"It wasn't you. It wasn't any of us," she comforted. "You know that. It isn't us."

"Did I kill?" He asked again, with more force this time. A general answer that he wasn't the wolf wouldn't suffice that time. A life had been taken, and he had to know what his role had been in it. He stood up straight, trying to feign confidence, but kept looking at the ground.

"I don't know. What I do remember from the night, we weren't even with them."

He breathed a sigh of relief and ran his fingers through her hair. She slowly reached out her hand. He didn't take it. Instead, he grabbed her arm and pulled her toward him, holding her in a long embrace.

"I'm sorry," he told her.

"It's okay."

"I love you, Hayden. I love you."

"Is something troubling you, Garrick Elliott?" Tyler asked as they sat in the cafeteria. It had been obvious this conversation was coming. Garrick and Tyler didn't spend many full weekends apart, and Garrick very rarely ignored his friend's texts. He just wished he had a good excuse – or that he could tell his friend the truth.

"Just had a tough weekend," was what he said instead.

"Did anything in particular happen? Would you like to converse?"

Garrick looked at his friend. Even after all the years he'd known him, Garrick still couldn't determine exactly when Tyler's dialect was intentional for humor. Tyler wore a comforting smile that just made it even harder to hide the truth from him. If Garrick could trust anyone in the world, it was Tyler. Why was he fighting so hard to keep half of his world a secret from his best friend? Didn't he owe Tyler some kind of honesty?

"I…" He knew he couldn't say anything. Questions swarmed through his mind. If he were to finally open up, where would he even begin? How would he prove that he was telling the truth? He'd sound crazy. It was best, like Aldric had taught them, to not tell humans about their existence.

"Can I talk to you?" Cailean asked from behind Garrick. Garrick wasn't sure where he'd come from – but it was as if he had a sense for any thoughts of divulging confidential information. Garrick wasn't sure he'd have said anything, but Cailean's timing was uncanny.

"I think we'd prefer you didn't," Tyler said with a smirk.

"Good thing I meant him," Cailean replied confidently, "and it wasn't really a suggestion."

"Interesting," Tyler said as he turned to stand, clenching his fists. "Because I wasn't actually stating a preference."

Garrick could see Cailean's eyes light up. He always enjoyed toying with people – pushing whatever buttons he could. He was trying to get Tyler worked up for the sole purpose of proving he could.

"It's okay, Tyler," Garrick told him, placing a hand on his friend's shoulder as he stood. Tyler sighed and relaxed his shoulders, but he still appeared ready for a fight. Garrick wanted to believe Cailean wouldn't let this altercation escalate to a brawl in the lunchroom, but he wasn't convinced. He knew that Tyler would go that far to protect his friends. He also knew, unfortunately, that Tyler would have no chance in that fight, so it was his turn to be the protector for a change. As he followed Cailean to the door, Garrick could feel Tyler's gaze burning a hole in his back. The distrust in his eyes demonstrated that his regard for Cailean was about as high as Garrick's.

The moment they rounded the corner, Cailean turned to face Garrick. Grabbing his shoulders, Cailean slammed him against the wall. Garrick gasped for breath, but quickly recovered and struggled to break free, though he knew it was a completely futile effort. Cailean held firm, pinning Garrick's arms to his sides; any time Garrick moved too much, he would just pull him forward and thrust him back into the brick. Finally, Garrick gave up.

"What have we told you about telling people?" He snarled.

"I am not going to tell him," Garrick sighed, more exasperated than anything else. He wasn't completely convinced he was telling the truth, but he thought he was. Before Cailean had shown up, he'd already made the decision that it was safer not to tell him. He didn't need to hear the lecture again.

"You better not. I won't let you put us all in danger like that."

"I told you I won't say anything. I haven't for a year. Why would I now?"

"Maybe you need someone to cry to when you saw what happened. Well, trust me, Garrick. It is going to be worse if they find out."

"Let go of me."

Cailean didn't budge. He just stared at Garrick with animalistic fury. More unsettling, though, was the fear. Cailean wasn't just angry – he was concerned about what might happen if someone discovered what they were. Before Garrick had a moment to process, he was free. A split second passed where he actually thought Cailean had let go, but then he saw that the young man was about a foot off the ground. He soared through the hallway, impacting the lockers with a bang and sliding down to the ground. Garrick saw Chase standing where Cailean had been.

Chase turned, towering over Cailean as he stood up straight and glared down at him. Cailean quickly stood up – any semblance of fear now replaced with anger.

"He's one of us," Chase spat. "Treat him like it."

"I'd do the same to you if I saw a risk that you'd tell someone."

"And maybe it would work for me. But not for him."

Cailean just glared at Chase for a minute before his rage subsided. He turned and stormed down the hallway.

"Just in time," Garrick exhaled. "I almost hurt him."

"Right," Chase laughed as he turned to face Garrick.

"Seriously, I had him."

"No, you didn't."

"Thanks," Garrick offered after a brief moment of awkward silence.

"Any time. You okay?"

"I'm sick of people asking that. I'm fine!" Garrick snapped.

"I... meant about the being slammed against a wall by a werewolf."

"Oh. Yeah, that. Sorry."

"Come on," Chase said, wrapping his arm around his friend's shoulder. "Let's go eat."

Garrick sat on the stairs after school, waiting for Hayden to find her way to him. Tyler and Kayla walked by, hand in hand, but Garrick was confident he'd gone unnoticed. That was definitely preferable. As much as he'd have liked to say goodbye to Tyler. Garrick was just losing his ability to pretend to like Tyler's girlfriend – if there was ever an ability in the first place. While he was happy for Tyler, it also hurt to watch. Knowing that love existed, and having found someone who actually brought a smile to Garrick's face, made it harder to see Tyler wasting his time. He deserved someone who made him smile more than, on a good day, half of the time.

Completely lost in his thoughts, he didn't notice Hayden sit down. Silently, she leaned her head on his shoulder. Without a thought, he wrapped his arm around her. All of it felt instinctual at that point - the movements barely even registered. For a moment, it felt like all of the other people were gone. Finally looking up, he realized that feeling wasn't too far off. The school was nearly empty. Garrick had no idea how long he'd been stuck in his mind, or how long Hayden had been sitting there. Though he wished the only thing polluting his thoughts was Tyler's broken relationship – there was so much more. He didn't know how to cope with all of the news – but in that moment he was satisfied knowing, or at least believing, he didn't kill anyone.

"I need to talk to Aldric," Garrick said, skipping past the greetings.

"About?"

"Everything."

"Garrick, you know he won't like being challenged."

"I'm not challenging him. I just need to know how this is justified. People are dead, Hayden. And everyone is just pretending nothing happened. That isn't right."

"No, it's not."

He expected some kind of argument to follow, but she just agreed. She seemed to be lost in her own thoughts. Garrick allowed the silence to linger for a moment longer – giving her time to mention anything she wanted to. Standing up, Garrick kept his arm around her and led her to the car.

The drive was quiet too. It wasn't an awkward silence, and it didn't feel like there was some lingering issue they hadn't discussed. It was just a comfortable silence. Of course, that was probably because Garrick was in his head, trying to plan out the best wording for the conversation he didn't want to have.

"Alright," Garrick muttered as they pulled up to Aldric's house. He spent a moment psyching himself up – drumming on the steering wheel. "Alright."

"There's not really another way to get your questions answered," Hayden encouraged.

"Weren't you trying to talk me out of this?"

"I'm curious now," she shrugged. "Go on, I'll wait here."

"Oh? Not curious enough to hear him yell?" Garrick joked.

"You're such a great storyteller, I'd rather hear it from you."

He smiled, releasing his death grip on the steering wheel. Breathing in a few more times, he prepared to talk to Aldric. He wasn't afraid of him – at least not in the sense that he thought Aldric would ever hurt any of his own. It was just that none of the pack wanted Aldric angry at them. No one challenged Aldric – not even his son. Garrick knew that wandering in there and demanding answers wasn't one of his best ideas. More, though, he knew it had to be done.

He knocked on the door and a woman answered.

"Mrs. Phoenix," Garrick said with a smile. She welcomed him with a hug and smiled warmly at him. It baffled Garrick that this kind woman found a stern and stoic man like

Aldric. Maybe there was a bit of truth to the idea that opposites attract.

"Garrick, it's so good to see you!" She beamed. Closing the door behind him, she added, "and on a day when you're not camping, at that."

"Yeah, sorry," he blushed. He hadn't really thought about the fact that he never visited. While he didn't feel great about that, the house wasn't the most inviting place.

"Do you want something to drink?"

"No, I'm okay. I'm just here to talk to Aldric," Garrick responded. He didn't want to cut her off, but he was ready for the conversation, and he was concerned that if he waited too long, he'd lose his resolve.

"Well, you usually are," she said, walking to the kitchen. "Doesn't mean you won't get thirsty."

"I'm okay," he laughed. "Thanks, though."

"Alright then," she said, turning to face him. "He's upstairs in the study."

"Thanks." He hesitated for a second longer, but then took a deep breath and headed up the stairs.

"Come in," Aldric said when Garrick's hand was a few inches from the door. He opened it slowly.

"Hello," he said, barely audible over the creaking of the door. *Off to a great start,* he told himself.

"Oh, Elliott. I wasn't expecting you."

Garrick walked inside and closed the door behind him. Aldric was clearly able to see through his very poorly concealed agenda, and he looked at Garrick skeptically. Garrick expected him to ask what he wanted, or why he'd come, but that wasn't what was said.

"How are you doing, Elliott?" His voice had never sounded so soft.

"I think I'm okay," Garrick said. He inched toward Aldric and sat across from him at the desk. Aldric's intimidating presence loomed over him, even though all of his words so far were kind. Maybe Garrick was just anticipating the argument he knew he was about to start.

"I'm glad."

"I just have to know, Aldric. Has this happened before?" He knew the answer, but he had to hear it from him. Garrick needed to hear Aldric admit it if he was going to get anywhere with the conversation.

"Yes."

"Why do we let it? I thought we were going to the woods to protect people?"

"I lead you to a wildlife preserve. Campers are not permitted, and they are warned that it's a dangerous area. Sometimes people break those rules. While it is unfortunate, it isn't my duty to protect them."

"Isn't it, though? To stop yourself from hurting people?"

"My pack comes first, Elliott," he said. "This is the only way to guarantee I fulfill my duty to you. This is how we stay safe. You just have to trust me on that."

"But you haven't given me a reason."

"The reason is that none of you are dead."

"What about the basement? We couldn't hurt anyone."

"What if we got out? The whole town would be in danger. Innocent people who weren't trespassing. My wife would be in danger."

"I   just   think…"

"Don't," Aldric said, his voice growing harsh. "You don't have to think. It is not your responsibility to process anything about any of this. Trust that I will handle it. This is the only way."

"I can't accept that."

"What?" Aldric asked, genuine shock in his voice.

"I'm done accepting your word as law," Garrick said, standing. He wasn't sure where that surge of power was coming from – he knew it wasn't like him. Still, the pent-up emotions from over the weekend came pouring out. The vague reasoning over the past year had finally taken its toll. Garrick couldn't bite his tongue anymore. "You're wrong on this, Aldric. We can't just keep putting people at risk."

"Get out," Aldric said. Surprisingly, the anger had faded. His voice was calmer than Garrick had ever heard. That was more frightening, though, than a screaming match.

"Gladly. I'll find my own way to do this, and I'll show you that I can stop the casualties. I won't be a murderer."

Aldric was stunned – he clearly wasn't expecting such a strong reaction from Garrick. Maybe he just believed that the pack would perpetually and blindly trust his word. Still, he held a smirk on his face. He started to laugh, quietly at first, but then it grew louder. His shock became amusement. Confused, Garrick just watched Aldric, trying to determine what was possibly going through the man's mind. Before he even registered that Aldric had moved, Garrick felt an intense pain in his stomach. Aldric had leapt over the table and drove his fist into Garrick's gut without giving Garrick a second to respond.

The impact was enough to lift Garrick off his feet and send him a few feet back. He was convinced a few ribs broke, and maybe a bone in his back as he collided with the wall. For a second, he just sat there, trying to catch his breath. Even if he could breathe, he knew he'd be too shocked and too slow to fight back. Aldric grabbed his neck and lifted him into the air. Garrick struggled, but realized he had no hope of breaking the iron grip.

"The only reason you're still alive, Elliott, is because of me," he spat. "You think you can live alone, but you can't even survive one attack from me? You'll die out there, kid. The only reason that I haven't killed you yet is because you're one of us. As pathetic of a werewolf as you may be, you are still one. And unlike you, I don't betray my kind."

Aldric threw Garrick back toward the door. Garrick hit the wall and dropped to the ground a few feet from it, but he didn't have the strength to move. His throat was completely crushed, and he couldn't get a single breath in. Though he could feel his body repairing itself, it didn't ease the pain.

"Get out," Aldric said, not even facing Garrick anymore. He turned and walked back toward his desk. "And don't show your face in here again. You want out of my pack? Fine. But there are monsters out there far more terrifying than I, Elliott. And you had better not come crying to me when they get their hands on you."

Chapter 3

Twenty-two months ago

"We have been hanging out for a month," Hayden urged Garrick, tugging him along. He begrudgingly walked with her. "You can't avoid all of my friends forever."

"I know, I know," he groaned. Every fiber of his being wished he could. Hayden's friends were beyond intimidating, and – from what he'd heard – they weren't the kindest people. One of them was Cailean, and that alone was enough to make Garrick resist spending a moment with them.

"Come on," she tugged harder. He almost lost his balance as she moved more quickly than him, but he tried to play it cool. Her strength kept surprising him, but he tried to hide it as much as possible. It was emasculating, but he was just more concerned that she'd find it a problem if she caught on to how much weaker he was than she. Hayden held him tightly as they walked toward the lunchroom. Over the past two months, she'd eaten with him, but she had kept trying to get him to go eat with her friends.

"Do you realize your friends are terrifying?" Garrick inquired, trying to sound as though he was joking. She just laughed and kissed him on the cheek.

"They'll love you," she whispered in his ear.

Though he had agreed to meet them the previous day, he hadn't meant so soon. He wasn't prepared to set aside all the notions he had of this group. Hayden was wonderful, but her group didn't seem quite as great. Cailean Phoenix was a self-centered jerk – he'd witnessed that first hand. Cailean was the villain in any high school drama, the arrogant bully who seemed to take pleasure in other people's misery. Brooke Cassidy was a Cailean's perfect counterpart. She was the girlfriend anyone would expect Cailean to have. Tall, beautiful, and probably nearly as conceited as her boyfriend.

Garrick wasn't sure what he was hoping for. He was scared that they wouldn't like him because he didn't want them to convince Hayden to break up with him. That was probably a shallow thought. The two of them really liked each other, and he knew she wouldn't just give up on that because her friends didn't like him. Still, he knew from secondhand experience that it wasn't easy dating someone who didn't like one's friends. If nothing else, this experience made him feel worse about not liking Tyler's girlfriend.

On the other hand, Garrick was equally concerned that this group would like him. If they like him, and they weren't the kind of people he wanted to associate with, what did that mean about him? He didn't want to be the type of person who associated with people like that. Then again, Hayden was, so just being friends with them clearly didn't corrupt her too much.

Well, he tried to convince himself. *If Hayden likes them, they can't be that bad.*

"Hey guys," Hayden said. "This is my boyfriend, Garrick."

"Hey, Garry," Cailean greeted him with a smirk. Everything about his face appeared friendly, but his tone implied something sinister. His voice was dripping with disdain. *Or maybe they can be,* Garrick conceded.

"That's Cailean," Hayden said. "Don't worry; I don't care if you like that one."

Garrick laughed, grateful that she was able to ease his nerves. There was something special about her. It wasn't necessarily difficult to sense the tension there, but to know exactly what to say was more impressive. He wasn't even completely convinced that she was joking.

"I'm Brooke," the other girl told Garrick. She probably hadn't made a judgement about Garrick yet, but at least she didn't dislike him on sight. Given everything he'd heard about her, that was surprising. It was a good sign – maybe she wasn't quite as bad as he'd assumed. Nonetheless, he couldn't make that judgement after one greeting, and she still had the entire lunch to decide she didn't like him. He could already feel the nerves coming back as he sat down.

Another guy was sitting at the table. Garrick hadn't heard anything about him, so he had no idea what to expect. His presence wasn't quite as demanding as the other two, and Garrick guessed he was more of a quiet type. Somehow, he managed to avoid the circulating rumors that typically surrounded the "cool kids." Hopefully that meant he was a bit more down-to-earth than his friends. "I'm Chase," he said, extending his hand for Garrick to shake.

He seemed nice enough. There was a bit of sadness in his voice, but no bad intent. Something about him felt genuine, and that was comforting.

"Nice to meet all of you," Garrick said slowly, trying to feign confidence.

"So, how'd you meet Hayden?" Brooke asked, quickly breaking the ice. He appreciated that. She obviously already knew the story – being Hayden's best friend probably meant there wasn't much she didn't know. Getting him to talk about himself was a clever tactic to loosen him up, though. He knew it was a tactic, but it still worked.

"Funny story, actually," Garrick began. "She was moving into the house down the street."

They all looked at him expectantly.

"And, uh. I helped."

"That's not particularly funny," Cailean offered.

"It's not really much of a story," Chase added. At least he smiled. It made Garrick feel like he was just trying to be friendly, bringing him into the friend group.

"I dropped a couch on my toe," Garrick blurted out. It was more inquisitive than an actual statement, wondering if that would justify his opening.

"Okay, see, you should have led with that," Chase advised.

Garrick spent the next thirty minutes eating lunch with Hayden's friends and trying to impress them. Between Chase and Hayden, he started to feel like he was part of the group. Hayden's joke that he didn't have to like Cailean actually comforted him quite a bit because the other two were decent people. Cailean just spent most of the time scoffing and making snide comments. When the lunch bell rang, he practically jumped at the opportunity to leave.

"How bad was I?" He asked Hayden a few minutes later as he walked her to class, holding her hand. He was hopeful, and he definitely had expected it to go much worse. Still, his heart was pounding as he wondered if Hayden thought the same thing. "Be honest."

"You weren't nearly as awkward as I thought you'd be." She smiled and nudged him with her shoulder and squeezed his hand as she spoke, and the tiny laugh at the end of her sentence forced a smile onto Garrick's face as well.

"Oh, thanks," he feigned exasperation.

"You were great," she relented. "I think they liked you."

The two of them had reached her classroom, so they stopped a few feet away from the door. Hayden turned to face him and grabbed his other hand. She waited a few seconds, looking into his eyes and holding his hands. Hayden smiled at him with slightly parted lips as she searched his eyes. Garrick couldn't help but wonder what was on her mind.

"Thanks," she finally spoke up, "it meant a lot to me that you finally met them."

"Of course. I'm sorry I pushed it off for so long."

"It's okay," she smiled. She waited a bit too long to respond – as if she were trying to find the right words. "The first time is usually scary. I had to wait until you were ready."

A part of him was convinced she wasn't talking about meeting her friends anymore. As they gazed into each other's eyes, her words reverberated in his head.

Just do it, he thought. *That's definitely what she meant.*

She'd never been more beautiful to him than in that moment, and as the halls cleared out, they stood alone. Class was going to start soon, though, so he knew his window was closing.

Garrick leaned toward her, his heart beating out of his chest. His face was inches from hers, and he could barely make out the expecting smile on her face. He let go of her hands and wrapped his arms around her, moving his head to the side and pulling her in for a hug.

Garrick wanted more than anything to kiss her, but he didn't want to scare her away. He felt like there was something more between them, but what if he was just making it out to be more in his head? He wasn't willing to risk losing what they had.

Present
24 days until the full moon

"So, that happened," Chase said slowly, breaking the tension of the silence that had surrounded them. The two had been standing in Garrick's front yard tossing a ball back and forth for almost an hour before he'd finally spoken up. Garrick didn't feel like there was much to talk about – at least nothing words would change.

Garrick had tried to avoid any conversations about that night, but he had known it would eventually come back to him.

"Yeah," Garrick agreed quietly.

"I know it's hard to accept," Chase offered. "It sucks, and there's no way around that."

"You don't have to try to comfort me, Chase," Garrick sighed.

"Someone should."

"It won't help."

"I heard you got in a fight with Aldric," Chase changed the subject slightly – but still to something Garrick would prefer they didn't talk about.

"It was his fault, Chase."

"Do you really think he doesn't care?"

"Doesn't it seem like it?"

"I don't know," Chase groaned. With perfect timing, Tyler rounded the corner, walking toward Garrick's house. Seeing the two of them, Tyler's eyes lit up and he held his arms in the air. Garrick tossed the ball to him from three houses away, and Tyler caught it in one hand.

"Wow, Garrick Elliott. I don't remember you having such a good arm," Tyler teased as he approached.

"I've been working on it," Garrick smiled. He was genuinely happy – thankful that Tyler had arrived. It would allow him to spend a few more minutes with his friends and pretend his problems didn't exist.

"Hey, Tyler," Chase greeted, pasting on a smile and trying to pretend they hadn't been in the middle of a serious conversation.

"What did I interrupt?" Tyler, intuitive as ever, asked.

"Nothing," Garrick sighed – fully aware he wouldn't actually be able to hide anything.

"Garrick was just ranting about the physics of throwing a ball," Chase interjected. "Apparently it's more about math than actually possessing any skill."

"I never said that," Garrick defended.

"I don't know, it definitely sounds like you," Tyler shrugged, tossing the ball to Chase.

"I guess it does," Garrick replied. Chase was a quick thinker, which made him a good liar. The fact that those skills were necessary was just an unhappy side-effect of the life they lived.

The three of them tossed the ball back and forth for a few more minutes, talking about everything that came to mind aside from werewolves. Garrick laughed with his friends and, for the first time in a while, felt normal.

Garrick sat in the coffee shop across from Tyler. Tyler had insisted that they go, probably to give him a chance to try to find out what was wrong with his best friend. It was a sort of intervention. Tyler was going to text Hayden and Chase, but Garrick basically begged him not to do so. While he knew he couldn't tell Tyler the truth, he also felt that having them there would just make the lies worse. He didn't want Tyler to be the only one in the group unaware of his secret.

Garrick had barely talked to them over the past few days anyway; at least compared to how much he usually did. He saw them both every day, and he thought he had them almost convinced that he was over what had happened. Somewhere deep down, though, he couldn't accept the idea that all of them were so nonchalant at the loss of human life. Hayden wasn't as bad as Cailean, Brooke, and Aldric seemed, but he wondered if that was just his bias showing. They thought it was completely acceptable. Not entirely ideal, no, but something that just happened in nature. Hayden seemed to view it as a necessary evil. He couldn't read Chase, but he seemed to be somewhere between those views.

Garrick just had trouble accepting the 'necessary' part. There were other options which weren't even being considered. He just didn't understand why Aldric refused to talk to them aside from offering vague threats and asserting that he knew best.

He hadn't spoken a word to the other three since his fight with Aldric. Brooke, Cailean, and Aldric had only talked to him because he was in the pack. Without that, the only thing that tied him to Brooke was Hayden, and there was nothing between the others. He leaned back as he sipped his coffee. He tried to hold Tyler's gaze, but he found himself too distracted.

He felt like he had lied to Hayden. There was an inherent difference between lying and pretending to be okay, though. He was mostly just evading the appearance of moping around, but he hadn't lied to her. He knew she'd see right through him if he tried. He didn't even believe that she thought he'd accepted anything – she was just allowing him to process how he needed to. *I'm not okay,* he thought, *how is she?*

He couldn't come to terms with what was happening. He tried to pretend everything was okay, but he was falling apart inside. Despite all of his grand proclamations that there was another way, he was lost, and he didn't have much time to figure it out.

"What's going on, Garrick Elliott?"

Garrick wished he could tell Tyler the truth. Aside from feeling like he was lying to his friend, Garrick just felt alone. Being without a pack now, he just needed someone on his side. He wanted to open up and explain everything that he had been through over the past two years. What he needed more than anything was a friend who wasn't a killer; someone he could confide in without them feeling like he was throwing that accusation at them.

"I…" He was at a loss. Maybe he could come up with a half-truth. Like what? He'd witnessed a murder. No, that could lead to far too many questions. He was having relationship issues? No, Tyler might say something to Hayden. Instead, he just looked down into the darkness of the coffee which sat in front of him and said nothing. So many thoughts swam around in his head, but he had to keep them all inside.

"You know you can tell me anything, right? We've always been there for each other, but you've been acting incredibly peculiar recently. I can assist with whatever is troubling you, but not if you refuse to divulge any information."

Tyler was trying so hard to be there for Garrick, but he was clearly running out of things to say. What more could he offer if Garrick just kept shutting him out? He knew he needed a friend, and he was terrified to risk pushing Tyler too far away, but he knew there had to be a reason everyone was so scared to let anyone know. He had to stop himself from making any hasty decisions.

"It's just... Me getting stuck in my head again," Garrick said. Considering himself an honest person, especially with regard to his friends, lying was always painful. If there was any possibility he didn't have to, he wouldn't. So, instead, he just spoke in technical truths. He didn't have to tell Tyler the real problems plaguing his mind, but he could at least tell him they were there.

Tyler laughed. It didn't sound like a fake laugh – or even one of frustration – but as if there was actually something comical. It felt so out of place that Garrick didn't really know how to process the information. He just stared blankly at his friend for a moment.

"Do you see me as a fool?" Tyler asked, defeated. His laugh faded as quickly as it had appeared, and all that was left in his eyes was sadness.

"Of course not," Garrick blurted out defensively.

"There is evidently something wrong; it's clear to anyone close to you. Just... Just forget it." He seemed truly hurt. Garrick wanted to say something, but there were no words which could appease his friend. He just sat in silence and looked down toward his coffee, unable to hold Tyler's glare. "You need someone to talk to. If not me, find someone else."

The words, or even the tone, weren't particularly harsh – but the implication was. Tyler felt like Garrick didn't trust him anymore. Garrick wished there were anything to say to prove his friend wrong, but he knew it was a lost cause. Instead, they sat in silence for a few more minutes. Tyler closed his eyes and ran his hands through his hair, flustered. Garrick just fought to stay in the moment and keep himself from getting trapped in his mind again.

Tyler stood and left the shop without saying another word. He didn't look angry. Garrick wasn't even sure he looked hurt. His face was just expressionless.

After waiting another minute, Garrick sighed and stood. He slumped to the door.

"Bye Garrick," the girl behind the counter called out as he walked out the door. It caught him by surprise at first, but he settled down as he realized who'd called. She'd worked there for years, so she'd started to become an acquaintance. While it probably meant that he was there far too often, it actually felt nice to be recognized. Garrick faked a smile, attempting to conceal any form of emotion, as he turned around. He definitely didn't want more questions about that conversation.

"See ya, Sammi," he responded with as much cheer as he could muster.

He stepped outside and started on his way back home. He was a few blocks away and the walk would be pleasant in the setting sun. His mom had the car again because she was working the night shift, so walking was really more of an imperative than an option. Still, there could definitely be worse days to be wandering around in the open air.

He let out a loud sigh as he walked. He knew he was pushing everyone away – and all he wanted was to change. Garrick knew he didn't have much of a chance on his own, and he wasn't good at bottling up his feelings. What choice did he have, though? He didn't see any of his friends the same way when he looked at them. They reminded him that he himself was, at least very possibly, a murderer. If nothing else, he was an accomplice.

Tyler, however, was not. Garrick hated that he had to hide anything from his best friend. Aside from just wanting to be trustworthy, he knew he was shoving away the only friend he could actually trust – even about the lycanthropy. Tyler was the only one who wouldn't just say they were justified to appease his own conscience. Even if unconsciously, Garrick knew the others were hurting, and they just believed what they had to. All he needed was one person to just be blunt and honest. It was too dangerous to tell anyone, though; especially now that he wasn't in a pack. Being alone made a wolf an easy target, and anyone with information could be interrogated by the hunters. It was unfair to share his curse with people who had a chance to live normal lives.

While he'd never actually seen hunters, Aldric swore they existed. He would never divulge any information as far as how he knew; he'd just say that there were hunters out there who would kill werewolves for nothing more than what they were. As he kicked some stones in his path, Garrick couldn't help but wonder if that was actually a problem.

"Garrick," Hayden greeted him on his porch. She stood and walked to him as he approached. She wrapped her arms around him and he hugged back, weakly and not quite as convincingly as he wanted to.

He nearly collapsed, sitting down on the porch. Hayden sat close to him, their legs barely touching. He rested his arms on his knees as he leaned forward. She placed a hand on his arm and waited for him to say something before she talked.

He had always loved that about her. She was a very touchy person. No matter what they were doing, they were touching in one way or another. Whether it was just their legs barely brushing together as they sat near each other or her holding his hand when they walked. He felt like she really loved him.

He looked at her, poorly concealed pain dulling the shine in both of their eyes. Somber silence filled the world around them, and the seconds began to drag on.

"Hey," was all he was finally able to muster.

"Hey," she responded, quiet and inquisitive. "You haven't texted me all day. I thought you were dead."

"Sorry, I must have left my phone here," he said. He was genuinely apologetic. He was forgetful sometimes, and his phone was often a victim of that.

"Garrick, please come back. Apologize to Aldric. I can't keep wondering when they'll find you. It's killing me."

"I can't apologize for something I don't regret. I'm right, Hayden. You know that."

"It doesn't matter who's right. What matters is that he keeps us safe."

"At what cost?"

"Garrick…"

"I wish I could forget. That I could just convince myself it was necessary like the rest of you. But I just can't – it isn't that easy, Hayden."

"Why not?"

"I can't be with them anymore."

"With them?" she asked. "What about me? I'm with them."

"This isn't about you. You know I love you." It was only partially true. He did love her, and it wasn't entirely about her. He knew he could get over what she was doing just because of the way he felt about her, but a part of him was scared to. Garrick was terrified that he'd start to be accepting of murder because he was blinded by love. Still, it was mostly the others.

"Please, Garrick. Don't leave us. Don't leave me."

"I have to do this, Hayden. You can come with me. We don't have to obey his every command. We don't have to be like him." Words started pouring out as he finally confessed what had been weighing down on him.

"He's kept us safe."

"That isn't a reason to blindly trust him! He doesn't tell us anything – he just hides behind a veil of age and wisdom. That isn't a way to earn trust."

"We don't need to know everything!"

"Why not? What if he's wrong?"

"What if you are?"

"Then at least I tried."

"You could get someone hurt, Garrick."

"I could save someone."

"Garrick! You don't get it! He's protecting people! It's not his fault people are where they shouldn't be!"

"Stop defending him! He led us to murder, don't you get that?"

With that, an aura of silence filled the air once again. Garrick's heart dropped as though it were made of stone.

"I can't just sit back and watch you die, Garrick."

"Well, I can't just sit back and watch you kill."

"How could you even say that?" she asked – the shock and pain evident in her voice. "You think I enjoy killing people? It tortures me, Garrick. The dreams about what we might have done. I just know that I must move on. It's the only way we can be safe."

"When you saw it, you didn't even react."

"One of us had to be strong! You're blaming me for being that one? For being there when you needed me?"

"No! I just –"

"You what? Think I should be crying about it still? That I should let my life stop – let that tragedy mean nothing at all?"

"I think we should be finding a solution!"

"Like leaving the pack? Getting ourselves killed? Is that what you want?"

"Of course not."

"You're acting so selfish, Garrick. You think that we aren't all affected by this? Just because you can't handle it doesn't mean you have the right to judge us for doing what we have to do to survive."

"I'm not upset by what you've done! No one could help what happened in that forest. I'm angry about what you're doing now! What you aren't. What none of you are doing. I feel like I'm the only one who actually wants to be sure that no one else dies."

She didn't respond. Tears welled up in her eyes as the silence forced its way back into their surroundings. Garrick took a few deep breaths, trying to calm himself down enough to avoid yelling. It would only get worse if someone overheard their conversation.

"Being in that pack," he started again. "I can't help but see what we are, Hayden. We're monsters. Killers."

"I am not a monster," she said angrily. She stood and walked away from him, leaning against a post but refusing to look back. "I am a girl who's doing what I have to do to survive with this terrible thing that happened to me. I can't believe you would insult me for that."

"Hayden, wait," Garrick sighed as he followed her. His tone softened. It wasn't that what he said wasn't accurate, but he hadn't wanted to hurt her. He wished he could have just bottled it up.

"No, Garrick. If you can't stand to be around us, then don't be. Stay away from me. I can't keep looking into your eyes and seeing nothing but hatred replacing all the love that was there. Even if it's just a part of me you hate, it's still me. You go ahead and die trying to be a hero. But I am not going to have you on my mind all the time anymore. I can't have a boyfriend who may or may not still love me. And I definitely can't have one who could be dead tomorrow because he's so completely self-righteous that he won't even try to survive!"

She was screaming at him now, and he was worried that the neighbors would hear some of their conversation. A fire burned in her eyes, and she looked so angry that he was physically taken aback, moving a step away. He felt his own anger start to fade into sadness, and he just looked back at her expressionless.

She looked like she wanted a response, but he didn't have one for her. He continued to stare blankly as she scoffed angrily and turned from him. There wasn't even sadness anymore – his brain was overwhelmed to the point that it shut off.

The anger, sadness, and pure disbelief blended together and interfered with one another to the point that he just couldn't feel. Garrick wanted her to come back – he wanted to find the magic words that would make the argument disappear – but he wouldn't lie, and he knew no words he had could convince her. He just watched the love of his life walk away. The second she was out of site, he collapsed to his knees as the realization of what had happened hit him, and the tears fell.

Chapter 4

Twenty-one months ago

Garrick silently sat amongst Hayden's friends, chewing quietly and contributing as minimally to the conversation as possible. Though he'd been eating with them for a month, he didn't feel a part of the group. Hayden wanted him there, and that was enough for him, but it didn't mean he had to be talkative. Most of the others didn't seem to particularly care about his presence. Chase was the only one who seemed to notice him, but he was just a genuinely good person, and Garrick had grown to like him. They weren't the closest friends, but they were far closer than Garrick would have assumed he'd be with anyone in that group.

Over the past month, Garrick had begun to see Chase as a friend, and he started to feel a loyalty toward him. Hayden had told him that the two of them used to date, and they both seemed over it, but he still wasn't sure if it was right. He knew there was no obligation – it wasn't as if he was stealing Chase's girlfriend. Garrick didn't even know him before he'd fallen for her. Still, he decided he should at least talk to him about it. There hadn't been many opportunities, though, and he felt far too uncomfortable when they were alone.

Garrick was perfectly copacetic with his limited participation in any discussions anyway. It gave him more time to think – to lock himself in his mind like he usually did. From the impressions the others gave off, Garrick was the only introvert present – and he tended to prefer his thoughts to most human interaction – unless it was with Hayden. Though he'd only known her for two months, he couldn't shake the idea that he wanted to spend his life with her. Maybe it was just him romanticizing their relationship. After all, he wasn't sure she even knew he felt that way – or that he felt anything for her. Every time he tried to bring it up, he was paralyzed by the fear that she interpreted things differently, or that she didn't feel the same, so he just avoided discussing it.

As the lunch bell rang, Garrick mustered up his courage. There were two conversations he wasn't looking forward to, but he didn't want to avoid them. He had to pick one to tackle, so he chose the one which was awkward but not necessarily intimidating.

"I'll catch up with you later," he told Hayden.

"Oh, okay," she shrugged. Hayden stood and walked out of the room, and Garrick watched her leave. He was definitely not ready to risk losing her, and he lacked the confidence to try to label anything with her. Instead, he hoped to build up his confidence with lower stakes. Though it wasn't ideal, he'd rather lose Chase as a friend than Hayden as – whatever she was.

"Hey, man," Garrick said quietly after Brooke and Cailean waked away.

"Hi?" Chase laughed.

"I want to ask you something."

"What's up, Garrick? Is everything okay?"

"Yeah, I just... Well, over the past month, I've really started to consider you a good friend of mine."

"Well thanks, I appreciate that."

"I know you and Hayden used to be an item," he continued. Garrick had never felt more uncomfortable in his life, but he felt like this was something he had to talk to Chase about. If he wanted the two of them to stay friends, he couldn't ask Hayden out without at least giving him a heads-up. Aside from that, a part of him was actually happy to be pushing his comfort zone. He knew he wouldn't be able to skate through life only partaking in safe and amicable conversation.

"An item?"

"Together," Garrick clarified.

"Together?" Chase asked slowly, squinting.

"Dating," Garrick choked out, barely able to function through the difficult conversation. Chase was silent for a second, but then his inquisitive look finally broke into a smile.

"I'm just messing with you, Garrick. Can't make something easy for you, can I?" He asked with a laugh. He patted Garrick's shoulder and stood up. Garrick wasn't entirely sure what to say, so he just stood as well.

"That was a long time ago," Chase added, his demeanor becoming slightly somber and nostalgic.

"What happened?" Garrick asked. The two of them started walking out of the lunchroom and toward the hall. Garrick had no idea where Chase's class was, so he was just following him and hoping the path didn't take him too far from his own.

"Well," he responded hesitantly. Garrick felt like Chase was hiding something – selecting his words very carefully. "We really liked each other. But I don't think we were ever meant to be more than friends, you know? I guess the time came for us to decide if we really wanted to be with each other forever. And we just didn't."

"I see. So it's all in the past, then?"

"Of course."

"So you'd be fine if I asked her out?"

Chase smirked, stopping in his tracks and looked back at him. "You haven't? You two have been holding hands for a month, my friend. I figured you were both just terrible at hiding a secret relationship."

"Maybe it's a bit of that," Garrick smiled back. "I don't know, I guess I've just been too afraid to ruin it. But I want to officially go out with her, you know? I just couldn't do that without at least talking to you about it first."

"Why?"

"I don't know," Garrick shrugged. He felt himself loosening up and managed to find the confidence to add humor to his tone. "I just didn't want to ruin our blossoming friendship."

"You're a good guy, Garrick," Chase said as he placed a hand on Garrick's shoulder. "I guess that just proves that Hayden has good taste. I'm happy for both of you."

Chase turned and walked away, leaving Garrick to stand there with his thoughts for a moment. He started beaming for more reasons than he bothered to count. He felt triumphant that he finally had his dreaded conversation, hopeful for his future with Hayden, and glad to have a new friend.

Chase stopped again, turning around to look at Garrick harshly. "Oh, but one thing: if you hurt her, I will literally tear you apart."

"I'd be disappointed if you didn't," Garrick responded sincerely.

Present
21 days until the full moon

Garrick checked his phone. There hadn't been any sound, and he set the ringer to the highest setting, just in case someone called. Still, he checked it. Denial somehow made him question his enhanced hearing against all logic – and he convinced himself he may have missed the tone.

Hayden hadn't said a word to him all weekend. He had left her two voicemails and tried texting her a dozen times, but she never responded.

He had begged his mom to let him stay home from school while attempting to talk as little about the break-up as possible. He was lying on his bed staring blankly at the ceiling. Allowing himself to check the phone again, Garrick saw that it had been two minutes since he last opened it. Every minute seemed to drag on for decades.

He sat up and rubbed his eyes. Garrick could feel the lack of sleep affecting him. He hadn't moved, but he was also scared to close his eyes – lest he see Hayden. There was no motivation left for him to do anything. He hadn't showered or changed clothes in two days, and the only times he had left were when he needed to use the restroom. Even when he ate, he just hid in his room. His mom had been understanding and even ate with him once, but the entire meal was shared in silence as Garrick just looked at the wall. She hadn't said anything, but he knew she didn't want to see that again – so she'd taken to eating in front of the television.

He stumbled to the bathroom. His legs were weak, and he had to catch himself on the door. He wasn't sure if that was from a psychological side-effect or if his legs were simply protesting due to their lack of use over the past few days. Given the fact that anything physical was bound to heal, he was leaning toward the former. Unfortunately, simply understanding that it was psychosomatic didn't fend off the weakness.

He made his way to the bathroom and brushed his teeth, took a shower, and changed. He wasn't sure where he was going, but he knew he had to get out of the house. If Garrick didn't act upon his sudden motivation to move, there was no way to know when it would come back. After making himself slightly more presentable, he stepped outside and walked for about half of an hour, up and down random streets, just to find himself at the coffee shop he loved so much. He smiled weakly and went inside.

"Hey, Garrick," Sammi said. The shop was empty, but she went back and started preparing a drink. When he realized it was for him, he decided that he definitely did go there too frequently.

Though it made him feel special that the barista remembered his order, he hated that she was working. If he'd realized she wouldn't be at school, Garrick wouldn't have gone in. Even though she had mentioned that she'd graduated three years ago, his mind just wasn't up for putting things together. Since she was there, though, he had to fake a smile. At that point, she became another person he had to try to convince he was okay.

"Playing hooky?" she asked with a sly smile. She leaned over the counter. Her blond hair fell over her shoulder, and Garrick had to blink to stop himself from seeing Hayden.

"Don't tell," he joked. He walked up to the counter, pulling out his wallet. He thought about how many times he had been in there. Yes, he'd gone alone and with Tyler. But the painful memories were with Hayden. Those memories followed him everywhere he went.

Garrick handed her a few dollars and took the coffee, exchanging pleasantries before retreating to a table in the corner. It became his personal goal to forget that he wasn't alone in that room. The countertop with packets of sugar was directly in front of him. Hayden had never been able to stand drinking black coffee. Of course, he hadn't been aware when they started dating, but caffeine didn't even affect her at all. She basically used it as a conduit for cream and sugar. Growing up, Garrick had learned from his mother, who always worked late, that it was a way to help him wake up. After he was scratched, he just continued to drink it out of habit more than anything else.

"How are you doing?" Sammi asked. Though she'd blocked his view of the countertop when she sat down, Sammi had somehow managed to surprise him nonetheless. Garrick tried in vain to hide his startled reaction.

"Sorry," she said, smiling. "Thought you saw me."

"Yeah," he responded. "Guess I was distracted."

"So how are you doing?"

"With?"

"That girl of yours."

"She isn't mine. Not anymore," he said. Finally, he told someone the truth. At least something which was true. It felt like all he'd done for weeks is hide and reveal only the safe parts of anything he said.

"I know," she said. "It's written all over your face."

"Oh."

"I just wanted to make sure," she added slowly. She sounded hesitant – as if she were waiting for him to continue the conversation. At the moment, though, he wasn't particularly interested in any type of human interaction. Garrick just allowed the silence to continue.

"I was thinking," she finally added. Garrick wished another customer would wander in and distract her, but the next rush wouldn't arrive until after school. She seemed like a nice enough person, but she clearly couldn't read a room. He'd talked to her quite a bit, but this was bordering on the longest conversation they'd had, and he couldn't understand why she chose that particular moment to have it.

"Maybe I could make you some dinner," Sammi proceeded cautiously. She looked nervous, and Garrick could tell that she was as horrible at making friends as he was. "Take your mind off things. I'm a great cook."

Drifting through the sea of thoughts, Garrick barely registered that he was supposed to be providing an answer. He just stared blankly at her.

"I mean, it doesn't have to be a date, just two friends hanging out." She mistook his lack of a response as denial and quickly corrected herself.

"Okay," he responded, emotionless. Only half of his attention, if that, was dedicated to the conversation. "That sounds great."

"Wow," she replied happily. He used all of the strength he had to pull his mind from Hayden's voice and focus on Samantha's.

"Okay, how about Friday?" she asked, sounding a little too excited.

"Yeah, perfect," he said. For a second, he thought about whether he had plans with Hayden on Friday, and that just brought him even lower. "I'm not doing anything Friday."

"Your place or mine?" she asked.

"Uh, well, my mom isn't going to be home," Garrick replied. Realizing that he'd agreed to spend time with another person, he quickly searched his brain for excuses to reverse the mistake.

"So yours?" she jumped in quickly, not allowing him to stretch out the answer any longer. "That's great, it'll be better if we don't have to deal with my family."

Garrick searched his brain for any other excuses, but he couldn't think clearly. Her smile just made it more difficult. He felt more awkward with each passing second, and the silence was becoming painfully obvious.

"Yeah, that works for me," Garrick sighed. She gave him her number. They exchanged awkward goodbyes as he left and headed home.

Great, he thought. *I just agreed to a date. What was I thinking?*

Really, he hadn't been. Not about her at least. He wasn't used to girls being so forward with him. Garrick desperately racked his brain for a solution. Of course, he could always just cancel, but he knew he'd feel terrible. He could invite other friends to make it less awkward. If he brought Chase and Tyler, it would just be a group of friends eating together. As quickly as that idea came, though, it dissipated. She'd most likely be intimidated when she expected just Garrick. Anyway, he wasn't quite sure he was ready to explain the situation to Chase.

"Hey," he texted Tyler. Normally, Garrick sent messages in paragraphs, but as he gathered his thoughts, he sent

the singular word. As quickly as he could think, he typed, "*I need a huge favor. I sort of have a date on Friday.*"

"*What?*" Tyler texted back. "*You and Hayden made amends?*"

"*No. The girl from the coffee shop. I didn't think about it, she just asked me and I was distracted and I said yes. I don't know what to do. I shouldn't be going out with her, it isn't fair for anyone. But she was so happy, I can't just cancel...*"

Trying to type every thought into words, Garrick was hammering away at the keys on his phone. The words just flowed into texts as a stream of consciousness. While he was confident Tyler would understand exactly what was happening, he knew no one else would from the fragments of sentences he kept sending. In some twisted way, he was actually glad to have a problem with which he could trust his best friend again. There was some modicum of normalcy creeping its way back into his life. Of course, the circumstances were undesirable, but he was finally able to be totally honest with Tyler about something again – for the first time in years.

Garrick had sent at least a dozen messages, ranging from one word to multiple paragraphs, before he felt confident that he'd emptied his thoughts into the texts. Though Tyler's response only took a few minutes, the wait felt like hours. His heart was pounding – though he wasn't quite sure why.

"*No need to worry. I have a plan.*"

"*What is it?*" Garrick asked. He held his phone, staring at it intently as he waited for the message to come through. He didn't even notice where he was walking anymore.

"*I'll go. I'll bring Kayla and we'll make it a double date. Double dates are much less awkward.*"

That was a horrible plan. She had planned to make him dinner, and she would show up and see two extra people? Wouldn't she be just as off-put as she'd be if he cancelled on her? Maybe, but she wouldn't be as hurt. He hoped.

"*Good plan, right, Garrick Elliott?*" Tyler sent.

Without any other option, Garrick responded, *"No. Not at all. But it's the best one I've got. Be there at 6."*

Garrick looked up and found himself surrounded by trees. He thought he'd been walking home, but the texting had apparently set him off course. The woods were actually a very calming place for him when he wasn't going there to transform into a ravenous beast. Just being surrounded by nature, he felt the stress start to fade away.

He wandered around for a bit, taking in his surroundings. The sun was high in the sky, and there were patches of light sprinkled all around him. The leaves on the trees were blowing with the slight breeze which kept the air even cooler than it actually was. In front of him, there was nothing but dense foliage as far as his eye could see. Looking over his shoulder, Garrick wondered how far he'd gone. There was no sign of civilization. Subconsciously, he must have been avoiding running into trees for quite a while.

A tree a few feet to his right shook, disturbing all the life anywhere nearby. Squirrels darted down the trunk, insects scuttled away, and at least thirty birds angrily departed from the branches. Their squawking and the flapping of their wings drowned out any sound that there had been around him. He weaved to the side, avoiding a raven which passed inches from his face. As he watched, it dodged past the trees to his left until it disappeared into them.

Curiosity slithered into his mind, forcing him to question what force could cause so much commotion. Whatever it was, he knew he didn't want to be anywhere near it. Though his brain repeated that thought – telling himself to avoid looking at any cost – his legs seemed to disobey him. A low growling rose from the shrubs nearby as he approached the tree which had been shaken. He wondered if there were any bears around there. He hadn't seen any, but there weren't many animals powerful enough to force that much motion out of a tree.

Time to go home, he thought. It was more of a pleading with his own subconscious than anything else. He couldn't make himself leave, though. The part of him which was concerned for his safety was succumbing to the part which needed answers. He pushed a low hanging branch to the side and ducked down, trudging through the increasingly dense foliage.

Clouds blotted out the sun, covering the patches of light and plunging the forest into darkness. Fear started to flood his mind as the growling intensified. He could feel the sound reverberating through the ground underneath him, vibrating in his chest. The logical side of him knew it was time to turn and run. He should get back home. But something within him he didn't know existed kept him going. He'd come so far, and deep down, he knew that it was too late to turn back. There wasn't much waiting for him back in the town aside from an awkward meal and heartbreak – but here, there was more. Although he didn't know what it was; he knew there was some secret hidden just beyond his reach, and it caused him to keep pressing forward into the darkness.

He saw an outline of a dog dart past him. Maybe it was someone's pet that got loose. It probably heard the bear too, and it was running to get out of the woods. Every animal in existence seemed to be smarter than he was in that moment. They all followed the instincts screaming to run to safety.

Distracted by the dog, he didn't notice the much larger figure move. By the time he processed the motion, it stood only a few feet in front of him. He couldn't distinguish its full form, but the creature looked majestic in a sense. It radiated power – and he was drawn in by it. Every fiber of his being screamed to run, climb a tree, get to safety by any means necessary – but he just watched.

The creature's back was arched, its paws planted firmly into the ground. Garrick still tried to tell himself it was a bear. For a brief moment, he acknowledged the peculiarity of that being his preferred outcome. The bear rose to its hind legs and Garrick could sense its eyes looking at him. The ground reverberated as it opened its mouth and roared.

No, not roared. Howled.

The wolf dropped back onto all fours and circled Garrick. Panic started to set in. He couldn't understand why death at the claws of a bear seemed preferable to a wolf. Nonetheless, his brain started to react more when he realized what stood in front of him.

He'd lost sense of direction, but from where he thought was the direction of the town, he heard thunder. A flash of light illuminated the woods, and he saw the bright eyes of the wolf for a brief second. The wind grew much stronger, and the trees around him were shaking furiously.

He backed away until he hit a tree. The wolf inched closer to him until he could see its eyes shining through the darkness. They were the color the sky had been when he'd left his house that morning – a beautiful but pale blue.

"Good dog," he muttered, mustering everything he had to instill the slightest hint of confidence in his shaky voice. All he could do was hope the creature would respond to the tone in his voice. Maybe it wouldn't tear him to pieces if he whispered sweet nothings to it as it grew closer.

It pounced, and he ducked and rolled to the side. The creature caught on a second too late, but it was able to twist its body enough to slam his side into the tree instead of his head. The tree splintered, and Garrick could hear the sound of wood cracking even louder than the thunder that grew closer.

The wolf crawled toward him. He was paralyzed.

It stood directly over him. Its eyes stared into his. What he saw in them was confusing. It was as if there was a shred of intelligence – almost as though it recognized him. Behind what he knew to be a monster, a creature of nightmares, there was a shred of humanity.

Then, that shred disappeared as it bared its teeth, which reflected the glint of lightning as it bolted across the sky.

Garrick shot up in his bed, sweat pouring down his face. It was dark outside, but he had no idea what time it was. He vaguely remembered coming home, but he also remembered wandering into the woods as he texted Tyler about his date. He wiped the sweat from his forehead with his thumb as he breathed heavily. He scooted backward so he could lean his back against the headboard of his bed, needing the support to sit up.

He leaned his head against the wall behind him and closed his eyes, exhaling slowly. Willing his heartbeat to slow down and carefully monitoring his breathing, Garrick tried to calm himself down. Regardless of how many times he told himself it was just a dream, it felt like more, and he was unable to get it out of his head. He ran his fingers through his hair and sighed deeply.

The events of the day were all coming back to him, but he couldn't tell which of them had actually happened and which he had dreamed. They all flowed together. He wondered which part of the day he had dreamed.

Garrick reached over the side of the bed to his nightstand, grabbed his phone, and checked the time. It was after nine. He saw his text messages. His mom left one telling him to order a pizza if he wanted food. She'd left money on the counter. With his stomach in knots from the stress, he couldn't imagine any food sounding appetizing ever again. Even if he decided to eat, he was just going to make a sandwich. He refused to spend any unnecessary amount of her money.

He had another text from her. *"Ily Gar-bear. ;) That means I love you Garrick in teen talk. Mixed with a bit of mom talk."*

That brought a smile to his face. She texted just as much as he did, and she was handy with all the expressions people used throughout them. She didn't really understand emoticons, though, and it always made him laugh to see her use or misuse them.

"I love you too, Mom," he sent back. She'd texted hours ago, but he responded nonetheless. He knew it would make her happy to see it.

The third and final message in his inbox was from even earlier in the day, and it was from Tyler. *"What are friends for, if not devising mediocre plans to avoid potential awkward-ness? I'll bring some pie."*

So that part had not been a dream.

Chapter 5

Twenty-one months ago

"Tyler, I really need your help here," Garrick said. He was becoming frantic due to his inability to conjure up the right words.

"Settle down, Garrick Elliott. What's the problem?" Tyler asked. Sitting on the couch in his living room, Garrick felt himself teetering on the verge of a meltdown. He could ruin everything, and that fear was paralyzing. Nonetheless, he was equally scared of perpetually regretting a lack of action.

"I'm going to ask Hayden out."

"It's about time," Tyler laughed, leaning back a bit. It was clear that he felt a wave of relief – probably assuming there was something far worse hiding behind Garrick's fear.

"Well what if she says no?"

"What reason could she possibly have to reject you?" He smirked a bit, but Garrick wasn't sure if it was a serious question. His rationality wavered as he continued to panic.

"Have you seen her?" Garrick exclaimed.

"Indeed I have," Tyler said, placing a hand comfortingly on his friend's shoulder. "She is so far out of your league. I'm legitimately dumbfounded at the prospect that the relationship has progressed as far as it has already."

Garrick knew he was right, but it didn't calm his nerves in the slightest.

"But it has," Tyler continued with a shrug. "Logic isn't a factor here. This girl is crazy about you. She sees something far greater than anything you see in yourself. Trust me, I know it's there.

"Hayden wouldn't turn you down if she were paid to. The way the two of you are practically cinematic. It's so perfect that the rest of us are thoroughly convinced it's a ruse – the two of you are putting on a well-conceived show. Yet, against all odds, it's an actual relationship."

"Maybe she's just happy being my friend."

"If you honestly believe that, I find it hard to believe you weren't intentionally diverting your attention from her advances."

"I'm blind to signs! You know that. I can't do any of this subtle relationship development. What if I misread something?"

"She's been illuminating neon signs in your face for a month. At this point you should just be happy she hasn't given up on you yet."

"I don't even know what to say."

"Would the specific words make any difference? Just stand up, walk across the street, knock on her door, and blather on about how attracted you are to her until she kisses you. Any combination of the words 'will you go out with me?' will suffice."

"Okay," Garrick nodded forcefully, trying to convince himself he was prepared. He stood up and walked to the door, head held high and confidence overflowing. As soon as he reached it, though, he turned back around. His feigned confidence faded and he attempted to make a hasty retreat. Tyler was right behind him, blocking his path. He gave Garrick a friendly, albeit forceful, nudge through the front door.

"Don't make me ask for you, Garrick Elliott. I will, and that will embarrass all of us."

Garrick gulped overdramatically, nodded, and turned back around. He crossed the street and travelled the short distance to Hayden's door. As he knocked, he felt as though his lungs were collapsing within his chest. Even if she said yes, what was he going to do? Garrick didn't have the slightest idea on how to be a good boyfriend. The door opened, interrupting his thoughts.

"Hey, Garrick," Caleb greeted. "I don't assume you're here for me?"

"I was hoping to talk to Hayden," Garrick responded, trying to conceal his awkwardness.

"Well, a guy can dream," Caleb shrugged as he called to Hayden. She rushed down the stairs as her brother walked away.

"Hey Garrick," she smiled.

"Hi," he muttered, avoiding eye contact. He stood there in silence for nearly a full minute as she looked at him expectantly.

"Is everything okay?" she finally asked.

"Yes! Yes. Hayden, do you want to do something?"

"What?" she laughed. He wasn't sure if she was requesting details on his plan or just expressing confusion, so he did his best to clarify.

"I don't know. We could do something. Something convenient for you. Do you like eating? You don't look like you like eating, but I mean, you have to. Like to survive."

"I eat," she said, her expression changing to something more skeptical. He was losing her, and fast, but there wasn't a single suave cell in his body. How was he supposed to act like he was the kind of person she'd date?

"Yeah," he said. "I mean, I know. But do you want to do it with me? Eat, I mean?"

"Garrick Elliott, are you asking me on a date?" she asked.

"Yes," he responded inquisitively. A part of him was looking to her for affirmation, as if he were unable to confirm his own intentions, but another part was just scared of the direction of the conversation. Suddenly, he realized that since it was already out there, there was no going back. A bit of the tension faded away, and he was able to force a bit more confidence into his voice. "Yes, I am. I've liked you since the moment I saw you, and I've spent two months building up the courage to walk up to your door and ask you to be my girlfriend. So there it is."

"I'd love to eat with you," she laughed.

"Really?"

"Obviously," she said. "I was just starting to get worried you'd never ask."

Present
17 days until the full moon

"Garrick," Chase spoke quietly and almost hesitantly. For the first time all week he'd approached Garrick and Tyler in the lunchroom, and it was apparent his mind was struggling in search of the right words to say.

"Can we talk?" was all he was able to choke out.

In the brief silence that followed, Tyler looked at Garrick inquisitively. Garrick just shrugged, but nodded to him, assuring him that everything was fine. Tyler looked back at Chase skeptically. Between the three of them, it was rare that something was said in private – at least as far as Tyler knew. Conversations about their shared curse were typically something Garrick and Chase concealed a little better.

"I'll see you after school," Tyler told Garrick, shrugging as he tried to pretend he wasn't offended at being left out of a conversation with his friends.

"You're crazy, Garrick, you know that?" Chase whispered harshly as he sat across from Garrick and leaned in close in an attempt to avoid being overheard.

"What?" Garrick froze for a minute, genuinely shocked by the sudden shift in tone.

"Look, it's been two weeks since your fight with Aldric. We all expected you to be back by now. You can't keep doing this."

"I can't go back now," Garrick responded forcefully. His conviction wiped away the confusion that had gripped him only moments before.

"I know it's hard. Trust me; I hate feeling like a monster. I hate what I did. But we don't have another choice."

"I'll find one," Garrick tried to appear nonchalant, but he knew the odds were stacked against him. He was alone.

"You know what," Chase conceded, softening his voice a bit. He spoke slowly, selecting his words more carefully. "If you do, maybe we can start our own pack. Until then, please come back. You'll get killed out here. And maybe you'll take a few people down with you."

Chase stood, cutting the conversation short. He knew Garrick well enough to know that he wouldn't get an answer in that moment – Garrick would have to be left to ponder. As Chase walked away, Garrick took a deep breath, finding himself wondering if Chase was right. But how was he going to go back around them, especially after what happened with Hayden? She still looked away whenever he came into view. She still refused to say a word to him. There was no way the two of them could be near each other.

No, he'd have to find a way to handle the change himself. But he'd have to do that later. He had other things on his mind. He tried to calm himself down as he rubbed his eyes. Confident he'd contained himself enough, he walked out of the lunchroom, heading to his next class. As he crossed the threshold of the doors, Tyler stepped from the side and startled him. Garrick caught Tyler's wrist and locked it, spinning around and pinning his friend to the wall – adrenaline coursing through his veins.

"Don't startle me like that," Garrick muttered as his pulse slowly faded back to normal. He dropped Tyler's wrist and stepped back. Tyler shook his hand, trying to force away the pain, as he looked at Garrick disconcertedly.

"Well, that was unexpected," he finally admitted, raising his eyebrows as he spoke. His usual lightheartedness was ever-present. "So, are you prepared for this evening?" Tyler asked.

"Not in the slightest."

"You're going to be fine. I will prevent you from making too much of a fool of yourself."

"Thanks," Garrick said with a laugh. "Just don't forget the pie."

At five o'clock, his doorbell rang. Tyler was early. He'd asked his friend to get there before Samantha did in hopes the awkwardness would be somewhat appeased, but Garrick hadn't expected him to take it to heart so much. That meant he was going to have to spend extra time with Kayla too. There wasn't much of an opportunity for him to win in that situation.

He opened the door to see Samantha standing in front of him, beaming with two full bags of groceries in her hands. He quickly pasted a fake smile on, but he knew she'd already caught sight of his perpetual frown that he'd worn over the past few weeks.

"Everything alright?" she asked. Her smile died down as quickly as his had appeared.

"Yeah," he responded, shrugging off the question. It almost sounded convincing. "Come on in." As an afterthought, he added, "here, let me help you with those."

He took the bags and led her inside. As he placed the bags on the counter, his mom, having heard the door, came out from her room. She was in uniform already, and her badge caught a glint of the dim kitchen light. She was on night shifts recently, so she had to go in at six. He'd hoped no one would arrive until well after her departure, simply to save him a lot of awkward conversation.

"Hello," she greeted, shooing Garrick a questioning and jokingly suspicious look.

"Ms. Elliott, I assume?" Samantha asked.

"Yes," she responded, still retaining her suspicious gaze. She had become skilled in the art of feigning emotions through her countless interrogations, so even Garrick was starting to wonder if she was serious.

"I'm Samantha. You can call me Sammi if you want."

"Well alright Sammi," his mom responded with a quiet chuckle, breaking character. Garrick was so thankful for his mother. She wasn't a parent who would intentionally make an already awkward situation worse for him – at least not until after Samantha was gone.

A lot of moms would ask who she was, since he never mentioned her. Or say something to Garrick about how soon it was after Hayden. He would have agreed with that, of course, but he didn't want to explain all of that to her.

Instead, she just made a joke. "Went shopping for us?" she asked with a smile.

"Sorry," Samantha replied. "I just had to pick up a few things for dinner. Are you going to eat with us?" It sounded like an invitation – there wasn't a hint of concern that his mother would say yes. She was a genuinely nice person. He'd said his mom wouldn't be there, but Samantha didn't seem off-put or bothered at all by her presence.

"I can't," his mom replied. "I have to get to work as soon as Garrick here gives me the keys to the car."

Garrick didn't say anything. He just retreated to his room and strained his hearing, hoping they weren't discussing anything that could make his night go downhill. His hearing was slightly better than average thanks to the wolf senses, but those barely helped so far from the moon. All he could hear was some indistinct conversation and laughing. He sifted through everything in his room, desperately trying to remember where he'd left the keys. The more quickly he found them, the faster he could get back out there and perform the imminently necessary damage control.

"Silly me," his mom said from the doorway, startling him out of his trance. Somehow, he hadn't noticed the cessation of the conversation, or her make her way back toward him. She was dangling the keys in her hand, leaning against his door frame and smiling at him.

"You did that on purpose," Garrick muttered, exasperated.

"You know me," she smirked. Her expression changed quickly, fading from playful to concerned. "You alright, Garrick?"

"It's a long story," he said.

"Well I expect to hear it when I get home. And find you here. Sleeping. And no one else." She said it jokingly, but in a tone that let him know she was completely serious.

"I know, mother."

"Good. Well, she's cute."

"Yeah," Garrick said. His mom was heading back down the hall and out the door. She waved at him as she left to work. He turned his gaze to Samantha, who had already started laying ingredients for spaghetti out across the counter. He was so happy she'd chosen something so simple. At least he didn't have to deal with trying to pretend to like some overly fancy food. She was wearing a white tank top and shorts and had her hair tied back in a ponytail, probably to keep it out of her face as she cooked.

"Yeah, I guess she is."

Garrick had texted her earlier in the week asking if it was okay to invite Tyler and Kayla over as well. He had specifically avoided using the term 'double date' but it seemed to him that any way he phrased the question made it incredibly obvious. She was surprisingly okay with it, so he thought maybe she was nervous for their date as well. Though they most likely had very different reasons, it made him feel better to know that he wasn't the only one.

"Your friends better get here soon," she told him as she leaned over the oven, stirring the sauce which rested on the back burner. "It's almost done."

"He will," Garrick responded, careful about his word choice. Maybe it was petty, but he wasn't willing to call Kayla a friend. He left it at that for a few seconds, allowing the silence to hang in the air. "Thanks for this," he finally added.

"Of course," she told him. She stopped stirring and stepped back from the oven. She checked on the garlic bread and switched off the oven. Hesitantly, she moved toward him a bit – and he just felt dread. He recognized this moment, and he definitely wasn't as interested as she was. In a bold move, she threw her arms over his shoulders, pulling him into an embrace. Their faces hovered a few inches apart. Garrick awkwardly moved his head to the side and hugged her, careful not to hold on too tightly. No matter how long he'd been with Hayden, he always felt butterflies when they touched. Here, he felt nothing. It started to feel like the hug was dragging on a bit too long when the doorbell ringing gave him a valid excuse to pull away.

Garrick had to remind himself to walk normally – to avoid letting her see how excited he was to get a buffer. Trying not to bound toward the door, he cautiously meandered toward it and placed a hand on the knob. When he opened it, Tyler and Kayla stood in front of him. Tyler, holding a store-bought apple pie, beamed and silently bounded inside. As Kayla followed him, Garrick realized the day had finally come that he was actually happy to see her.

"Thanks for coming," he said to Kayla. She smiled and hugged him as she greeted him.

"Hi Tyler," Garrick called after his friend.

"I'm on a mission, Garrick Elliott," Tyler called back, continuing his trek to the kitchen. Garrick laughed as he closed the door and led Kayla to the kitchen. He introduced everyone as he caught up to Tyler, who placed the apple pie he'd brought on the counter in a rather exaggerated motion.

"I have procured a pie," he declared.

"He is very excited about that pie," Kayla whispered to Garrick. Her tone confused Garrick, as he wasn't sure if it was supposed to be a joke or a complaint. Either way, he overheard and didn't seem too offended.

"I am indeed!" he exclaimed. He reached out for her hand, and when she took it, he pulled her close and kissed her lightly.

When they weren't arguing, they both seemed so completely happy. It was as if they completed each other, and they wanted to spend every waking minute of their lives together. It reminded Garrick of what he had with Hayden. The problem was that the time they spent happy seemed to be significantly overshadowed by the amount of time dedicated to bitter arguments.

"It looks like a wonderful pie," Samantha laughed. "Thank you."

"I am glad to know someone is appreciative of this magnificent pie," Tyler said. Garrick was starting to get the impression that he wasn't kidding. Tyler was apparently just really looking forward to that pie. "You are most certainly welcome. I hope you enjoy watching as I consume it in its entirety."

Kayla smiled, seemingly perceiving that as the cutest thing she'd ever heard. Garrick was happy for Tyler. He and Kayla had been together for three months consecutively this time, and he had a small amount of hope that maybe things would actually work out for them. As much as he didn't think Kayla was the best choice, he was happy to see Tyler smile.

They all chatted for a while, talking about everything from school to their favorite movies. Garrick and Samantha shared a lot more in common than he would have expected.

After about ten minutes, Samantha turned off the burners and began plating meals for everyone. She insisted that they sit at the table as she brought them their food, although Garrick offered to help her.

The four of them sat and ate together. Everyone laughed and talked, and Garrick started to forget that he had thought the night was going to be a complete disaster.

Garrick shoveled one more bite of spaghetti into his mouth. It was possibly the best thing he'd ever eaten.

"What do you all think?" Samantha asked as they ate.

"It's delicious," Garrick said, trying to swallow his food before he spoke. "Thank you. I had no idea you could cook like this." The other two just nodded as they ate. They thanked her through full mouths.

"Thanks," she said, blushing a bit. "It's a family recipe, so I was a little nervous you wouldn't like it."

"Well, then I am grateful to your entire family," Garrick said with a smile.

After another few minutes, Garrick started to feel odd. His stomach churned, and his throat started to swell up. He'd eaten a lot, but he'd had a bigger appetite since his first transformation, and he couldn't imagine he'd managed to overeat. Especially with how careful he always tried to be. He wondered if he was allergic to something she had used, or if that was even possible. He started quietly gasping for breath, trying to avoid allowing anyone to see that he was having that reaction. He took a drink from his water, but it didn't help. Panic started to set in and breathing became near impossible before he felt an intense pain rise in his stomach. One that he recognized far too well.

"Excuse me," he choked out, pushing his chair out from the table. He walked to the bathroom, struggling to keep his balance. His vision started to blur, and the world shook around him as he bit back agony. As soon as he was out of their field of vision, Garrick leaned against the wall for support. He got to the bathroom and closed the door, splashing water in his face. His vision cleared up slightly, but the pain only continued to worsen. This could not be happening. It was impossible.

The next minute felt like it went by in slow motion. He heard the others talking from across the house.

"Is it time for pie?" Samantha asked.

"Absolutely!" Tyler replied enthusiastically. Garrick heard as a chair scraped across the floor, being pushed away from the table. He heard Tyler's footsteps. "I'm going to ask Garrick Elliott if he wants a piece before I decide how large to cut them."

Garrick stared at his reflection. He watched as a few shreds of blue cut through his eyes. He held tightly to the edge of the counter, trying to dig deep enough into his hands to cause him enough pain to hold the beast back. It was futile, though. The blue specs in his eyes spread like a plague until there was no other color left in his iris.

Panting with the intensified pain, he felt his canine teeth begin to grow. He watched as the nails on his hands began to change, and the hair on his arms grew in front of his eyes.

Time moved at a crawl – every second felt like an hour. Each footstep brought Tyler that much closer, and Garrick didn't have the words to stop him.

There was a knock on the door.

"Just a minute," Garrick growled.

"Would you like a slice of pie?" Tyler asked through the closed door.

"I'm good."

"You sure?"

"Yes!" Garrick barked, a little too loudly.

"Well, sorry," Tyler responded, playfully sarcastic. Garrick heard as he turned to leave, and he breathed a sigh of relief. His solace had been premature, though, because Tyler stopped only a step away. Garrick lurched forward and bit his tongue to hide a scream. When the wave of pain subsided, he spat blood into the sink.

"Are   you   alright?"   Tyler   asked.
"Yes!"

"Okay." He wasn't convinced. Garrick couldn't hold back the pain anymore as he felt his shoulder break, only to start to change shape. He grunted too loudly as he dropped to his knees, unable to support himself with the sink any longer.

"Garrick Elliott?"

He couldn't respond this time. What was happening? It wasn't late enough to turn, even if the moon was full. Was there an eclipse he didn't know about?

"Okay, my concern for your safety has overpowered my desire for your privacy. Cover yourself." Tyler opened the door. How had Garrick not locked it? He had other things on his mind but locking the door should have been a pretty simple idea when it came to protecting his friend from himself.

Tyler stared at him, eyes widening. His mouth fell open, and he didn't say a word. Tyler was completely paralyzed.

"What..." He finally managed to speak, but he couldn't form the full question. Tyler stumbled back a step, but he didn't turn to run. All things considered, he was actually taking it a little better than Garrick himself had. Then again, Garrick had been transfixed watching the change too. He hadn't run until it was too late.

Garrick grabbed the edge of the counter and forced himself to his feet. He didn't look at Tyler; he just stared at the ground. One of his knees broke as his body protested his movements. Biting back the pain, he managed to remain standing.

"Tyler," he groaned slowly, trying his best to formulate the words through his changing vocal folds. "I'll explain everything. Right now, I need you to get everyone out of here."

"What do I say?"

"I don't know," Garrick said. He paused for a second, another wave of pain rushing over him as he felt his other shoulder dislocate itself. He probably looked absolutely horrifying. "Something. Cover for me."

"What's happening?"

"I can't…" Garrick could hardly force out any more words. They were sounding more monstrous and hoarser as he spoke, and his voice was quickly becoming inhuman. Soon, it would disappear entirely.

"Can't talk. I'll explain. Go."

Tyler nodded, but didn't move straight away. Garrick felt the femur in his left leg split in two, and he fell to the ground. Tyler nodded again, but still didn't move, eyes glued to his friend. Garrick pushed him back a little, and he stumbled backward, barely catching himself. Finally, he broke the trance and turned, walking quickly down the hallway. He was trying to be calm, but Garrick could smell the fear on him.

Garrick reached up and closed the door, locking it as if the lock would be of any use. Tyler had already seen him, and the wolf would likely just break it down. He tried to hear what Tyler told them. With his changing ears, it wasn't hear, but multitasking proved difficult. Still, he couldn't let go until he knew they were safe.

"I presume it's an allergy," Tyler justified. "Since childhood, he's had a strong reaction to garlic."

"Oh no," Samantha sounded genuinely concerned. "I'm so sorry. Is he okay?"

"He's fine," Tyler said. "He'd just rather not make an appearance at the moment. His face is puffy and his eyes are red. Also, I'm not sure if it's a good idea for him to leave the bathroom, if you know what I mean."

"I should have asked," she said, ignoring his joke.

"Honestly, he probably should be better at making it known."

There wasn't much that could excuse his behavior, and he was grateful that Tyler was even helping him out at all. Garrick wasn't sure he would have been able to do the same thing had the positions been reversed. He probably would have been too scared to think of anything to say other than "Garrick is becoming a werewolf, let's run for our lives."

He heard the door open and close, then listened as the footsteps faded away. When he couldn't perceive any trace of any of them, he finally gave up. Garrick collapsed to the floor and exhaled deeply. The pain dulled as he stopped fighting and let the wolf take over.

Chapter 6

Twenty-one months ago

Hayden smiled at him. She had a strange way of making him feel like he was exactly where he should be, even with every part of his mind screaming that he didn't have a chance. He stood on her doorway with flowers. At first, he'd felt like it was a good idea, but the longer he stood there, the more he questioned himself. Garrick couldn't help but wonder if it was too cheesy and overdone. For someone like Hayden, he should have found something more unique than roses.

In his eyes, she was the most beautiful girl in existence. She had long, blonde hair that she had curled for their date. She wore a blue dress, and it just made her eyes shine even brighter. With her heels on, she was slightly taller than him, but her confidence made him feel as though she towered over him. He fumbled for words as he looked at her.

"Are those for me?" she asked with a smile, glancing at the flowers.

"No," Garrick responded, snapped out of his daze. It was a few seconds before he even processed the question, then his inaccurate response. In a panic, he blurted out, "I mean yeah. Yup. Yes!" He had sifted through every affirmative word he could think of until he found the right one.

"Garrick," she spoke calmly, her smile unbroken. She placed her hand gently over his on the flowers and breathed out deeply. In an almost unnaturally soothing voice, she added, "Calm down."

"Can we start over?" He asked, taking solace in her calm demeanor. Being around her relaxed him, even when he was terrified and making a fool of himself.

"Sure," she agreed lightheartedly. She closed the door. Not exactly what he'd meant. She peeked her head outside, gazed at him intently, and her tone took a serious turn as she asked, "Did you mean the last five minutes, or should I bring the couch back outside?"

"No," he laughed. "This is good."

"Okay, good," she responded as she closed the door again. Garrick took a deep breath, preparing himself before he knocked on the door again. As he waited for her to open it, he straightened out his shirt and stood taller.

"Hello," he said as she opened the door.

"Hi," she laughed.

"Wow. You look beautiful. Perfect. Like, in a good way."

"How can that be in a bad way?"

"Look, I brought you flowers!" He handed her the flowers, and she disappeared inside to put them in a vase. He turned and hit his head against the wall, muttering *"in a good way?"* to himself. Before she returned, he quickly composed himself and stood, attempting to hide any negative emotion.

"You look nice too," she told him as she stepped back outside. He was thoroughly convinced she'd seen his reaction to his own greeting, but she didn't say anything about it. She just wrapped her arm around his and waited for him to lead her to the car. She had to take the first step, dragging him slightly behind, before he was able to stabilize himself on his weak legs and actually walk.

"I'm warning you," he said as he opened the door for her. He'd run through the part of the date where he went up to the door dozens of times in his head. He wanted it to go perfectly. Through all of his rehearsal, he'd been confident there was no way he'd make a mistake. Clearly, though he was mistaken.

"I think that was the best I'm going to do all night," he finished. She laughed as she ducked her head under the roof of the car and pulled her dress down to keep it from bunching up. Before he closed the door behind her, she had to readjust herself and retrieve a part of the dress which was still hanging outside of the car.

Garrick walked around the back of the car, still trying to convince himself that Tyler's advice was true. All he had to do was be himself, she obviously liked him if they spent so much time together already. Anyway, she'd already said yes. That had to be the hardest part, right?

"You could do a lot worse," she sympathized as he sat down next to her.

"Really?" He closed the door and started the car, then looked at her with a grin.

"No," she admitted. "I don't think so."

He was deflated. There was no way this was ever going to work out. He'd already started off absolutely wrong twice.

"It's cute, though." Garrick was shocked to hear that. A single compliment from her washed away his doubts as if by magic.

"You're not a normal girl, are you?"

"It would seem not."

"Still perfect," he replied, still staring at her eyes. Trying to avoid an over-reaction, he bit back the smile, but it continued forcing itself to grow larger. When he looked away, he gave up and just beamed as he put the car in drive and headed to the restaurant.

Present
17 days until the full moon

Garrick woke up on the bathroom floor. He looked around, trying to gather his bearings. It didn't look like too much was broken. He did see his shirt, torn to rags, near him though. That had been a nice shirt, too. The rest of his clothes were also ripped up, shreds scattered around him. It didn't look like he had torn them apart, though. It looked like they just ripped because he didn't have time to remove them from his changing form.

He grabbed a towel from under the sink and wrapped it around his waist. Then he retrieved his phone from the pocket of his jeans. He checked the time. He wanted to know how early it was, wondering if his mom had come home from work already. Garrick couldn't think of any way to possibly explain the mess to her.

It had been thirty minutes. How was that possible?

He decided to save the mystery for later. There were more pressing things for him to address at the moment. For one, he had to apologize to Samantha for running out on her in his own house - which was going to be incredibly difficult to explain. Then he had to talk to Tyler. If, of course, Tyler was willing to talk to him. It had taken Garrick weeks to finally talk to Hayden after he found out about her. While it would be nice to finally be able to talk to Tyler about this part of his life, he had to respect his friend if he needed time. Before he could do anything else, though, he had to clean up the mess in the bathroom and get rid of those torn clothes. He had broken apart a hand soap dispenser, and the clear contents were scattered across the floor, leaving the tile coated in a slippery film. He had also taken down the shower rod, but somehow didn't damage the curtain itself. The damage was actually surprisingly minimal. He would have expected to find holes in the walls, leaking pipes, or pieces broken from the sink and bathtub.

Garrick decided to get dressed before worrying about anything else. He struggled to his feet, using the sink and the wall for support. Leaning on the walls as he recovered his strength, he made his way to his room and selected the first outfit he could find in his closet.

He sat on the edge of his bed and rested his chin in the palms of his hands, contemplating what he was going to say to Samantha. He could always just claim he got sick, but he didn't want her to think it was her cooking. Maybe it would be best to go along with Tyler's claim that it was his allergy to garlic, about which she'd have had no way of knowing. He hadn't eaten the bread, but maybe he could convince her that he did – she probably wasn't paying too much attention to what specific foods he ate. Additionally, any type of allergy would be something he should have mentioned to her before she cooked him food.

Settling on cleaning the bathroom first, he set his towel over his shoulder and made his way back. Cleaning would help clear his mind, and maybe even give him time to develop a script for the people to whom he had to explain. He dropped the towel on the floor and retrieved the remains of his torn clothes. He also picked up the broken pieces of the plastic hand soap container and wrapped the plastic in the shreds of fabric which had been the outfit he'd worn earlier. Holding the mess of clothes and plastic in one hand, he checked with the other to make sure there were no soap leaks. It would minimize his work if he didn't drop soap all over the house as he walked. Garrick headed outside and moved aside one of the trash bags in the trash can and hid his garbage under it. There was no reason to suspect anyone would be inspecting his garbage, but he wanted to be safe just in case.

He went back inside and quickly set the shower curtain back up. He twisted the rod to try to size it, but it kept sliding down the sides of the shower. He groaned dramatically as he tried a few more times, and finally extended it enough to stick in place. Though he would still trade it if he could, there were perks to his lycanthropy. That curtain would have grown rather heavy in the past. He wiped down the floor with the towel to clean up all of the soap, but it seemed to just be spreading it. Trying a different approach, he dampened the towel in the sink, then went back to cleaning the floor. The soap started to bubble up and just create more of a mess. After a few rounds of ringing out the soapy water, it finally started to look like the floor was just wet. He retrieved another towel to dry it up. Because he wasn't quite sure if all of the soap would make too many bubbles and wreak havoc in the washing machine, he carefully rinsed the soapy towel in the bathtub first. He swung the towels over the side of the shower. Finally, he grabbed a new soap dispenser from the cabinet under the sink and set it up where the old one had been.

The kitchen looked just as it had before he'd changed. He was just happy that he hadn't done anything truly damaging, like shredding the shower curtain or breaking the mirror. Or tearing the appliances out of the wall. At least all the damage was easily remedied without informing his mom.

He had done everything he possibly could to distract himself, but he knew he had to have the conversations eventually. He took out his phone and stared at it, willing the perfect excuses into his mind. It was just before 9:00 pm. He wondered if that was too late to show up at Tyler's house. He knew Tyler's family was strict about certain rules, so he didn't want to risk waking his parents. However, since he'd built up the resolve, he also had to try to talk to his friend before he lost it. He looked for his jacket but quickly gave up when it wasn't in the first place he checked. Instead, he just changed into a long sleeve shirt and headed outside. He locked the door behind him and started walking to Tyler's house. As he walked, he pulled out his phone and sighed deeply. Best to just get them both over with.

"Hey," he texted Samantha.

"Hey there," she sent back almost instantly.

"Sorry about tonight."

"It's okay. I had a great time."

"Until I disappeared?"

"Well, that was a little odd. What happened?"

He didn't respond for about a minute. He hadn't been prepared for her to answer so quickly, and he was still struggling with the wording on his response.

"I think I get it." That would definitely impress him. He himself didn't get it. It would be amazing if someone who didn't even know that werewolves existed could explain why one just changed for a few minutes on a random night in the moon cycle.

"?"

"I know you just broke up with Hayden. Tyler explained it all. I didn't know how recently it was."

"Yeah," he said. Because it was the best excuse he had, he tried to use it to his advantage. He was shocked that she'd given it to him. It would make the explanation easier, if nothing else. *"I guess I was a little freaked. I'm sorry."*

"I didn't mean to freak you out."

"I know."

"We don't have to be anything more than friends. I didn't even think that was a date, to be honest. Until Tyler told me it was."

"Oh. Well I feel dumb"

"No, don't. I was happy when he told me."

"Good. I'm glad."

Garrick was walking up to Tyler's house. He saw that lights were still on in the second story window, which was Tyler's room, so at least he was awake. He walked up front and saw a faint blue glare shining through the living room window. He'd been there enough to realize that was likely the television, which implied someone was watching it. Still, he didn't want to knock so late, in case they'd fallen asleep in front of the T.V. again. But he also didn't want to call Tyler; he didn't want to give him the chance to ignore the call or to freak out before he saw him. Garrick had no plan, so he just stared at the door as if it would open itself.

"Maybe, eventually, we can have a second date," Samantha sent. He didn't know what to say. He didn't ever want to date her. It wouldn't be fair to her. He loved Hayden. As much as he liked Samantha, he could never give her that.

"For now, how about we hang out next week? As friends." She was being understanding. She was nice, caring. He really wanted to feel something for her, but he couldn't muster up any type of emotion whatsoever. Nothing more than a possible bond of friendship.

"Okay," he conceded. *"I'd like that."*

He called Tyler. The phone rang, but he didn't answer. Garrick took a deep breath and knocked on the door.

"Garrick!" Tyler's mom exclaimed as she opened it, beaming at him. She hugged him, pulling him inside. In his peripheral vision, Garrick could see Tyler's step-dad sitting on the couch, watching some sport with a beer in his hand. "How are you?"

"I'm great, how are you?" he asked, pasting on a fake smile and trying his best to avoid allowing her to detect any difference. He didn't need to owe another explanation to anyone.

"I'm glad you got a date," she cheered. "I always thought you could do better than Hayden." She was trying to be nice, but there really was no better than Hayden. She didn't even sound convinced as she said it.

"Anyway," she added slowly, detecting the awkwardness lingering in the air. "Tyler is up in his room."

"Thanks," Garrick told her. He climbed up the stairs, taking his time. He had no idea what to say when he saw Tyler.

He knocked on the door. Nothing. When he tried again, Tyler opened the door. He pulled Garrick into the room, closing the door roughly behind him. He didn't say a word to him. Instead, he just sat in the chair and glued his eyes to the book which lay open on his desk.

"Tyler?" Garrick asked hesitantly. "Is everything okay?"

"Okay?" Tyler asked, his voice not carrying the tone Garrick would have expected. He almost sounded excited. "My best friend is a lycanthrope!"

"That's not really something you should be screaming."

"Sorry," Tyler whispered. His voice was much quieter, but it was still full of excitement.

"So, I just wanted to make sure we were okay."

"What are you talking about, Garrick Elliott? I'm not going to despise you for what you are. That's the definition of racism. I'm wounded that you didn't tell me sooner, but that's unimportant at the moment."

Garrick sat on the bed, and Tyler spun his chair to face him. They were both silent. Tyler's face grew grimmer over the minutes that neither of them spoke, as if the silence of the room was so full of dread that it drained his emotion straight from his face. Garrick wondered if the enthusiasm was fake or if the reality was just starting to set in.

"Why," Tyler finally asked, "Why did you hide this from me? We're best friends. I thought you trusted me."

"I wanted to, really. I just had to protect you. Aldric always told us that hunters would chase us down and use the people closest to us to find us. He said it's safer for everyone if we don't say anything. But I know that doesn't make it better. I'm just telling you the same thing Hayden told me, and I didn't feel better. I'm sorry."

"Woah. Slow down. Hunters? And Aldric is a werewolf? I guessed Chase, Hayden, and Cailean. Maybe Brooke. But I didn't guess Aldric."

"You got all of them except Aldric. I'm impressed," Garrick didn't want to reveal everyone else's secrets, but he wasn't going to lie anymore. Anyway, there was no convincing way to change Tyler's mind when he discovered it already.

"It wasn't difficult, just a simple deduction. You and Hayden have to have something in common, with how far out of your league she is," he joked. At least, Garrick hoped it was a joke. "There's no other justifiable reason to spend time with

Cailean. I've begun to feel as though Chase was hiding something recently, given your increased frequency of conversations to which I am uninvited, so to appease my own emotions I hoped it was about this. I just assumed Brooke was in on it too because she's a part of the group. So, how about you just start from the beginning? I have a lot to catch up on."

"Okay," Garrick empathized. He tried to take it slow and not throw too much information at Tyler at once. He'd had over a year to learn about werewolves and hunters. Garrick pulled his sleeve up and showed Tyler his arm. "It started when I was scratched by that wild animal. Remember when I told you about it, and this scar? It really was a scratch, but it was from a werewolf." He went on to explain everything that happened. His fights with the others, how he had learned to cope, all the way to how he had left the pack.

"But tonight wasn't a full moon," Tyler pondered. "You still have another, what, two weeks? Also, you said you change for the full night, but it hasn't been much more than an hour since I left your house."

"I don't really have answers to those questions, either."

"And you can't ask Aldric."

"Exactly."

"What about Chase? I'm positive he'd do everything in his power to help."

"I'll ask him about it on Monday. I... I'm not really ready to talk to him about the circumstances of the random transformation."

"Understood. Alright, then we will have to try the next best thing. There exists an expansive collection of knowledge – from generations past. They keep records in an ancient technology known as 'books.' I happen to know of the location of these artifacts."

"Okay, Tyler," Garrick laughed as Tyler spun the chair back around and began flipping through the pages of one of the books on his desk. He was absolutely amazed by how well Tyler was handling this rush of new information. He didn't even seem fazed by the sudden discovery that creatures he'd spent his whole life believing to be myth were wandering his town. Of course, he had probably been processing it for the past hour, or at least suspecting, since he'd seen Garrick half-transformed. Still, it had taken Garrick much longer than that to accept his new reality.

"Are you sure you're alright?"

"I am," Tyler said. There was a twinge of sadness in his voice, but Garrick couldn't detect any reason to think Tyler wasn't telling the truth. "I'm just glad I finally know."

"I'm sorry I took this long to tell you. I hated hiding everything."

"No, I understand," Tyler spoke with the same degree of sadness, but there was empathy in his tone. He didn't take his eyes from the screen as he continued flipping through the pages and reading up on werewolf lore. "The most popular opinion seems to be that it's triggered by emotion."

"That isn't true," Garrick said. "I've been pretty mad at times, and I've never changed if it wasn't a full moon. Anyway, tonight I wasn't upset at all."

"Fair point," Tyler conceded.

"Hey," Garrick started quietly, interrupting Tyler's research. Recognizing the tone, Tyler dropped what he was doing and turned back around to face his friend. "Can I ask you something?"

"Anything."

"Objectively, do you think I'm being a complete moron? About leaving the pack?"

"Objectively? I do. I completely sympathize with what you're feeling, and I honestly don't know what I would do in your shoes. However, it also seems exceedingly unlikely you can handle any of this on your own. It sounds to me like you need them."

"I guess."

"But now, you have me to help."

"How?" Garrick asked skeptically.

"Well, you and I are going to take a drive around town tomorrow. We can find you an old abandoned building where you can change this month without the risk of crossing paths with innocents.

"That would definitely get one thing off my mind," Garrick admitted, realizing that he still had no idea what his own plan was. There was quite a bit to figure out, but finding a safe place to handle the transformation was definitely the top priority.

"And I'm going to use my amazing research prowess to find you a cure."

Chapter 7

Eighteen months ago

"Are you sure you don't want to go?" Garrick asked Hayden. He and Chase were going to open mic night at the local coffee shop. They held the event every weekend, and Garrick tried to go as often as he could. Tyler played there as often as he could, and Garrick wanted to support his friend.

"I don't want to ruin Guy's Night," she said with a smile. She kissed Garrick before pushing him lightly. "Anyway, Caleb is going to college at the end of the year, and he's feeling a bit down about leaving. He insisted we 'partake of the bonding.'"

"Your bother is weird," Garrick laughed.

"They were my words," Hayden joked.

"Weirdly wise. That's where I was going." She laughed and patted his chest.

"I'll miss you," he said.

"Yeah, yeah, yeah," she laughed. Garrick walked from her door and headed to his car. Though he still had an hour before the actual event started, he had to pick Chase up and get to the shop, or parking was going to be a nightmare. Open mic night had only grown in popularity since they'd started a few years back. It probably brought as much business to that shop in one night as they got during the rest of the week. Honestly, Garrick thought that was in large part Tyler's doing. The night had seemingly become a bunch of people opening for Tyler, the main act, and then some others. Then again, Garrick couldn't deny his inherent bias toward his best friend. That bias didn't make it any less true that the crowd always blew up when Tyler stepped up to the microphone.

Garrick pulled up in front of Chase's house. His friend, already waiting outside, jumped into the car, barely allowing Garrick a chance to slow down.

"Alright, so where are we going again?"

"Wait, really?" Garrick asked, dumbfounded. To him, it was just a weekly event, so it hadn't crossed his mind that Chase didn't know about it.

"Yeah. I didn't really care, honestly. I just wanted to hang out, and your text said 'support Tyler' so of course I'm in."

"Well, alright. We're going to open mic night," Garrick explained as he drove. "Tyler's there pretty much every week, and I like to do my best to go for him."

"That's sweet."

"Yeah, well," Garrick started. He didn't really have anything to say, though, so he just let the statement fade away.

"I didn't realize Tyler was a singer. I mean, I know he talks about it, but I didn't know it was actually a thing," Chase offered, breaking the silence in the vehicle. As much as Garrick loved spending time with Hayden, he was actually grateful for the chance to spend some one-on-one time with Chase. He could see the two of them becoming good friends, but he knew he was going to have to get through his own awkwardness a bit more.

"Oh, really?" Garrick asked, his voice perking up. The chance to talk about someone other than himself always brightened his day. He found it easier than trying to make small talk. "Yeah, he's really good. He picked the music teacher's guitar up in middle school and I swear, this twelve-year-old was playing like a professional. He refused to put that thing down. She was so impressed – the teacher – that she actually gave Tyler the guitar. She taught him how to play and sing after school, even after we moved to high school. He still goes over there sometimes just to practice, but she told him she has nothing else to teach."

Garrick laughed as he told the story. He wouldn't have believed it if he hadn't witnessed it first-hand.

"Really?" Chase asked. "That's so cool."

"Yeah," Garrick responded, excitement still seeping into his tone. "He's a natural."

"So you've known each other since middle school?"

"Oh, no. Well, I mean technically. We met in first grade. I was trapped in Physical Education class playing kick-ball. All the kids teased me because I was not very good, but one time I finally got myself a good hit. I was running to the base, but Tyler had the ball and he was running toward me. He was always faster than me, but he tripped over his shoelace and I made it to safety."

"So he's a klutz? There's another fun fact."

"No," Garrick laughed. "Even as a six-year-old, Tyler looked out for me. He pretended to trip so I could get the win."

"You're kidding?"

"No. I confronted him about it after class, and he admitted it, but said not to tell anyone. We've been glued together since then. I can't count the number of times he's stood up for me since then. So, if there's any way I can be there for him, I do. Even if it's just sitting and listening to him sing."

"Wow, I had no idea you guys were so close."

"He's my brother," Garrick replied with conviction.

"Well, I can't wait to see if he's as good as you say he is."

Garrick just laughed as he pulled up in front of the coffee shop and parked his car. There weren't too many people there before them, but he could see that Tyler was already there getting ready. Garrick and Chase went inside to get a good seat, finding a table as close to the make-shift stage as possible.

After five minutes of terrible karaoke singing, Chase looked at Garrick with agony on his face. "Are you trying to torture me?" he whispered. "What have I done to you?"

"Some people think they can sing."

"Someone should really tell them they can't. This is embarrassing."

"You can tell them if you want," Garrick shrugged.

"Are you kidding? I'm not completely heartless. I'll leave that to their friends. Or talent scouts," Chase smirked. The two waited through a few more singers before Tyler finally made his way to the stage. He brought his own guitar, like usual, so the background music shut off as he introduced himself.

Tyler had a gift. His singing was always so raw with emotion. If there was one good thing about his relationship with Kayla, it was that she was always giving him fuel for his art. Garrick just hoped, for his friend's sake, that the right person would show up one night and hear Tyler's music. Maybe Tyler could find his way out of their small town.

Now that he had Hayden, Garrick wasn't plagued as constantly with the thought of escape, but he still dreamed of the two of them getting away from that town. He didn't know where, but he always felt trapped. He tried to shake it off; He was there for Tyler – that was where his attention should be. Garrick could allow himself to dwell on those thoughts at any other point.

"You were right," Chase said after Tyler finished singing. The crowd, following Garrick, stood and clapped for Tyler. He still had more time, and even if he didn't the crowd would be chanting 'encore' until whoever was running the night allowed him to play another song, but Garrick couldn't hold back his excitement for his friend. "He's good."

"Yeah," Garrick said. "He's something special."

Garrick was happier for his friend than he knew how to express. There wasn't a single part of him that he'd describe as jealous. Still, though, he couldn't help but wish that 'special' were a word that could be used to describe himself as well.

Present
16 days until the full moon

"So," Garrick's mom said, sitting on the edge of his bed. He'd been sleeping when she got home, but she'd snuck into his room probably as soon as she'd heard him stirring. She was still in uniform. "Sammi?"

"Yeah," Garrick said. He didn't know where to start. Or what was safe to say. Not only did he have the awkward mental block of this being his mother, but also the problem that he had to exclude anything involving being a werewolf, which occupied most of that night in his mind.

"Where did you meet?"

"She works at the coffee shop," he told her. "She could see that I was upset last time I went in there and she offered to make dinner for me."

"Most girls would think of that as a date," his mom said. She clearly caught on to the idea that he was trying to act like it wasn't. Garrick couldn't hide subtleties like that from her.

"Yeah, well, I didn't really think about that. I didn't really think about anything, I was kind of in my own world. I just said yes."

"Well, I like her. She's cute and she seems really nice," his mom said. She slapped her hands against her knees and stood up. She was just partial to anything that made Garrick get out of his room. He knew she'd been worried about him over the past week. She'd had it written all over her face, although she refused to mention it, knowing it would only make him feel worse to have someone concerned about him on top of everything else.

"Yeah," he responded absently. She was a great girl, but it was far too soon for him to think of anything along the lines of a relationship. If he ever thought of it, it would be too soon.

"I'm going to go take a shower," she said as she walked out of his room. "I'm really happy for you."

"It's not like that," Garrick responded defensively. He could have just let the conversation end there, but he felt the need to defend his actions.

"Why not?" His mom turned back around, her expression suddenly very sad. Garrick wished he'd just kept his mouth shut. Everyone would have been happier.

"It's only been a week…"

"Yeah," she said. "But who knows how long this girl will wait for you? You can't push her away because of something in your past."

"I know," he told her.

"Do you like this girl?"

"I guess." He did like her. A lot. But it felt weird. She was a good person, and he liked spending time with her, but he didn't love her. She wasn't Hayden, and she never could be.

"Getting over your first love is tough," his mom consoled. "But we all have break-ups. You just gotta move on and put yourself back out there."

He didn't want to be back out there. She meant well, but she couldn't understand. He wished he could tell her that. He wanted to explain that he would never get over his first love; it was just not an option. She had never felt anything like he and Hayden shared. But he would just sound like any other teenager full of angst over a lost relationship, thinking they're alone in the world.

"Thanks, Mom," was what he said instead. She smiled again and nodded, turning around. It was best to just let her think he was taking her advice. At least he wouldn't hurt her that way. Garrick sighed deeply as his mom left, closing the door behind her.

"I think I have an idea on how you changed when it wasn't the full moon," Tyler said. He'd told Garrick to go to his house as soon as he could, so Garrick thought he had more questions about lycanthropy. He'd groggily forced himself out of bed and changed, rushing over to meet his friend. He didn't think Tyler would have found an answer – or even a possible one – so quickly.

Garrick sat on Tyler's couch, expectantly. It was rare that the two of them actually spent any time at his house, but Tyler's parents weren't there. When they were, Garrick could feel the tension. He had wondered before if that was why Tyler enjoyed spending so much time at Garrick's house, but he'd never asked him about it. It was never the right time to bring it up, and he figured Tyler would mention it if he wanted to.

"So?" Garrick asked. "What are you thinking?"

"Hear me out. Garlic."

"Garlic? There are so many things wrong with that. When did I even eat garlic?"

"Most people don't think of it as an ingredient in spaghetti, but apparently Samantha does. So she cooks a meal in which garlic is an ingredient, you unknowingly consume the garlic, and then you transform." Tyler clapped his hands, as if he'd come up with a brilliant answer. Garrick appreciated his friend's attempt, but he was not at all convinced.

"Tyler, I'm not a vampire."

"No," Tyler responded, running his hands through his hair as he turned his back to Garrick. He clearly felt annoyed that Garrick wasn't understanding. Garrick wondered how long his friend had been awake. He looked lethargic, and there were bags under his eyes. Maybe he'd been up so late thinking that he was missing steps when trying to convey his idea, but it just made sense in his mind. Whatever the case, Garrick couldn't see the logic in his idea. "But you are allergic to garlic."

Suddenly, it clicked. Garrick had been allergic to garlic since he was a child, but he hadn't thought about that in months. He just assumed that being a werewolf meant his allergies faded away. After all, his body would just heal from any allergic reaction. Unless for some reason, it affected the human part of him, and the wolf had to rush forward to protect him while he healed.

"Shoot," Garrick responded, his eyes lighting up as he snapped his fingers. He leaned forward, and Tyler excitedly stood up, clearly happy that his friend was catching up. "Maybe you're right. Okay, we have to test this."

"Don't worry Garrick Elliott, I have you covered," Tyler said. He sprinted to the kitchen. Garrick wasn't sure what he was expecting Tyler to come back with, but he figured it would be something with garlic in it. Even just some garlic powder would do. Instead, he walked into the living room holding a clove of garlic.

"What is that?" Garrick asked. He knew the answer to the question, of course, but he didn't know the words to express his confusion at the situation.

"Take a bite," Tyler responded, holding the garlic out for Garrick to take.

"Are you kidding? I'm not going to take a bite of pure garlic, Tyler. That's disgusting."

"No, really. It's not that bad," Tyler said. "Here, look."

Before Garrick could try to stop his friend, Tyler took a bite. His face started contorting in disgust, but he did his best to disguise it. He smiled and held a thumbs up as he chewed through the pain. "See?"

Garrick didn't want to get anywhere near that garlic. His eyes were already starting to water just from the smell, and he was nearly certain eating it wouldn't cause him to transform. As he hesitated, his mind started presenting every reason that this plan didn't make sense. Why wouldn't Aldric have said anything about allergies? It seemed like an important note if they were attempting to prevent transformations

in public. Anyway, before his first transformation, he had actively avoided garlic. Since he had not thought about that in
months, he was bound to have accidentally eaten garlic in
more than just that one dish of spaghetti. Still, what if he
hadn't? There was a chance that this could give him an answer.

"Just give it to me," Garrick said. Tyler handed it over,
and Garrick closed his eyes. Slowly, he raised the clove toward his mouth, the smell assaulting him with every second.
If he breathed through his mouth, though, he could taste it.
Neither was a reasonable option, so he decided to just hold his
breath.

"Wait," he hesitated, lowering the clove.

"It's for science," Tyler encouraged Garrick.

"I'll do it," Garrick accepted. "But I am going to hide
in your bathroom. If I tell you to run, you run as fast as you
can. Do you understand?"

"That," Tyler responded, "is a rather reasonable request." He led Garrick to the bathroom, and Garrick closed
and locked the door behind him. Looking at the mirror, he
raised the clove to his mouth.

"Why am I doing this?" he muttered to himself. He
exhaled deeply and took a bite. It wasn't actually as bad as he
thought it would be, but the aftertaste hit him like a rock.
Then, he started to feel the acidity as he continued to crunch
the garlic. His mouth started to burn and his eyes watered.

"Oh, gross. This is the worst idea you've ever had,"
he exclaimed through a full mouth. He tried chewing faster,
just wanting to get the garlic out of his mouth, but it didn't
help much. Spitting it out wasn't an option, though, because
he'd already gone that far to test Tyler's theory. Even though
he was thoroughly confident at that point that it wasn't the garlic, he was going to see it through. He started groaning and
muttering in anger as he swallowed it. He couldn't believe
he'd actually done that.

Garrick felt sick to his stomach. It was actually
vaguely similar to what he'd felt the other night, and he was

starting to get concerned. He leaned against the wall and slid down, breathing deeply and closing his eyes. The spaghetti had taken a few minutes to take effect, but if the garlic were the problem, a whole clove would probably be faster. A minute went by, but he didn't feel any different.

"Are you changing?" Tyler asked eagerly through the closed door.

"No! No, Tyler!"

"Oh. Well at least we know."

"Yeah," Garrick muttered, opening the door. He looked at Tyler as he wiped the tears from his eyes. "I'm going to go chug a gallon of tap water to get this taste out of my mouth."

"I didn't think it was that bad. You're overreacting."

Part of Garrick wanted to laugh at everything that had just happened, but a larger part of him just wanted to be sure he never ate garlic again, even if it didn't mean transforming into a wolf.

"Please just start the car," Garrick ordered as he made his detour to the kitchen.

Tyler was sitting in the driver's seat of his car, pointing out random buildings that looked old and had basements. Garrick really did appreciate his friend's enthusiasm, but it wasn't necessarily the most helpful thing he could be doing. They couldn't be sure if the buildings were abandoned, or how exactly they could gain access.

"What about a storage shed?" Tyler finally asked, apparently realizing that Garrick was probably not going to think any of the buildings they could find were suitable.

"Yeah," Garrick pondered. "That could work."

Tyler drove them to the nearest storage facility and parked the car. He sat for a few more minutes and rubbed the steering wheel nervously. Garrick looked at him, slightly confused.

"Alright, so here's the story: We are two young men moving to a new place as we start college. We have to store some of our belongings, given the lack of space in our new apartment. Does that sound reasonable to you? I think we can pass for a few years older."

"Tyler," Garrick interjected, "They don't care. I'm just going to go ask how much a unit costs."

He laughed silently as he climbed out of the car and closed the door. When he walked into the building, he saw one man sitting behind a desk reading a magazine. The office was actually very small. There was the desk, which had a computer on it, and the chair in which the man sat. The office held no other furniture whatsoever – not even a poster or calendar to lighten up the dull brown walls.

"How can I help you?" The man asked, his eyes glued to the magazine, his feet on the desk as he leaned back in the chair.

"I need to store some furniture," Garrick said awkwardly. He'd talked a big game with Tyler, but he didn't particularly enjoy communicating with people. "How much does it cost here?" That had gone better in his head.

"Eighty bucks a month," he said. He offered Garrick a quick glance before returning his gaze to the magazine. "Just ask your mom to hold your stuff, kid."

Garrick was offended. Despite the fact that he was still technically one by law, he hated being treated as a child. *"At least I'm a reasonable age to still live with mine,"* he thought, smirking to himself and wishing he had the self-confidence to respond in turn to people who treated him rudely. Instead, he just nodded and left the building without another word. Although he hated to admit it, the man was correct in his assumptions. There was no way Garrick could get that kind of money without a job of any kind, and he didn't have a large base of people he could ask. Even if he did, there was no valid explanation for his reasoning.

He stormed back to the car and opened the door a little more forcefully than he intended. There were still times that he had to remind himself that things tended to be lighter than he expected them to be. Back in the car, Garrick closed the door and explained the situation to Tyler. In retrospect, Garrick wasn't sure why he hadn't been aware that the plan would fall through. He didn't have an income stream at all – any amount of money would probably have been too much. There were always odd jobs he could do, but nothing steady. Tyler sighed and put the car in gear, but he hesitated for a minute.

"You know, you really don't have to do this," Garrick told him solemnly. He was grateful for everything his friend had tried, but it was clear they were both out of ideas. That was why the car still hadn't moved.

"Yes, I do. We are going to find a way to make this work, Garrick Elliott."

"How are you so confident?"

"I have to be. Anyway, maybe I just haven't had the time to become as jaded as you," Tyler said with a smile. As always, he tried to lighten the mood. Suddenly, his eyes lit up and he sat up straighter as he asked, "What do you think about the abandoned warehouse outside town? It's vast and completely desolate. No one has been there in years. Except maybe serial killers, but that was never confirmed. Anyway, you get a serial killer out there it's survival of the fittest." Garrick laughed, unsure of whether he found Tyler's joke funny or if he was just amused by the fact that his friend was trying so hard to keep the situation as light as possible. He knew he'd be far worse off without Tyler to help him.

"Seriously though," Tyler added after waiting for a second, draining the humor from his tone, "I think it could be exactly what you need."

"I don't know," Garrick objected. "I think it would be possible for me to just break through the doors and run toward town. I don't know how thick walls are to those types of places, but that wolf can get pretty determined."

"You don't want to make this easy for me, do you, Garrick Elliott?" Tyler asked, exasperated but understanding. He looked left and right, as if a perfect idea would suddenly appear on the side of the street. Garrick wasn't even paying attention to their surroundings. It was apparent to him that he wouldn't find the right place anywhere in town.

He needed a place with a basement; that much he knew. The wolf wouldn't be able to climb the stairs, so it would be trapped for the night. Underground walls also meant it wouldn't be able to break through. He also needed somewhere a bit out of town, because people would hear the wolf slamming into things if it were next door to their house.

He searched the depths of his mind, clawing for any idea. There was an underground level of the school, and that building was in a neighborhood of its own. It would be far enough out of the way that he could be quiet, and no one in their right mind would want to be at the school at night. The problem was that it would be locked down during the evenings. He could break the locks, but he would prefer not getting caught breaking and entering. Anyway, there were bound to be cameras there as well, so he'd have to find a way to navigate around them.

As Tyler drove, Garrick stayed trapped in his mind. Weaving through neighborhoods, Tyler just kept searching. As he turned past again, Garrick noticed the trees which bordered to town to the west. There were woods surrounding the town, with a river to the south. To the east, where they typically changed with Aldric, the landscape was flat. Just past the trees, where he couldn't quite make out, on this side, was a hill.

Garrick thought about the surroundings a bit more. This side of the woods was more popular – probably because the hike made things more interesting. However, just past the common campgrounds, he'd heard there was an old house up at the top of the hill. He hadn't actually made the journey himself to see it because he'd never been incredibly interested, but from what he had heard, it was more like a ranger station, or even a watchtower. It was a building which had housed people who'd worked in the woods and monitored game hunting. That was years ago, before the jobs moved closer into the city and the building was left abandoned. That was one story. Another was that it was, in fact, a house where an old man had lived alone until he died and left it unattended. Then, there were the obligatory ghost stories. A few years back, the building had caught fire, and no one was around to do anything about it. Of course, since then, people claimed it was haunted.

Whatever the truth was, Garrick didn't care much. The reason for its existence, or that for its abandonment, didn't particularly matter. What mattered was the fact that it was in fact abandoned, and that it could be exactly what he needed. He informed Tyler of his thought process, and Tyler was more than willing to go out of his way for a chance that they find the place. He sped through the trees as long as the trail would allow, but eventually, the two of them had to park the car at the bottom of the hill and hike the rest of the way.

The trees started to grow taller and denser as they went deeper into the woods. Garrick was completely unfamiliar with his surroundings. There was something he found comforting about the woods, but he was also uncomfortable feeling lost. He wasn't used to being unable to pinpoint exactly where he was. Nonetheless, the adventurous side of him enjoyed hiking and exploring new territory with his best friend. He'd seen plenty of maps of that side of the woods, but he'd never actually been there.

"Up here," Tyler called out. He had walked slightly faster than Garrick, who spent more time admiring the trees and getting lost in nature. It was a surreal feeling. There was something familiar – as if he'd been there before, although he could recognize differences in the patterns of the foliage. It all looked the same, but different. Then again, he supposed, trees were trees, so it should look relatively similar to the other side of town. He sped up to catch up with Tyler.

An old, two-story, wooden building rested in front of them. Garrick walked up to it, examining it carefully. The windows were mostly broken, and a few had boards nailed to the frames from the inside. Some just had planks resting

against them as well. Garrick couldn't tell if they were intentionally pressed against them or if they'd fallen during the fire.
He was confident, though, that there was at least a fire. There
were scorch marks along the wall – black burns in the wood.
As he approached the porch, Garrick climbed the three stairs
that led up to it. An old wooden door rested in its frame in
front of him, but the screen door that covered it was hanging
off from one hinge. It reminded him of something pulled
straight from a horror film.

The stairs creaked loudly as Tyler climbed them to
catch up to Garrick. Hesitantly, he placed his hand on the
doorknob as Garrick continued to look around the perimeter.
Garrick walked up to one of the windows. The glass was completely shattered, and he could see remnants of it lying around
the ground near it. No one had even bothered to try to clean
up after the fire. Maybe they'd deemed the condition too severe for repair. Garrick reached his hand through the broken
window and pushed some of the debris to the side.

He felt a prick on his arm. Startled, he pushed the
beam over and pulled his arm back. The beam landed angled
in front of the window. Looking more closely, Garrick realized there was still a piece of glass in the frame. His arm bled
more than he'd expected, and he watched as a few drops fell
to the floor beneath him. He realized he had made it worse by
pulling his arm out suddenly, because beneath the blood was a
deep gash in his flesh. Garrick wiped off the blood as the
wound closed up. Attempting to get a better sense of the interior of the house, he peered through the window. He wanted
to make sure that it wouldn't collapse on them when they
walked in. With the dim light barely making its way through
the trees, Garrick wasn't able to make out much more than a
few feet inside.

"Garrick Elliott, this door is stuck," Tyler called from
the patio. "It won't budge. We're going to have to find another way inside."

Garrick backed away from the window. It was barely
large enough for him to fit through, but the beam had planted

itself in the middle. As a last resort, he could knock the remaining glass out of the frame and try to squeeze through, but
he hoped there was an alternative. He wasn't sure what would
happen if he pushed that beam forward, and he was definitely
trying to avoid causing any more movement than he had to
before he trusted the integrity of the building.

"Let me give it a shot," Garrick replied, confidently
walking toward Tyler. He met his friend at the door and
grabbed the handle. Expecting resistance, he pushed against
the door. It opened with ease but creaked loudly.

"Right," Tyler said sheepishly, "I keep forgetting
about that."

As Garrick pushed the door open another few inches,
they heard a loud crash from inside. He froze the arm on the
door, careful not to push or pull at all, as he put his other arm
in front of Tyler. After a second, Garrick peeked inside, only
to see darkness. He pushed gently against the door, trying to
let more light into the room.

"Hold on," Tyler warned, placing a hand on Garrick's
shoulder. "Were you able to determine what happened?"

"No," Garrick admitted. "I assume it was a beam from
the roof. The place looks like it really took a hit from what I
saw over at the window."

"Whatever it was, you might cause more problems if
you force this door open. Let's take a look around. Maybe
there's another way in."

"Yeah, that makes sense," Garrick concurred. He took
another step back, carefully holding on to the door. As gently
as possible, he let go of the handle and backed away. The two
of them crept down the stairs and walked around the side of
the building. Tyler had his eyes glued to the bottom floor, trying to find another way in, but Garrick had been trained to
search his surroundings much more efficiently. His mind
wasn't just focused on a door or window on the first floor. He
was looking for an entrance from the outside to the basement,
or even a window on the top floor he would be able to climb
to.

As they turned around the side of the house, Garrick was able to see the back for the first time. A piece of the wall and roof were missing from the second story. Garrick was starting to understand why no one bothered to repair the house. Due to the age, there was no question that the renovation costs would exceed any value.

"There's a door down here," Tyler mentioned. "It looks like there is more debris in front of it, though. I don't know, Garrick Elliott, I'm starting to realize this may not have been the best idea. This place could fall apart any second."

"I'd survive. Look up there," Garrick said, pointing out the second story.

"That doesn't make me feel any more secure, strangely enough."

"I'll check it out."

"Do you see a ladder? I'll follow you up," Tyler asked as he looked around the yard. Garrick started running toward the building. He jumped at the wall, pushing down against it with his foot as he reached for the second story. He grabbed at the broken wall, but he just missed it. Instead, he drove his hand into a sharp edge of the wood and slid back down the wall. He groaned as he wiped blood from his hand, and Tyler watched in awe as the puncture wound closed.

"So you can't run up walls?" Tyler asked wryly, clearly choosing not to mention anything about the healing.

"I guess parkour isn't as easy as every video I've ever seen makes it look."

"Do you want me to give you a boost?"

"Maybe I should have thought of that first," Garrick accepted with a laugh. Tyler walked over to him, cupping his hands together. Garrick placed his foot in Tyler's hands.

"Be careful, Garrick Elliott. I'm not exaggerating when I say it looks like this place could fall apart in an instant."

"I'm sure it's a lot more stable than it appears. It's been standing like this for years." Tyler just shook his head as he lifted his friend. Garrick jumped up, grabbing the landing and pulling himself up.

The ground underneath him didn't present any imme-
diate danger of caving in, but he was still sure to tread carefully. There were burned pieces of wood all around him, and
the floor looked scorched.

Garrick carefully navigated his way to the door of the
room. Upon reaching it, he pushed it with caution, listening
for any falling debris. He wasn't particularly afraid for his life
if the building collapsed, but he didn't like the idea of the pain.
When he stepped through the door, he was able to faintly discern the staircase. Realizing that stairs might not be his best
idea, he contemplated just jumping to the lower floor. At least
then he would know what he was in for. A quick and painful
fall, but there was no anticipation of anything deteriorating under his feet as he walked. He decided against it, though, and
placed his hand on the railing.

Garrick tested each step before he placed his full
weight on it. Only one of them felt as though it would break
under him – it bent as he put weight on it – so he took a larger
step to skip that one. As he reached the bottom floor, he saw
the beam that was blocking the front door. It looked like it had
fallen a while back. The beam had probably been resting
against the door, and Garrick had dislodged it when he pushed
against it. It was lying nearly horizontally covering the door
and wall. If Garrick had continued to push it, it may have just
broken through the fragile wall near the front door, turning at
a diagonal.

Garrick carefully lifted the edge of the beam which
was in front of the door and carried it in a semicircle before
setting it back down.

As Garrick gave himself a moment to examine the
room, he was inclined to believe the story about the old man.
There was furniture that looked practically ancient in the
home. It was a pretty nice place, though, despite the creepy
vibe it gave off. The burn marks weren't as bad on the bottom
floor as they were on the top, either, and the furniture didn't
look too destroyed. If anything, it looked like there was just
water damage – maybe from fighting the fire, or maybe from

the years of rain leaking in through the destroyed ceiling. The fire must have started upstairs and been put out before it was able to reach too much of the bottom floor.

Garrick walked around the staircase, going through an archway which led to the kitchen. He saw the kitchen door, but there wasn't any debris in front of it. Wondering what it was that made Tyler assume it was blocked, Garrick walked up to the door and tried to open it. The fire had melted the knob, making it impossible to twist on this side, and forcing the door locked. Garrick was having trouble rationalizing the path of this fire in his mind, but that wasn't incredibly important at the moment.

Garrick pushed hard against the door, snapping the hinges as he broke it open. He could have gone back around and opened the front, but he knew Tyler would be on the other side of this door waiting for him. Part of him didn't want to walk back through and redirect him, and another part just wanted to show off.

"So what do you think?" Tyler asked, ignoring the cracking of the wood.

"I don't think it's going to fall apart on us. Some of the support beams on the roof have fallen down, but I think they stopped the fire before there was any real structural damage. You know, aside from the second story missing a section. We have to see if there's even a basement, though."

Tyler laughed nervously in response, and Garrick smirked. He knew he would be terrified if he were in Tyler's position, but he was having fun being the brave one for once. Of course, it was easy to be brave when there didn't seem to be any consequences. The worst that could happen was he get some scrapes which healed in an hour. Tyler had a lot more to risk if he explored a decrepit old house.

"You know," Garrick started earnestly, "It's totally okay if you want to stay outside. I can keep looking around on my own and have you as back-up."

"Right," Tyler laughed, "There's not a chance. My curiosity greatly outweighs my fear for my life."

"I'll keep you safe," Garrick laughed. He wouldn't have allowed Tyler to walk inside if he thought there was any chance anything would happen to him. Having wandered around the house, though, he was confident it would stand, at the very least.

Tyler laughed, and Garrick led him into the house. They walked back toward the living room, sticking close to the wall, testing doors until he found a staircase that led down to the basement. Garrick couldn't hide the excitement as he started to believe this was exactly what he'd been looking for.

Tyler followed him as he descended the staircase. Garrick looked around – unsure of what exactly it was he needed. He'd never had to find his own place to transform before. Of course, he had his general ideas, but he wasn't even entirely positive that the stairs would keep him down there, but it made sense to him. As long as he locked the door before he went downstairs, the wolf would have no reason to try to get out, and it wouldn't be able to gain enough momentum to knock down the door at the top of the stairs. That was based on speculation, but he was also far enough away from civilization that the wolf wouldn't be searching for a way out, and if it found one, it wouldn't run into town.

"This is petrifying," Tyler muttered.

"This, Tyler, is perfect."

"Yeah, I know. Perfection doesn't change the fact that it's harrowing. Honestly, I think the fact that the two of us are standing here discussing this place as a viable option for anything only serves to add to the sinister vibe."

"Fair enough."

Garrick snapped a picture of the room and sent it to Chase. Although he wasn't convinced Chase would actually go there with him, he wanted to prove that there was another option. He looked around, satisfied with himself. He had proven Aldric wrong. There was another way. Garrick had found his own method, and he felt victorious.

"Great, so that's done," Tyler blurted out eagerly. "Let's make our way back home and guarantee that you never have to make use of this place."

Tyler seemed so confident that there was a way to cure Garrick's ailment. Although Garrick wasn't sure if he believed it himself, it was definitely worth looking into. Not that he hadn't before, but what he was doing wasn't working. He could fight against the change all he wanted, but he knew that it would never actually stop the beast. Maybe the two of them could find something that would. The worst thing that could happen was that nothing worked, and Garrick was stuck in the same place where he was already trapped. The best case, though, was that he would find a way to ensure that he never had to worry about the wolf again.

"Yeah," Garrick affirmed. He actually started to believe that he could be human again. That he could find some way to get rid of this curse.

Chapter 8

Fifteen months ago

Garrick sat with Hayden in front of her television, willing away the boredom. There was nothing he liked more than spending time with her, but that didn't make him a fan of her taste in movies. Since they'd started dating, he'd only been inside her house a few times, but her mother and Caleb were gone for a few days touring a college a few towns over, so Hayden had asked him to bring over a romantic comedy to watch with her.

He sat next to her, his arm wrapped around her. She was lying on his chest with her legs resting on the couch behind her. The smell of her hair wafted up toward him. That was something Garrick could never get tired of. Her hand was flat on his chest, just over his heart; a perfect symbol for their relationship – his heart was in her hands.

"Are you comfortable?" she asked, turning her head from the screen to look into his eyes. She seemed to be enjoying the film far more than Garrick was, so for her to divert her attention felt like an honor. He smiled and looked down at her, brushing her hair behind her ear. She inched even closer to him.

"As long as I'm holding you, I don't think I can be uncomfortable," he told her. Of course, he was aware that most of what he said around her felt cheesy, but it didn't alter the validity. Garrick was just thankful that he found a girl who appreciated his failed attempts to be smooth.

She nuzzled her head deeper into his chest, burying herself. Garrick gently ran his fingers through her hair.

After a few more minutes, she sat up next to him. Scooting close to him, she then planted a kiss firmly on his cheek. He turned to face her and kissed her back. Time froze as he gazed into her eyes.

Her expression was pensive, as though she were trying to formulate a thought. He couldn't tell what it was, but also didn't want to press the issue and ask her about it. He decided to just let her say whatever it was that came to mind. If she wanted to tell him, she could. Still, he was starting to get worried. She kept taking breaths as though attempting to start a sentence, opening her mouth slightly to form the words, but then stopping short. For the first time in their relationship, Garrick was witnessing Hayden speechless.

"Garrick," she finally said, still hesitant.

"What?" he responded as patiently as he could, attempting to conceal his racing heart.

"I love you."

Garrick's breath caught in his throat, and for a moment his vision blurred. He couldn't process the words, although their meaning seemed clear. Neither of them had spoken those simple words yet, but he'd felt it for a long time. Garrick had just spent countless hours waiting for the perfect moment – trapping himself in his mind with the fear of scaring her away. Now, she'd finally said it, and he couldn't bring himself to respond. She stared at him expectantly, clearly as nervous as he'd been only moments before. Garrick mustered up all his courage to force a reply.

"I love you too," he stuttered, tripping over the words. As he said them, he felt himself get lighter. The metaphorical weight on his chest was replaced by a physical one as she pressed herself closer to him and kissed him.

Hayden stood, leaving the movie to play as she grabbed his arm and gently pulled him to his feet. Entranced, he stumbled to his feet, not quite convinced he believed his reality. Garrick forced himself to follow her though his legs shook with each step. At the doorway to her room, she let go of his arm and turned to face him again. Gently placing her hands on his cheeks, she pressed her lips against his. Garrick refused to let himself believe any thoughts racing through his mind, and he just tried to focus on the moment.

Hayden's arms slid down his face, wrapping tightly around his waist as she backed up, pulling him with her. She turned around and nudged him, pushing him onto the bed. Sitting on the bed, he looked up at her, masking his disbelief. She stood over him, looking deeply into his eyes. Garrick's heart was pounding, and he didn't know what to do. He'd never felt this way about anyone, and he felt like any action he took could completely ruin everything. However, he was equally concerned a lack of action would be interpreted as a lack of interest, and he'd ruin it that way.

"Are you sure?" he asked – finally deciding on a course of action. He didn't want her to take any step she wasn't ready for, or to start doing something because she felt like she should.

Hayden didn't respond. She just smiled as she climbed onto the bed, straddling him on her knees. She leaned down and kissed him again.

Present
11 days until the full moon

"You are not going to that house, Tyler," Garrick said adamantly. "I don't care if the king of werewolves showed up and told you that was the only way you could cure me."

"There's a king of werewolves?"

"I have no idea if there's a king of werewolves."

"You've deceived me, Garrick Elliott. I trusted you," he smiled. Garrick didn't return the gesture. His friend had gone completely crazy, and he wasn't going to support it.

"Listen, a vast majority of the possible cures I've found require you to be in your wolf form. I want to help you."

"Yeah, well find a way that doesn't involve me eating you," Garrick quipped.

Tyler's desk was covered in books, most of which he'd already read through at least once. There were open books strewn across the room, left open to pages with morsels of information Tyler had deemed worth retaining. Garrick couldn't imagine how much time his friend had poured into that research over the past few days. He was starting to get concerned for his friend's sanity.

Tyler and Kayla had broken up once again a few days before, and it seemed apparent that he was using Garrick's condition as a distraction. That, combined with his innate desire to help, made a dangerous combination.

"Hey, Tyler," Garrick spoke up. "Are you alright?"

"What do you mean?" Tyler asked, avoiding eye contact by keeping his focus on the book.

"About Kayla."

"I'd prefer to focus on this," Tyler responded shortly. He covered a cough before returning his attention to his book. The constant movement was bound to be taking a toll on Tyler, but the best Garrick could do was be there, and make his appreciation as clear as possible. Maybe all Tyler needed was a distraction, but Garrick was determined to at least be present and ready in case he needed to talk.

They were both silent for a while. Tyler had found a multitude of ways to cure a werewolf. Garrick knew that most, if not all, were just rumors. One was to call the beast's name when it was in the shape of a wolf. He shot that down instantly. He'd said Hayden's name before while they were changing. Anyway, he wasn't even there when the beast took over, it didn't make sense that he would be able to respond just because he heard his name. Of course, there was a nagging idea in his mind that it was still a possibility, but he refused to put Tyler at risk – so there was no chance he'd allow his friend to get close enough to speak to him.

Tyler had conceded that that one wasn't likely, so he suggested another. This one required him to draw blood from the wolf. Garrick doubted it was that simple. If it was, the hunters wouldn't kill wolves, they'd just cure them. Even if it was a cure, though, it would once again require Tyler to get too close for comfort. He would most likely end up tearing his best friend to pieces, and he doubted Tyler would actually be able to harm a werewolf.

"Who turned you?" Tyler asked, finally breaking the silence. He turned to Garrick, holding a closed book with his finger marking a page.

"I don't know," Garrick said. "The night is such a blur, and I couldn't tell which is which. It could have been any of them."

"Well, I suppose that negates this option," Tyler said with a sigh. Garrick looked over his shoulder. He couldn't believe Tyler had even thought about that one – killing the one who had scratched him. This author actually had a lot of information on the topic, and they claimed that when the one who scratched him was killed, his scar would slowly fade, and so would the rest of his wolf powers. Even if that were the case, he was not going to kill the people who'd been in his pack. That wasn't who he was.

"Any ideas that don't involve homicide? Or at least not me committing it? That's the whole reason we got into this mess in the first place," Garrick said, recognizing the irony. He had tried to escape the curse because he was afraid he had killed and may do it again, and the most plausible theory to stop him was to simply have him kill someone else.

"Alright," Tyler said as they finished reading that section, "I may have been a bit eager. I just saw the phrase 'confront the wolf who scratched you,' and assumed it would be viable."

"No, I know," Garrick sighed, dropping his head back and closing his eyes. He took a deep breath and sat up straighter again. "I'm sorry. I know you wouldn't expect me to kill someone."

"Here's another possibility," Tyler offered after reading a few more pages.

"What?" Garrick asked. He knew that it was almost definite that Tyler was wrong, but he still allowed the smallest amount of hope to seep through into the question. He peered over Tyler's shoulder.

"So, Romans believed that if you completely exhaust yourself, you can rid yourself of the curse."

"You want me to run off the wolf?"

"Don't say it like that, it sounds significantly less convincing."

"I have to go meet up with Sammi," Garrick groaned as he checked the time. "I told her I'd walk her home from work again. Meet me at the gym in two hours."

"Finally, another solution warranting an experiment."

"You can't count the first one," Garrick argued jokingly. While he was still more than a little bitter about the garlic, he was able to look back and see the humor in it. At least their first experiment set a low bar both in efficacy and Garrick's desire to participate.

"How can we gauge success?" Tyler asked. "Shouldn't we wait until it's closer to a full moon?"

"I'll know if it's going to work, trust me." He wasn't lying; he knew that he'd be able to feel it. He always felt the wolf just underneath the surface. If somehow the beast weakened, he'd know that it had worked. While he didn't believe that it would for a second, anything was worth a shot.

He shook his head. He hadn't been to the gym since Cailean had 'trained' him. That felt like a lifetime ago.

"Alright," Tyler said. "I'll be there."

"Hey," Garrick said, catching up to Samantha as she walked out of the coffee shop. The sun was setting, and the purple hues in the sky started to fade to black.

"Hey," she said, a smile spreading across her face. "I didn't think you'd make it."

"Of course I made it," he responded.

The two of them walked a few blocks, talking about their days. It was mostly Samantha telling Garrick stories about how ridiculous some of the customers had been and Garrick trying to find little truths in the events of his day that he could share. He hid behind half-truths, telling her that he'd spent the day with his best friend. He told her that since his break-up with Kayla a few days ago, Tyler had needed him there.

That was mostly true. Only, he didn't really need Garrick. He needed a way to distract himself, which presented itself in the form of researching cures for lycanthropy. That part, though, he decided was something that should stay unsaid.

"One of them asked me for a decaf drink, alright? That is totally a normal thing. Then, as I hand them the cup, they tell me, 'thanks, I needed a boost. I probably would have fallen asleep at work.' I'm like 'yeah, so that isn't exactly what you needed then,'" she rolled her eyes as she finished the story.

"You actually said that?"

"Of course not. I laughed at him. He thought I was laughing with him. I don't know, maybe he was kidding. Whatever," she said. She smiled. Garrick did too.

They stopped in front of her house, and she turned around to face him as she leaned against the door frame. She was studying his eyes, and he wasn't exactly sure what it was she was looking for in them. Whatever it was, Garrick tried to keep her from finding it. He did his best to keep any emotion he could from being reflected.

"You are hiding something, Garrick Elliott," she said. Her using his full name felt strange. It wasn't like he didn't hear it every day. It had actually become a sort of nickname that Tyler used, saying that it just rolled off his tongue. Over the years, though, it had become something vaguely personal, like an inside joke between himself and Tyler. It almost felt like an intrusion for someone else to use it.

"Oh, you think so?" he asked. Inside he panicked, but he recovered as well as he could. He didn't want to give her any further reason to suspect she was right – she may not want to be his friend anymore. It was great to have another friend, even if it didn't mean anything more. Even worse, though, she may be inclined to investigate, and he didn't want her anywhere near that side of his world. He'd already roped Tyler in, he didn't want anyone else to have to bear his burdens.

"Yeah," she said. "And I'm going to find out what it is." She leaned forward and tapped her finger against his nose. He smirked, leaning back subtly as she'd inched uncomfortably close.

They looked at each other for another moment. Garrick couldn't tell if the thing he was feeling in the air was some kind of tension or just the awkward silence. Either way, he wanted it to end. He was starting to feel uneasy.

He was just about to break the silence when the look in her eyes suddenly changed. She closed the distance between them and kissed him. Garrick froze, not certain how to process the information. He felt a confusing wave of emotion rush over him, and he couldn't sort through the racing thoughts.

She quickly stepped back, looking into his eyes, gauging his response and probably deciding if she should apologize.

"That was…" Garrick muttered, unable to find the proper words. It wasn't that he was necessarily stunned, but more that he was unsure of what exactly it was. Part of him was happy, but a much larger part was unsettled.

"I'm sorry," she said.

"No," Garrick told her. "Don't be."

"I just thought that it was a good moment."

"Yeah," he said, still trying to think of how to handle the situation. What he did was one of the worst ways he could possibly have responded. "I have to go. It has nothing to do with what just happened; it's just that I promised Tyler I'd be somewhere. Really, I'm not leaving because of…"

"The kiss?" she finished when Garrick trailed off.

"Yeah. I mean no. I'm not leaving because of that. I really do have to leave, though. I'm sorry about the timing."

After a few seconds of a pause, he waved his phone and added "Best friend duties," goofily. He turned and walked away, embarrassment adding to the mixture of all of the other confusing emotions swimming in his head. He absolutely did not want that to happen again. He felt like he was cheating on Hayden, even though they weren't together anymore. He still loved her. He shook his head as his heart began pounding.

Garrick found himself distracted by every sound as he passed. The streetlights buzzing became deafening, and the light blinding when he looked up. His stomach churned as he tried to focus on simply moving forward.

"Okay, breathe," he muttered under his breath, willing himself to heed his own advice. Though he was shaken by what had happened with Sammi, he knew his body's reaction was drastically exaggerated. It was only a kiss, but for some reason, he'd lost all capability for rational thought. His head started pounding as every thought raced through his mind, and he could feel his lungs closing up, refusing to accept oxygen. It was unlike anything he'd ever felt before – as if his own body was fighting him.

Garrick pushed himself forward, moving one foot after another. Believing that focusing on a task would help him come to his senses and get over the pain, he tried to forge a path to the gym.

He breathed deeply for a few minutes, slowing down as he tried to catch his breath. Nothing seemed to work, and he felt the panic set in. Not long after, the unfamiliar feelings began to be replaced with far more recognizable ones. He felt the pain pushing itself forward, the beast inside clawing its way to the surface. Agonized, he collapsed on all fours on the sidewalk, lurching forward. He stared at the lines in the concrete, willing his pounding migraine to fade. The pain was starting to get too powerful. He watched claws grow from his hands. Biting it back with everything he had, he stared at his fingers. The wave of pain passed by relatively quickly, and the claws retracted. He stared in awe at his hands. Last time had only been about half an hour, but this time he hadn't even lost himself. He didn't know if he should be excited by that or terrified by the fact that he was still so close to changing when the moon wasn't full.

Garrick stayed on all fours, panting as he tried to breathe. His vision was blurry, but at this point, he knew it wasn't the wolf – it was the shock. He dropped to the ground, lying on the cold, hard concrete and staring up into the night sky. After a few minutes, he allowed himself to stand up slowly. He wiped the sweat that had been dripping from his face and continued his walk to the gym. Now more than ever, he had to find a way to stop this.

"Wait, you stopped it?" Tyler asked. Garrick nodded. For the past five minutes, Garrick had been running on the treadmill at maximum speed and incline. In that time, he'd explained the situation to Tyler, and he still wasn't short of breath at all. As much as he'd love to dispel the curse, he couldn't deny that there were perks to being a werewolf.

Still, he felt like he wasn't reaching his maximum speed on that treadmill, and he was getting concerned that he might never even get tired. For the most part, the strength that wolves had just came from the frequent tearing and rebuilding of muscle, but their healing factor was how the muscles rebuilt so quickly. That same healing, though, would keep his body intact when a human would be gasping for breath. Aside from that, his heart was just another muscle which was torn apart as he transformed into a wolf. He'd never tried to push himself to the limits, but with everything that his body went through, he was beginning to doubt there were any.

Even as a werewolf, though, he was at least in part human – so he was bound to run out of energy eventually. Especially as far from the moon as it was, Garrick was sure that he didn't have the full force of the wolf backing him, and eventually, they'd be able to determine the validity of Tyler's newest idea.

"I don't know," he responded. "I mean, yeah, I fought it. But it didn't fight back as hard as it usually does."

"Maybe it wasn't strong enough to, given the fact that it isn't a full moon. It's possible that the wolf's power just grows with the moon, and then the full moon is the only night it's strong enough to take over."

"That makes sense," Garrick said. "But the moon is bigger now than it was last time, so why would it be weaker now?"

"Well, could it have been triggered by something?" Tyler asked.

"Such as?"

"I don't know. Sammi seems to be the common factor. Perhaps somehow she brings it out of you."

"I've spent a lot of time with her without anything similar happening, though."

"Well, the first time was a first date, right? I know you were trying to avoid that, but deep down you were bound to have some inclination that it was still interpreted that way. What about this time. Was it special?"

"No," Garrick said.

"Nothing?"

Reluctantly, Garrick offered, "She kissed me."

"Well, that certainly explains it. She's triggering the transformation!"

"That doesn't make any sense, though. I've felt emotions much stronger than any of these with Hayden, but that never forced a change."

"Maybe you're right, but it's the best lead we have. Humor me; how does she make you feel?"

"It's hard to explain," Garrick said. For the first time since he'd started running, he began to take note of his breathing. He was beginning to have to focus on breathing correctly as he ran. There was no fatigue setting in yet, but it was a start.

"Try."

"She doesn't make me feel like anything. Wolves mate for life," he started, using the same explanation Hayden had offered him a year ago. "So that means I can't ever love anyone like I loved Hayden."

"Fine, but does that mean you can never love anyone at all?" Tyler asked.

"Yes. I really like her, but I don't have those kinds of feelings for her."

"Right, but think about this, Garrick. The way you explain it to me, the human and the wolf are basically separate entities – the two of you constantly vying for supremacy. That struggle proves that even though you're a werewolf, part of you is still human."

"Okay."

"So there is a part of you driven by the wolf, and that part will love Hayden forever. But maybe the human side is able to move on – and to start having feelings for a new girl. If that's the case, it follows that the wolf would be angry, because it doesn't think you should be with anyone else. When you get too close to her, it takes over and tries to stop you."

Garrick tried to process the suggestion. It made sense on some level, but he didn't want to accept it. He didn't think he loved Sammi, but he wasn't over Hayden, so he couldn't distinguish that feeling quite yet. Maybe the wolf was picking up on something that he was trying desperately to hide from himself.

"This is going to sound absolutely insane," Garrick said.

"What?"

"That might actually make sense."

"Appreciate it," Tyler said sarcastically. "Well, now that we have a working theory, what's the next step?"

"For now? I just avoid her. Our number one priority is finding a cure. If she is the reason for the mistimed transformations, I have to stay away from her in order to protect her. And if she's not, then I am right and I just don't love her. If that's the case, then I can only ever love Hayden; I shouldn't be leading Sammi on. Especially after tonight."

"Okay," Tyler said hesitantly. He clearly wasn't enthused with Garrick's response. Garrick had been moping around since the break-up – he was well aware of that. His friend just wanted him to be happy. Still, Garrick was confident that his logic was sound, and though Tyler wasn't happy with the conclusion, he couldn't argue with it. "Then let's get this cure."

Neither of them said anything for the next twenty minutes, but Garrick's breathing slowly became more labored. An hour later, he started to feel like he couldn't move his legs anymore, but he kept going. According to Tyler, he had to be so exhausted that he actually lost his ability to move.

Tyler eventually just gave up and started thumbing through a magazine he found. He was clearly amazed at Garrick's endurance, but even his awe had its limits. Garrick himself was surprised, but for the opposite reason. He hadn't pushed himself since his first transformation, so he was only now discovering that he had limits at all.

After another ten minutes, Garrick just collapsed face-first onto the treadmill. The belt continued to rotate at its maximum speed as he dropped down. Garrick turned his head as he fell, avoiding connecting with his nose first. Still, the rub-

ber scraped layers of skin from his face as it thrust him backward. Thrust from the machine, he rolled onto his side – but
his arm twisted around him and snapped, the bone splitting in
two. Garrick hit the wall behind him, his head snapping back
as he connected. His vision blurred for a brief moment, and
he had no question in his mind that he was concussed.

Tyler's shouts as he jumped toward his friend melded
into the cacophony of screeching noise that filled Garrick's
ears. The shattering of bone had clearly been loud enough to
hear over the roar of the treadmill. Garrick looked down at his
arm. Though he was seeing double, it was still blatantly obvious that it shouldn't be bent that way. Hearing heavy footfall,
Garrick looked up to see the man who'd been working at the
desk running toward him. Dizziness set in due to the quick
rotation of his head, but he tried to focus. As he gathered his
bearings, he noticed that the treadmill's screams began to die
down. The safety key was dangling from Garrick's collar.

He struggled to catch his breath, but was more worried
about the worker getting across the gym and to him, because
it wouldn't be difficult to notice the scrape already starting to
close on Garrick's face. If he trapped them in conversation
long enough, he'd watch Garrick's arm twist back into its
proper shape.

"Get me out of here," Garrick managed to force out
through his gasps. He blinked rapidly, trying to regain his vision. The double vision he had was starting to blend together
to one, but everything was still vaguely blurry. Tyler reached
down and helped his friend up. He wrapped Garrick's good
arm around his shoulder and the two walked toward the door.
The worker approached them, but Tyler turned to keep Garrick's more injured side facing away.

"Are you alright?" The man asked. "I think I should
call the paramedics, just in case."

"No," Garrick argued unconvincingly.

"We just have to get him home. He was trying to break
a record – pushed himself too hard," Tyler said. The man
looked at them skeptically, but he didn't stop them as they

gently nudged past him. Garrick's vision returned to normal as they stepped into the darkness of night, and he felt confident he could stand on his own. He straightened himself out, standing taller and taking his arm from around Tyler's shoulder.

"I'm sorry," Tyler apologized.

"Don't be," Garrick told him. The wound on his face had stopped bleeding, and the blood which was already there began to dry. All he wanted to do was get home and clean himself up. There wasn't a part of him that regretted trying Tyler's solution, because at least there was one more thing to cross off the list. He could still feel the wolf just under his skin, and the healing was clearly present, so he knew it hadn't worked.

"I probably should have planned this better," Tyler ruminated, his eyes downcast. He was probably realizing, as Garrick had, that if it had worked, Garrick wouldn't have healed very well from that injury. To Garrick, that would have been a small price to pay – but it was evidently weighing on Tyler.

"No," Garrick said. "I thought it was worth a shot. I still do. Anything that may or may not work, as long as it doesn't put my friends at risk. A little pain passes, Tyler. I just want to be rid of this thing."

"You broke your arm, Garrick Elliott."

"Yeah, well," Garrick said, snapping the bone back into place with his open hand. He felt the muscles and tendons begin to reform around the bone and hold it in place. "At least we know that that doesn't work." He moved his arm which had been broken, showing Tyler that the bones had all grown back to normal.

Chapter 9

Fifteen months ago

"Hey, Chase," Garrick muttered. He and his friend were eating lunch with Hayden and her friends again, but he'd pulled Chase away the first time an opportunity presented itself. With that group, it was difficult to find time to speak to any one person individually, but he knew he had to talk to someone.

He wasn't sure exactly how tasteful it was, but Chase had become one of his best friends, and no one knew Hayden better than him. He was the best one to ask for advice. Garrick was getting concerned, and he thought maybe Chase would have some idea how to tell what was going. Maybe, if it was something Hayden felt more comfortable talking to friends about than Garrick, he'd know exactly what was bothering her.

"Yeah, what's up?" he calmly responded. Chase didn't seem off-put by Garrick's tone or the fact they'd steered away from the others for this conversation. Garrick couldn't help but wonder if that was because Chase was just a good friend – and a good actor – or if he was overplaying the awkwardness of the situation in his mind.

"Do you know if Hayden's alright?" Garrick forced the question out, fighting through his perceived awkwardness. She'd been acting differently for a while. He had a creeping suspicion that it had something to do with the fact that they'd slept together the previous week, but there was no chance he was going to bring that up to Chase. Still, maybe Chase would have another idea – one which would make Garrick feel a little better.

"Well, I'm significantly less confident than I was a few seconds ago," he laughed. "Why do you ask?"

"I don't know. She has been pretty distant these last couple of day, that's all."

"Well, you know girls."

"No. No, I really don't."

"I'm sure she's just fine," Chase sighed. His expression screamed to Garrick that he was trying to be a good friend and avoid lying, but there was something he was hiding.

"It's probably just not a good time of the month," Chase added with a laugh. There was something forced about that laugh. Chase was choosing his words carefully, attempting to avoid divulging some piece of information.

"I don't know," Garrick groaned. He didn't want to push Chase, he'd already asked him for a lot. Anyway, of course he was going to be more loyal to Hayden – they'd known each other far longer. Garrick just wished Chase would come out and say that he wouldn't talk about it.

"I'll talk to her," Chase offered. "I mean, I'm not as close with her as you are, obviously. But maybe it's just something that she doesn't feel comfortable telling you, you know?"

"Is that normal? For girlfriends to hide things?"

"Just breathe, Garrick," Chase comforted. He was trying his best to make his friend feel better, but it was just making things worse. Garrick could see that there was something that he knew about. He just wished there was some way for him to find out what it was.

"Maybe it's just the full moon," Chase suggested. "It makes people crazy."

Present
3 days until the full moon

Garrick lazily strolled toward his car, not in any particular rush to get anywhere. The ten-minute drive home was the worst part of his day. He wasn't typically bothered by driving alone, but specifically driving home from school had become something he'd done with Hayden. That trip, every day, just adding to the ever-growing list of things which reminded him of her. Recently, even things completely unrelated to her started to make him think of her. He would either mourn the fact that they'd never done something together, or he would momentarily cherish the fact that something didn't remind him of her – only to realize he was thinking about her again.

He unlocked his door and slumped into the seat. As he started the car, he heard someone softly say, "Garrick, wait for me."

The voice sounded like a whisper right into his ear, and his head shot up and darted around. How had he missed someone getting that close to him? Garrick spun his head in each direction, scanning the car in a panic, but there was no one within a ten-foot radius. Just as he was beginning to accept that he was losing his mind, he noticed through his peripheral vision that Chase was walking toward him. He shook his head, scolding himself silently as he saw the smirk forming on his friend's face. Garrick wondered if he'd ever get used to the sensory changes which accompanied the full moon. As foreign as the concept still felt to him, he was still surprised that he hadn't understood the second he'd heard Chase. He caught his breath, sitting sideways in the seat with one foot on the ground and the other on the frame of the car, as Chase closed the distance between them.

"You know, people are going to think you're crazy if you keep talking to yourself," Garrick teased as Chase approached.

"Whatever," he laughed. "If that's the one thing about me deemed crazy, I'd say I'm doing something right."

"Can't argue with that logic," Garrick shrugged. He waited a second before adding, "Need a ride home?" He desperately hoped that Chase would say yes, but tried to bury that feeling in a friendly question. Any company would be great, and it would distract him. Chase's house was in the opposite direction, so it would make his trip alone longer, but it wouldn't be a trip home from school alone. That practically semantic difference meant the world to Garrick.

"That would be great," Chase accepted gratefully. He walked around the car and sat in the passenger seat, closing the door a little too hard behind him. "Thanks," he told Garrick, his friendly tone starting to become forced. Garrick sighed, once again surprised that he hadn't caught on to what was actually happening. Chase never asked for a ride home, so there was clearly some ulterior motive. Turning around, Garrick closed his door, hoping it would allow Chase to actually say whatever what was on his mind.

"You need to come with us," Chase blurted out the second the door closed. It had worked even better than Garrick had expected. Garrick was silent for a moment as he shifted the car into gear and started driving toward Chase's house. He waited a few minutes, Chase's comment lingering in the air, before he finally gave it a response.

"I can't. You know that."

"It isn't safe out here. Aldric has told us a lot more about the hunters. He's scared for you. Mad, yes, but scared too. He wants us to get you to come back. Of course, he'd never say that and risk his pride faltering, but he doesn't want you to get hurt, Garrick."

"Didn't you see my picture?"

"Yeah, that looks great. But I really don't think that it's going to work. I showed Aldric and he just rolled his eyes. He told me they'd catch you."

"Thanks for the concern," Garrick replied, trying to hide the anger and sarcasm. He was genuinely glad to have friends who cared about him, but he wasn't even convinced that hunters existed. Anyway, no amount of concern would change the fact that Aldric refused to do anything to protect innocent lives. Maybe his pride truly was the issue, and he was just angry that Garrick found a solution to the problem that Aldric hadn't been able to solve. He flipped his blinker on and turned left through a light. His phone vibrated. Assuming it was a text from Tyler, he let it beep without checking it. "But I can't go back there. I don't think anyone will find me, but even if they do, I'd rather risk myself than innocent campers."

"Then I'm going to change with you," Chase demanded.

"No. Let me at least do it once, make sure it's safe," Garrick argued.

"I'm not letting you do this alone. I told you we could start our own pack if you found a better alternative. Well, let's do it."

"Next month, Chase," Garrick implored as he pulled up to Chase's house. "I just want to know that it will work. And I want to test my theory that hunters won't come after me. I don't think I'm wrong, but I'm not confident enough to bet your safety on it."

"Okay," Chase resigned. An air of silence filled the car when Chase didn't get out. He leaned forward, elbows on his knees. He took a deep breath and checked his phone, clearly trying to procrastinate the remainder of the conversation.

"Hayden's a mess, Garrick."

"Please, Chase. I can't."

"I know."

1

"I have to go to Tyler's," Garrick changed the subject as he checked his phone. "We're working on something."

"He knows?"

Garrick blanked for a second. He didn't realize that the rest of the pack didn't know that Tyler had learned about him. The thought that it was a secret simply hadn't crossed his mind. Although he knew his face gave him away, he desperately searched his mind for any possible explanation. Garrick wasn't sure what Aldric would do if he found out Tyler knew.

"It's a school project," Garrick said, almost inquisitively. He tried to sound convincing, but he'd never been a good liar. Chase shook his head, not even pretending to believe the weak attempt at an excuse. With them being so close to the moon, their wolves were pushing their way out, and Chase would be able to hear his heart.

"Your heartbeat raced when I asked that," Chase explained. "What are the two of you working on?"

"A cure. It's far-fetched, but there are tons of ideas in the books we've found. Most of them are pure mythology, but it's still worth a shot. Maybe, somewhere hidden in all the myths, we can find a way to stop the change."

"Let me help." Chase didn't give Garrick room for an argument. Garrick just sighed and put the car in drive, heading to Tyler's house. "So, how did he find out?"

Chase had agreed to ask Aldric what may cause a change outside of the full moon. He seemed to be convinced by Garrick and Tyler's theory as well, but they all decided it would be better to see if Aldric knew of a way. Of course, Chase was going to exclude any of the bits that involved Garrick – which was basically everything. He was going to have to find a time for it to come up, because there was no question Aldric would put it together if Chase just asked it as a random question.

In the meantime, he wanted to help find a cure. He was lying on his back on Tyler's bed surrounded by open books and holding one above his face. Tyler sat at his desk, leaning over his own book and studying it intently. That left Garrick to skim the books they'd already searched, hoping they'd missed something. At the moment, he sat in a chair and tossed a ball in the air, catching it absentmindedly. Even when his eyes drifted away, he didn't miss the ball once. He wasn't sure if he could just sense its presence or subconsciously hear the wind displacement.

Tyler caught Chase up on the methods they had already discussed, which was practically everything they could find. As he spoke, Garrick pondered each solution. Chase and Tyler would look to Garrick any time they had a question, apparently expecting him to have any more answers than they did. Tyler seemed particularly interested in the idea of drawing blood from a wolf, but also admitted that it was too dangerous for any human to attempt.

"What about this," Chase suggested, turning the book toward Garrick and Tyler as he held his finger under a bold heading. "Exorcisms. I mean, we are, in a sense, possessed by a beast, right?"

"It's worth a shot," Garrick conceded. There was no counter-argument that made sense in his mind. The only thing that he felt was that sometimes, the wolf didn't feel so much like an evil presence. Those moments were always fleeting, and he repeatedly fell back to the conclusion that it was malicious – but something still felt wrong about performing an exorcism on it.

"That also says running water would stop a werewolf, though," Tyler combated, squinting as he read the paragraph.

"We have crossed a few streams," Chase joked. "If I remember correctly."

"I know I've woken up on opposite sides of them. I don't know if I used a bridge, but I don't think the wolf would have gone out of its way," Garrick added, not acknowledging Chase's joke. Garrick was too focused on determining the validity of the source.

"Still, it doesn't discredit the entire article," Tyler empathized as Chase's chest fell with a heavy sigh. "Just because not every piece of information is correct."

"No," Chase acknowledged hesitantly. Still, when he turned the book back around, he flipped through the remainder of the pages with significantly less enthusiasm. Garrick's faith in that source began to waver as well, and he found himself questioning whether any of the books could actually hold an answer.

At some point, Garrick left and found his way to the woods. All he wanted was to rest in silence and solitude, hoping it would help him concentrate. Maybe he could find some way to fix everything that was going wrong in his life if he just gave himself a few minutes to think about it. Even if not a cure, he hoped he could just find solutions to the personal dilemmas plaguing his mind. Every waking minute his head swarmed with thoughts; he couldn't help but think all he needed was a minute to quiet it all down.

But he didn't really do much thinking. He actually just let the sounds of nature calm him, and he almost felt himself drifting off to sleep. For the first time in as long as he could remember, his mind went completely blank, and he didn't have the burden of thought pressing down on it.

Placing his elbows on the fallen tree behind him, he leaned against it for support. The crunch of the leaves beneath him startled a bird, which flapped its wings violently as it flew away. Garrick breathed deeply, accepting fresh air into his lungs as he admired the trees in front of him. The air felt cleaner – purer – than anything he'd experienced, and with each exhale, he could feel the stress and anxiety leaving his body.

Suddenly, Garrick noticed a shape dart out behind a few trees in his peripheral vision. He didn't even have to wonder for a second what it was. The beast was too large to be an animal in that forest, and it was far too fast for its size. It was the wolf. He looked around, wondering where he actually was. This couldn't be real. It never was.

Still, he was terrified. No amount of logic or rationalization could quell the now intense beating of his heart. Garrick lurched forward, staggering to his feet, and ran as fast as he could, uncertain of where he was going. He just kept trying to get away from the sounds of rustling branches and breaking leaves behind him that indicated that he was being chased. He darted past a few trees, ducked under branches, and jumped over fallen logs. Despite his best efforts, he could hear the wolf gaining on him, rapidly closing the distance.

In an instant, the sounds of the pursuing creature were silenced. He broke the line of trees and stumbled into a clearing. There was a single tent set up, but it was torn to shreds. Two human bodies lay not very far from the site.

He dropped to his knees, staring at the image that continued to haunt him. Blinking furiously, Garrick willed the vision to dissipate. He even repeated "it's just a dream," fully aware that he couldn't be witnessing this again. It was to no avail – regardless of what he told himself, the tent wouldn't move. The bodies wouldn't vanish. He could feel his heart rate climb as his breathing became more shallow and he descended into panic.

He saw the wolf walk powerfully out from the trees in front of him and to his left. It moved diagonally toward him, almost as though it were being careful to avoid the campsite. The beast paused for a moment at the body and looked down, seemingly only noticing the bodies in that moment. It inched and nudged the corpse, which obviously didn't respond. The wolf whimpered a bit, but it wasn't distracted for long. As quickly as it had been distracted, its attention shifted back to Garrick and it continued its path toward him.

He could see himself reflected in its eyes – a broken boy collapsed to the ground, his will shattered.

"What do you want from me?" he asked angrily. The wolf, presumably incapable of speech (but who knew, in his twisted head?) didn't respond. Projecting his anger at himself, at the weakness he could see in the image in the wolf's eyes, he raised his voice. He yelled, "What do you want?"

It just motioned toward the site, its eyes downcast. If he didn't know better, Garrick might believe the wolf was showing remorse. Unwilling to humanize the beast in front of him, he refused to accept that. Still, there was a sadness in its eyes. Garrick's expression softened as he looked back down at the wolf, catching its gaze.

"You didn't do this, did you?" He didn't know who he was talking to. The wolf wasn't even there, not really. It was all in his head. But he felt a need to speak his thoughts out loud. The wolf looked innocently at him. Then, as quickly as his own expression had changed a moment ago, the wolf's did. Its mouth opened in a snarl and it dove at Garrick.

"Garrick?" Chase prompted, shaking him awake. Garrick's eyes shot open and he twitched violently as he tried to sit up. Chase, whose hands were on Garrick's shoulders, let go of his friend and moved backward, holding his hands up. "You looked like you were having a nightmare."

"Sorry," he muttered absently. He tried to gather his thoughts and stabilize his breathing as he sat up and looked around Tyler's room. "I must have fallen asleep."

"You did indeed – about four hours ago," Tyler retorted. "I made the executive decision to allow you to get some rest."

"I'm sorry," Garrick repeated.

"Don't mention it," Chase sympathized.

"Did you guys find anything?" Garrick asked groggily, stifling a yawn.

"Not really," Chase sighed. "I found a few people claiming they had a way to prevent it. Not really a cure, but it can supposedly stop you from changing. I don't know. It was a lot of meditating and talking to your inner beast. It was really weird."

"Thanks anyway," Garrick accepted. "Sorry."

They both just brushed it off and buried their noses back into their respective books. Garrick hadn't realized the two of them were so focused. For Chase, it made sense. If they actually found an answer, it would change his life forever. The curse, though, didn't affect Tyler directly. To him, it wasn't anything more than helping a friend who had a problem once a month. Garrick found himself speechless, honored to have such good friends. They'd been researching for hours, and he'd already found himself losing hope, then drifting off. The two of them, though, just kept going – trying to find an answer despite the odds.

He checked his phone to see a text from Samantha

"Garrick, can we talk?" She asked.

"Are you at the coffee shop?" Garrick replied.

"I get off in an hour."

"I'll meet you there."

"Guys," Garrick spoke to the two people actually in the room. "I need to talk to Samantha. I have no idea what to tell her, but I can't just keep ignoring her forever. I hoped we'd have cured it by now, but that was a little ambitious," he admitted.

"Unfortunately, I don't think I'm an authority on this subject," Tyler joked. Garrick wasn't sure if that was just his way of getting out of giving advice or if he was acknowledging his imperfect relationship history.

"The girl from the coffee shop?" Chase asked skeptically.

"It's a long story," Garrick sighed.

"My warning still stands," Chase said menacingly, squinting at Garrick with feigned malice.

"At this point it might be a mercy," Garrick groaned. "Don't worry, I'm figuring it out."

"Okay. We'll get us a cure," Chase offered, his tone so convincing that Garrick actually believed him. He knew there had to be something that they could do. Watching the two of them work so hard gave Garrick determination to pursue a cure more – he couldn't give up if they weren't. He still had a dozen books back at home that he'd checked out from the library, so he resolved to get back into reading after he made it home from his awkward conversation.

"Do you need a ride home?" Garrick asked Chase as he stood and stretched.

"Nah, I'll walk, thanks," Chase said. "I'm going to stay here for another few hours and try to figure this out."

Tyler nodded absently, devoting rapt attention to the book.

"Do you guys need my help?" Garrick asked, hesitating at the doorway before he left. He felt awful leaving them to try to fix his problem. Aside from that, he was procrastinating dealing with Samantha.

"You're no help," Tyler joked, finally peeling his eyes from the book and turning to Garrick. His tone shifted as he gave his friend sincere advice, "Honestly, though, Garrick Elliott, we're alright. You've been depriving yourself of sleep for weeks, desperately searching for any morsel of information, and it's wearing you down. Give yourself a break, go talk to the girl, figure out your personal life without the wolf weighing you down. Then go home and go to bed, because we're going to need you functional."

"Thanks, guys," Garrick smiled. Tyler nodded, waving him on. Steeling himself with a few deep breaths, Garrick headed outside, hoping the words would come to him in the car. All that presented itself was more confusion. He knew he didn't want to date her, but part of him wondered if the human side did, and what that would mean if he found a cure. A larger part couldn't imagine ever loving anyone else – and if he found a cure he'd share it with Hayden, and all of their issues would vanish. Except, of course, the fact that he needed her support, and there was a piece of him angry at her for not being the one where Chase was.

Regardless of whether or not he wanted to date Samantha, though, he cared about her. At the very least, he wanted to make sure he didn't hurt her, but that seemed inevitable. If he told her they couldn't even be friends, she'd probably be devastated, but she'd be safe. Otherwise, he was putting her at risk – and he didn't want to bring more people into his world.

Confusing thoughts racing through his mind, Garrick drove to the coffee shop and parked outside. Waiting for Samantha, he realized he hadn't even begun to think about what to say, so he tried running through the conversation in his head. Every scenario he imagined ended with her angry at him, and most ended with them never talking again.

"Hey," she greeted as she got in his car. Garrick hadn't actively noticed her approach, but he wasn't startled as she opened the door and got in. Subconsciously, he must have known. If he'd been thinking about it, he would have heard her footsteps before she even left the shop.

"Hey," he replied awkwardly.

He started the car and drove to her house. They spent the entire drive in silence, but she just sat in her chair after he stopped.

"I'm really sorry," she finally found her voice.

"Really," he told her. "It's fine. I'm just going through a lot of confusing stuff right now. It really isn't about you, as horrible as that is to hear."

"Want to talk about it?"

"I can't."

"Why not?"

"It's... complicated. I don't think you'd understand."

"I'd understand a lot more than you may think," she implored, hurt. "Try me."

"I'm not over Hayden yet, you know? And I don't know what that means for us. You don't want to be friends, and I get that. I don't know if I do either. I just don't think I'm ready for anything more. And I don't want you to wait. I don't know if I ever will be."

"You will be," she comforted, setting her hand atop his. His instincts screamed to pull his hand away, but the conversation was going far better than he'd anticipated and he didn't want to ruin that. "I'm not going to push you, Garrick. I really am sorry."

"It's okay. I'm sorry for being so hard to be around."

"Well, you are kind of difficult," she joked.

"Do you want to hang out sometime?" Garrick asked after a few minutes of silence. He knew that he shouldn't have asked it, but she looked so hurt, and she was just sitting there awaiting some response. He wanted to do anything he could to get that look off her face.

"Yeah," she beamed. "I'd love that. I work pretty much all weekend. Is Monday good?"

"Monday is actually really bad for me," Garrick said cautiously. She looked confused, probably wondering why he'd ask her to hang out just to decline her invitation. "Tuesday, though, I'm free."

"Okay," she replied. "Tuesday." She got out and walked to the door. He watched as she went inside, making sure she got in okay. Then he drove off, heading home and thinking about how much of a complete moron he was.

Chapter 10

Fourteen months ago

Not for the first time, Garrick watched the clock tick away to the end of the school day. As usual, he couldn't bring himself to focus on the teacher's dull lesson, but now he couldn't even keep his attention on his own daydreaming. He was lost in his head – something completely typical for him – but in a way which was completely unfamiliar. Normally, his thoughts gave him hope and comfort, and he dreamed up scenarios where he could be a hero, or just live out his own dreams. Recently, all of those thoughts involved Hayden, so even that wasn't a new concept. However, that day he hadn't been able to conjure up a positive thought. Stubborn doubts and fears pushed their way to the forefront of his mind, and no amount of internal screaming could drown them out. Garrick had convinced himself that he knew what Hayden's evasive attitude and her avoidance of him over the past few days meant. As much as he wished he didn't, he knew.

The bell rang, and he stood up groggily, wishing that he didn't have to move on with his day. Although anyone else would say school was a complete bore, it wasn't too bad for him. It gave him a chance to sit and stare off into space – to wallow silently, and an excuse to ignore the constant vibrating of his phone. Communication with another human being took far more energy than he could muster, and at least class gave him a reason to give people for his absent responses. With the dismissal of school, he had to go home, where he was under no social obligation to pretend to be okay, and he knew that would just lead to an even deeper well of tears and self-pity. He slung his backpack over his shoulder and trudged toward the door.

Garrick watched his feet as he walked, keeping his eyes pinned to the ground in front of him. A vibration from his pocket demanded his attention, and he finally pulled his phone out with a groan and flipped it open. He had four texts. One from Tyler, making sure he was okay – claiming that Garrick had been acting strangely the whole day. He'd hoped he'd been able to mask it, but he knew himself well enough to know that there was no chance he'd actually pulled off any sort of ruse. Garrick was horrible at lying and acting, and Tyler had known him his whole life. Another was from his mom, letting him know that she'd be home late from work again. The other two were from Hayden, one asking him to meet her somewhere, and the other just saying she had to talk to him. It was evident what was coming, and he planned to procrastinate it to a time when he was alone and could break down as he saw fit. Whatever her texts said, he wasn't going to meet her; he was just going to go home and send her a text acknowledging that he understood. Looking at her as she broke his heart wasn't something he could handle.

As he rounded a corner, he heard her voice muffled by the sounds of people rushing past. He couldn't make out the words, but the tone was a whispered rage. Garrick inched closer to the noise, trying to avoid being seen. A voice in his mind screamed that he didn't want to know who she was talking to or what was being said, but his curiosity took over. Knowing full well the knowledge could do nothing but hurt him, he gave in to his lust to learn everything there was to know.

"I have to tell him," she whispered. "He deserves to know."

"No, he doesn't," a familiar voice argued. His stomach churned, but he tried to maintain his composure.

"I hate lying to him."

"You knew what it meant when you made your choice," Cailean scolded her. "There's no taking it back now."

Everything started to fall together in his mind. She'd been avoiding him for days, and he'd seen her going to Cailean's house the other day. She just refused to talk to him about what was going on, probably unable to formulate any adequate story on the spot. The pieces of the puzzle just fell into place, though, and everything became painfully clear.

"I'm not going to let you risk everything, Hayden. Stop thinking about yourself. I don't care how lying to your boyfriend makes you feel – I won't let you ruin my life over it. And I definitely won't let you ruin Brooke's."

There it was. What could she possibly tell him that would ruin Brooke's life? Garrick leaned against the wall to prevent himself from falling over. Even though he'd started to suspect something, he didn't think it would be so drastic. Everything pointed to it, he saw that now, but he'd been blinded by his unparalleled hope and his desire to trust her.

There was a sudden break in speech, and he could hear the shuffling as they both jolted their heads toward him. He hadn't thought he'd made a significant amount of noise, but maybe he'd fallen into the wall harder than he'd realized. Garrick stumbled backward, trying to find a place to hide and avoid detection as he heard Hayden's footsteps approaching him. He walked into someone, who pushed him forward and glared as they walked by. The crowd behind him was large enough to just blend into, but his balance was still off from being pushed, and he couldn't recover quickly enough. Hayden turned the corner, almost running into him, and he watched the expression on her face morph through a dozen expressions before she settled on remorse.

"Garrick," her voice broke as she spoke. There was pain in her tone, but he couldn't bring himself to feel any pity for her. Maybe he should have felt guilty for eavesdropping, but the only thing he could bring himself to think was that he was vindicated. Hayden's gaze dropped from his eyes to the floor as she fumbled for the words to say to make anything better.

"What did you hear?" she finally asked meekly.

"Enough," Garrick said. He forced anger into his voice, even though all he could feel was sadness. If he spoke any more, he was worried he'd just choke up. He couldn't let her see that, though, so he tried to sound powerful and angry. Breaking down was for another time – not with her in front of him.

"It's not what you think, Garrick. I can explain everything, I promise. Please," she said. Her eyes lifted back toward him, sparkling as the light reflected from the tears brewing within them. The same shine that always filled him with comfort and joy now brought forward pain and anger.

"Don't bother," he interrupted, turning his back to her. He wouldn't be strong enough to leave if he stayed for another second. He already felt his legs trembling, but he forced himself to walk away. If he allowed her an explanation, he might forgive her, but he refused to let himself. He had to be stronger than he'd ever been, because he wasn't going to let himself be a victim. Garrick Elliott wasn't going to be someone who got cheated on.

One step at a time, he forged his path home. As he did, he found himself coughing, choking on the tears. Keeping his gaze on the ground in front of him was all he could do to stop himself from collapsing to the sidewalk and sacrificing his ability to move. When he was safe in the privacy of his room, he could allow himself to feel, but he didn't want to cry as he walked down the streets. To distract himself, he started daydreaming about fighting Cailean. He wished he had the guts to do it. He knew things wouldn't end up the same way that they always did in his head. He probably wouldn't even get one good hit in before he was completely unconscious. But at least then he wouldn't be a coward.

Present
The night of the full moon

Garrick walked down the street, heading to the abandoned station, granting himself the leisure of wandering around the woods a bit rather than taking the most direct path. He was nervous for his first change alone, so he'd given himself plenty of time to make it to the cabin. As he watched the sun set, his confidence grew, and he knew he could manage. He walked to his sanctuary – the building Garrick hoped would be his refuge from the beast. All of his hopes were placed in that one structure – one which could keep him from being heard or hurting someone else, but also eliminate the risk of running into Aldric. After he was confident his plan was working, maybe he could actually convince Hayden, Cailean, and Brooke to come with him. Aldric would have no choice if his whole pack decided together that this was a better plan. Of course, Garrick hoped it would solve his problems with Hayden, but at the very least it would prevent anyone else from dying.

He climbed the steps and pushed the door open. It squeaked, once again protesting Garrick's entry. He walked through the darkness, his eyesight barely faltering in the darkness. Able to discern at least the shapes surrounding him, he quickly navigated to the cellar door. Cautiously, he opened it and stepped inside. As soon as he was secure inside, he closed and locked the old wooden door behind him, exhaling deeply. For the first time all month, Garrick was starting to feel relaxed. He'd actually managed to do what his pack claimed was impossible.

Walking down the stairs, Garrick took his shirt off and tossed it into a corner. He was actually happy, despite the fact that he was about to change and was completely unable to stop it. He was proving to himself, and to everyone, that he didn't need Aldric. Even Aldric would have to recognize that he was stronger – better – than that pack gave him credit for, and he was going to be the only one who wasn't at risk of killing someone that night. At the moment, that was enough of a victory. The cure could come later.

"I thought I might run into you here," a voice in the darkness said. Garrick panicked, not even concerned about placing a name to the voice. He wasn't sure, and didn't care, if it was a friend or a foe, all that he knew was that anyone in there was not just in danger; they were already dead.

"No, no, no," he groaned. Maybe if he said it enough, it would stop being true. More than anything, he wanted to believe that he had just been hearing things, but he couldn't deny reality. He picked up his voice, speaking with more conviction as he added, "No, you need to get out of here."

"I thought we were friends," Samantha muttered. He was going to kill her. The wolf struggled against Garrick, pushing its way to the surface. "Why do you so desperately want to get away from me?" If he were in any other condition, he would have noticed the peculiar tone in her voice, but it barely registered in his mind. At the moment, he was just focused on saving her life. Somehow, he had to get her out of there before he changed and put her at risk. Either she would get killed or she'd become a werewolf, and Garrick wasn't sure which would be a worse fate to inflict on her.

He knew she couldn't see much, because he couldn't. If even his eyes were struggling to adjust to the dark, barely able to make out her outline, he knew hers were useless with no light coming in from outside. Nonetheless, she was able to locate him, and she turned to face him as they spoke.

"Sammi, there are things that I can't explain to you right now; things that you probably wouldn't believe if I tried to, but you need to leave."

"How naïve do you think I am, Garrick Elliott?" she mocked, stepping toward him as she followed the sound of his voice. A small window near the top of the basement, secluded in a corner, allowed the slightest sliver of moonlight into the room – but that sliver was enough to reflect from something dangling in Samantha's hand.

Before he could react, she drove the blade into his ribs. Stunned, Garrick staggered backward, his hands clasping the wound. He fell to his knees and barely caught himself from falling forward. As he tried to process what exactly was happening, he felt her foot slam against his side, and he dropped to the ground, rolling over twice before colliding with the wall. He coughed, leaving blood on the floor in front of him.

He didn't know exactly what was happening; his mind was spinning with so much new information. What he did know was that she had betrayed him. The whole time that he was so worried about hunters, and he just let one get so close to him. He'd allowed himself to begin to believe they didn't exist, and apparently they had to give him a neon sign that he was wrong.

Garrick fumbled for the blade, his coordination absent in the pain. When he finally found it, he ripped it out of his body and threw it against the far wall, as far from Samantha as it could get. Garrick tried to force himself to stand, but he couldn't manage. He placed his hand over the wound, pressing it down and willing it – to no avail – to heal.

"What did you do?" He forced each syllable from his mouth with extreme effort.

"Silver," she said. "You may find that it has some unique properties." She was now crouching down, right in front of his face.

"Why are you doing this?" he asked, a fit of coughing punctuating his question. The words not so much a demanding, forceful question as a plea for help. "What did I do to you?"

"Well, that one is for me to answer." A different voice – a male voice, and much older. "You see, Garrick, your kind killed my brother. Samantha's dad."

"I suppose you could say that I caught your scent," Samantha taunted, caressing his face. "That first day I saw you. I knew something was off. And then you suddenly started covering up your beautiful arms. I tried testing you a couple times, but you never stuck around long enough for me to be absolutely sure. Then, when you told me about the things I wouldn't understand and your unavailability of the full moon, I knew."

"That wasn't me. I haven't killed anyone." He was only able to process a few pieces of information, and it felt like the man was more important to respond to at the moment. Given his limited capacity for thought and responses, he decided against humoring her supervillain monologue. Anyway, in his possibly delusional mind, he actually believed there was a way to get through to them – and his only idea was appealing to his own innocence.

For a brief second, Garrick questioned himself. He wondered why he was so convinced that he didn't hurt anyone when this whole crusade had been because of a fear that he had. Did his dream really change his mind so much? Or was the wolf – which was just under the surface – trying to use its control to speak to him. It wanted to clear its name in the last few seconds of its life.

"Not yet," the man conceded, "but you will." Garrick looked around the room, but he couldn't make out more than a few dim shadows in the moonlight. The wound in his side wasn't pouring blood anymore, but it still hurt. It wasn't likely it would close before he changed, and he wasn't sure what that meant for himself. Maybe the reason they were so confident was because he was already dead.

"So you're going to kill me?" Garrick whimpered, failing his attempt to sound defiant.

"No," Samantha said. A spark of hope flashed through Garrick's mind, only to be crushed when she added, "I like you, Garrick. I am going to cure you. To set you free."

The words themselves weren't sinister, but they were accompanied by an almost unrecognizable tone. Normally, she put on a good show, but here, he could sense a brokenness as she spoke. She actually believed what she was saying, but any semblance of sanity had vanished.

"That's what you tell yourself? Does it help you sleep?" Garrick scoffed. He may have done horrible things, but at least he took responsibility for them. Still, he couldn't judge Samantha – she thought she was helping. The poor girl was just deranged.

"Then why wait? I'll be able to kill you both in seconds," Garrick snarled. He could feel the beast pushing forward, even more now that he was in danger. Somehow, it granted him the power to be defiant that he'd lacked before.

However, he also knew that he was bluffing. He knew he had to wait at least a few minutes before the wound from the silver would wear off, and he'd be able to change. If he stopped fighting against it before that, it would just be an attack while changing, to which Aldric had always told him he was vulnerable. These two knew their stuff, it seemed, but he could only hope they would fall for his ruse.

"Good point," Samantha said. Garrick heard a gun cock. He tried to move, but agony tethered him to the ground. She aimed the gun at his head.

"How could you do this to me?" he asked, resorting to the last tactic he could think of. He hoped to appeal to some humanity, or at least buy enough time for a miracle. Aside from that, though, there was a deep desire to understand. Garrick just wanted to know why any of this had happened. He had never felt so betrayed. He tried to believe that she wasn't hunting him the entire time, but that wasn't something he could convince himself of. "I–"

"You what, Garrick? You loved me? I doubt it. I'm pretty sure your chances of love left with Hayden. With me, you just fell for an act."

She'd seemed so nice. He didn't believe it was all a lie. Maybe she had been brainwashed to hate werewolves, but she wasn't actually the manipulative killer she seemed to be. She had to have cared for him at least a little bit – he could hear it in her voice, so he tried to use that opening.

"I could have loved you," he lied. Listening carefully, he thought he could hear footsteps up above. Whoever was coming couldn't possibly make his situation worse – so he had to try to just buy himself a few more seconds. "Werewolves choose who we love, and I was just scared to choose you so soon. But that was wrong."

"What?" she smirked, apparently amused that he'd even tried.

The man laughed. "You couldn't even fool someone untrained, kid."

"Yeah," she added, hardening her face again as she cocked the gun.

Her focus was drawn to the creaking near the stairs. Garrick wanted to take the opportunity to attack, but he couldn't move.

The door, locked from the inside, shook vigorously. For a split second, the shaking stopped – then the door caved in violently, splinters of wood scattering across the floor. Chase sprinted down the stairs and jumped from halfway up the staircase, landing directly in front of Samantha's uncle. He lifted the man and threw him against the wall. Samantha quickly turned and shot, in his direction, but Chase was faster. He dove to the ground and grabbed the knife Garrick had thrown, rolling away. Blinded in the darkness, Samantha shot where Chase had stood, not realizing he'd moved. The light from upstairs started to filter in, but it wasn't enough.

Chase stabbed the knife into Samantha's rib. She cried out, dropping the gun and falling to her knees. Her uncle quickly got up and rushed to her side. Taking advantage of his concern, Chase kicked his knee and shoved him to the ground. Chase reached a hand out to Garrick, pulling him up. Garrick put his arm around Chase for support, and the two of them staggered to the steps.

They ascended the stairs as quickly as they could, but it took too long in Garrick's condition. When they reached the top, Samantha's uncle – the hunter – was directly behind them. Without turning around, Garrick heard the creak of the steps only a few below him. Garrick fell forward, grabbing the handle as he stumbled through and slammed the door shut as he dropped to the ground. The door barely stayed closed as it hung on one hinge. The other two, along with pieces of wood from around the lock, had fallen down the stairs. Garrick reached up, searching for the lock on the low chance it would work. The hunter slammed into the door, but Garrick held the knob as he turned it.

Garrick moved out of the way as Chase pushed over a beam to block the door. "Okay," Garrick tried to catch his breath, resting on the ground. Chase, standing next to him, lifted him up, forcing him to continue walking as the hunter pushed against the door, pointlessly spinning the knob.

"We aren't safe yet," Chase cautioned, urging Garrick to keep walking.

"They're locked in," Garrick argued.

"Garrick," Chase retorted, barely a whisper. "When I kicked it in, I pretty much destroyed that door. It won't be long before he realized he can pull instead of push."

"Oh." Garrick tried to pick up the pace, but his legs collapsed under him. He lurched toward the ground, but managed to catch himself on the wall near the front door. Garrick leaned against the wall, holding his stomach with as much force as he could muster, begging the blood from the reopened wound to stay in his body. He could all but hear the beast inside of him begging to be set free, begging to save his life from this threat. He had pulled the blade out of his body fast enough to limit the effect of the silver, but he was starting to regret it. He knew that the beast could force itself out at any moment in time. Did it know it would put him in danger? Or maybe it knew he was wrong, and it wouldn't, since the wound was inflicted early enough.

Chase fell to his knees and slammed a fist to the ground. He looked down at the floor as he clenched his jaw.

"What are you doing here?" Garrick asked, angry at Chase for putting himself in danger. Of course, that anger was overshadowed by how thankful he was that his friend just saved his life.

"I told you I'd be here for you," Chase said. The hunter pulled the door open, and Garrick listened as he cursed the two of them for their back-up plan. He was even more thankful for Chase in that moment, because he never would have thought of it. With the blood pouring from his side, he could barely think straight, and he'd actually believed he'd locked the door.

"We have to go."

"We'll never make it to the others in time."

"Then we'll go deeper into the woods this way. We just have to go."

Garrick could hear the hunter ramming against the beam with all his might. The faintest scraping of wood against the floor told him it wouldn't be long before the hunters were out of their cage.

Chase looked up, his green eyes shining with a light that seemed to come from inside him. He nodded as he tried to stand up. Garrick could feel the wound in his side closing again, and the realization that Chase's life depended on him gave him stronger conviction. Garrick wasn't going to let Chase suffer for a decision he'd made himself. Or for the people that he'd chosen to trust. Chase was there, willing to fight for Garrick. And Garrick was going to help him get out of it. His friend had saved him from the hunters, but he wasn't going to get far without transforming, and Garrick had become much better at that. It was his turn to return the favor.

Garrick pushed himself away from the wall, standing on his own. His weak legs wobbled beneath him barely able to push him forward. He pulled Chase up using all the strength he could muster. The exertion opened the wound in his stomach once again, and fresh blood poured to the ground. Chase could barely stand as he fought through the pain of his own transformation, and Garrick saw blood on his friend's shirt. The bullet must have made contact, and Chase had just kept going because he had to. He and Chase supported each other as they walked to the front door. They made it outside, but before he closed the door, Garrick saw the support beam finally slide far enough for a person to squeeze through. He shut the front door again, but realized that he couldn't lock the door from the front. Garrick let go of Chase, advising him to continue walking. He stood between Chase and the door as he backed away, trying to get farther from the hunter who was after them.

One too many steps backward and Garrick dropped down the stairs, landing hard on his back. It knocked the breath straight out of his lungs, leaving him light-headed, as he was already gasping for air from the transformation. He saw the doorknob turn, and quickly returned to his senses, and to his flight. Chase was stumbling down the staircase as the door opened, and the hunter shoved him down.

Garrick forced himself up, and he tackled the hunter to the ground. He felt his wound beginning to close again, and his strength started to return. He punched the hunter once drawing blood from his mouth. He punched him again, three more times, unsure of what his plan was exactly, but he was using his strength to his advantage. Skill won over strength, though, as the hunter bucked him forward, then rolled over, pinning Garrick to the ground. He slashed Garrick's shoulder with a silver blade, but it wasn't deep. It was more of a distraction, which worked because he backed away. The hunter drew a crossbow and aimed at Garrick's head. This time, he wasted no time – firing the arrow. Garrick felt the world move in slow motion. Lying on the ground, he watched the arrow move toward him. A figure fell in front of him first, though, as Chase dove toward Garrick.

The arrow went straight through his heart – something that he should have been able to heal from. He'd always heard that werewolves were most vulnerable when transforming, and he'd been concerned about it, but he didn't know what that meant exactly. Seeing the arrow hit Chase, though, in his half-transformed state, it was clear.

"No! Chase!" Garrick screamed. He could practically feel the wolf's howls as well. He stopped fighting it. The anger of what had happened to his friend fueled his transformation further. The wolf was begging to come out. Fully aware that he didn't have the strength anymore, he finally stopped fighting it.

Garrick watched as claws erupted from his fingernails. He growled at the hunter, who had already reloaded his crossbow and was aiming at Garrick. Another arrow shot by, but Garrick rolled out of the way. He bared his teeth, laughing as if it were a game. He could feel his grip on his own mind fading, but it wasn't as terrifying as usual. Another arrow was on a path for Garrick's face, and it would have killed him if Garrick's newly formed tail hadn't swatted it out of the way. Garrick ran toward the hunter, who gave up on the bow and drew a gun.

Garrick sidestepped and was behind the hunter before the gun was even level. He kicked the man, bring him to his knees. Garrick grabbed him to pull him back up, slamming his back against a tree. He caught the hunter's wrist and pulled it back, driving it with as much force as he could into the tree. Multiple bones in the man's hand shattered and the gun dropped to the ground. Apparently accustomed to the pain, the man reacted quickly, pulling his blade and slashing toward Garrick.

Garrick jumped back, narrowly avoiding contact with the blade. He seized the opportunity of the man being stunned to step forward and slash his throat. He didn't leave the man in pieces, but he definitely left the corpse as an unquestionable animal attack.

Attempting to deprive himself of any time to process, Garrick turned toward Chase. He could think about what he'd done when they were safe. For now, he had to get himself and his friend somewhere far away from the hunters.

Garrick ran back to Chase and dropped to his knees. He held Chase, in his arms as blood continued to pour from his chest. Garrick pressed his hands against the wound in an attempt to cease blood flow. Trying to divide his attention equally, Garrick focused on helping his friend while attempting to reign the beast back in. It was harder than ever before, because he'd already started his transformation, but he could not allow himself to give up on Chase. His vision was getting blurry; his eyes obviously in the process of changing to those which didn't truly belong to him.

"I'm so sorry," Garrick cried, tears streaming down his face. All he wanted to do was find a way to help Chase, even if that meant taking his friend's place, but he knew there was nothing he could do. He didn't notice the beast pressing against him quite as much. He looked at his claws only to see that they weren't claws. They were nails.

"Don't be, Garrick. I don't regret anything. You're my best friend, and you were worth saving. I would do it again."

"We can save you," Garrick implored. "You're going to be okay." He knew it was futile. Since Chase was hit during the transformation, it was only a matter of time before he bled out. At least, that was what Aldric had always told them. Looking down at the light fading from Chase's eyes, Garrick knew deep down that it was the truth. He just held his dying friend in his arms and lied, hoping to give him some peace.

"No, I'm not," Chase admitted with a sad smile. He paused, as if searching for the words, and added, "Garrick, there's something I want you to do for me."

"Of course, anything."

"Kill me."

"What? No!"

"Please, Garrick. We both know the only real cure for this curse. It's the only one that makes sense. You have to kill the one who scratched you. For all we know, that could be me. Make my life mean something, please."

"No. I'd rather live every day as a monster than one day having paid that price to be human."

"Then do it for me, Garrick. Who knows how long I'll lie here in pain, waiting to die. Help me."

"Chase... I can't. I... I can save you. Come on, we'll take you to a hospital. They'll stitch you up – help the healing process."

"And what, Garrick? I wolf out there and kill them all? Assuming that even works. If not, then you kill them."

Garrick knew he was right. He knew there was nothing at all that could be done. He took a deep breath, trying to steady the heaving of his chest, and moved his hand toward Chase's neck. He watched as claws once again came from his nails.

"Thank you," Chase said. There were tears in both of their eyes. Garrick wanted to believe it was merciful, but he couldn't help but feel that he was justifying murder. Still, he could see the pain in his friend's eyes, and there was only one way to allow him any type of rest. Solemnly, Garrick drew his nails across his friend's throat, granting his request in one swift motion. Chase breathed one last breath, almost resembling a sigh of relief, as he closed his eyes for the last time.

He held Chase's body in his arms as he silently cried for a few seconds. Then he let go and pushed himself back against a tree. He drew his legs up and rested his elbows on them. He placed his head in his hands, the claws running through his hair, not taking a moment to think about the blood which still soaked his hands. His canines grew, and his ears changed shape, but he stayed still for as long as the shape of his body would allow it.

After ten minutes had passed, he was on all fours. Garrick was locked somewhere in the deep recesses of his own mind with no control over his own body. The wolf walked toward Chase, who still lie half-transformed on the ground. It nuzzled against him, as if trying to restore life to his still body. Its attempts proving futile, it turned and headed off in the other direction. As it glanced back once more before departing, a tear fell to the dirt beside its paw.

Garrick walked into town, sniffing out his pack and trying to find exactly where Hayden was. The buildings came into view, lights from the houses and businesses twinkling in the moonlight. The streetlights continued to change color, even with no cars on the streets.

He saw a girl, probably no older than ten, who just happened to be in her front yard. She was probably just an innocent child, playing with chalk on the sidewalk before she had to go inside for bed. She was just in the wrong place at the wrong time, and Garrick couldn't do a thing to save her life.

When she saw him, she screamed at the top of her lungs and turned to run inside. He jumped, blocking her path to the door. Garrick snarled at the child, ready to pounce, even though every human piece of him screamed not to. The wolf, the animal, was threatened by the presence of a human, and it needed to defend itself.

A blast from behind him. He didn't know what it was; he couldn't process the explosion of sound. The animal mind in control of him just rendered a terrifying noise, and he turned around. This was the girl's alpha. It must have been. He was much larger than she, and he had made bursts of light and sound erupt from his hands.

Garrick ran, jumped onto the roof of the house, and kept running. He made a break for the trees, where he knew he'd be safe. Humans didn't like the trees, they weren't usually there. And if they were, they were weak. And in the trees, Garrick had a pack. Within minutes, he crossed the tree line. That was where he saw her.

She stood near the edge of the woods, waiting for him. It was as if she had been looking for him, and she knew he'd be coming back to her. Her eyes scanned the town; not full of hunger, but loneliness.

Everything that their human selves had done, it all faded away as he sheepishly paced near her. She welcomed him by rubbing her head up against him. He felt at home as Hayden cuddled herself closer to him.

Garrick's eyes fluttered open. He was lying in the leaves, and he had a jacket laying over him. His jacket. He didn't remember getting it back from Hayden, but assumed he must have. Not completely aware of the events of the previous night, he couldn't imagine any other reason he'd have it. Until he heard her voice.

"I thought you might be cold," Hayden said. She leaned against a tree, smiling at him as he rubbed his eyes. His face lit up as he saw her, apparently forgetting it wasn't supposed to smile in response to her anymore.

"A little bit," he admitted. She tossed him a pair of pants.

"I hoped you come," she said as he pulled on the pants. "I have to be honest though, your timing could have been better."

He walked up to her and pulled her into an embrace. It was a hug that said everything that had to be said. He apologized for everything – for abandoning her and blaming her for those people getting hurt. And she just hugged him right back, leaning her head on his shoulder, apologizing for not supporting him and for walking away. Neither of them was willing to let go until they heard rustling in the leaves.

Hayden glanced up. She looked past Garrick's face with the slightest pinch of fear. He knew who was going to be there when he turned around. He'd have to face Aldric sooner or later, but he'd hoped he'd have a few more minutes to prepare himself first.

"What is he doing here?" Aldric asked, glaring at the two of them. Garrick didn't know how to respond, with so many words floating through his head. He still wanted to hate

Aldric, but after what happened the day before, he couldn't blame him for anything. He knew that.

Aldric wasn't intentionally leading them to hurt people, and Garrick couldn't go one turn alone without putting himself in danger. Without putting Chase in danger.

"Please, don't do this," Hayden begged.

"Not right now," Brooke added, stepping out from some trees behind Garrick. Cailean stood silently next to her. If even Brooke was stepping up to defend him, they definitely sensed that Aldric's temper was much worse than even Garrick had thought. Garrick could obviously tell as well, but he wondered if his leaving really had that much impact on the pack. Or, maybe Brooke just didn't want to ruin her day after she'd just woken up naked in a pile of leaves – presumably beside a dead animal, judging by the blood on her face.

"I'm not going to write this off," Aldric said, giving each of them a miniature glare before returning the entire focus of his anger to Garrick.

"I'm sorry," Garrick offered.

"I told you to stay away, Elliott."

"I know, Aldric. And I was wrong. I see that now. I thought that I could handle it better on my own. I thought that I could stop myself. But I killed someone yesterday. It was self-defense, but that doesn't make it easier. I can still see the face he made as I forced that least bit of breath from his lungs.

"I almost killed an innocent little girl. I would have, had her dad not shown up. It was hungry, that's all I know. It was hungry, and it just wanted something to eat. I saw the fear in her eyes, Aldric. And it didn't care.

"I thought that being with you all kept me tied to this, to being a wolf, a monster. But I was wrong, you all keep me human. I need you, or I'll get myself killed. Myself, or worse, someone else. I'm sorry, for everything Aldric. I really am."

Garrick could see all of the others' faces full of surprise. He didn't know if it was at the fact that he remembered so clearly, which they all knew wasn't characteristic of him, or due to the tears welling in his eyes, but they were all shocked.

"I gave you a chance. You denied me. I can't protect you anymore," Aldric sighed.

"Dad," Cailean stepped up from the shadows. His dad was still full of rage, and they all knew that no one crossed Aldric when he was angry. Cailean may have been a jerk to everyone else, but he would never speak out of turn to his father. He was just as scared of him as everyone else was. Garrick was in shock as he watched the scene unfold in front of him. "He's one of us. We can't just leave him on his own. Give him another chance."

Garrick could see the rage boiling up inside Aldric. Not only was his son against him, but so was the rest of the pack. Garrick expected him to explode, but something shifted in his face. The anger was gone in an instant, and it was replaced with something possibly more unsettling. The best way Garrick could describe it was longing.

"Do you remember what I said, Garrick? The last time we talked?"

"You... You said never to show my face to you again."

"Ah, that I did. But before that. I told you that I would never turn my back on my own." Aldric sighed and turned away. He rubbed his face before turning back to Garrick.

He reached his hand out, and Garrick hesitantly grabbed it. Aldric pulled him in and hugged him. "You were always one of mine, Elliott. You're not just one of us – you're my son. I'm glad you've returned."

Chapter 11

Fourteen months ago

Garrick found Cailean behind the gym, effortlessly running laps around the track, after school was dismissed. Countless thoughts racing through his mind, Garrick took a deep breath as he walked up to Cailean. Each step was a mistake, and he knew that, but he couldn't just let everything happen without standing up for himself. He had no idea what that entailed, though, or what source of bravery he was drawing upon to continue walking.

"Cailean," Garrick muttered, courage absent from his voice – apparently expended by the walk. His fist balled up at his sides as he focused on his anger. That was the only way he could see himself actually following through with any sort of confrontation.

"Well, hey there Garrick," Cailean smirked, slowing to a stop as he finished his lap and walked up to Garrick. Garrick could feel the blood boiling in his veins – and he wanted nothing more than to wipe that smug look off his face. What could she possibly see in this guy? Apparently, arrogance was all women wanted.

"How are things with Hayden?" Cailean continued, poorly feigning innocence.

That was it. Garrick rushed him, pinning him against the brick wall to the side of the track. He pressed one arm hard against Cailean's throat, holding him against the wall with all his might. Garrick drove his other hand into Cailean's stomach and Cailean lurched forward, only to have his movement restricted. Though he was coughing and gasping for air, Cailean's eyes looked oddly calm.

"How dare you?" Garrick spat.

Cailean's smirk didn't falter for a moment. He punched Garrick in the ribs, and Garrick dropped his arms, freeing Cailean. Winded, Garrick stumbled back and Cailean grabbed him, spun him around, and threw him into the wall. At the last second, Garrick turned his face to the side to avoid plunging his nose into the brick, but he wasn't able to save himself from a painful impact. Garrick turned to Cailean, raising his fists. He couldn't even take a guess at what his next step should be, but he'd always heard fighters say to keep their hands up.

Garrick threw a punch, hoping to catch Cailean off guard, but Cailean easily ducked under it and countered with a punch to the stomach. Garrick dropped to the ground, his breath fleeing from his lungs. He struggled to climb to his feet, but Cailean placed a foot on his chest and kicked him back to the ground before he could rise up.

"I dare you to get back up," Cailean challenged. Garrick did, and Cailean punched him again, knocking him back to the floor. As he fell, he hit his head on the track beneath him, and his vision blurred. He tried to will himself to stand, but there was no strength left in his body. Cailean laughed as he walked away.

Garrick wasn't sure how much time passed before Hayden came into view near the side of the building. It probably wasn't more than a few moments, because it barely gave him time for his sight to return. Cailean must have sent her as soon as he could to go admire how much better he was than

Garrick. Picking up the pace to a sprint as she rounded the corner, she closed the gap and dropped to her knees next to him.

"Garrick," she cried as she pressed her hands against his shoulders as if that would help him in any way. "Are you okay?"

"I'm fine," he responded angrily, shoving her hands away. The rapid motion made him dizzy, but he tried not to let her see that.

"What were you thinking?"

"It doesn't matter," Garrick groaned. He struggled to his feet, trying to catch his breath. Hayden tried to help him, but he pushed her away, unwilling to acknowledge that he needed her.

"I need to get home," he muttered. Recovering slowly with each step, he walked away.

"Let me help you," she offered.

"No! I don't need you," he yelled, facing her again. "Alright?"

"I know," she told him. She seemed to sense that the problem was much deeper than what was currently happening, and tears started to fill her eyes. "But what if I need you?"

There was nothing left for him to say, so Garrick just turned away and kept walking.

Present
29 days until the full moon

"What happened?" Hayden finally asked. The previous morning, Aldric had told them all Chase wasn't coming back, but no one pressed Garrick too hard for answers. Maybe they could see in his eyes that he'd break. Garrick wasn't sure how Aldric knew, but he'd probably been alive long enough to know what it meant when he saw Garrick come back alone.

Now, Hayden was searching, as gently as she could, for the answers they all wanted.

Over the past few hours, with her sitting next to him on the bed, he'd been trying to recap the events of the past few weeks. He expected her to be fuming, but she wasn't even upset about what had happened with Samantha. Granted, he had left out the part about Tyler's theory on what it meant for him to transform on nights when the moon wasn't full.

Still, she took everything surprisingly well, but Garrick couldn't help but wonder if that was just because she hadn't fully decompressed yet. She was bound to be having trouble processing the sheer volume of events. What had probably been a slow, painful three weeks for her had passed surprisingly fast for Garrick, given everything that happened.

After he'd finished telling her about his accidental date all the way up to that kiss and his awkward exit, silence filled the air for at least half an hour, but she never moved her foot from where it sat under his leg. Between the two of them, that was almost like a secret language that meant everything was going to be okay. If she'd moved away from him that would have seriously concerned him about the possible future of their relationship.

Still, he didn't want to push it. He kept his arms folded in his lap and leaned against the wall, his legs extended sideways across the bed. She sat next to him, her hands placed atop each other on her knee. She had her legs pulled up, her feet on the bed. Garrick wanted to place his hand over hers, but he wasn't sure how she would respond to that. Instead, he resolved to just be happy with what he had.

Garrick looked at her sadly, his mouth opening slightly as he tried to formulate words. Unable to produce any more sound, he kept quiet and turned his head forward. With a sigh, he dropped his head and closed his eyes. Breathing deeply, Garrick rubbed his eyes and realized he hadn't slept enough. He deeply doubted he would ever be able to sleep well again. Images of the previous night flashed through the darkness, but he didn't try to escape them. He deserved to be haunted by these ones.

He felt her hand on his left arm, and he reached over and placed his right hand on hers. He could feel the tears forming in his eyes, and he closed them tighter in hopes that would fight them off.

"What happened?" she repeated, her voice so gentle it actually put him more on edge. He didn't understand how she could be so perfect in every situation – how she managed to have such good composure even after everything Garrick had said. It was in that moment that it dawned on him, though – it wasn't that she was unaffected by the news; she was just strong enough to contain her emotions and focus on the issue at hand.

With her hand in his, he could feel some of her strength add to his own. He opened his eyes and blinked the tears away. One more time, he took a deep breath, preparing himself to continue to the hardest part of the story – and to finally answer her question.

"I went into the basement," he mumbled. Trying to speak up, he continued, "my plan was just to change there. I thought it would be perfect, and I wouldn't hurt anyone." He watched her nod patiently as he divulged this new segment of his story. It seemed like everything he had to say was just going to be more painful than the last. Everything that happened with Samantha was bad enough. Then there was the betrayal. And Chase.

She didn't even know that Tyler knew yet. That information didn't seem too pertinent, though, and he'd save it for another time. It felt like he was already throwing so much at her, and he wanted to try to focus on the actual events for the most part. Anyway, how was he supposed to explain to her that he found out? He wasn't even positive that they were right about what was happening. But it hadn't happened since the kiss, so it didn't seem unlikely. Still, he wanted answers before offering her conjecture, and she was mostly asking about Chase, so he didn't need to drag anything out longer.

"Samantha was down there. I have no idea how she knew where I was going to be. I may have mentioned the building, I guess. I don't know why I would have, but I was excited, you know? Obviously, I never said a word about the change, but I guess she was able to put two and two together.

"She stabbed me, and she was going to kill me, but Chase showed up. He saved my life. We got out of the building, but her uncle was there. Another hunter. He shot Chase in the middle of his transformation. So I fought back. I killed him, Hayden. And it wasn't the wolf, either. It was me. I..." He hesitated, unwilling to continue the sentence. He had to tell her the truth, though. "I wanted to. All that the wolf did was make me able, but I did it."

"You did the right thing. He would have killed you," Hayden sympathized.

"I know. At least, that's what I tell myself. I don't feel bad about it, though. I should, shouldn't I? I killed a man, Hayden." Maybe he just had too many negative emotions over everything else to waste any on someone like that man. Maybe it was anger for what happened to Chase. Whatever the case, though, he couldn't muster up any semblance of remorse for what he'd done.

"No. You saved yourself."

"I wasn't the person I should have saved!" Garrick yelled in misplaced anger. He was well aware that Chase wouldn't have been there if it weren't for him, and he still hated himself for that fact. Hayden just looked back at him, her eyes simultaneously sympathetic and hurt.

Garrick sighed, trying to reign in his emotions. He knew he had to finish the story. He had to tell her everything.

"He wasn't dead yet. Chase. He was fading out, but he wasn't dead. I told him that everything was going to be alright. I held my friend in my arms and lied to him as I watched him die."

"I'm so sorry."

"I killed him," Garrick blurted out. He didn't know how he was planning on working up to that, but what happened was definitely not part of that plan.

He felt sick to his stomach as he said it out loud. Even with his eyes wide open as he stared at the blank wall in front of him, he saw the night again. Every second had been seared into his memory.

"No, you didn't. You can't blame yourself," Hayden comforted. She wrapped an arm around his shoulder, but he pulled away in shame as he turned to face her.

"No, Hayden. I killed Chase. He was shot in the heart, and he was dying. He was in pain. He asked me to kill him. I tried to convince him it would be okay, but we both knew I was lying to him. My claws came out and I killed him."

She pulled away from him, and he thought that was the last thing they'd ever say to each other. That had finally been too much, and she was just going to leave. That's what he deserved.

She didn't. She sat on her knees facing him and held his face in her hands. Even though his vision was blurred, he could see the tears falling down her cheeks. She didn't say anything for a minute as she struggled to avoid sobbing.

"Garrick," she tried to say. She was choked up, and she had to repeat herself twice more before what she said was audible and coherent. "You did what you had to do. Just like we all do."

"But…"

"No," she interrupted, "no. It was a horrible situation, but you did what you had to do in it. It would have been cruel to…" She stopped. He knew what she was going to say. It was the same thing he told himself to try to make it sound better. It would have been cruel to force Chase to keep going through that pain just to die anyway. It didn't sound any more comforting coming from her than it did from himself, though.

She shook her head, unable to say anything else. Garrick pulled her closer. Her arms wrapped around him and she collapsed forward, her chest heaving as she cried on his shoulder. He held her close and placed his head on top of hers.

He wanted to be the strong one for once. He wanted to show her that he could protect her, that he could be there for her, and that he could hold her and make her feel better. Instead, he just cried with her.

"Seriously?" Tyler asked, tears welling up in his eyes. Garrick had explained everything that had happened, and Tyler wasn't one to face his problems head-on. He had merely tried to bury his emotions and keep finding a cure. The more he worked, the less he had to think about Chase. Garrick, however, wasn't willing to sacrifice any more, and he wasn't able to divert his focus like that. "You don't even think it's worth taking a chance?"

"I've tried controlling it," Garrick reasoned. "I thought we wanted a cure."

"I concur, but that appears to be a dead end, Garrick Elliott."

Tyler was starting to become borderline obsessed with lycanthropy. Garrick stood in his friend's room, staring in awe at the printed pages strewn across the floor. All of them were pages of notes he'd taken from different books, and there appeared to be an organization to them that Garrick was unable to comprehend.

There were also multiple library books across the floor. A few were closed, displaying the ominous titles and cover art. Multiple books were illustrated with a silhouette of a werewolf. No two depictions, however, looked exactly like another. The open books were littered with sticky notes, marking either Tyler's place in the book or an important piece of information. Most of the sticky notes also had writing on them, presumably referring him to other pages or saying which part was especially useful. His notes, both on the small pads and the pages scattered around, were highlighted in green, pink, and yellow, which Tyler had explained were to mark true, false, and questionable information.

Tyler wanted to be of some assistance to his friend, but Garrick was concerned that it was taking a toll on him. He looked like he hadn't slept in days, and he was behaving strangely, constantly looking over his shoulder. As he spoke, he would get excited and start to raise his voice, then quickly correct himself to a whisper. The texts Garrick kept receiving at five o'clock in the morning supported his theory that his friend severely needed a good night's rest.

It was evident that Tyler felt as though he had failed his friend by allowing him to change the night before – as if he had any bearing on that curse. As little sense as it made, Tyler probably blamed himself for Chase's death. He had been trying to find a cure, so he thought it was his fault that the two of them were out there.

Now, though, with his attention turned to methods of prevention rather than disposal of the beast, he seemed to have renewed vigor.

"Fine," Garrick conceded. "What do I do?"

"Meditate. This is dependent on you discovering a way to speak with the wolf. It's locked up there in your head somewhere, and you just have to find it.

"Great," Garrick groaned. At first thought, it sounded completely insane, and the fact that it made any sense to Tyler just made him question his friend's judgement. Maybe Tyler was starting to get desperate, so he clung to any miniscule possibility. The more he thought about it, though, the more the idea grew on Garrick. He was starting to feel like this was a useful piece of advice. He had seen the wolf before in his dreams; maybe there was a way to find it when he wanted to. But it was always trying to kill him. Even if it was a possible option, was it a likable one?

He decided that if the wolf killed him, so be it. He wasn't going to make everything that Chase and Tyler had done for him be a waste. There had to be some better way to cope with his affliction, and he was going to find it – even if that meant facing the wolf head-on.

Garrick sighed as he found a clear spot on Tyler's floor and sat down, cross-legged. He didn't really know what meditating was, but to his understanding, it was nothing more than sitting there in silence and focusing on his breathing. Something that he'd done countless times before.

Tyler collapsed to the floor and quietly sifted through pages in a book. The background noise wasn't particularly distracting, but Garrick found himself wondering what might happen if the wolf did attack him in his mind. Would his body be surrendered to the beast permanently? He wondered if he should retreat to his own house before trying anything, but his limbs started to feel heavy.

"I'll let you focus," Tyler whispered, somehow able to sense Garrick's concern. He snuck out of the room as silently as possible, but Garrick was able to hear as he walked down the hall and retreated to the bathroom. Garrick could hear his friend's muffled sobs as he finally allowed himself to feel – thinking he was out of earshot.

Clear your mind, he thought. That was the most difficult task he possibly could have assigned himself. It sounded simple, but it really meant so much more. It meant he had to stop focusing on everything that he had done wrong. He had to stop wondering if he could really make things right – the way they had been – with Hayden; stop regretting everything that had happened with Samantha. He had to let go of that feeling of betrayal he'd felt as she'd literally plunged a knife into his body. And he had to stop hating himself for what happened to Chase.

One by one, those thoughts drifted out of his mind. All of his concerns and fears drained away as if he'd found a switch in his brain.

He looked up, watching as the darkness of his mind was illuminated by a bright, shining sun. The trees started to appear around him, seemingly phasing into reality from nothingness. Unsurprisingly, he found himself back in the environment he'd seen in his dreams as frequently as in reality. As he glanced around, examining his surroundings, Garrick tried to figure out what part of the woods he was in – but he wasn't able to place it.

Garrick beamed to no one. He couldn't believe it had actually worked. He allowed himself a few moments of quiet celebration before calming down and focusing on the task in front of him. In the emptiness surrounding him, the painful fact that the easy part was over dawned on him. Now he just had to find a monster that wanted to kill him and reasonably ask it to stop taking over his body when the moon was full.

He listened to the crickets chirping and the birds singing melodically from the otherwise silent brush. A slight breeze picked up, cooling him as the leaves began to sway. Though he'd had similar dreams to this, the roles were reversed here. Normally, he was pursued – always futilely running from a monstrous piece of his subconscious. Now, though, he was the hunter. Garrick was seeking out the wolf.

After what felt like an hour of steeling himself, waiting for the wolf to make an appearance, he finally decided to take the initiative. He walked a few feet past some of the trees, trying to get a better feel for his location. Still unable to recognize anything specific, he accepted the fact that it was quite likely this wasn't a part of the woods encompassing the town. In his dream world, it didn't technically have to be somewhere he'd been. It didn't even really have to exist. All that mattered was that he found the wolf.

Instead, he found an old building, clearly out of place. The nearest wall was mere inches from a tree, there appeared to be vines growing from one of the windows. He had a familiar feeling, as if he'd seen it before, but he had no recollection of such a place.

What is this? He thought. It seemed as though his brain was distorting a memory, or blending a few. He knew he was supposed to recognize it, but his semi-conscious mind was dumbfounded.

Cautiously, he walked closer, approaching the building. As he took a few steps, though, he saw himself and Chase break through the front door. Though in an unfamiliar location, the events themselves were ingrained in his memory. He watched in slow motion as the arrow meant for him lodged itself into Chase's half-human chest. His friend collapsed to the ground. Every fiber of Garrick's being attempted to propel him forward, trying to get closer, fruitlessly hoping that he could change the outcome this time – but his legs didn't move.

Garrick panicked. Overcome by the knowledge that there was no way to alter the scene unfolding before his eyes, he became determined to escape it – even if that meant abandoning his chances to find the wolf. He looked around frantically, as if he truly believed there was a secret door out of his mind, desperately searching for a way to break free from the nightmare.

He watched himself kill Chase again, his friend's blood staining the ground around them. Garrick wanted to cry out, but he couldn't interact at all with the painful image in front of him. He was able to turn his head, though, as he heard a rustling in the trees. Fully expecting the wolf, he braced himself, but it was Hayden who came running from the woods.

"Garrick," she muttered shakily as she got close enough to see the version of him holding Chase. "What have you done?"

Brooke and Cailean were close behind her. The agony on all three of their faces shifted to pure rage as they glared at him. The dream Garrick tried to justify himself, but neither he nor the real one could find any words to say. The real Garrick just watched in horror as his best friends looked at the dream Garrick with such contempt.

Then, the dream version of himself looked past all of them. Right at him.

Garrick's eyes shot open. His hands shot out in front of him, finally responding to his plea to reach out toward his friends. Claws had grown from his nails, though, and those hands were a strange mixture of himself and the wolf. Terrified, he blinked rapidly. After a minute, when his heart had settled back down, he examined his hands again, only to find that they were completely normal. He was going crazy.

Garrick took a deep breath before he knocked on Aldric's door. He had to tell him everything. If anyone would have the answers to all of his questions, it would have to be Aldric. Though he wasn't looking forward to the conversation, he knew he had to get information. Garrick needed that just as much for Tyler's sanity as his own.

Constantly pondering the cure, or preventative measures, was already taking a toll on Garrick, and he could see it wearing his friend down as well. He had burdened Tyler with too much, and he hoped that with some answers, his friend would finally be able to get some sleep. Tyler was trying to find any book or article he could to explain the changes outside the full moon – anything that supported his theory, or even just a single resource that mentioned it.

Garrick looked at the door as if it would have some kind of note written to him. He was going to have to repeat the entire story to Aldric. He'd have to divulge every painful detail. Ideas about how he would respond to what Garrick had done to Chase terrified him, and Garrick felt that he deserved the worst of the responses he could imagine.

Cailean opened the door. Garrick couldn't read the look in his eyes.

"Hey," Cailean mumbled, avoiding eye contact. He motioned for Garrick to go inside, so he did.

"Look," Garrick blurted out. He wasn't sure exactly where to start with his sentence, though. Between the vast list of apologies and the debt of gratitude he owed Cailean, he couldn't find the words. Aldric may not have let him back into the pack if it weren't for Cailean.

"Don't say anything," Cailean interrupted, "It's okay. I understand. We've all been there."

Garrick was confused, and Cailean clearly saw it on his face. He wandered to the couch and dropped down, leaving Garrick behind. Cailean patted the seat next to him, pulling

Garrick's attention back to him, and Garrick caught up. Cailean sighed deeply, searching his mind for the best way to begin his story.

"When I scratched Brooke," he laughed, shaking his head. "The two of us thought we would be better off without my father. With him, it was all about being a werewolf. Seriously, like all we ever talked about. It happens once a month, you know? It isn't that interesting.

"Anyway, we thought we'd have a chance at really being human if we got away."

This was a part of Cailean which Garrick had never seen. He was opening up, and it seemed like he actually felt something. Sure, he wasn't as terrible of a person as Garrick had always assumed, but he still didn't particularly like the guy.

Before he was scratched, Garrick had seen Cailean as a complete bully. After he joined the pack, he saw a different side of the young man – a side that cared deeply about his kind. He cared about werewolves significantly more than humans, but that worked out in Garrick's favor. Still, he had never seen him as anything other than the alpha's son. He was entitled, proud, and arrogant.

But he also had a past – and that was something Garrick hadn't taken the time to acknowledge before. Garrick suddenly found himself interested in what had happened that caused Cailean to become the person he was.

"How'd it go?" Garrick asked. He already knew the answer, but he thought that maybe if he asked questions he could pry a bit more information from his pack member.

"How'd it go for you?" Cailean laughed sadly. He had already changed his smile to his typical smirk and brought out his sarcastic tone.

"Absolutely miserable," Garrick admitted.

"Well, there you go, buddy," Cailean responded, patting Garrick on the shoulder as he stood and walked away. "We all come back."

"Where are you going?"

"I assume you wanted to see my father," Cailean responded. He didn't look over his shoulder or even wait for a response as he walked off. Garrick stood and followed Cailean to his father's office.

Garrick sat in front of Aldric, awaiting judgement. Aldric looked down at him, his gaze angry and his lips locked in an unsettling frown. His imposing figure had always been intimidating, but it had never bothered Garrick more. The man sat at least six inches taller than Garrick, and his broad shoulders made him seem even larger. His brown eyes seemed to be full of darkness. Aldric sat across the desk from Garrick, wearing a dark grey suit which served to make Garrick feel underdressed, adding to his insecurities.

Garrick had just recited the entire story of what had happened to Chase. He didn't talk to Aldric about his relationship issues at all, not yet. Aldric was sort of a father figure, sure, but he was the father figure who would send him to his mother for those things. He wasn't the type of person to discuss emotions.

"I'm so sorry," Garrick finished his story. Garrick wasn't quite sure who he was speaking to, but he knew it extended beyond Aldric. As if he were present to hear, Garrick felt himself apologizing to Chase as well.

"You put him in danger when you told him. Somehow, you managed to convince him this idea was feasible. He risked his life to follow you."

"I didn't want him to!"

"I know. You tried to stop him. He believed in you. That was not your crime."

"He shouldn't have trusted me."

"He was right to. You had a good idea, Elliott. You couldn't have known what was waiting for you there. I always told you about the hunters, but I never said what to look for. This isn't your fault, it's mine."

"I'm the one that killed him."

"Don't say that," Aldric growled, setting his fists slightly too violently against the table. He took a breath to compose himself before continuing. "No. You did not kill him. They did. What you did was a mercy, and you know that. You saved him."

It shouldn't have mattered to Garrick, he had still done it. It wasn't something he should just be able to be okay with. Somehow, though, Aldric backing him on it gave him a boost of confidence that maybe he had done the best he could.

"I buried him this morning," Aldric added melancholically.

"What?" Garrick inquired, the shock apparent in his voice. He hadn't really thought about what was going to happen to Chase's body, and he hadn't wanted to. He'd assumed there would be some kind of funeral, at least, when someone found him.

"We can't have anyone asking questions," Aldric explained. "To the rest of the world, Chase ran away last night."

"That isn't right," Garrick argued.

"None of this is right. We do what is necessary. We have to do anything we can to cover up our existence. We can't have people asking questions."

"But how will this raise any questions?" Garrick snapped, raising his voice. He was still trying to convince himself that he'd been doing the right thing, but this was just too far. Garrick was torn apart inside, no matter how many times people assured him he made the right choice. Deep down, he felt like there had to have been a better option. When Aldric started talking about covering it up, though? That was just too far.

"An eighteen-year-old high school senior stabbed in the woods? That would flood the papers. The hunt for his murderer would occupy the entire police force. Any vaguely intelligent person would question the wounds."

"He deserves a funeral," Garrick muttered under his breath, refusing to give Aldric the satisfaction of audibly admitting he was right.

"The rest of the world can't know. The pack can get together here tonight in his memory, but that's the best we can do."

"We can't even tell his parents?"

"Elliott, you're well aware of why that's a horrible plan. You witnessed first hand what the hunters are capable of. The fewer people who know about us, the better – for their sake."

Garrick was so frustrated that he didn't even think about asking his other questions. He just stood and started to leave the room.

"Training begins tomorrow," Aldric called out, causing Garrick to stop and turn back around. "We can have one day to mourn."

"Training for what?"

"Survival. I intend to teach each of you everything you need to know about the hunters. Chase didn't know what to expect – I failed him as an alpha. I won't make that mistake again."

Garrick looked at Aldric with more respect than he ever had before. Aldric had a fire burning in his eyes at the loss of one of his pack. Garrick honestly didn't think he'd cared about them that much – he had assumed they were nothing more than a burden to him. Witnessing Aldric in that moment, though, he knew they were a family.

He turned toward the door again, but hesitated. He wanted to be angry, but he could tell how much Aldric was hurting from everything that had happened. Somehow, he still had the strength to accept Garrick, and to protect him. He couldn't blame Aldric for having the responsibility of making the tough decisions. Softening his eyes, he looked back to his alpha.

"Aldric, there was something else," Garrick started cautiously.

"What is it?"

"You try to teach us about wolves, right? Everything you can?"

"Yes, of course. I see no reason not to share all I know about what we are. Where are you going with this?"

"What do you know about a wolf transforming outside of the full moon?"

Chapter 12

Fourteen months ago

Garrick had tears welling up in his eyes by the time he got home – but seeing Hayden sitting on his porch, he quickly wiped them away and attempted to compose himself. She was sitting on the top step, with her feet on the step below her. Her elbows were on her knees, and her head in her hands. She hadn't looked up, so it was safe to assume she hadn't seen him. Unprepared for the conversation, Garrick tried to stay silent and avoid detection for a moment. He'd had the entire walk home to decompress, but he still wasn't completely in control of his emotions. Finally, he sat next to her as quietly as possible, and she didn't flinch at all. Garrick wondered how she'd managed to arrive before him, and how long she'd known he was there, but he decided there were more important questions to ask at that moment.

He was still limping from his fight with Cailean as he grabbed the rail of the steps and tried to ease himself down quietly. His body ached, and he knew he would have quite a few bruises the next day. That wasn't what he cared about, though. He couldn't stop thinking about Hayden. He'd out-lined this conversation a dozen times, accounting for every type of emotion or response she could give. He thought he was ready for yelling, for crying, or just for neutrality. Now, there she was, sitting on his porch, and he knew all his plan-ning was for naught. He didn't know if he should be hostile or try to give her a chance to explain. He was in too much pain to start off the conversation angry, though. Instead, he re-solved to sit in silence and allow her to start the conversation.

"I love you," she mumbled into her hands, still avoid-ing eye contact. Finally, she looked up and took a deep breath. "I want you to know that."

"I... I love you too," he responded, caught off guard. Still, he kept his defenses up – Garrick couldn't let himself fall for anything. Anyway, given her tone, he didn't like her start.

"It's just –"

"I know," he interrupted, unwilling to hear the rest of it. Garrick decided that he didn't want to hear an explanation. There was no good to come from that – he'd rather just get it over with. "I heard you and Cailean."

"What?"

"When I left. He said you couldn't tell me about you two."

"What? No! It's not like that!"

"Then what is it like?" he snapped, raising his voice in anger. As much as he didn't want to hear the words, he felt like he needed to. He wished at least she would have the de-cency to admit when she'd been caught.

"There are things that I just can't explain," she mut-tered, turning her eyes away from him. There was a genuine sadness in her eyes, but Garrick couldn't find it in himself to have any pity for her. "I'm sorry. Please, I need you to trust me."

"I don't think I can anymore," Garrick said. He stood and walked to his door turning his back on her as he steeled himself – concealing any emotion.

"Garrick," she cried, following him with her eyes. Tears streamed down her face, and she choked up as she called to him, but he turned his face away, trying not to be affected.

"I think it's best if you leave," Garrick told her as he unlocked his door.

"Please, at least talk to me about this," she begged.

"I just… need time," he sighed, the anger slowly giving way to sadness in his voice. "I need to figure out what I want."

He walked into his house and closed the door behind him without looking back. He knew she didn't leave – he could hear her on the other side. But he didn't open the door; he just sank to the ground and cried.

Present
29 days until the full moon

"It's impossible, right?" Garrick continued. The silence which had filled the air after his last question was uncomfortable. He'd never actually seen Aldric appear speechless – caught off guard.

"Why?" Aldric questioned carefully. There was unease in his voice. Almost fear.

"It happened to me."

"When? I need you to tell me exactly what happened."

"Okay, so I have this theory. You know how you always said wolves mate for life? Well, there was this girl who was really friendly after… Everything. And I didn't realize it, but I invited her over for dinner. Then, I ended up transforming. I think the wolf was angry with me because it thought I was trying to move on." He felt bad not giving any credit to Tyler, who really came up with the idea, but he wanted to procrastinate telling Aldric about Tyler's knowledge of them for as long as possible. He wondered if it would be better to just come out and say it – Aldric may be able to help keep Tyler safe. Maybe he'd try to somehow work it into the conversation.

"That is completely ridiculous," Aldric muttered. There was still something he was hiding, though.

"I know, it sounds weird. But the second time was after she kissed me, it was about a week later. I didn't want her to!" Garrick felt the need to defend himself, but it was clear Aldric didn't care about his relationship drama. He was focused on the, admittedly more important, werewolf aspect of his story. He sighed and continued, "And it never happened other than those two times."

"Who is this girl?" Aldric asked, an unusual sense of urgency filling his voice.

"Oh… Uh…" Garrick fumbled for his words. Although the question was a completely logical one, Garrick hadn't been prepared with an answer. "Her name was Samantha."

"You need to stop talking to her. Get away."

"She…"

"Is a hunter."

"No! No she wasn't. They must have gotten to her, tricked her or something. I don't know." This was the first time Garrick had actually allowed himself to think about it. There had to be a better explanation. Could she possibly have been using all of that time as cover? Spending years working in a coffee shop just to find werewolves

"Hunters live normal lives, Elliott. They're still human beings, depending on your definition. They have jobs and friends and families. But by night, they kill our kind. Where does she work?"

"She worked at the coffee shop."

"Worked," Aldric mumbled, thinking the word over for a moment. He was clearly putting all of the pieces together in his head, and Garrick was impressed. He didn't have too much to go on. But he'd known about them much longer than Garrick had, so he had no idea what to expect.

"Oh," Aldric sighed. "She was the other hunter. You knew this, and you didn't tell me?"

"I…" Garrick searched for a defense for himself, but there wasn't one. He wasn't sure if he'd been afraid to share the details or if he'd just wanted to pretend they weren't true, but he knew he should have divulged everything to Aldric days ago.

"Look, Elliott. As you know, wolves are most vulnerable during the change. Your body is trying to heal, but it's also breaking apart in an attempt to transform. If they hit a wolf in the right moment, your body won't know which form to heal into, and it will just continue to deteriorate until you finally can't fight anymore. They have a variety of weapons to use during that brief window. They've found a way, though, to avoid waiting – and to catch us off guard. Have you heard of wolfsbane?"

"Yeah, I thought that was just legend. Well, I know the plant exists. But I figured the effects it had on us were a myth."

"They are. Mostly. Wolfsbane brings the beast out. It forces the change. They use that in order to test people and find out if they're wolves. Small amounts are typically unnoticed by humans, but it would cause a wolf to change for a few minutes. That's long enough for them to stab you, and you won't heal."

"But how…" Garrick truncated the question as he racked his brain for an answer. He knew Aldric would be able to understand exactly what he was asking.

"She cooked for you. That's pretty obvious."

"And the other time?" Garrick knew he shouldn't have to ask these questions. He could tell, even though his mind was spinning, that the answers were obvious. It felt like when a word was on the tip of his tongue, but he couldn't quite find it. His answers were in his mind, but didn't seem to be attainable.

Aldric, looking only slightly annoyed, pointed to his lips. Of course. She had kissed him. She must have had it on her lips. And the first time she just put some in the food.

Garrick laughed nervously and leaned back in the chair. He stared blankly at the ceiling above him, trying to process the new information. He felt stupid for believing in his own theory for so long – but this one made so much more sense to him. It didn't require him to wonder if he was subconsciously experiencing feelings he knew he wasn't.

"I left you all so unprepared," Aldric said sadly. Garrick barely heard him, but he got the impression that he wasn't talking to him anyway. He was just saying the words, probably unable to believe what he had done, and clearly blaming himself for everything which had happened. Garrick understood the feeling all too well. How had he fallen for a trap which was, in hindsight, so blatantly obvious?

He had known that he could never love Samantha, but he'd *still* allowed himself to be tricked by the idea. Garrick's phone beeped, pulling him from his self-pitying mind and back to reality. As he looked up, he noticed Aldric set his own phone down on the table. Garrick hadn't even noticed him retrieve it.

"Aldric," Garrick cautiously added, swallowing hard as he tried to find the right words to say. "There's something else."

"What else could there possibly be?" he groaned, exasperated, but no longer sounding angry.

"The first time I turned, I had people at my house. The first time outside of the moon, I mean. I'd asked Tyler to bring his girlfriend and make things less awkward, so it was the four of us."

Aldric looked at Garrick intently, but it seemed that he already knew where Garrick was going. There was understanding mixed with some confusion in his eyes, which was an odd blend to see. Garrick continued, trying to break the news as lightly as he could.

"I ran to the bathroom when I started turning. I didn't know what was happening. Tyler came back to help me, and I told him to get everyone out of the house. I had to do it to protect them. I might have killed them all."

"You told him?"

"He saw me."

"How much does he know?"

"Pretty much everything that I do. He's been helping me try to find a cure or control the change. He also helped me find the place to turn."

"Is that how they found out?"

"What do you mean?" Garrick hesitated, completely shocked by the answer. It took him a moment to realize that Aldric was actually asking if Tyler had tipped off the hunters to the location. Garrick couldn't believe that Aldric even thought it for a second, and he was offended by the thought.

"No, of course not. I have complete faith in Tyler. Anyway, he's been working too hard at helping me to even be considered to be a hunter."

Aldric paused for a few minutes. Garrick understood that his word didn't mean much when it came to the character of people at that moment, so Aldric really had no reason to believe him, but he knew that Tyler wasn't working with the hunters. Still, he tried not to respond too harshly. Tyler had been Garrick's best friend since first grade, but Aldric didn't have that history with him. It only made sense for him to be skeptical.

"Bring him."

"Where?" Garrick asked. Aldric nodded toward his phone that still sat on the desk. Garrick pulled out his phone to see that he had a message from Aldric. The text was a group message between the remaining five members of the pack.

"I have failed all of you as an alpha. I've warned you of a threat, but never prepared you for it. The hunters are here. All of you report to my house at seven o'clock tomorrow, and every day until further notice. We have a lot of work to do. Now, we begin training for this threat."

"Hey Mom," Garrick called absently as the front door opened. He sat in the living room, skimming through yet another book on werewolves, and didn't look up. "I made pizza, if you want some."

"That's the first thing you have to say to your mother when she gets off work? Not 'I love you,' or 'how was work?'" She laughed as she closed the door behind her and hung the keys up. Garrick tried to finish his page, but all the sound distracted him, so he sighed and set the book down next to him.

"That should always be the first thing anyone says to anyone," Garrick responded, looking toward the kitchen.

"Well, thanks." Despite her joking, she walked into the kitchen and grabbed a piece of pizza before sitting next to him on the couch.

"So how was work?" He smiled as she fell onto the couch.

"Well, no one got murdered today, so that's a plus," she laughed. She always made vaguely morbid jokes like that, claiming that precincts in larger cities would get calls about murders or armed robberies weekly. This time, though, the joke made Garrick sick to his stomach.

"I guess that's a win," he choked weakly. He tried not to sound unsettled, but he had never been a good actor. Or a good liar, for that matter.

"Hey, Garrick, I wanted to ask you something," she said, straightening up as she took another bite of pizza. She set the slice down on the table and rubbed her hands together as if that would actually clean them.

"What?" He questioned – his heart racing. Garrick knew that when someone did something wrong, they assumed everyone else knew about it. However, in this case, it wasn't an unrealistic expectation. His mind raced through everything she could possibly ask about – ranging from werewolves to hunters and to Chase – in the brief second before she verbalized her question.

"Have you heard from Chase?" she inquired. Garrick's heart sank as his fears were confirmed. At least he wasn't being completely paranoid thinking that she was going to ask about something he didn't want to talk to her about. That wasn't much comfort, though, as he tried to search for a convincing answer.

"Not today," he admitted, feigning a nonchalant attitude as well as he could, but failing miserably. "Why?"

"Oh, it's nothing. I shouldn't say anything, I just wanted to know," she shrugged. She reached back to her pizza and took another bite. She clearly wasn't concerned about anything, but it had been brought to her attention. She'd just been conditioned by the years of being a detective in a town with minimal foul play to assume that cases like this didn't point to the worst possible outcome.

Garrick didn't know how to respond. He was trying to act normal, but in his frenzy of trying to hide information, he didn't know what that meant for himself. He felt like he should ask her if he was okay, but he also didn't want her to have any follow-up questions. Garrick wondered what he would do if he found out Chase was missing without knowing why. Would he ask her about it or just text Chase?

"I'm sure everything is okay," she comforted, picking up on the very clear distress on his face. "I'm sorry for scaring you. His parents came into the station today and said they hadn't heard from him, but I'm sure they're overreacting."

"Did they try calling him?" Garrick scrambled for the right question to ask. He knew that Aldric had destroyed the phone, so there was no way they could have reached him, but he thought that would be a question that would throw suspicion off him a bit.

"Yeah, they said his phone is dead. Hey, it happens all the time, honey. He probably just stayed at a friend's house without saying anything, and his parents overreacted."

"I guess," Garrick conceded.

"I just thought maybe he'd gone camping with you, so I figured I'd ask."

"No, he didn't," Garrick lied. He could try to pretend like he was telling the truth, because technically none of his words were lies, but everything hidden under them was. Even if just a lie of omission, he hated misleading his mom. He was grateful, though, that she took the clear discomfort in his voice as concern for his friend rather than the typical reaction of Garrick trying to lie.

"We'll find him," she assured him. She was trying to comfort him, but it just made Garrick feel even worse. All he wanted to do was tell her the truth – that there wasn't a chance that they would. But Garrick bit his tongue, letting her think that she was making him feel better.

A few hours later, the pack was gathered around in Aldric's living room. Everyone sat there in complete silence. Garrick had convinced Aldric to allow Tyler to come. After all, he'd lost a friend as well. Clearly unsure of how to interact with them, though, he just sat on his own, eyes downcast. It was the worst funeral service Garrick could imagine. He felt like someone should be sharing memories or something, but no one was speaking up. Aldric had set up a slideshow with pictures of Chase, which was a nice touch, but it just felt impersonal.

Garrick didn't feel like he really deserved to say anything, either. He was responsible for what had happened to Chase. Everyone in that room knew it, but most of them didn't know exactly how responsible he was. Aldric had told Garrick that he shouldn't say anything. They should just believe the hunters had killed Chase. Garrick had already told Hayden, but Brooke and Cailean were completely in the dark. That didn't feel right, either, but Garrick was at a complete loss. He didn't know what was right anymore, and everything about the situation felt broken, so he just decided to do whatever Aldric told him. After what had happened last time he tried to disobey him, he couldn't see a reason to try again.

After a few minutes, though, a few words slipped out of Garrick's mouth. "I'm sorry," he said. Tears were building up in his eyes, but he tried to keep them back. Garrick couldn't stop thinking about the family Chase left behind. His parents were frantically looking for him, asking the police for any leads. His little sister was probably at home, wondering where her brother went. Nothing felt right, and he had to apologize for it, but he knew it didn't make anything better.

"What?" Cailean snapped. He was clearly on edge too. Chase had been just as much Cailean's friend as Garrick's, and Cailean was demonstrating that he didn't know how to handle himself either. Garrick hadn't spoken loudly enough for the others to hear him, so Cailean had probably just heard some muttering. He wasn't even sure who he was talking to – whether it was Chase, his family, or the rest of his pack.

"Nothing," Garrick choked out.

"Do you want to say something?" Hayden asked Garrick under her breath.

"I shouldn't," he whispered back.

"Just talk about a memory," she urged. "I think it'll help everyone."

He nodded. Garrick slowly stood up and walked to stand in front of the slideshow. With as much time as he spent in his head, imagining conversations and speeches, Garrick would have assumed he'd be more ready to give one. Still, though, as he tried to start talking about his friend, he lost all ability to formulate sentences from his ideas.

"We all loved Chase," he lamented, fighting back the tears. "He was such a great friend – right to the end. He gave his life to save mine. And he deserves so much better than this, but if this is the best we can give him, I want to spend this time celebrating Chase's life, not dwelling on his death.

"Chase spent hours – days – working with me and Tyler to find a cure. He'd already done this by himself, and he knew that nothing would come of it, but he was there for me to help in a quest he knew was futile. His actions speak volumes for the kind of person he was.

"I could tell hundreds of stories of days that he brightened. He had a way of finding a silver lining in anything bad I could come up with. Even when I tried to out-negative him and counter his retorts, there was always some way he turned every situation around. I don't know how he did it, honestly, but that pure optimism just made him see this world without any flaws. Chase was a lot of things. He was a great friend – he was funny, kind, altruistic, but if I had only one word to describe the kind of person Chase was – it would simply be 'good.'

"I could sit and try to find any example – any mistake he made to try to prove myself wrong – but there is just nothing. The only mistake Chase made was trusting the wrong person, and I would give anything to take his place right now. But since I can't, I just hope that all of us will let his example sit well with us. Because this world needs more people like him."

The next day, Garrick stood in Aldric's basement, looking around at the others. The rest of the pack was gathered around a table with a variety of different weapons on it. It was an assortment of knives, bows, and guns that Garrick hoped he would never have the misfortune of seeing someone wield against him. Aldric stood at the head of the table, holding a small knife in his hand. Tyler, who had never seen the basement before, looked around in awe. There was nothing particularly impressive to Garrick in the room, but Tyler was probably just excited to be part of the group now.

"Silver," Aldric explained, spinning the knife and holding it up for the others to see. "They use this because it temporarily stunts our healing abilities." That was something they all knew, and Garrick thought he may have been saying it for Tyler's benefit. Garrick had explained that to him already. At this point, Tyler knew as much as Garrick about werewolves – and maybe more. Still, a lot of it was based on myths, so it was probably best to just rebuild his knowledge from the start anyway.

If Tyler was going to be a target for the hunters based on his knowledge, they had two options. The first was to make sure he had absolutely no knowledge, leaving the hunters with nothing they can extort from Tyler. Since Garrick had already made that plan impossible, they had to go with the second option. Arm him with enough knowledge and weaponry to fight if he had to defend himself.

Aldric explained wolfsbane to the group, and they responded practically the exact same way Garrick had. Tyler, suddenly understanding everything that had happened with Samantha, slapped his forehead with an open hand. He turned to Garrick to explain it, but Garrick just nodded, indicating that he already knew.

"They only use guns in three circumstances," Aldric said. "The first is when they're completely desperate, and you've gotten rid of the rest of their arms. You see, the gun isn't incredibly effective against us, because we can typically just heal from a bullet wound."

"What if the bullet gets lodged?" Cailean inquired. The amount of interest he had was almost frightening. He was staring intently, desperately absorbing every word that came out of Aldric's mouth.

"Your body will reject it. It can just push the bullet out, given the size. Typically, while healing, the foreign object will just be forced out." Cailean nodded, showing his understanding. His eyes were alight. Garrick assumed it was just because he was appreciative to finally have all of this new information about his enemy. He had heard about the hunters much longer than Garrick had, but even he didn't know the first thing about them.

"They also use guns, though, when they've already hit you with the silver blades. Since your healing is weakened, a gun can do much more damage."

That made perfect sense to Garrick. It also cleared up why Samantha had aimed a gun at him. They didn't need to use her uncle's crossbow when he was already too weak to heal. A gun would be faster.

"What's the third reason?" Tyler spoke up. He was quieter than he usually was, and Garrick got the sense that he didn't quite feel like he belonged. Maybe he just didn't feel safe. Aldric had that effect on others of his own kind, so it was probably even more intimidating for a human.

"You," Aldric responded bluntly. "Humans will die from one bullet. So, if there are any of them who want to help our kind, they can dispose of them with a gun."

"Perfect," Tyler muttered under his breath.

"In terms of ranged weapons, they will mostly use bows or crossbows," Aldric continued. He didn't even pause for a minute to try to give Tyler the smallest amount of reassurance. After waiting so long to explain anything to the pack, he was apparently treating this as a crash course, and he had to stay focused. That was probably for the best. Tyler had found himself in a nearly hopeless situation, so reassurance wasn't what he needed at that time. The only thing that would help was learning how to deal with what he was up against.

"We can heal from those wounds just as easily, of course. The wound will close mostly around the arrow, but that still leaves a large injury that can't recover until the weapon is removed. Your options here are to fight through the pain and tear it out instantly, or wait until after the fight. If you let it heal, then remove it, you'll be reopening a wound, and there is no point in granting them another opening."

Aldric didn't have to explain it too much. Since the arrow would pierce all the way through them, their bodies wouldn't be able to just push them out. Even if it just lodged itself, it had more mass and a larger circumference than a bullet, so it wasn't as easy to just force out. They would have to remove an arrow before they could fully heal from the wound. And a mass of arrows could mean enough wounds that even a werewolf would succumb to the blood loss.

"Why?" Brooke finally asked the question on everyone's mind. There was a general understanding between all of them that the hunters just wanted all of their kind dead, but it didn't make sense. Why not just try to corral them or something? Help them change in a safer way? Keep tabs on them and only kill the ones that were actively hurting people? Genocide was never a rational answer.

Even Garrick, who saw himself as a monster, couldn't understand the logic behind killing all of them. His own pack was made up of five innocent people, four of whom weren't even twenty years old. They had issues on one night of every month, and he believed that they should be focusing on a way to keep that from hurting anyone. But did that really mean that every single one of them deserved to die?

"They all have their reasons," Aldric said. "Some were raised by hunters and taught that we are all monsters. Some are extremists who believe that we are abominations, an unacceptable mixture of man and beast. Some lost families to a wolf and begin to believe that all should pay for the sins of one. Their logic behind what they do isn't what's important. What is important is that it is happening, and we must be prepared."

"What else should we know?" Hayden pitched in, trying to gather as much information as possible.

"I'm currently working on collecting all of the information I've been given or have gathered in a more orderly fashion. For now, I've covered everything that is extremely pertinent for you all to know."

"So, now we get to fight?" Cailean stood, a little too excited. He slammed his fist into his other hand in a showy display.

"Yes," Aldric said. They had all learned how to fight off attackers, just in case of this. Aldric had taught them multiple forms of martial arts over the years, but it was always just a few defensive tactics meant to escape or de-escalate a situation. Cailean had tried to spar more often, but Aldric was rarely a part of that. Now, however, there was a clear sense of urgency, and Aldric wasn't going to stand back. It was apparent that he intended to take a more active role in their training. Garrick knew that this meant more running and more fighting, probably every day for the foreseeable future. After what he had experienced a few days ago, he didn't have a problem with that. He actually welcomed it.

"Brooke and Hayden," he said as he motioned his head to one of the mats he'd set up. Throughout their training, Aldric had expelled any notion that the two of them should always spar due to their gender. They had all given each other significant amounts of bruises, and hunters wouldn't attempt to keep any societal standard. Anyway, Garrick knew for a fact that both of them could outmatch him in an instant. The only reason Aldric paired them up this time, Garrick assumed, was because their fighting skills as humans were relatively equally matched. He guessed that meant he was with Cailean. At least it would force him to push himself. Pairing the best up with the worst had always been Aldric's way of training Garrick. Garrick had always preferred working with Chase, but maybe that was because his friend had taken it easy on him.

"Tyler, you're with Cailean," he directed as he pointed to another mat.

"What?" Cailean groaned, deflated.

"He's the farthest behind," Aldric explained. That was an understatement. "And I trust you the most to be able to hold back. I want you to teach him everything you know. And try not to kill him."

Tyler was visibly terrified, and Cailean looked annoyed, but the two of them marched over to where Aldric had told them to go. It made sense to put the two of them together. Cailean wouldn't take any pity on Tyler, but he was also the best at channeling his strength, and he would be able to stop himself from doing any serious damage. Cailean punched Tyler in the stomach the second they stopped at the mat. Tyler doubled over and fell to his knees.

"Lesson one," he said over Tyler's fit of coughing. "Always keep your guard up."

Whatever could be said about Cailean, Garrick couldn't deny that he was a good teacher. He'd always pushed

Garrick, but never beyond what he knew he could handle. Even when Garrick himself wasn't sure he was able to push anymore. He would even hold back when they sparred, practically every time Garrick could remember, and pretend that he wasn't.

"What about me?" Garrick asked, concerned that he already knew the answer.

"We all know you're the weakest wolf, Elliott" Aldric started. That was a great way to start the sentence.

Thanks for the confidence boost, Garrick thought.

"And you're probably the worst fighter here. Excluding your friend, of course."

Cruel, he thought, feeling deflated. *But fair.*

"You, Elliott, get me."

Garrick sighed, his fears confirmed. Trying to avoid displaying his general fear or concern, he stood tall and met Aldric on the mat. The two of them stood, facing each other, as the other pairs were already fighting behind them. Aldric smirked, searching Garrick's eyes for any sign of his first action.

"When do we start?" Garrick asked. Aldric smirked, opening his mouth for an answer, but Garrick threw a left hook, trying to take advantage of the element of surprise to get the first hit. He had never actually fought him before, but he was still intimidated. He thought if he could get a hit in, he'd impress Aldric – even if it was the only hit he landed.

Aldric weaved backward, avoiding the attack. Garrick hadn't planned a follow-up, and he wasn't prepared when Aldric drove his open palm into his chest, knocking him back. Garrick stumbled backward, barely able to maintain his balance. He rushed in again, throwing a fake to Aldric's face and a punch to his ribs. Aldric didn't flinch at all from the fake, apparently able to see through Garrick's ruse. Aldric caught the punch, twisted Garrick's arm around, and kicked him toward the wall all in one smooth motion. Garrick's face slammed against the wall. He was almost positive he had broken his nose, but he just turned back around and wiped the blood with the back of his hand. He refused to go down that easily. He was determined to become stronger, and this was just the first step.

He ran back to Aldric and threw a few more punches, all of which Aldric easily deflected. He brought his knee toward Aldric's stomach, and the man just stepped to the side and swept his leg under the one that Garrick was standing on. Garrick fell back, slamming his head into the mat as he landed. He jumped to his feet and faced Aldric again.

Garrick threw another punch, and Aldric leaned back, avoiding the blow. When he came forward, he brought his fist full force into Garrick's stomach.

Aldric fought very defensively. He was an expert at avoiding getting hit, as well as using Garrick's own momentum as a weapon. Garrick had hoped that meant that he wasn't as strong as he looked. As Aldric connect that punch, however, Garrick realized that was not the case.

Garrick flew across the room and hit his back against the wall. His head slammed into the wall, and the world went dark.

After what was probably not more than a few seconds, Aldric was reaching a hand out to help him up. He couldn't see straight. He tried to accept Aldric's hand, but he ended up reaching out to the air.

Aldric grabbed Garrick's arm and pulled him to his feet. Garrick could feel his body repairing from what was obviously a concussion. He leaned against the wall and waited for his breathing to slow down and for his double vision to return to normal.

He noticed that the others were still sparring. Hayden and Brooke were employing everything Cailean had taught them to try to get the best of each other. They ducked, weaved, and dodged, each landing a few good hits on their opponent.

Tyler looked beaten up. He was panting heavily, but he didn't stop. Cailean, of course, didn't have a single mark on him. But Garrick saw Cailean stumble backward a step when Tyler landed a hit to his jaw. Cailean, seeing that Garrick was defeated, apparently decided it was time for his own fight to end as well. Tyler ran toward his opponent, but Cailean stepped to the side and pushed Tyler against the wall. Dazed, Tyler stumbled back, and Cailean caught him in a headlock.

Aldric stood in front of Garrick as he watched the others – completely silent as he watched them all fight, judging their skills. Garrick assumed the only thing which could possibly be running through Aldric's mind at that moment was how much work he had to do. Even Cailean, as good as he was, was nowhere near Aldric's fighting skill. If he was right, and the hunters grew up believing they had to kill werewolves, they would be training for their entire lives. Aldric was trying to whip a group of people together in a month – if they even had that long. There was no guarantee the rest of the hunters would wait until the next full moon to come after them, given that they had the option of wolfsbane.

Garrick, however, took his focus off of the fighting in front of him. He turned his full attention to Aldric. *Lesson one,* he thought, remembering what Cailean had taught him. *Always keep your guard up.*

He wrapped his arm around Aldric's neck and tucked his hand into the crook of his elbow, making sure his hands weren't available for Aldric to grab.

Before any feelings of pride could make their way to Garrick's mind, he was flying through the air. Aldric had slipped from the hold as he flipped Garrick over his head. Garrick's back slammed against the ground, since they were no longer on the mat, and his breath was knocked out of him. So much for that plan.

"Nice try," Aldric commended. Garrick, disappointed, just gasped for air. He definitely had a long way to go.

Chapter 13

Fourteen months ago

Garrick was leaning his back against the wall, trying to look as if he were occupied. He held his phone, occasionally tapping random buttons. It was only 11:43, and he had 17 minutes left of lunch. He didn't feel up to sitting with Tyler. He could barely keep himself together already, and Garrick was someone that would much rather be alone when upset. As much as he loved spending time with his best friend, he knew he couldn't hide his emotions, and Tyler would try to cheer him up. Garrick wasn't quite ready for that.

He stood by the gym, hidden behind the building, where he could be alone. No one was supposed to be that far from the cafeteria at lunch, but he had snuck around the security guards. They didn't usually ask for hall passes from people who looked like they had a reason to be wandering around.

So Garrick tried his best to keep himself busy. Aside from just hoping to appear busy and avoid looking like the miserable wreck he was, he assumed that finding a distraction would actually help him a bit. It had only been a few days since his break up with Hayden, and he was still completely torn up about it. Well, break-up wasn't the right word. He hoped. He had only seen her once, and she was with Cailean, during those past few days – and that just served to make him feel even worse. Garrick wanted to trust her, but it didn't look good, and he wasn't going to allow himself to be made a fool.

He could pretend not to think about it, but it was obviously a futile attempt. For someone who was always locked in his head, his mind was an inescapable weapon. As hard as he tried, there was nowhere he could run to escape from himself.

"Are you okay?" Garrick read as the phone buzzed. He'd accidentally opened the text as he played with his phone.

"Yeah," he sent back. Tyler would know he was lying. It didn't take someone any special knowledge of Garrick to see something so obvious. He and Hayden had been inseparable for the past few months, and when that ended, Garrick felt like half of a person. Any passing stranger could see that, so there was no doubt Tyler would see through his empty words. Of course, that wouldn't stop him from trying. "I just needed some time alone."

"I don't believe you," Tyler texted him. A second message followed closely after. *"But I will let it rest. You know where to find me if you decide you wish to talk."*

"Thanks," Garrick said. This was obviously not the first time Tyler had noticed Garrick was hurting, but it was the first time Garrick wasn't sitting with them at lunch. Garrick was grateful to have a friend who cared so deeply for him, and who was actually interested in listening if Garrick needed someone to talk to.

"Garrick," a voice said as he hit send. Startled, he jumped and his phone fell from his hand. His desperate attempt to catch it only served to knock it further away from him, and the second attempt just grabbed air. A hand quickly shot out from nowhere and secured his phone. Brooke, Hayden's best friend, held the phone out to him.

"You dropped something," she told him, handing the phone back to him.

"Thanks," Garrick responded, awkwardly taking the phone back and placing it in his pocket.

"No problem," she laughed, clearly hiding the intention behind her deliberate search for him. There wasn't a high chance that she'd unknowingly stumbled upon him, especially given that Brooke wasn't one to wander around alone at lunch.

"What are you doing here?" Garrick finally broke the silence.

"Look," Brooke explained, "I just wanted to talk to you about Hayden."

"Did she send you?" Garrick asked. He didn't know what he hoped the answer would be. It would have been nice to know that she wanted to fix things, but he also wasn't sure how he felt about her sending someone on her behalf. Still, it was probably better than dealing with her face-to-face. He didn't know if he had the strength to turn away from her again.

"No," Brooke groaned, apparently annoyed at the suggestion. "Just hear me out. Hayden has been a wreck without you. I've never seen her happier than when you're with her. I get that it's hard, because she has some things she can't tell you. But I swear to you, it's nothing to worry about. She's crazy about you."

"What is it, then? What is so important that she has to hide it from me?" Garrick snapped, standing up from his position on the wall. He relaxed for a second, realizing that she wasn't the person he was mad at. He didn't care if Hayden had secrets. Sure, he hoped she'd open up one day and tell him, but he didn't mind secrets as long as he could trust her. That, however, had been violated after what he'd heard.

"Sometimes you just have to trust someone, Garrick. I know it's hard, and it isn't fair," she admitted. "Just talk to her, alright?"

"Alright, fine," Garrick conceded, "I'll stop by her house tonight."

"Do it tomorrow. Tonight she's camping with me," Brooke responded.

"Of course she is," he laughed, turning away. He had figured it would be the perfect night to show up and tell her he was sorry and he was ready to listen. This would have been the day they were together for seven months, but she was going to be out camping with her friends.

Present
27 days until the full moon

Garrick sat in the coffee shop. He wasn't sure why he still went to that one, with everything that had happened. There were a few other stores in town with the same set-up. Maybe he liked the memories, though. Even all of the bad ones.

He looked at the bulletin board as he sipped his coffee. He wasn't reading anything specific, just staring blankly like he normally did when he was trapped in his thoughts. He tried to scan the information posts, reading to distract himself from his own mind. A name stood out and snapped his full attention to the real world.

Samantha.

Her name was hidden in the middle of a page pinned to the bulletin board. Garrick started from the beginning of the page, reading through the notice thoroughly. The family appeared to be having a memorial service for her at their house on Saturday. Garrick wondered if it was completely wrong for him to even consider attending. He shook the idea off, knowing it was not for the best.

Over the past week, he hadn't learned much more about the hunters. Even Aldric's information on them was incomplete, but he had quite a bit to teach them. Garrick had learned, at the very least, that he had to be more careful. Samantha had caught his scent simply because his physique had changed so rapidly. They were trained to notice the slightest abnormality.

The worst part was that they could be anyone, and they were dangerous every day. The threat had grown, and it wasn't limited to the monthly transformation anymore. They were hunting down him and his friends, who only had real means of defending themselves one night a month, and they weren't in control on that night. Even with all the training they'd crammed in over the past week, which was a lot, he knew he wasn't prepared to take on people who'd spent their entire lives learning how to kill him.

His best defense was staying hidden. He hoped Samantha hadn't told everyone about him – because that would mean the only two hunters who had known about him were dead. That didn't seem like too far of a stretch, because most hunters wouldn't face a wolf in a group as small as two. The only reason he could imagine them sending such a small force to kill him was that they didn't know she was going to do it. Her uncle must have found out somehow, but that was it. That meant he had another chance to stay hidden, and to avoid putting his friends in danger.

Garrick peered up at the clock, verifying that he still had a few minutes before he had to get to Aldric's house. There was supposed to be an incredibly important training, and he was expected to be there early, which was relatively unsettling.

He tried to be calm as he drank his coffee. His life was suddenly spinning out of control. He hadn't even talked to Hayden much outside of Aldric's house. He had no idea what he was expecting of her. It made sense that it would take her time to forgive him, if she ever did. He just wished he could know exactly where she was on that.

She seemed to avoid him at school, and he'd waited a couple of times to try to offer her a ride home, but she was always somewhere else. Neither of them had texted each other. At the training, though, she didn't seem to have anything against him.

Maybe she was just better at acting than he had ever been, and she really was harboring resentment.

His mind drifted to Chase again. He'd been trying to convince himself that he made the right choice, but he couldn't accept that. He still felt as though there had to be more he could have done for his friend.

Garrick violently shook his head, as if trying to dislodge the thoughts from their home. He stood and retrieved his jacket from where it rested on the back of the seat. Walking outside, he put the jacket on and brought the hood up over his head. He kept his head low; making sure no one was following him, and broke into a jog toward Aldric's house.

"Good," Aldric greeted him. "You're here."

It was only 6:30, so no one else had arrived yet. Even Cailean wasn't there, because he was out somewhere with Brooke. Hayden would probably be showing up soon. Tyler had the night off, though. It was good for him. As much as he needed their help, he was still only human. He was simply not capable of pushing as hard as they were.

"Yes, sir," Garrick responded. "Why did you need me here early?"

"You know what it feels like."

"What?"

"Wolfsbane. You've felt it before. You know how to tell. I want you to teach the others."

"Why me?" Garrick asked, shocked. While he'd felt it before, he had been too preoccupied with panicking to recall all of the symptoms he had experienced. Anyway, was Aldric saying that he had never gone through it? That seemed simply unbelievable to Garrick, given his knowledge on the subject.

"Because," Aldric groaned, annoyed to be explaining himself. He clearly wasn't used to running the pack as anything other than a dictatorship, and he hated being questioned. Still, he was trying to be more communicative with his members. "You, my son, are being tested. I need to know what you remember."

"Can't I just tell you here?" Garrick protested.

"Maybe. But my way is more interesting."

Garrick fell silent, resigned to the fact that there was no point in further arguing with Aldric. He'd made his mind up, so that was how it was going to be. He dropped his head and walked down to the basement, where he waited for everyone to show up. He had no idea what to tell them, or why Aldric was forcing him to be the one to do it.

Hayden came down the stairs first, and she sat next to him. Her knee brushed slightly against his. His fingers were interlocked and his hands were on the back of his head as he leaned his head against the wall. He moved one of his hands, placing it on the ground in between them. It was a code, in his mind, wanting to know if she'd place her hand on his. She didn't.

"Hayden," he started cautiously, "I'm sorry."

"For what?"

"Everything."

"I'm not mad at you," she sighed. She turned to face him, but slid away as she did. Her body language and her words were telling Garrick two completely different stories.

"Really?" he stuttered, surprised at her response. He figured she had to be at least a little upset; he knew he would be. With everything that happened with Samantha, and the fact that he was directly responsible for the death of one of their friends. He couldn't really forgive himself. How could he expect her to?

"Chase wasn't your fault," she comforted, as if reading his mind.

"What about –"

"That one," she interrupted, sadly. "Will take me time."

She didn't say anything for a minute. Hearing footsteps coming down the stairs, he realized their conversation was coming to an end. He nodded, accepting what she had said and the fact that he wouldn't get any further information. It was only fair, and he accepted that he just had to give her all of the time she needed.

He started to stand, but she grabbed his forearm and held him down. She didn't say anything, though, and he wondered what was on her mind. His heart raced, and he felt hopeful, as if she'd changed her mind in those few seconds.

"I do love you," she finally told him, "and I know you love me."

"I do," he confirmed.

"You kinda have to," she smiled weakly. "It's going to work out. I promise. I just need time."

She leaned forward and kissed his cheek before letting go of his arm. Cailean and Brooke came down the stairs and scanned the room for Aldric. When they didn't see him, they both looked confused. Hayden, apparently catching on to what they were wondering, adopted the same look of confusion. It wasn't like Aldric to be late to a training session – he was usually the first in the room. Garrick was actually confused too, because he had assumed Aldric would be down there to monitor his instruction, but given the fact that he wasn't there, Garrick assumed that meant he was just expected to begin on time. If Aldric hadn't shown up yet, it meant he wasn't coming.

Garrick stood, breathing heavily. What was he supposed to say?

"Okay," Garrick hesitantly began, carefully choosing his words. "Aldric told me to explain to everyone what the symptoms of being on wolfsbane are, just so we all know how to tell exactly what it feels like. I guess so that we can start running if we're poisoned by it."

"How would you know?" Brooke inquired.

Garrick had forgotten she didn't know. This was the major reason he hated hiding any information from anyone – it was impossible to keep track of who knew what. Cailean and Hayden supported Brooke's question by giving Garrick questioning looks of their own. At least he'd already told Hayden about the kiss. This would have to be a horrible way for her to find out. Still, he was walking on thin ice with her, and finding out that he'd been hiding something from her wasn't going to help their relationship. Anyway, it wasn't something he wanted to keep bringing up and making her think about.

"Oh, wow," he muttered. He fell into one of the chairs that Aldric had set up near the stairs last week.

"I have something I need to tell you all," he admitted. "When I was gone, I ran into a hunter. That's where all of this came from. You all know how Chase died. It was my fault."

"It was not," Hayden defended. She glared at him. He wasn't sure if she was angry at his self-pity, the fact that it was clear he'd hidden something from them, or the fact that he started his explanation with that. For Brooke and Cailean, who didn't know the rest of the story, that was a very incriminating confession.

"It isn't your fault he followed you out there, Garrick," Cailean offered softly, trying to be supportive of his pack, but also not completely convinced that his own statement was true.

"That isn't what I mean," Garrick corrected. He wasn't sure exactly what to say, so he decided to just start the story at the beginning. "There was this girl. She made me dinner one night. I didn't want to be there with her alone, so I asked Tyler to bring Kayla over. After dinner, I started to feel weird, and I had Tyler get them all away from me. Tyler saw me transforming, and that's why he knows. That's how he found out."

"You were dating someone?" Brooke exclaimed. They all knew that he couldn't love again, and even for humans that was too short of a time for that to be acceptable. Still, he wasn't sure if that was the part of the story to be focusing on at the moment. He'd just disclosed to them that he had been caught transforming outside the full moon.

"It wasn't that simple," he explained, trying to defend himself. It was a difficult task, given that he agreed with her harsh reaction. "I wasn't thinking and I just accepted her offer."

"Did you stop seeing her?" Brooke pushed, "Why didn't you cancel?"

Hayden was clearly torn. She looked happy to see her best friend standing up for her, and she clearly wanted answers to all of those questions herself. However, she also didn't like seeing Garrick be accused like that, and she clearly wanted to come to his rescue. For the time being, though, she just listened.

"I told her that I couldn't see her like that. I just wanted to be friends. She said she was okay with that, and nothing happened."

"At all?" Brooke asked. "She just backed off like that?"

Garrick froze. He didn't want to finish the story. Garrick wanted to just forget and move on, and he wanted Hayden to do the same. Still, it was better to just put everything in the open. He didn't want to hide it anymore, and it would come out eventually anyway.

"The second time I turned, she kissed me," he sighed.

"Oh my…" Brooke groaned. She looked at Hayden, whose eyes were filling with tears. She hugged her friend. "How could you?"

"I swear," he implored, turning his attention from Brooke and to Hayden. Even though he'd already said it, he didn't know if he'd ever be able to stop apologizing for how much he'd hurt her. "I didn't mean to. I didn't kiss her back. I left in a hurry, and I didn't see her again."

As an afterthought, Garrick realized that wasn't entirely true, so he added, "Except when she tried to kill me."

He hadn't, that much was true. He had agreed to, but that wasn't a date. He was going to tell her that he couldn't do it, and if she wasn't able to be friends, he couldn't spend time with her anymore. He was going to tell her that he couldn't love anyone else, because he was thoroughly convinced of that fact.

As a matter of fact, he had told her. He didn't really know why he was going to meet her again. He did know, though, that nothing ever could have happened between them. Still, it didn't change the hurt he saw in Hayden's eyes. Or the anger he saw in Brooke's. Even Cailean looked at him with disapproval.

"Look, this sucks, and I don't mean to cut this short, but how does any of this relate to what happened with Chase?" Cailean finally spoke up. Hayden was crying on Brooke's shoulder. Cailean was obviously less concerned with the emotional aspect and more interested in how his friend met his untimely end.

"The hunter was after me. Chase saved my life."

"Then he didn't die in vain," Cailean muttered. Garrick wondered if that was true. Chase was much better for the pack than he was. He let that sink in for a few minutes, until he just couldn't take it anymore

"Alright, just stop," Garrick declared, standing up. There was more confidence and force in his voice than he had known he could muster. "Look, I deserve every ounce of judgement you're all casting on me. I messed up, big time. I know that. Right now, though, there is something else we need to be focusing on."

"No," Hayden argued. He was surprised that she would refuse any discussion of wolfsbane, but his confidence faltered, leaving him unable to take control of the situation. "I love you, Garrick, but Brooke is right. You had so many chances."

"Hayden –"

"Let me finish. You had so many chances. But I know it was a confusing time for you. And I should have been there for you. I love you more than anything, and yet I wasn't there to support you. Chase was there, and I wasn't."

Garrick hadn't exactly made it easy for her to be there for him, but a part of him was thinking the same thing. Out of the entire pack, he hadn't expected that Chase would be the only one who would have chosen to stand with him.

"None of this would have happened if I had been a good girlfriend. If I'd stood up for you and tried to help you."

She walked forward and grabbed his hands. He didn't know what had changed, except that maybe she'd just heard a sincerity in his voice that wasn't there the last time. He had apologized, and he had meant it, but this time, he truly regretted everything that he'd done. Last time, he would have given anything to change it. This time, he would have settled for doing anything to stop Hayden from hurting. Somehow, that had gotten through to her, and she looked into his eyes with more love than he'd seen in weeks. Still, though, love wasn't all that was in her eyes. It was wrapped under layers of both pain and guilt.

She wrapped him in an embrace. He could sense from how weakly she was holding him that some of what she'd said was just talk. She wanted to forgive him, he knew that, but it wasn't easy. Nonetheless, he felt right being in her arms again.

He didn't want to push her away, but he knew that he'd have to tell them what he knew. It could end up saving one of them, and he couldn't let his desire for that contact with Hayden to get in the way of the little that he could actually do for the pack. After all the pain he'd caused, Garrick owed it to them to make up for it to the best of his ability. Just when he was going to gently push her off, however, she let go and stepped back.

"Tell us what you have to say," she commanded. The others still didn't look particularly happy with him, but they hesitantly nodded.

"Alright. Well I didn't know what was happening either time," he began. "I wish I could explain everything that happens, but I don't think I can. I can remember my throat closing up. It felt like I couldn't breathe. Suddenly, all of my senses started to get stronger, and that's how I knew the wolf was fighting its way to the surface. Somehow, you can just feel it. Honestly, the only advice I can give any of you is that if you start feeling like you can't breathe, you get far away."

"I can't stay here for this," Cailean angrily blurted out. "I can't stand here and listen to you, acting like this is okay. Like I'm supposed to learn from you. I can't act like you didn't just tell us that. I don't know how the others can, but I just can't. You've had us convinced that the hunters did this. You lied to us, Garrick. And you killed Chase."

"Cailean," Garrick responded. He didn't have a follow-up, but Cailean didn't give him time for one anyway.

"No! You didn't do what was right. I wanted to think you did, but this? There had to be hope! You gave up on him! You're toxic, Garrick! I told him that this would happen, but he left anyway! He thought he saw something in you, but all you did was fail him!"

Cailean took a few steps closer to Garrick, but he collapsed on the floor before he made it. As Cailean coughed violently, Garrick felt his own throat start to feel tighter. He wondered if something was wrong with him, but he saw the others darting their eyes back and forth in panic. Hayden's blue eyes started to glow brighter, and Brooke's started to glow a bright green. Cailean was still looking down toward the ground, coughing, but Garrick could see claws starting to push their way from his fingertips.

Garrick turned around and looked up the stairs, wondering how the hunters had gotten into Aldric's house. Had one of them followed someone? Did this mean they had already gotten through Aldric? And how had they gotten to the others?

He growled, feeling his canines grow in his mouth. He felt his nails grow into claws. By the time he turned back around, he saw all three of his friends on the floor. He heard their bones breaking as they started to change shape.

He felt the wolf pushing itself forward, but he couldn't give in yet. He didn't know where the hunters were. He had to make sure he was there to protect his friends when they were vulnerable. Just like Chase had been there for him.

He looked up the stairs, but the door was closed. Garrick closed his eyes, focusing on listening to what was happening upstairs. He couldn't get past the pained moans of his friends. He was trying to use the transformation to his advantage, but it was too painful.

"Don't give up, Garrick," he heard. He couldn't place the voice, and it wasn't anyone in the basement. Maybe it was just in his head. His inner voice giving him the confidence he needed to focus and to fight off the transformation long enough to find out what was happening.

He caught himself promising the wolf that it could take over soon; he just needed a few minutes. He needed to make sure that they would all be safe first.

He heard footsteps. Two heartbeats. Aldric and his wife. That was it.

Garrick screamed, his eyes shooting open. He breathed heavily, examining the area around him. His hands had gone back to normal. The others were lying in their human forms, their clothes torn but not completely destroyed. So they hadn't transformed fully. It was less of an exposure, like his second time had been.

Breathing heavily, Garrick raced toward the stairs. He had to check on Cailean's parents. If the hunters had managed to poison the vents somehow, they could still be in danger. The door opened, though, and Aldric stood at the top, completely uninjured. Thoughts flooded through Garrick's mind as he wondered how Aldric had managed to fight everyone off on his own, but his head hurt too much to think about it. Instead, he set his jacket over Hayden, then collapsed into the chair and closed his eyes.

"What happened back there?" Garrick asked Aldric.

"I wanted everyone to experience it. It isn't something that can be described; you just have to know what it feels like to go through it."

"So you did that? This was your plan the whole time? Some warning would have been nice."

"You wouldn't have been able to keep the secret."

Garrick couldn't argue with that. No matter how hard he tried, he wouldn't have been able to hide that plan from them. He would have acted differently. Still, he would have liked to know that he was going to have to go through that.

"So what? You wanted to see how we'd respond without warning?"

"In a sense."

Garrick felt like he'd been played. He had believed that he was going to do something important for the pack – finally be able to do something helpful rather than harmful. Really, though, he'd just been a tool Aldric used to gauge the pack's reactions and their transformation times when surprised with wolfsbane.

"This was all just a test," Garrick laughed bitterly. "You told me you needed my help, but you lied. Again. You were just testing us."

Maybe he didn't deserve Aldric's trust. He hadn't earned a place in this pack. He'd already abandoned them once, and that had gotten someone killed. He felt like he was over-reacting. As much as he hated being distrusted, it was a fair reaction. He knew that the pack's confidence, and especially Aldric's, was not going to be easy to earn back.

"No, I wasn't," Aldric replied calmly.

"No? Then what were you doing?" Garrick yelled, getting annoyed and no longer trying to hide it from his alpha.

"I was testing *you*, Elliott. To see how much you could fight."

"I... I didn't change," Garrick realized after a minute. He took a breath and tried to relax, trying to see things from Aldric's perspective. If that really was his intention, then of course he wouldn't be able to inform Garrick. Still, why test Garrick, though?

"No one did. It wasn't enough."

"They got claws. Their bones broke. I didn't. I just felt my eyes and teeth start to change. I didn't get as far as them."

"Of course not, Elliott. You have always fought it more than everyone else. That's why the transformation hurts you the most. You refuse to just let it happen. It only buys you a few extra minutes, but that is sometimes enough to out-last a dose of wolfsbane. That's what this was. I wanted to see how much time you could buy."

So there was something Garrick could contribute. Maybe his ability to fend off the effects of wolfsbane could actually help the pack. Maybe he could teach them how to stop – or at least slow – its effects. Or maybe he was just getting ahead of himself again.

"Well, at least it's good for something," Garrick muttered. He paused for a moment before adding, "How do you know all of this?"

"You think you're the first person to try to fight the wolf?"

Chapter 14

Fourteen Months Ago

Garrick sat in his room, sincerely trying not to overthink his relationship. He and Hayden had been together for seven months to the day. That was supposed to mean something, but to her, it didn't seem important. Instead of spending the day with him, she chose to go on a camping trip with her friends on which he was very intentionally excluded.

He wasn't sure what to make of it, but it didn't sit well with him. They'd been in a tough place for a while, but in his mind it was the perfect day to reconcile. With Brooke's nudge, he had finally built up the resolve to give her a chance to explain. He had told her that he wanted to talk before the camping trip, and tried to explain the problem with her choosing camping over him, but it only led to a bigger fight. He hated the thought, but he couldn't move on from the idea that there was something going on between Hayden and Cailean. Garrick would have to be blind to miss every sign pointing toward it. Cailean was always hovering around her, and he saw her texting him constantly.

With everything that was going on, he would have thought she'd show up. He hadn't officially broken up with her, and that would be a great time for her to come in with some romantic gesture. He truly hoped that the whole camping trip was a ruse, and that she was planning something big. He knew she wasn't, though. She had someone else. He'd always known she was out of his league, but he couldn't say it didn't hurt more that it was Cailean who stole her from him.

He heard a knock on his door and his heart leapt. Maybe she really did have some semblance of a romantic side, and she was showing up and surprising him. He opened the door and beamed.

At Tyler.

"Hello, Garrick Elliott," Tyler greeted.

"I was not expecting you to show up," Garrick muttered, trying not to sound too disappointed. He invited Tyler in, and the two of them sat on the couch. Since Kayla had broken up with Tyler, he and Garrick had hung out practically every day. Tyler knew it would be a particularly difficult day for Garrick, but he also knew Garrick well enough to know the best thing for him was probably to be left alone. Nonetheless, Garrick couldn't hold it against his friend – he was just trying to do his best.

Garrick was constantly trying to convince Tyler to stop being friends with Kayla. She was already talking about some cute boy in her class, and Tyler was the friend she talked to about it. Tyler claimed he was just glad to have her in his life. Garrick wondered if he could ever feel that way about Hayden. Could he listen to her talk about Cailean after he confronted her? He didn't think he had that capacity in him. It was almost admirable to see the loyalty in his friend, but it was mostly just painful.

"I have come to converse," Tyler proclaimed.

"Clearly," Garrick acknowledged with a feigned smile.

"Seriously, though, the texting was getting confusing. So, you tried to reconcile things today, but she's going on a camping trip?"

"Yeah. With Brooke."

"You have to go find her."

"I don't know where they are," Garrick groaned.

"I didn't claim to know how, just that it must be done. If nothing else, just for closure."

Tyler pulled at Garrick and practically threw him out the door.

"Get in my car."

"No," Garrick argued. "You're right; I need to go talk to her. Maybe this is all a big misunderstanding. I owe it to myself to figure this out – I can't dwell on it all anymore. But I need to do this alone."

Present
26 days until the full moon

As hard as he tried, Garrick couldn't get Cailean's words out of his mind. Maybe he was right. Chase would definitely have been safe if it weren't for Garrick; he couldn't argue with that. Being around Garrick was obviously dangerous for Tyler, too. The hunters would go after him for information, even though he wasn't a werewolf. It seemed like Garrick was just putting the people around him in peril.

To make matters worse, the police had officially launched an investigation to try to find Chase. That was unavoidable. Unfortunately, it wasn't an uncommon occurrence for teenagers to go missing without being found. Aldric had resolved to use that fact to their advantage, attempting to steer the investigation away from a murder and toward a missing person. At least that was a less noticeable case. Even if the scheme was effective, though, it didn't help Garrick forgive himself for what had happened.

Garrick had told his mother he was sick in a successful attempt to stay home from school. Thankfully, she was too involved in work, being the lead on Chase's case, to ask for any specific information. Anyway, she probably assumed that he was old enough to make his own decisions and stay home if he wanted to. It wasn't possible for him to get sick like a normal person, but he did feel nauseated – so it wasn't actually a false statement. He couldn't think straight. A virus or bacteria would have no effect on him, but his own mind could still do quite a bit of damage on its own.

He felt like he had to do something, but it was apparent that there was nothing he could do to make everything okay. Still, the complete lack of action just intensified the pain in his stomach. He sat up, looking around his room. Garrick wondered if getting out of the house would be enough to distract him – at least slightly. He didn't know where he could go, but he felt like he was never going to be able to move on from the past few days, and he knew wallowing wasn't the best option.

Maybe he shouldn't get over it, though. He deserved to be going through the agony that he felt. He shouldn't have survived that, and he knew it.

Cailean was handling the grief in his own way. He had refused to talk to Garrick since his outburst the previous day. Brooke was better at hiding her anger at him, if she felt any, but she didn't seem to want to talk to anyone. Hayden was clearly still having trouble moving on. Chase had been a large part of her life in the past, so Garrick couldn't blame her for taking it so hard.

Somehow, it seemed to just be hitting everyone that Chase was actually gone. It seemed like the first few days, on some level, they all expected him to just show up – as if Garrick's memory had failed him. The pain was finally settling in with everyone, and Garrick didn't know who to go to, but he needed to talk to someone. He didn't have a right to expect anyone to try to comfort him – they all had to move on in their own ways. However, his normal coping mechanism of locking himself up and working through his issues alone was not going to suffice that time.

Garrick stood up and grabbed his keys, shoving them into his pocket. He couldn't stand lying down in his bed anymore. If nothing else, he needed to go for a walk. A little exercise would get his blood flowing and hopefully help clear his mind a bit.

Garrick walked out the door and closed it behind him. He wasn't sure where he was planning to walk, but he hoped the fresh air would help him feel better. Aimlessly, he began wandering around the streets, hoping an answer would find its way to him.

Garrick had replayed that entire night in his mind hundreds of times over the past few days, but he found himself picturing every aspect of that night once again. There must have been a way that he could have helped Chase. He could have tried to put pressure on the wound, or run him to a hospital. Maybe he would have been able to fight the wolf if he had a purpose – like carrying his friend back into town. Or maybe Chase would have healed given more time.

Deep down, he was fully aware of the lack of logical consistency in his arguments. Each time he thought of a new possibility for what he could have done, the pragmatic part of his brain just shot it down. Still, the idealistic part felt that there had to be something more he could have done.

Of course, he could have just not led Chase there in the first place. That was a stupid mistake. What made him think that he could handle everything on his own? He could barely handle being a werewolf in a pack. It should have been obvious that he wouldn't be able to do it without Aldric's guidance. If Garrick had been so set on making his own mistakes, he realized in retrospect that he shouldn't have told Chase where he was going.

Garrick looked around him, examining his surroundings. Paying no attention to where he'd been walking, Garrick found himself in a part of town he barely recognized. He was in a beautiful park, with a few trees planted in the green grass surrounding him. Apparently, his subconscious mind always found a way to lead him to nature. Civilization was still present, but most of the buildings were beyond the park. There was only one small building to Garrick's left which was within the perimeter of the park. Garrick recognized it, but he wasn't sure from where. A few feet away, he saw a bench, so he sat and admired the view. A few small fir trees were growing throughout the park, in various stages of life. One beside the bench provided just enough shade for Garrick to rest in.

Calming chirps filled the air around him as the birds called out, but the rest of the park was quiet. A middle-aged man wandered through the park, but he appeared to be making his way toward Garrick. Silently, he sat next to Garrick on the bench. Reaching into a bag, he retrieved a few seeds and tossed them out for the birds to eat. Everything suddenly felt so calm to the rest of his life – he felt as though he had found himself in a scene of a movie. It was hard for him to comprehend the possibility of people living this life.

"How often do you feed the birds?" Garrick spoke up, trying to break the awkward tension. Usually strangers wouldn't sit next to someone else on a bench, especially when there were plenty more around the park. Still, even if it were with a random person feeding some birds, Garrick would have been grateful for conversation. This was one of the very rare times that he wanted a way out of his head.

"Only when I need to look busy while I wait for someone to talk to me."

"Sounds lonely."

"I have other people to talk to," the man laughed, "It's not for me."

"So you think I'm looking for someone to talk to?"

"You look like a young man with a lot on your chest. You ditched school today, and now you're sitting on a bench behind a church. It seems like you're looking for something."

Garrick looked up, finally recognizing exactly where he was. He hadn't been to the church since he was a child. He wasn't sure what had happened, really, or why he hadn't been back, but he recalled the entire area in that moment. Maybe the man was right. Maybe he was looking for answers, and some part of him felt like he'd find them there.

"What's on your mind?" The man pressed gently. He didn't look directly at Garrick. His gaze was fixed on the birds in front of him. It was almost like he was intentionally trying to avoid looking at Garrick. Not because he seemed uncomfortable, but because he was trying to avoid making Garrick uncomfortable. It wasn't until Garrick looked closer at the man's face that he actually recognized him as the pastor of the church. He must have dealt with quite a few people who really needed to talk about their lives.

Still, Garrick was relatively certain that he'd never dealt with something of this magnitude before. This was a burden that Garrick couldn't share with someone else. Yet he found himself compelled to talk. The man sitting next to him seemed so easy to talk to, and Garrick really did need to talk about everything running through his mind. If Garrick opening up and sharing too much information with someone was an inevitability, at least this person was likely to be trustworthy.

"I don't go here," he explained.

"I know."

"Why do you care? You don't know me."

The man just smiled, finally looking to Garrick. "Because you're lost."

A tear started welling in Garrick's eye. Despite his best effort to hold it back, the tear rolled down his face. He didn't deserve anyone to look at him with such compassion – such sympathy. This stranger, though, was the first to catch him when he fell.

"You don't have to talk to me," the man offered. Garrick didn't realize how long he'd been in his head, but it must have been a few minutes. "But if you need to, I'll be here."

"What if you can't help me?"

"I probably can't. But sometimes it makes it better to talk things through."

"Have you ever done anything bad?" Garrick finally opened up.

"More than I'd like to admit."

"I don't mean getting angry at someone and saying something you shouldn't. I mean something really bad. Something you aren't sure you can come back from."

"Trust me, there is nothing you can't come back from."

"What if it's too late to make it alright?"

"It's never too late. There is no way that you can ever be too lost to be found."

Garrick knew that this wasn't going anywhere. He could tell that this man wanted to help, but there was no way a human could understand what had happened. It wasn't his fault, but he couldn't say anything to comfort him, and Garrick couldn't be specific enough for any real advice.

"Right," Garrick muttered, deflated, "thanks."

"Do you want me to tell you what you need to do to repent? To be forgiven? That isn't what I do. I think that whatever you've done, you are clearly tearing yourself up over it. Things get better. You just have to find your peace. It's up to you to decide how to make it right. What I'm here for is to tell you that you can."

"What I've done... There's no making it right."

"What did you do?"

"And what if I can't stop myself from doing it again?" Garrick continued, ignoring the man's question. He was more talking to himself – just venting without regard for the listener anymore. He realized, though, that he had to be very careful, because that was a dangerous mindset.

"It might be hard, but you have to hold on to your strength. Don't give up. You can find strength within yourself, and whatever this is, you don't have to do it again."

"I hurt someone," Garrick finally admitted. He knew he shouldn't be talking about it, but he couldn't stop himself. It felt great to have someone to talk to – someone from whom he could expect no judgement. Of course, if he let too much information pour out, there had to be a time when even this man's kindness would die.

"I'm sorry," Garrick quickly added. "I need to go."

"Do you think you're going to hurt someone else?"

"Thanks for the talk," Garrick responded. In that moment, he was thankful that the pastor didn't recognize him. In his desperation for connection with a normal human being, he'd opened up too much, and now this man was concerned Garrick was going to commit a crime. He'd be obligated to report it if Garrick wasn't careful, and he knew he didn't have the self-control at the moment to keep himself from pouring out his heart. He stood and walked away as he finished his sentence. "But this burden isn't yours."

A few more hours of walking led Garrick to the lake just outside of town. He had no gauge of how long he'd been walking, but it had probably been a few hours, because the sun was starting to set – reflecting orange and purple hues from the surface of the water. Sitting on the dock, his shoes just barely grazed the surface of the water. He tossed a rock across the water, watching it skip a few dozen times to the other side of the lake. Garrick remembered taking trips to the lake and skipping rocks with his mom when he was younger. Back then, they'd never made it even a quarter of the way across – only jumping two or three times across the water. There hadn't been a change in his skill, as far as he knew, but he assumed the increased force alone was enough to get that extra distance.

It had been a while since Garrick had spent time near the water. He used to go there a lot with his mom as a kid, but as he grew up, he started to get more interested in the woods. His mother had been promoted and taken a detective position, so she didn't have as much time, and he had started spending weekends with Tyler and later Hayden, so it didn't seem worthwhile to travel so far out of town. The woods seemed so much larger – like they hid beautiful mysteries that he wanted to find – while the lake just seemed to have its beauty displayed on its surface. Whenever he needed to think, he'd often go somewhere he could find himself surrounded by trees. Now, though, the rest of the pack was aware of that. Though he wasn't sure if any of them would try to find them, he wanted to be somewhere they wouldn't be able to.

Garrick felt as though he was at the end of his rope. The last place he thought would have his answers only proved to make him feel worse. He always wanted to believe that he was a good person, but how could that possibly be true? Garrick was lost – drowning in mistakes that he'd made – and a simple conversation with someone wasn't going to change that.

If he were as good as he thought – as he hoped – he was, surely he'd be able to think of one person whose life was better because he was in it. Instead, though, all he did was put the people he cared about in danger. It was just like Cailean said – Garrick was toxic.

Garrick heard a quiet splashing in the water, and his head darted to the side. Not quick enough to see whatever had caused the sound, he only noticed the ripples in the water. It was just a fish swimming around. He audibly laughed at how paranoid he'd become. Ever since he got scratched, his life was just spiraling downhill, and it didn't seem like there was anything he could do to slow the momentum of his descent.

Garrick would have given anything to go back in time and change that night. He should have trusted Hayden more. Of course she wouldn't do anything to hurt him – she never would have. He had gotten jealous, and because of that, he trapped himself in a constant nightmare that the lycanthropy brought along with it.

Since his first turn, Garrick spent so much of his life trying to be normal. He ended up with Samantha not because he loved her, that was obvious to him, but because she was human. With her, it felt like he had something normal again. Of course, that had backfired.

Even Tyler knew, so that took away one of his last normal, human relationships. There wasn't much tying him to that old life of his, and he could feel it rapidly slipping from his reach.

Was that why he killed Chase? Garrick had no idea which wolf scratched him – there was a chance that it had been Chase. As little as Garrick wanted to believe it, was it possible that he killed Chase because he thought it could cure him? He hoped that wasn't it – he believed that he had done it for Chase – but he was starting to question himself. He wasn't even sure who he was anymore.

There were a few quiet footsteps on the dock. Garrick didn't bother turning around, because he recognized the foot-fall. Garrick sighed. As much as he knew he fully deserved whatever verbal abuse was coming his way, he also knew he wasn't emotionally prepared for it.

"How did you find me?" Garrick muttered as Cailean sat next to him on the dock. Neither of them looked at the other, but Garrick recognized Cailean's shoes as they dangled over the water.

"Tyler told me you used to come here a lot."

Garrick remained silent. He should have been a bit smarter if he didn't want to be found. He picked a place that someone knew he'd go to. While he hadn't picked the single most obvious place, he had chosen the second most predicta-ble place.

"You weren't at school."

"I'm not feeling well."

"None of us are," Cailean concurred. His tone sounded harsh, but he looked down at the water after he said it, appar-ently regretting his tone. He looked like he had something on his mind, but he couldn't bring himself to say it. Garrick had been impressed when the pastor had noticed that look on Gar-rick's face, but in that moment realized that it wasn't too dif-ficult to see when someone had something that needed to be said.

"I'm sorry, Garrick," Cailean finally mustered up the courage to say.

"For what?" Garrick was shocked that Cailean would ever admit he was wrong or apologize for anything.

"I was out of line. I was upset when I found out what happened, and I turned on you. I know you're torn up, and you don't need me making that worse on you."

"Nothing you said was wrong. All I do is hurt the people around me."

"Don't say that. You know it isn't true," Cailean sighed, finally looking away from water and looking Garrick in the eye.

"You were right, Cailean. I'm toxic." Garrick looked away, unable to face the shame of looking at his friend in the eye.

"Shut up. I've never met someone who tries harder than you to do what's right. And yes, Garrick, that includes Chase. He was always a great person, of course, but he changed when you joined us. You weren't becoming more like him, Garrick, he was becoming more like you."

Garrick almost said something, but Cailean held up a finger to tell him to wait. Garrick knew how hard it must have been for Cailean to be talking about this, so he didn't want to interrupt him. It wasn't any easier for him to hear, but he knew Cailean had gone far out of his way and set quite a bit of pride aside to prepare that speech.

"If I were ever in trouble, you're the first person I would have expected to be there for me. Chase saw how hard you were trying, and he was inspired. I know that I told you his death was your fault. It wasn't. What was your fault is that he died feeling like he had a purpose. He believed in you, and he wasn't wrong to. You're a good man, Garrick. And I'm sorry for acting like that isn't true."

Garrick could see tears welling up in Cailean's eyes. He was developing a new respect for his friend. Though he wasn't convinced that anything Cailean was saying was true, he knew that Cailean believed it, and it meant a lot to hear.

"You don't get it, Cailean. I didn't leave him there."

"Don't," Cailean interrupted."

"I can't keep hiding things."

"No, but I know. I know, Garrick. That's part of why I reacted so strongly," he sighed, placing his hands on the dock behind him and leaning back. He sighed, clearly struggling to find the right words. "Don't worry, no one told me. It's just… obvious. I mean, I pieced it together from your reaction and everything. You don't have to say it."

"How can you still think I'm good?"

"My father has explained to me how agonizing death is when you're attacked during the change. Your body tries to heal, but it heals to a broken state, and it just falls apart. That is a horrible death, and avoiding it is merciful."

"But Cailean," Garrick argued, for some reason still trying to convince Cailean to hate him. "What if that wasn't my motivation? I thought there was a chance that killing him might cure me."

"You think that didn't cross my mind? You're always talking about finding a cure, and there's only one that I know works. That isn't why you did it. We both know that. I know you too well to believe that you would have killed him to benefit yourself."

"It should have been me."

"If it should have been you, then Chase died for nothing. He believed in you. And so do the rest of us, Garrick. Don't let Chase's death be in vain. You have to find a way to move on and to live your life. That's what he wanted. That's why he went there that night. You owe him one thing – and only one thing – and that's to honor his wish."

Garrick let Cailean's words sink in for a moment. Maybe he was right. There was nothing Garrick could do to make everything right, but it was done. Chase had sacrificed himself, and Garrick was going to do everything he could to make sure that his friend didn't die for nothing. If that just meant living his life as well as he could and fighting off the hunters, he would. Rather than dwelling over the past, he owed it to Chase, and to his memory, to live in the present.

"Thanks, Cailean." An awkward silence drifted over them, and Garrick looked at Cailean, tears welling up in his eyes.

"We're not hugging," Cailean said, standing up. He patted Garrick's shoulder, trying to mask the fact that he was quietly sniffling. He wasn't going to sacrifice his image, even when it was just the two of them, but Garrick knew that Cailean cared about him. It was a good feeling to be forgiven, even if he wasn't ready to forgive himself.

As Cailean left, Garrick continued looking into the water, as if there would be answers there. As if the water really did have more answers than it let on – lurking just beneath the surface. Garrick wasn't sure what else he could do to move on, but for the first time since it had happened, he felt like he might be able to.

Chapter 15

Fourteen months ago

Garrick broke into a jog toward the woods. With each step, he was able to muster more confidence. Defying all logic, he was beginning to convince himself that his trek was a good decision. Maybe chasing her down while she was camping with her friend was the grand romantic gesture they needed to work through everything.

By the time he broke the tree line, he was already short of breath. He stopped running and just walked deeper into the woods, trying his best to stabilize his breathing. To kill time as he waited to catch his breath, Garrick checked the time on his phone. The trees filtered out the minimal sunlight, and everything around him was dark. For the most part, Garrick was only able to make out the shadows of anything lurking in front of him. Despite his best attempts to keep mental notes of the paths he took through the darkness, after a few more turns, Garrick was aware that he was completely lost.

"Hayden" he called into the emptiness around him. Garrick wasn't expecting her to hear, especially with the trees blocking perpetuation of sound waves. Nonetheless, he had to try, because he was starting to get concerned that he had no idea how to find his way home, and he'd need some direction. "I have no idea where you are, but I really need to find you."

"Hayden," he repeated desperately. At first it had seemed like a good idea, but he was starting to question himself for going out there. If he found her, he could talk to her and try to work things out. Regardless of how much thought he put into it, though, there was no conclusion other than the one he'd reached. Garrick felt naïve for being compelled to follow her – and for hoping there were any way things could work out for them.

Garrick let his distractible mind wander, peering around at the trees near him. He had always attributed a sort of supernatural, mystical vibe to these woods. As he was walking through them, though, he had no idea why. There was nothing special or unique about any individual tree, and to-gether all they did was served as a border for the town.

"Garrick?" He heard her voice from somewhere be-hind him. Startled, Garrick jumped and turned quickly. He hoped her vision was as inhibited as his own, and maybe she hadn't seen his reaction. As his eyes focused a bit more on her, he was able to tell that Hayden was wearing her under-wear. Garrick wore a sweatshirt and pants, and he was still cold – so he instantly ruled out any possibility that it was just comfortable sleeping attire.

"What's going on?" he inquired, confusion apparent in his voice.

"Why are you here?" she responded with a question of her own. Her voice was filled with fear, and all of his confi-dence instantly drained from him. In hindsight, it seemed ra-ther obvious that running blindly into the woods to find the girl that he loved – who happened to be with another guy at the time – was not a good idea.

"I was looking for you," he started, wondering why it was him who began justifying himself. He had caught her red-handed but still was sheepish. Garrick froze, unsure of what emotions to feel or what words to add to his response.

"Now is not a good time. You need to leave, Garrick. Now," she ordered. Her harsh tone surprised Garrick; he would have expected something much softer given the circumstance.

Then Cailean walked out from the foliage behind her. "Hayden," he growled, "what are you-" he stopped when he saw Garrick. Cailean wasn't wearing a shirt, either. And of course, Brooke was nowhere to be seen. "Ah, well what do we have here?"

"He's just leaving, Cailean," Hayden snapped.

"No, I'm not," Garrick argued. Garrick refused to leave without an explanation, an apology, followed by his issuing a clear statement that he was done fighting for this relationship. Right there, he was going to fight through all of the relationship drama which had been building up. Even remembering what had happened last time he fought Cailean, he was ready for that altercation to become physical. He wasn't sure what had come over him, but he was done being a victim.

"No," Cailean agreed with a smirk. "You're not."

"How could you do this, Hayden?" Garrick snapped

"It's not what it looks like!" She implored, sounding defensive and even hurt. Garrick couldn't find empathy for her emotions anymore, though. It couldn't possibly measure up to how much she was hurting him.

"Then what is it?" Garrick asked angrily, raising his voice at her for the first time since he'd known her. "What could this possibly be?"

Hayden looked down, obviously unable to answer. Silence filled the air. Garrick could feel his blood boiling as he looked at the two of them. Hayden's eyes were downcast, filled with shame and despair. Cailean's smirk never faltered, but his eyes betrayed the slightest hint of confusion

"Wait," Cailean broke the silence, his eyes lighting up as if he suddenly understood what was happening. His grin became more of an amused smile. "You think she's cheating on you? With me? You're so completely ignorant, Garrick."

"Then go ahead and offer a more reasonable explanation. Anything at all," Garrick spat. He still had some of that anger in his voice, but he sounded more defeated than anything else. If she was cheating on him, there was no way that he could have stopped it. Garrick considered himself a nice person, but he was fully aware that he was scrawny and nerdy as well. There was no possible way he could compete with Cailean.

"Go ahead, Hayden," Cailean shrugged, backing away. "It's too late for your little boyfriend anyway."

"Garrick…" Hayden started. She hung her head low and took a deep breath before looking back at him. "There are things you don't know about this world. All I wanted was to keep you away from them."

"What are you talking about?"

"There are monsters, Garrick. That I wish you'd never had to find out about. Cailean and I, and a few others, we're different. Normally we're just people, but once a month, we change; we become something else. We're werewolves, Garrick. Aldric always told me not to tell anyone, because it's dangerous for humans who know. I wanted to tell you, I really did, but the others just wouldn't let me. That's what you caught us arguing about, and that's why I need you to leave right now, Garrick."

Garrick allowed the statement to linger for a minute, unsure of how to respond. He was baffled that she would go to such ridiculous lengths to try to avoid being caught. How could she actually think a story like that would convince him to just believe her and walk away?

"You're kidding, right?" Garrick finally responded. All that was left in his voice was the anger. She was actually pretending to be a mythological creature. First she cheated on him, then she lied. Garrick had actually been deluded enough to believe there was a logical solution. He had wandered into the woods, looking for her in the middle of the night, because he thought she would have something better to offer than myth.

"No, she isn't," Cailean chimed in. He was looking down at the ground, so his face was a shadow. "You really should have learned to just keep your nose out of where it doesn't belong." As Cailean looked up, his irises shone a brilliant gold in the moonlight.

Present
25 days until the full moon

Garrick parked his car on the street about a block from the service. Torn between whether it was distasteful for him to attend and whether it was right for him to pay some form of respects, he procrastinated opening the door. He was still unsure of whether their entire relationship had been a lie or just the last part of it, and he was unsure of whether anyone else would know of his involvement in her death, but she had been a part of his life, even if only a month of it. It seemed only right to at least bring some flowers. Selfishly, he hoped that would be enough to appease the guilt which tore at his heart.

Building up the resolve, Garrick forced open the door and stepped out. He was committed. Even in the worst case scenario, if they all recognized him, the worst they would do is tell him to leave. He couldn't imagine the hunters would be bold enough to attack him in broad daylight. Garrick walked around the corner, onto a street where all of the houses looked the same. They were all painted the same off white color, with the same gate out front. The lawns were all well-trimmed, most with a small garden somewhere along the walkway. Each of the houses had at least one nice car – far more expensive than anything Garrick and his mother could ever afford – parked in the driveway. The uniformity of the street gave it a completely fake feeling, and it felt to Garrick like it was the perfect place to hide secrets. The perfect place to hide an underground battle of hunters versus werewolves. Who would expect such a dark world to be brewing underneath such a beautiful neighborhood?

Garrick walked up to the gate of Samantha's house. He reached for the handle, but when his hand wrapped around it, he felt his hand start to sting. Quickly withdrawing his hand and shaking it, he noticed the handle shone particularly brightly compared to the rest of the gate. He muttered under his breath as he looked for another way in but couldn't find one. Just as Garrick was about to accept the handle as a sign that he shouldn't proceed, he saw the latch turn and the gate opened inward. An older woman, maybe Samantha's grandmother, with tears streaming down her face, pulled it open and looked intently at him.

"Are you here for Samantha?" The woman choked through her tears – her words nearly inaudible and unrecognizable. It seemed like a question with an obvious answer, given the event and the fact that he held flowers, but he didn't say anything about it. She deserved to ask a simple question without receiving a sarcastic response.

"Yes," Garrick answered solemnly, nodding as he spoke. He looked down, silent for a moment, then added, "I brought these." Unsure of what the actual etiquette was, he simply held the flowers awkwardly in front of him. Standing in front of the door and looking at a member of what was most likely a family of people who wanted him dead, Garrick realized he'd made a mistake going. He wanted to turn around and run, just to get as far away from that place as he could before any of them found out about him. Something deep down was refusing, though, to let him leave. At least, he consoled himself, she didn't seem to have any perception of who he was.

The woman took the flowers, thanking him with a nod and inviting him inside. He fought back the instincts that screamed that he was making a mistake as he stepped into the door, and it was closed behind him. At that point, it would be far more suspicious for him to turn and leave. If they didn't know about him, they would start looking into him after behavior like that. Garrick had trapped himself, and he just had to pretend to be a normal friend of hers. As he looked around, grasping for any face he recognized, Garrick realized that he didn't know anyone related to Samantha.

Anyone except her uncle, whom he'd also killed – but it was probably best not to bring that up.

It seemed that every single one of their neighbors was in this house, along with quite a large family. Garrick chastised himself for his decision once again. Secretly leaving flowers at her grave could have been a much more appropriate, and less dangerous, way to pay his respects. Instead, he'd waltzed into a house he could only assume was populated by hunters.

"Hello," a young man, probably a few years older than Samantha had been, greeted him with a flourish. He paused for a moment before smiling at Garrick and pointing. "I think I know you, right?" An uncanny aura of charisma surrounded this man, but Garrick sensed something off about his demeanor. He waved it off, though, realizing it was probably due solely to the fact that – though he hid it well – he was distraught.

"I don't know," Garrick answered honestly. He was almost positive that he didn't know the man, but he couldn't say for sure what the hunter knew about him. His brain searched for a proper response, but 'Yeah, I'm the guy that killed Samantha', probably wasn't the best ice breaker. He wished he were better at making up stories, but Garrick found himself at a loss for words. Finally, he just muttered out the first thing that came to his mind. "I was a friend of Samantha's. My name's Garrick."

"Ah, yes," the man replied with a dramatic snap, as if the pieces suddenly fell into place. Garrick tried to hide his panic. Should he have come up with a fake name? "I have heard quite a bit about you. It's a pleasure to finally meet you,

Garrick. My name is Darren. For lack of a better word, I'm Samantha's elder brother. We took her in after the accident."

Darren extended a hand, but Garrick froze for a second. The accident to which Darren referred must have been when her parents were killed by werewolves. Garrick didn't know to what degree he should question it, though, because she probably wouldn't have told him in such detail if he were a human. Deciding it was in his best interest to just ignore the comment, Garrick shook Darren's hand. Garrick breathed a sigh of relief under his breath. Maybe Samantha had mentioned his name, but nothing about the fact that he was a werewolf. Then, with a wave of his other hand, Darren thanked Garrick for coming and told him to make himself at home; eat food, socialize.

"Nice grip there," Darren smirked, winking at Garrick. Hoping he didn't appear as frantic as he felt, Garrick released Darren's hand and backed away.

"Samantha would have appreciated it," Darren offered. Garrick nodded with a half-smile, simply thinking how wrong Darren was. Samantha probably wouldn't have wanted him there at all. He was more there for himself – grasping desperately for any niceties which would soothe his agony of emotion. He just wanted to do something to make up for everything he had done.

Garrick studied the area as much as he could; worried he'd need an escape route. He told himself he was simply being paranoid, but a voice in his head kept screaming to run: to find the nearest window and break through it. Contrary the instincts demanding he fled, Garrick could feel moral pressure to stay.

There was a staircase to the left, up against the wall of the living room. To the right was the door to the kitchen, where the majority of the guests stood, eating and telling stories. Compared to the extravagant exterior, the inside wasn't insanely lavish. The couch that sat in the living room, resting not too far from a small television with two antennae protruding from it. There was a cheap coffee table in front of the couch, and a loveseat against the wall perpendicular to that. Other than that, there wasn't much. It was a charade, and Garrick knew it – he could feel it – but he kept fighting that instinct, hoping that these people were just not interested in interior design. After all, he couldn't guarantee they were even hunters.

He walked toward the kitchen but couldn't handle the crowd. After grabbing a cup of water, he just headed back to the much less densely populated living room. There was another door, almost hidden by the wall in the upper left-hand corner of the living room. Garrick continued scanning the house, trying to avoid getting disoriented by the number of people present.

Nervous, he sipped the cup of water without realizing it. He had told himself that there was one condition to going to this memorial, and that was to consume absolutely nothing the hunters offered. He'd broken that rule within the first five minutes.

He decided it was time to go, even before he felt his throat closing up. Garrick was concerned it would make too much of a scene to try to get past the grandmother, who was practically guarding the door. He decided he would have to find a window he could open upstairs and jump down that way.

He climbed the stairs as quickly as he could, trying to be completely silent. With each step, though, it became harder to breathe. By the time he reached the hallway above, he was nearly gasping for air – but he fought to remain as quiet as possible – refusing to draw even more attention to himself.

He hadn't had much of the water, so he was fully confident he could stop himself from changing. It would just be uncomfortable for about a minute. Still, he had to find a safe place, and a safe excuse, to let the wolfsbane take its course – and then he had to get as far away from that house as he could.

As he walked through the hallway upstairs, he heard footsteps closing in on him. He felt a hand clasp on his shoulder as Darren said, "Fancy yourself an explorer, Garrick Elliott?"

"Darren," Garrick groaned, composing himself as much as he could. He tried to hide the fact that he was completely terrified. Garrick felt like every decision he made just walked him into another trap. "Do you have a bathroom?"

"Why, of course, my boy. I'd be pleased to be of assistance. Right this way, if you will." He released Garrick's shoulder and began walking without missing a beat. Darren seemed so sincere that Garrick actually questioned whether he was just paranoid. There was something about his conduct, though, that screamed to Garrick that he knew.

Darren showed him to a strange door which didn't look like it belonged in a house. It was a stained glass double door which was impossible to see through. Garrick quickly opened it, searching for his escape but finding what looked like a bedroom. The room was only decorated with the most basic furniture – a bed, a dresser, and a nightstand – and there was not a second door anywhere to be found. The only decoration that seemed slightly personal was an abstract piece of art that hung above the bed. Garrick was transfixed by it, feeling like he should know what it was.

Then he felt a kick to his back that launched him forward. Garrick stumbled, tripping over himself and falling forward, slamming his head on the floor. Dizziness overpowered him as he tried to stand, so he just fell back to the ground. Garrick could feel the wolf fighting against him, trying to break free. He wasn't sure if he had been hit with a larger dose of wolfsbane than he had realized or if the wolf sensed danger, but it seemed to be growing more vicious.

"You know, Garrick, when I first heard of you, I was suspicious," Darren admitted. "You exclusively occupied Samantha's mind. I think her pride begged her to take the kill for herself, so she never mentioned what you were. Samantha had never felt so strongly about a boy, you see. I couldn't help but wonder if there was some secret. When she didn't come home that night she went out with you, every doubt was confirmed."

Garrick's mind was swimming. Fighting back the wolf and trying not to kill someone else split his focus from Darren's words. Darren held a palm open as he spoke, but he closed it and pulled it back, kicking Garrick in the ribs and rolling him onto his back. Garrick was convinced that Darren was a good fighter, but his form was questionable at best, and his movements were overdramatic. As Darren dropped his head to the side and stepped closer, Garrick questioned whether his flamboyant behavior was just part of his personality or if he was intentionally taunting his helpless victim. He slammed a foot down on Garrick's chest before swaying backward. The more pain Garrick went through, the more the wolf rushed forward, trying to defend the body that it was inhabiting.

"Honestly, I was less convinced when you showed up here, because I thought no one could be that stupid. Your kind continues to surprise me."

Garrick forced himself to his feet, and Darren let it happen. He smirked as Garrick struggled to stand, almost falling over, apparently enjoying witnessing his pain.

"Run," Garrick warned.

"Your incompetence continues to astonish me," Darren taunted. He reached his arm around his back, retrieving a knife from a holster on his belt and twirling it in his hand. "When you showed up here, I thought you had to be innocent. It had to be a coincidence, right? Because who would kill someone, and then go to their funeral?

"I should have realized that a monster doesn't have human morals, doesn't understand that that's not something you do, Garrick Elliott."

Darren squatted down next to Garrick, a mixture of inquisitiveness and disdain covering his face. "I hoped for you – trusted that there was a shred of humanity somewhere in there," he taunted, touching the tip of the knife to Garrick's chest

"That's why I tested you – instead if ending your life on sight. There was an herb in that water you drank. All you had to do was pass, and you could have walked out of here alive, no questions asked."

Garrick couldn't fight it anymore. Not because he didn't have the strength, but because he didn't have a chance alone. His nails sharpened and grew into claws, and his molars became pointed as his canines doubled in size. He didn't want to hurt Darren, but there was no way both of them were going to make it out of that room.

"You failed," Darren finished his monologue as he trailed the knife downward. Just as Garrick tried to move, Darren plunged the silver dagger into his stomach. Stunned, Garrick grabbed the end of the blade with one hand and reached behind him, looking for something to brace himself on with the other. He managed to pull himself backward with his free arm until he felt himself pressed against the wall.

He realized as he fell that he'd made another mistake. He'd given up fighting it, leaving himself vulnerable. He just let himself get stabbed in the middle of a transformation. His mind flashed to Chase struggling for his life, and Garrick began to lose hope.

"You know the best combination to deal with vermin such as yourself? Silver and wolfsbane. Their effects clash and just make your death so much more imminent than even thirty stab wounds from the blade alone. Plus, it makes it so much more painful," Darren mocked as he stood. Casually, he stepped forward, closing the small amount of distance Garrick had made.

Garrick let out a pathetic attempt at a howl – more of a begging whimper – as he coughed up blood. He pulled the knife out, throwing it at Darren in one last desperate attempt to save himself. Darren stepped to the side to avoid the blade and reached his hand out to grab the handle as it flew past him. He spun the blade in a half circle, taking a step closer to Garrick.

The doors behind Darren flew open, and Garrick tried to make out the figure that was standing in them. His vision was rapidly deteriorating, and he could barely make out the shapes of the people in front of him. He could only hope that this was someone once again coming to save him. Darren turned around, distracted from torturing Garrick, to face the figure. Garrick tried to use that moment of weakness, but he couldn't make any kind of move. He could feel the wolfsbane wearing off, and the effects of the silver began to face since it was no longer in contact with his body, but healing was still slow. Worse, it was agonizing, because every time his wound would start to heal, it would tear itself back open – almost as if his body had been tricked into believing the open wound was the natural state of his body. He struggled, but he knew it would be far too long before he could make a move.

"Darren," a recognizable voice boomed. Garrick couldn't place it, but he knew it to be friendly.

"What are you doing here?" Darren spat.

"I have to protect my own," Aldric warned. Garrick couldn't make out Aldric's figure, but it looked like he was holding something. He walked toward Garrick, feigning surrender with his hands in the air as he walked past Darren. As Aldric approached, blocking Darren's path to him, Garrick could see a glass in Aldric's hand. Garrick noticed a window to his left. If he could just muster the strength to throw himself out of it, he was sure he'd be able to pull himself away and start healing before Darren made it downstairs.

"This one killed in the city. Your wretched dog killed my dear sister, Aldric. Regardless of my father's inexplicable fondness of you, that will not be forgiven."

"No, I wouldn't suppose it would. It will be forgotten, though, because your father and I had a deal. I turn in the forest with my pack, and your family doesn't meddle in our affairs. He made a mistake – one which will not be repeated. Now, Darren, I would suggest you walk away before you make one of your own. Samantha's death was unfortunate, but Garrick was defending himself. Don't make this anything other than it has to be."

"My father taught me to always hold our honor. His word was law in this family. So I haven't broken that pact.

But this one did. He left the forest, so he dies." Darren was brandishing the knife, holding it between him and Aldric, but Aldric remained calm, lifting his cup for a drink. "You don't have to pay this price with him, but if you refuse to walk away, you'll share in his punishment."

"Aldric…" Garrick tried to force out of his mouth the words, but they wouldn't leave. He couldn't get the warning out. He knew, though, that Darren was just distracting Aldric. If he could get Aldric to take a drink of that water, then he'd be in the same place as Garrick. Darren would have them both trapped.

"Elliott, I'll explain everything later," Aldric offered. "Now, Darren, leave. Pretend you never saw this."

"No, the pact stands only if your pack turns in the woods. If you stand with him, be prepared to fall with him."

"Well, then you've brought this upon yourself. You want one of mine? You'll get a war." Aldric was now standing tall, towering over Darren, but the young man didn't back down.

"Aldric… Don't…"

"Relax, Elliott," Aldric dismissed Garrick's concern as he drank the entire glass.

"Wolf…"

"Focus on healing," Aldric started, but was interrupted. He choked back a fit of pain before continuing. "I can smell it. You see, Elliott, purebreds can use it to their advantage." His attention turned to Darren, a smirk covering the pain as his claws erupted and his mouth reformed to hold his new teeth. Darren dove toward Aldric, swinging the knife for his throat. Ducking underneath the strike, Aldric drove an elbow into Darren's gut. He punched the man, lifting him off of his feet as he flew toward the wall behind him. The knife clattered away from Darren as he slid to the floor.

"We're more in control when we have wolfsbane," he threatened. He dropped on to all fours, and Garrick watched as his shoulders broke, rising far above his back, one by one. His body changed to accommodate the new bones. Darren stood to his feet, grabbing the knife from the floor near him. His goal was clearly to stop Aldric from finishing the transformation, but he wouldn't make it in time. Aldric's transformation was more rapid than Garrick had ever seen before.

"This is your final chance to flee," he managed to say before he was entirely a wolf. "And clear this place out. Or this war will have early casualties."

Ignoring his warning, Darren rushed at the wolf, who jumped out of the way, easily dodging the swipe from the blade. The wolf circled around Darren, dodging swipe after swipe. He pounced forward, but Darren dropped to the ground and rolled to the side, avoiding the attack. The wolf skidded to a stop and quickly turned around to face Darren.

Darren raised the blade as he ran at the wolf. The wolf swung his tail at Darren's wrist, breaking his grip on the knife. The beast jumped on top of him, knocking him over and pinning him to the ground, growling at the hunter. Darren struggled for the knife, but it was a few inches out of his reach. As Aldric lowered his mouth for the killing bite, Darren grabbed the knife with one last reach of his arm. He managed to maneuver the knife so that the tip of the blade pressed into the wolf's neck. Darren didn't have the space to gain the momentum to pierce Aldric's skin, but it was enough to distract Aldric, granting Darren the opportunity to throw him off and roll backward, standing back up.

The wolf ran and dove at Darren, hitting him with all of its weight and pinning him against the wall. It stepped back and scratched at him, but he drove the knife forward in an attempt to parry the attack. The wolf hit Darren's hand with its paw, and the knife clattered to the ground again. As if it were planning this, the wolf placed its paw on the handle and pushed the knife back toward Garrick. Weaponless and practically defenseless in the wake of the beast in front of him, Darren backed away toward the door. The wolf swiped at him, and Darren jumped back to avoid it. The wolf didn't pursue him as he ran; it just stepped back to stand between the door and Garrick. It looked down at Garrick.

For the first time, when Garrick was looking into the eyes of that wolf, he didn't see what he always had before. There wasn't rage, hatred, and death. In those deep blue eyes, all Garrick saw was compassion. The wolf was worried about him.

Maybe it wasn't the wolf. Because finally, Garrick understood what Aldric meant. He'd never grasped the idea that they could be one, but now he did. Because he wasn't staring into the eyes of a cruel monster that happened to suddenly care about his existence. Garrick was staring into the powerful eyes not of the wolf, but of Aldric Phoenix.

Chapter 16

Fourteen months ago

Cailean's teeth began to grow, and his jaw cracked, then reformed. There was nothing Garrick could do but watch in horror as the boy turned into a beast right before his eyes. Cailean's face elongated and his arms bulged out, any fat fading and collapsing on the muscle. He dropped to his hands and knees, and his legs began to form into those of an animal. His feet took a completely different shape as the nails became claws. His skin stretched and darkened, and fur grew to cover his legs and back. He looked unreal – unlike anything Garrick had seen in the world before. As a final touch, Cailean bared his teeth and let out a growl.

The monster which was once Cailean pounced at Garrick, who quickly stumbled backward, barely fast enough to avoid getting bitten. The beast swung its paw at Garrick, who fell to the ground, narrowly avoiding the swipe. He crawled backward, kicking his feet frantically, hoping to scare the beast off.

"Cailean!" Hayden yelled, to no avail. "Stop!" Suddenly, she doubled over in pain too. Garrick was distracted for a second, and that gave the wolf time to pounce again. With pure fortune on his side, Garrick was able to kick the beast in the nose with as much force as he could muster.

The wolf stumbled back, shaking its head as it quickly recovered. That distraction gave Garrick just enough time to scramble desperately to his feet and lean on a tree for support. The wolf dove at the tree, and Garrick ducked to the other side of it, dodging and placing the tree between himself and the animal. He turned to run, but there were two more of them in the bushes behind him – one about the same size as Cailean and another almost twice as large.

The smaller one jumped at Garrick, so he ducked down, dropping to the ground as the wolf flew over him. He rolled over quickly, landing on his back as he saw one of the wolves already in the air pouncing toward him. He pushed himself toward the tree and used it for support to stand. Garrick could only attribute his reactions to adrenaline, but even that would only last him so long if he couldn't find a better solution. A third wolf came from the bushes on his right, leaving him surrounded. Even if he managed to get past those three, the large one was still hiding in the woods watching, so it would surely catch him. Any hope of escape Garrick had started to fade away.

He still tried. He spun and took cover behind the tree as the wolves ran toward him. He ran as fast as he could, hoping he was headed toward the town. On either side of him, he saw wolves keeping pace. Then he slid to a stop and fumbled backward, barely maintaining his balance. One of them had managed to cut him off and was standing in front of him

One of the wolves jumped at him, scratching his upper left arm, tearing through the sleeve. Garrick cried out in pain and fell onto his back. He covered the wound with his right hand, but blood was seeping through his fingers. The wolf jumped at him once again, but he pushed his way backward, with his right arm and kicked, as if he would find safety behind him. Nerves in his left arm had been torn, and he had no motor control over it at all.

He clumsily sat up and leaned back against a tree, trying not to panic as he noticed the trail of blood he was leaving behind. One of the wolves walked around the tree, growling, and Garrick jumped to his feet. The adrenaline rushing through his veins almost countered the agony that had taken over his arm. He ran faster than he ever thought possible, but they were faster. A wolf dashed from behind a tree, positioning itself in front of him. Another was behind him. One dove, knocking him to the ground and pinning him down with its paws.

He could feel the wolf's drool drip onto his neck, and he closed his eyes, waiting for death. Suddenly, he didn't feel the pressure on him anymore. He opened his eyes to see that one wolf had rammed into the other, knocking it off of him. Were they fighting over which one would eat him?

He tried to crawl away, but he couldn't move. The adrenaline was fading out, and he could feel himself bleeding out. He just watched one wolf scratch at the other, leaving a gaping wound in its front leg. It limped away, but the other wolf was already running toward Garrick. He turned his head away, only to see a third wolf on that side. He looked up again, finally giving up.

A wolf jumped over him and time seemed to slow down. Garrick noticed three lines on the beast's uncovered stomach. It looked like the beast was scarred from one of them. Maybe it had fought the others before.

That wolf tackled the other which had been near him, and then turned back to face him. Its eyes were a beautiful blue color, shining more brightly than any human iris could possibly have. Still, he could see something familiar about those eyes.

"Hayden?" he mumbled, the words slurred. Blood still poured from the wound in his arm, and he was starting to feel it taking its toll. The other wolf was back on its feet, and it swiped at Hayden. She turned around to fight the beast. Hayden bit down on the other wolf's neck, and she threw it back against a tree. She walked back to Garrick, but she didn't harm him. She licked his arm and nuzzled her head against him.

The other wolves stood about fifty feet away, on the other side of the clearing, all of them staring at Garrick as he lay on the ground. Hayden walked slowly and gracefully to Garrick's feet, where she positioned herself between him and the other wolves. When she growled, Garrick could feel the ground beneath him reverberate with the sound.

Garrick fumbled to his feet, hoping that with her help he could find his way home. He tried applying pressure to the wound in his arm again, hoping that would lessen the bleeding. Hayden continued to stand between him and the other wolves, growling at them, forcing them to keep their distance. Finally, the big one barked, as if issuing an order, as it turned to leave. The others followed, but seemed to be more reluctant to abandon their prey than their leader was. Garrick took deep breaths, and he rested his left hand on Hayden's head. She nuzzled her head up to his chest, and he just stared into the darkness where the other wolves had been.

Present
24 days until the full moon

"You can control the wolf?" Garrick pressed Aldric for answers. After the memorial service, Aldric had just sent Garrick home, clearly annoyed and refusing to give answers. Of course, Garrick had taken a few detours on his way home. He'd stopped by Tyler's to see if there were any new ideas. When he finally made it home, he had spent the entire night up researching different ways to control the wolf. Aldric had told him – and proven to him – that it was possible. Granted, he was specifically referring to purebreds, but if it were possible for them, it had to be possible for Garrick too. As expected, though, Garrick was completely unable to find any leads, and he'd been too scared of angering Aldric to push too hard the previous night, but that time he wasn't leaving without answers.

From Aldric's statement, Garrick gathered that it was possible for pure wolves to maintain control while under the effects of wolfsbane, which didn't guarantee anything different. Garrick, who wasn't a purebred wolf, wanted to gain control during a full moon, which was basically as different of a circumstance as possible.

Aldric's comment had convinced him that there was some hope for him, though, and that had given him renewed energy to pursue his research. Earlier that week, he was questioning whether control was ever possible.

All he'd gained from his search were a few more ideas about meditation, but he wasn't planning on trying that again. Last time he had, he'd fallen into a nightmare which he would rather not revisit. His only other idea was to repeatedly subjugate himself to the effects of wolfsbane. He could ask Aldric for help to find it, then just take small doses until he learned to maintain control during his transformation.

"No," Aldric sighed, crushing Garrick's new hope with a single word. It wasn't enough to make Garrick give up – not after what he'd seen. Garrick had recognized Aldric in those eyes – it wasn't just the wolf. Still, he was discouraged to discover that he wouldn't get any help from Aldric.

"You said that purebreds can use wolfsbane to their advantage," Garrick retorted, trying to pry some information from his alpha.

"I meant that I can control when I change. That way, I can fight the hunters as a wolf, not human. As a purebred, and with more experience, I can change faster than you, so the window of vulnerability is much shorter."

"Oh. But when you're a wolf, you still…"

"Can't control myself, no. And I don't remember it. Just flashes. It's like any other transformation."

Garrick was crushed. He had finally found a lead, but it vanished within a day. Garrick took solace in the fact that he hadn't brought the idea to Tyler in too much detail, because his friend would have been devastated as well.

"Is there some way to control the change?" Garrick desperately clung to his hope.

"Elliott, you need to give that up. It's impossible, trust me. I've tried, and stronger men have tried as well – yet success has evaded us all."

"You tried?" Garrick stuttered, unsure of where to proceed with his question. He had assumed Aldric had always just been accepting of what he was.

"As a child, I was raised to believe the wolf and I were one, so I assumed that meant I could control it. Throughout my entire life, though, there hasn't been a single time where that has proven true. Perhaps you and the wolf are just two beings inhabiting the same body."

"What did you try?"

"Everything. Meditating, fighting the change, even spells. For about ten years I became addicted to wolfsbane because I thought that changing when I wanted would eventually make me able to control myself when I was transformed. I tried talking to the wolf as I changed, as if it could understand me."

"So, everything I'm doing…"

"There's no point. I wish I didn't have to be so callous, but you're just causing yourself unnecessary pain by lengthening the change. It's impressive, Elliott. It's further than I ever got, but that's all that it will amount to: a delay."

Back to square one, he thought.

"But I saw you, as a wolf you pushed a knife away from Darren. You *thought* about it!"

"Not me. You've experienced enhanced senses and wolf-like traits around the full moon, right? Well, when you turn, it has some of your traits – especially if it's further from a full moon when your body is more human. That's why the wolf is such a dangerous predator. It's animalistic, but at times it can almost be rational. Even without rationality, instinct would demand the hunter be disarmed. You're reading too much into that. Elliott, I know it's disappointing, and I wish I could give you better news."

Deflated, Garrick stood to walk out of Aldric's office. It had become apparent that he wasn't going to get any good answers, so he wanted to take a few minutes to decompress before training.

"Sit back down," Aldric demanded.

"What is it?" Garrick obeyed, falling back into the seat as he asked the question.

"What possible reason did you have to go to that service?"

"I had to," Garrick asserted. With nothing to back up his statement, Garrick silently hoped that Aldric wouldn't ask him why.

"Why?"

"I don't know," he admitted hesitantly. "I mean, she may have been a hunter, but she was still a human being. It didn't feel right to just pretend she was never alive. I... I owed it to her."

"To pay your debt to a liar, you walked into a building occupied solely by hunters?"

"It wasn't my best plan. I just wanted to... I wanted to make it right."

"I know you're hurting over what happened to Chase," Aldric sympathized. "You need to honestly think about this question, though. Were you trying to make up for what happened, or were you trying to get yourself killed?"

The question struck a nerve for Garrick. Aldric brought up a good point. Garrick had never contemplated suicide, but he couldn't deny that there was a part of him which felt as though he deserved to be punished for his mistakes.

"I don't know," Garrick answered slowly.

"I understand." Aldric leaned forward on his desk, his expression solemn as he looked at Garrick. Garrick tried to scan his eyes and for any hint of what Aldric was truly feeling. Garrick himself didn't entirely understand – how could Aldric.

"We have to be smart. There is more at stake than just you and your emotional burdens here. Listen to me, son. Chase died for something he believed in. That isn't your fault."

"Yes, sir," Garrick nodded, although he wasn't fully ready to accept that yet.

"It gets easier," Aldric consoled as Garrick stood once again.

"Killing people?"

"No. Living with it."

Garrick sat on his couch, his head in his hands. He recognized that he'd fallen into a dangerous rut, and he wanted nothing more than to break out of it. It was clear that he'd make a lot of mistakes, but if he didn't start being more careful, he was only going to make things worse. From that moment forward, he decided, he was going to have to move on and stop dwelling on what had happened – no matter how much it hurt.

As he stood, Garrick heard the knob on the front door. He wasn't sure if his hearing was enhanced because of the wolf or his paranoia, but his eyes darted to the door. His mother, still in uniform, walked inside. Garrick relaxed a bit, but she wasn't supposed to be home for hours, so he was still concerned.

"Hey Mom," Garrick greeted cautiously. "Is everything okay?"

"Yeah," she feigned a smile. "I just need to talk to you."

"It couldn't wait until after work?" Garrick tried not to sound on edge, but his heart was pounding. Her tone clearly indicated that there was a serious problem, so his mind ran through every possibility. It had to be about Chase – was there new evidence?

"Everything's fine, Garrick," she tried to comfort, but it was clear she was lying. "Come sit with me."

The two of them walked back toward the couch and sat down. He wiped sweat off of his palms. Garrick hoped there was no reason to be nervous – this was his mother after all. Still, he just couldn't shake the feeling that something was dreadfully wrong.

"When is the last time you talked to Chase?"

Without a decent answer, Garrick froze. He'd spent so much time trapped in guilt about what had happened and the fact that they'd had to cover it up, then worrying they'd left something behind, that he hadn't come up with a decent alibi.

"I talked to him the day he ran away," Garrick admitted. "But he didn't tell me. I never would have let him do it."

"And he wasn't going camping with you?"

"No, he didn't."

"We recovered his texts," she informed him. "You were the last person he talked to."

Garrick's heart skipped a beat. He searched his mind for anything that could have been said in those texts which was incriminating, but he was drawing a blank. He was relatively sure that they never used words like "transform" or "werewolf" just in case someone ever did manage to read their messages, but Garrick had no idea what they'd talked about the day before he disappeared.

"We talked a lot," Garrick defended after a pause which was far too long.

"It said 'I'm coming.' You guys were talking about the camping trip beforehand. So why are you saying he didn't go?"

"He didn't," Garrick tried to sound convincing, but he was talking to a detective and a mother.

"You're hiding something. Just be honest with me, Garrick."

"Mom, I don't know where he is. He told me he was coming, but he didn't. That's all I know!"

"Why does it feel like that isn't true?" Her eyes shimmered with a tear and her expression had a mixture of sadness and betrayal that was hard for Garrick to see.

"I don't know," Garrick replied. *Maybe because it isn't,* he thought.

"I want to trust you."

"Then do. I don't know where he went, or why he left. All I know is that he didn't show up. I swear."

"His parents filed a missing person's report. Since he's still 17, he's a minor, and a runaway. We're not going to stop investing this, Garrick."

"What do you think I'm hiding, Mom?"

"Just tell me if there is *anything* else you remember, okay? Even if you're positive it won't make a difference – that there's no way it can help find him. Just tell me."

"Okay, I will."

She didn't say anything else as she stood up and walked out the door. They weren't in a town so small that everyone knew each other, but it was small enough that most people knew the police officers by name. She'd known Chase's parents for years, and they were obviously putting a lot of pressure on the police – and specifically her – to find their son. Garrick just wished he could do anything at all to make it easier on her.

"She caught me in a lie," Garrick explained to Cailean. Desperate for help, and with no one else to ask, Garrick had gone to see him as soon as his mother had left. Tyler wouldn't have been able to provide advice on the werewolf world to which he was so new, and his relationship with Hayden was still too unstable for him to do anything to jeopardize it.

"Who?" Cailean asked, clearly confused at Garrick's opening remark. Garrick had been thinking about his conversation on the walk to Cailean's house, so he hadn't thought about the fact that Cailean wasn't aware of it.

"My mom. She asked me what I knew about Chase earlier, and I said he didn't go camping, but she saw my texts where he said he was."

"Seems easy enough to talk your way out of it."

"I don't know. It just feels like anything I say will just be incriminating."

"That's typically how it feels when you actually did something wrong."

"Anyway, it's wrong to lie to her. She's my mother. I wouldn't even be able to. I've been looking for a way to make things right, Cailean. Maybe this is it."

"What are you talking about?" Concern quickly flooded Cailean's voice.

"I can tell her. I'll come clean. I'll serve my time, just like I should."

"No, you won't, Garrick. You clearly haven't thought this through. You just tell your mom you turned into a werewolf and killed your friend?"

"Of course not. I tell her we got in a fight while camping. Things got out of hand. I don't know, maybe there was alcohol involved."

"You can't get drunk."

"She doesn't know that," Garrick groaned, exasperated. Cailean was getting hung up on the details. Obviously, Garrick was going to hide the parts of the story about his curse, but at least he'd pay for the murder that he committed. Cailean was trying to be helpful, but Garrick realized that he'd asked the best person for advice on the werewolf world, but the worst for the morals of the human one.

"Sorry," Cailean muttered. "I forgot." He wasn't used to people close to him not knowing these subtle details about the lycanthropy. Of course he knew Garrick's mom wasn't aware he was a werewolf, but things like the rapid healing were just completely normal to Cailean, so it seemed he forgot humans weren't aware of those things.

"The point is, I'll tell her that things got out of hand and it was all an accident."

"And then what, Garrick? You go to prison. In twenty-four days, you change. The guards are shocked, and they don't know what to do. Then you tear through the bars and rip out their throats. You're in the middle of a buffet, and you kill everyone in sight.

"Maybe, miraculously, the police officers manage to get enough bullets in you to keep you down for good. Then, the hunters hear about this, and they come in to wipe out any witnesses. The rest of the city is eradicated, and we just become another Roanoke.

"If you want to condemn yourself, Garrick, I can't get in your way. But you're not taking the rest of this pack – or this city – down with you."

Garrick could hear genuine care in Cailean's voice. Although he would never say it, he wasn't only interested in the rest of the pack. He was worried for Garrick. He didn't want him to do something that would ruin, or sacrifice, his life.

"So what should I do, then?" Garrick asked.

"You choose," Cailean told him. "Either you tell her everything, or you tell her nothing."

"Why would I tell her about us?"

"Because she would understand that it wasn't your fault, and she's on the inside. She'd be able to help."

"But that puts her in danger."

"I'm aware."

"I can't do that."

"Then it doesn't sound like you have much of a choice."

"But I can't lie to her."

"Lying is easy," Cailean shrugged.

"Not for me, Cailean. I wasn't raised like you – I was taught not to lie. Anyway, I'm just not good at it. And she's a police officer. And my mom. She'd see right through me."

"I'll teach you."

Garrick thought for a minute. Was lying a skill he could really be taught?

"I don't want to know," Garrick finally decided. "I try so hard to tell the truth, and now you're trying to convince me to lie to my mom. That isn't who I am. This curse changes me once a month, but I don't want it to change who I am – not beyond that."

"Having this as a tool won't change you, Garrick. Because you're a good person. Lying isn't bad – it's just how people use it that is bad. We use it to save ourselves from trouble, or to keep avoiding someone finding out we've done something to hurt them. It's not inherently bad, and sometimes you have to do something you don't want to if you want to protect the people close to you."

"I guess that makes sense," Garrick conceded, feeling foolish.

"Like I said, Garrick. You have two options. You tell her about us and put her in danger, or you lie to protect her. Honestly, either one works for me. It wouldn't hurt to have her in our corner."

Garrick was silent, but Cailean clearly knew what that meant.

"Come over before training tomorrow. I'll teach you what I can."

Chapter 17

Thirteen Months Ago

Garrick was lying on his back, tossing a ball in the air above him. His phone buzzed, vibrating the bed next to him. Once again, he tried to tune it out, ignoring what had to be the tenth text from Hayden in the past hour. Distracted, he missed the ball, and it clattered to the floor and rolled away. With a deep breath, he reached for his phone, but he dropped it back onto the bed before flipping it open. Every time he thought he had the strength to talk to her, he lost his resolve. Regardless of how hard he tried, Garrick couldn't bring himself to talk about what had happened. Thinking about the monsters he'd seen that night, Garrick rubbed the scar on his left arm. Garrick felt like he had to find peace in his own mind with the monsters he'd seen before he would be able to talk to Hayden about any of it.

Deciding to try to take his mind off the werewolves, Garrick stood up. As he caught a glimpse of himself in the mirror, though, his mind fell back to the beasts. Garrick took his shirt off, tossing it to the ground beside him. He didn't look any different. He still had the same eyes, the same hair, the same scrawny arms. Physically, his body still looked like his own, but for some reason, he felt changed. He couldn't explain it, but somehow, he knew that he wasn't the same as he used to be.

Garrick looked more closely at his arms. The little fat that had existed on his arms already seemed to be disintegrating, as if that scratch had somehow introduced something into his bloodstream that destroyed triglycerides. In reality, something was affecting his metabolism – he'd already noticed that.

Slowly, Garrick hovered his hand over his right forearm. When he was eight, he had broken his arm falling off a trampoline. The wound had healed completely, of course, but there was always a small scar from where they'd had to operate. It had barely been visible, but he'd always been able to find it. Now, though, even as he inspected his arm for that small scar – that piece of his personal history – he couldn't find any trace of it. It had simply vanished overnight.

When he was fifteen, his appendix had burst. The doctors had to operate to remove it, leaving a somewhat sizable scar on his stomach. Looking at his shirtless body, though, Garrick was unable to locate that scar on his abdomen. The only scar that was left was the one from the creature that had attacked him.

Tearing himself from the mirror, Garrick grabbed his phone and walked to the bathroom and stood over the sink. In an attempt to clear his mind, he splashed water on his face. The second he looked up, though, he was trapped by looking at a mirror again, searching his face for any blemish. Thoughts were rushing through his brain faster than he could acknowledge them. Garrick's phone vibrated again, so he set it down on the counter.

Garrick rubbed his chin, feeling the prickly hairs that he'd intended to shave days ago. Hopefully a task would start to pull him out of his mind. Garrick slowly grabbed his razor, mesmerized by the blades as they shimmered in the bathroom light. He turned on the sink and covered his face with more water before running the blades across his chin.

Garrick exhaled sharply as he felt a slight sting in his chin. It was rare that he cut himself, but he was unfocused on the task at hand. As hard as he tried to distract himself, his mind continued to linger somewhere he didn't want it to be. He realized that shaving probably wasn't the safest distraction from that.

Placing the razor down on the sink, Garrick rubbed his finger across the wound, wiping off the blood. He'd expected there to be more, but nothing else came. Leaning forward, he looked closely at his chin in the mirror as he searched for the cut, but he couldn't find it.

He picked up the razor again, holding it in his hands. Well aware of the fact that it was a bad plan, Garrick still decided there was something that he had to do. He had to find out what was going on and what the implications were for him.

Garrick popped the blade out of the razor and held it between his thumb and index finger, slowly tightening his grip until he felt the blade pierce his skin. Instinctively, he flinched, dropping it into the sink. He ran his fingers under the faucet to rinse the blood off before examining the cut. The discovery that there was no cut wasn't nearly as shocking as he assumed it should have been. Something in his body was changing, and he wanted to know just how much. Maybe small cuts were just healing more quickly, but a voice inside told him that he wasn't seeing the big picture.

Unconvinced, Garrick picked the razor blade back up and pushed it hard against the back of his hand. He saw a small drop of blood, but there wasn't a wound when he wiped it away. That wasn't good enough; it proved absolutely nothing.

He turned his hand over and pushed the blade against the bottom of his palm. As the blade pierced his skin, he dug it deeper and dragged it down his forearm. He grunted quietly, trying to fight back the scream of pain that was building up. His mom wasn't home, but he didn't want the neighbors thinking he was getting murdered. Still, he couldn't help but let out a quiet yell as his wrist opened up, spilling blood into the sink.

There was a deep gash in his arm. He held it over the sink and turned on the water, trying in vain to wash the blood away. He was bleeding faster than he could possibly hope to clean himself off. Garrick started to get dizzy and realized he had done something even more stupid than he'd originally thought. His mind raced as he thought of solutions. Mentally, he was in a dark place, and he wasn't sure what was going on, but he still wanted the opportunity to find out.

Garrick could feel himself start to panic as the world became blurry. The increased heart rate only pushed more blood out of the wound. He could barely even see his own face in the mirror. He reached for his phone to call someone, but it slipped from his hand as he picked it up – tumbling to the floor. The phone was at his feet, but with his lack of coordination at that moment it might as well have been in another room.

Garrick grabbed the edge of the counter with his good arm, using all of the energy he could muster to stay standing. Strength started to drain from his muscles, so he leaned onto his elbows, placing as much weight as he could on the counter to keep from falling over.

Then the blood clotted. The running water rinsed away what was still on his skin, and no more poured from the wound. He could still see the deep cut – an open wound – but it wasn't bleeding. Garrick wasn't sure if he was delirious, but it looked like the blood he could see was thicker. Still dizzy, he managed to stand back up using the counter as support.

Garrick watched as the skin on his arm seemed to sew itself back together. Watching the process with utter amazement, Garrick lost track of time. A thin layer of new skin stitched itself together, and though he knew it was impossible, he felt like he could see the individual cells dividing before his eyes. Layers formed on top of layers, sealing the wound, and within half an hour, it was as if it hadn't been there in the first place. Where there should have been a scar, there was nothing; no way at all to tell that there had just been a gaping wound – one which should have been fatal – in his arm.

Continuing to stare at his arm, Garrick stumbled back and fell against the wall, sliding to the floor. For the first time since it happened, he allowed himself to think about what he'd seen. It had been plaguing his mind since then, but he hadn't granted himself the luxury of actually sitting and just thinking about it. All he'd done was tried to forget it – tried to keep the thoughts out of his head.

Garrick had watched Cailean turn into a monster. He had seen another – he assumed Hayden – save his life. He'd watched beasts fighting and had been caught in the middle. Now, the only possible explanation he could think of was that he was one of them. A werewolf.

His phone rang again. Hayden. Not ready to talk to her yet, he let it ring, ignoring the call. He didn't know how to feel. He still loved her, and his problem wasn't even accepting what she was – it was the fact that she'd been so good at hiding it from him.

He was also scared to talk to her because he didn't know how to act. Part of him felt like he should apologize to her. He'd accused her of cheating on him – but how could he have suspected what was really happening? Every sign pointed to exactly what he'd thought before there was some sort of supernatural explanation. He felt justified, and was actually angry that she hadn't been open with him before. They'd dated for over half a year, so she'd transformed at least six times during their relationship. Any one of those times would have been perfect to talk to him about it. Instead, she just waited until he caught on that something was going wrong. That just made him feel even worse. Somehow, as close as they were, he'd been stupid enough to let her hide something so big for so long. How had he not caught on?

Maybe he should have trusted her more, though. She had never given him a reason to question her. Except acting strange, sneaking around, and hiding a big part of her life from him. He ran his hands through his hair, frustrated. Anyway, how was he supposed to trust her when she obviously didn't trust him? How was he supposed to feel about all of this? And how could she expect him to know the answer to that so quickly?

He sunk further to the ground and stared up at the ceiling. Eventually, he'd find an answer. Eventually, the conflicting thoughts in his mind would settle on one answer. Eventually, he'd stop arguing with his own thoughts. Until then, he just had to wait.

Present
23 Days until the full moon

"Let's start with the easiest part," Cailean began, "but also the most vital."

"What's that? Don't get caught?"

"No. Breathe."

"Oh good, I have practice with that one," Garrick tried to joke.

"You have to control your breathing. You're going to be nervous – terrified that you'll say the wrong thing. You have to get over that. Say what you're going to say with confidence – convince yourself it's the truth. You'll have to watch your movements. But at the core of it all, you're going to have to breathe."

"Right," Garrick acknowledged, matching Cailean's serious tone.

"It's a lot harder than it sounds, and it isn't really something you can practice on its own. That's why I started with that – because it has to be in your mind through everything else."

"Okay, so what is something I can work on?"

"I think we should start with movements."

"Right. I mean, I know in theory that I shouldn't twitch or fidget, but I think the hard part is actually doing it."

"That's a good start," Cailean offered, "but you need to do more than just stop yourself from twitching. It's everything. Your head jerking, looking away, shuffling your feet. It's about acting natural."

"Easier said than done."

"Much. Give it a try. I am going to be your mother, and you have to lie to me."

"I hate chocolate pudding," Garrick lied, looking Cailean straight in the eye.

"That was an easy one, but I still heard hesitation. You had to think of something to lie about. If you were telling me the truth, and I asked about pudding, you'd tell me you liked it instantly," he explained with a snap.

"Yeah, but that's just because I had to think."

"Okay, what's your favorite class?"

"Art," Garrick lied again, focusing on everything Cailean had told him. He tried to keep his eyes pinned on Cailean and stay perfectly still. Garrick was a math person, art was the single worst class he'd ever had to take, and it was back in elementary school.

"I thought you weren't in art?"

"I'm not," Garrick answered truthfully. Then, he added, "But it was when I was in it in third grade, and it's just stayed at the top of my list."

"Do you want the good or the bad first?"

"Surprise me," Garrick groaned.

"Good news: you have a good technique. You sprinkle in a little bit of truth because it helps you convince yourself that you aren't lying."

"How'd you know I actually took an art class in third grade?"

"That's the bad part," Cailean continued. "That is the only part you convinced me of, so I figured it was true. You were focused so much on not twitching that you didn't allow yourself any natural body movements; you were stiff as a board. Also, you didn't pay any attention to your breathing. The nerves of trying to impress me with your lying prowess got to you, and your breath sped up. Finally, you looked away for a second, then looked back at me, trying to maintain eye contact."

"This isn't going to be easy, is it?" Garrick sighed.

"I can be easy on you, or I can teach you what you'll need to know."

"Okay, okay."

"So we'll try again. Something trivial like the art class, because it's easier to start lying about things that you know I don't care about at all. What's your favorite color?"

"Orange."

"Why?"

"Because it makes me think of a sunset," Garrick fumbled for a response. He sighed, knowing that the response took too long.

"Maybe I'm going about this wrong," Cailean grunted, standing. "You're just too tense."

"I'm trying."

"I know. Let's try some training that you might be better with. Close your eyes."

"What? Why?" Garrick asked.

"Just do it."

Garrick closed his eyes, but he could feel the nerves start to build. His breathing was intensifying. Fear was starting to set in as he felt blinded, and Cailean spent over a minute in perfect silence. Suddenly, Garrick felt Cailean's fist slam into his stomach with enough force to tip the chair over. Garrick opened his eyes and rolled over the back of the chair as it landed, then jumped to his feet, instinctively landing with his fists up, blocking his face and chest.

"What was that for?" Garrick accused, relaxing his arms.

"I wanted to take away your trust," Cailean explained calmly. "Now lift the chair up, sit back down, and close your eyes."

"Why? Why on Earth would I do that?"

"Because I said to, and I'm currently training you."

"I'm not sure of that," Garrick muttered, but he still did as Cailean instructed. He kept his eyes closed for about four seconds, but his instincts pulled them open.

"Keep them closed."

Garrick tried again, closing his eyes, breathing deeply. He had to fight to keep them closed, but he was sure a punch was coming. Just as he thought that, Cailean's fist connected with his face. Garrick fell out of the chair and onto the ground.

"How is this going to help?" Garrick rubbed his jaw as he stood.

"We're used to learning with violence, so I'm going to teach you how to relax. If you weren't so tense, you could stop me. Relax, breathe, and focus on the sound. You'll hear me move, you'll hear my shirt snap, you'll feel the air."

Garrick tried a few more times, but he kept getting hit. After getting knocked out of his chair a fourth time, he got angry, and it was even harder to focus. Four more times and Garrick had completely lost faith in Cailean's training. Given the fact that he had no other options, though, he tried to compose himself. He breathed slowly, attempting to remain calm. He sensed something coming from his right, and he raised his hand to catch Cailean's wrist just before his fist connected with Garrick's head.

"Good," Cailean congratulated Garrick with a smile.

"What did that prove?" Garrick asked, breathing slightly more heavily than usual. He was excited that he didn't have to get punched anymore – at least until they started training with Aldric in an hour.

"You have proven to both me and yourself that you can breathe and stay calm in a stressful situation. I want you to do the same thing as you lie to me. Control your breathing. So, have you ever been to the beach?"

"Yes, of course." Garrick smiled. He wasn't a fan of Cailean's methods, but he didn't have anything better to suggest. He just focused on his breathing, the same way he had when he knew that he was about to get punched.

"When?"

"Last year, I took Hayden for a night because she'd never been."

"Oh, that's interesting." Garrick felt incredibly uncomfortable as Cailean's eyes bored into his own. He sat perfectly still, but kept telling himself to loosen up. He took a deep breath, instantly regretting that. In a normal conversation, he didn't breathe like that. Trying to stay out of his head, he tried to keep his breathing steady. The lie was easy to tell because it wasn't life-altering but it was still nerve-wracking because he was trying to do it well.

"What was her favorite part?" Cailean asked.

"She loved all of the shells. She tried collecting a bunch to bring home, but she ended up leaving them there anyway," Garrick told him. He tried to fake a laugh, because he was lying about a good memory, but he was aware of how forced the laugh sounded.

"Oh, I see. What did you like about it?"

"I got to see my girlfriend in a bikini all day," Garrick said with a light laugh. It was faked, but it wasn't as painful as the last one had been.

"But really," he added. "It was the smile on her face. The look of pure joy that she had when she didn't have to worry about anything that would happen when we came back, and for the first time in a long time, she got to just live in the moment." A smile came to his face as he pictured the scene which never happened in his head. He saw Hayden standing in the sand, the sunset lighting up her eyes as she looked back at him. Her hands were safely wrapped in his as they faced each other, the world around them fading away and leaving just the two of them.

"That is what I'm looking for," Cailean cheered, clapping.

"What?" Garrick asked, snapped back from his fantasy.

"You know that didn't happen, but I almost believed that. If I didn't know you were lying to me, I'd have had no way of knowing. How did you do it?"

"I guess I stopped thinking about you. I just pretended you weren't there, and I lived in a daydream. In my mind, it was true, so I didn't have to lie to you about it."

"Perfect."

"So you think I'm ready?"

"Not even close. You had what, one good sentence? Now you need to step it up."

Garrick rolled his eyes, but he kept going. He was grateful that Cailean was helping him out, but he just wished none of it had to happen. He didn't want to have to get so good at lying, but he would do what he had to.

For the next hour, Cailean kept asking Garrick questions – answers to which Garrick would make up – and then picking out very minor details to criticize. It seemed that Cailean had begun to scrutinize Garrick even more after he managed to lie well once. Garrick learned to stop thinking of it as lying, and to start imagining the story in his mind.

As they were talking, there was a knock on the door and Aldric let Tyler in. Tyler was usually the first one to get to training, probably because he felt like he had a lot to prove. He definitely had more catching up to do than any of the others.

"Hey, what are the two of you discussing?" Tyler called to Garrick. Cailean gave Garrick a very subtle nod. Garrick was thinking the same thing, but he was glad to see they were on the same page. This was a perfect chance to try what he'd been learning. In the moment, though, it felt much harder.

"Cailean was just tea-" he started to say 'teaching' but cut himself off. "Telling me what he thinks I should do for Hayden. I wanted to do something extravagant. To tell her I'm sorry."

"No, he wasn't," Tyler said.

"Yeah, I know," Garrick sighed.

"I'm teaching him to lie," Cailean shrugged. "He clearly needs more work."

"Why do you want to lie?"

"Gotta get the cops off my tail," Garrick joked, futilely trying to diffuse the horrible feeling in his stomach.

"Oh, I suppose that makes sense," Tyler acknowledged sadly.

"So, speaking of Hayden," Cailean changed the subject, trying to avoid the awkward silence. Garrick could see in his eyes, though, that he felt just as awkward talking about anything personal. "How are things going?"

"Fine," Garrick replied. "I'm giving her space."

"What does that mean?" Tyler chimed in.

"We haven't talked in days, other than when we're here and we exchange a few awkward words; it's tearing me up inside, but I feel like she needs to come back to me on her own terms, or she'll never really forgive me."

"She'll come around," Cailean comforted, patting Garrick on the back reassuringly.

"Yeah," Tyler agreed. "You two are unnaturally perfect for each other. It's actually disconcerting at times. Don't worry about it, Garrick Elliott."

There were a few seconds of silence, and Tyler smirked at Garrick.

"What?" Cailean asked, picking up on the silent conversation.

"Nothing," Tyler responded. Cailean turned to Garrick for answers, clearly annoyed.

"He said we were 'unnaturally' perfect for each other. Well, it's not 'unnaturally.'"

"What do you mean?" Cailean questioned, still not catching their joke.

"It's supernaturally," Tyler delivered the punchline. He laughed softly.

"Really?" Cailean asked. "Is this a thing that I just heard?"

"Yeah, it is," Garrick laughed.

"Don't be bitter, Cailean," Tyler teased. "It was humorous."

"It was cheesy humor, which is subjectively the best form of humor," Garrick added.

"Are we just going to pretend that it isn't at all weird that you two are in each other's heads all the time?" Cailean asked.

"Probably," Tyler shrugged. There was another knock on the door. Tyler just sat down, and Cailean stood up. Garrick assumed he was going to the door, but he was just walking to his dad. He held up a hand, asking his dad not to answer it, then gave Garrick a nod.

"No," Garrick mouthed.

"Just do it," Cailean urged. He and Aldric left. Aldric was slightly annoyed by the charade, but he didn't seem to care too much because it wasn't holding up the training, since they were still waiting for Brooke. They all knew it was Hayden at the door, though, because Brooke would just walk in when she arrived.

"Get the door," Garrick begged Tyler.

"I would rather avoid further infuriating Cailean. My hands are metaphorically tied."

Garrick walked to the door and opened it, standing awkwardly in the entryway as he did. Hayden stood in front of him. She gave him a quick smile, but neither of them said anything, so they both stood still.

"Hi," Garrick finally spoke up.

"Hey," she responded, not looking him in the eye.

"Oh." Garrick realized that he was in front of the door so he stepped to the side to make room for her. "Come on in."

"Where is everyone?" she inquired.

"They're hiding, I think," Garrick answered.

"Okay."

"So, uh, how are you?" Garrick asked.

"I'm fine," she laughed quietly.

"Yeah, okay," Garrick muttered. "I'm going to go find the others."

He retreated in the direction that he'd seen Cailean walk and found him hiding behind the wall. He stepped into the hallway with him, making sure he was out of Hayden's line of sight before angrily whispering.

"What was that?" Garrick growled.

"I was trying to help," Cailean smirked. Garrick couldn't find anger in himself because he could see sincerity in Cailean's eyes.

"That was exactly as awkward as I thought it would be."

"You just need to make a move, Garrick. It's like winning her over all over again."

"No, it isn't like that. The first time she didn't have a preconceived notion of me, and I didn't have anything to make up for. Trust me, Cailean, I just need to give her space."

"What happened when she gave you space?"

"Good point," Garrick admitted. "But she isn't me. She is so much better than me. That's why I have to try so hard to make this work."

"By giving her space?"

"Exactly."

"Fine. Sorry I pushed," Cailean responded, annoyed. "But Garrick, it's about time you quit feeling sorry for yourself. It's annoying."

"That isn't what this is about."

"Yes, it is. I know you're hurting about Chase, but part of it is that it was you who did it. I would have in your shoes."

"You wouldn't have been there."

"If I were. I would have done it. I know the consequences, the suffering, if you didn't. Look, Garrick, you're a good guy. You deserve her. And I know things will work out. I just don't like training with you both like this. But I'll back off. As long as you promise to stop with the pity parties. And quit acting like you're the scum of the Earth."

"Okay," Garrick accepted. Cailen was right, to an extent. Garrick would at least try to honor that request.

"Hey guys," Hayden said, walking around the corner. Garrick turned to face her, but in an attempt to look natural, he placed a hand on the wall near Cailean's head. As he did so, he leaned uncomfortably close to Cailean. Hayden gave him a questioning look, and he just nodded at her with a smile. "Brooke's here. You ready?"

Chapter 18

Thirteen months ago

Garrick stood in front of Hayden's door, working up the nerve to knock. When he thought he was ready, he placed his hand on the door, but was unable to force himself to knock. Frustrated, he leaned his head against the door. He could hear Hayden's muffled footsteps on the other side of the door. Every day for the past week, he'd done this same thing, trying to finally talk to her with no success, and she had never known he was there.

This time was different, though. This time, he had the courage to lift his hand and bring it back down against the door. It was one simple knock, but he could hear her heartbeat speed up through the door, and he wondered whether it was from fear or excitement. When she opened the door, she was able to hide both of those emotions well.

"Hey, Garrick," she greeted.

Overwhelmed with how much he'd missed her, Garrick pulled her into a hug, failing to keep up his resolve to avoid tears. She buried her face in his chest, sobbing as she kept muttering "I'm so sorry," into his shirt. After a few minutes, when they let go of each other, she turned and walked inside, wiping tears from her face as she did. Garrick followed her, sitting on one end of the couch. Hayden sat awkwardly, her hands folded in her lap and her legs closed tightly around them, her eyes downcast.

Waiting for her to speak up, Garrick just stared at the coffee table in her living room. He could practically smell her anticipation. Clearly, she was unsettled – with no idea how to begin the conversation. If Garrick had any ideas himself, he would have broken the ice, but he was also at a loss. He leaned forward, resting his arms on his legs and sighing.

"What are you?" he finally muttered, looking toward her. Tears still pooled in her eyes, but the sobbing had died down as they sat in silence, so she was able to answer.

"I'm Hayden Faye. I'm the girl you fell in love with."

"Except on a full moon."

"One night a month, Garrick. That doesn't change who I am. That doesn't mean I don't love you."

"Then why didn't you just tell me?"

"I wanted to. But Aldric said it was safer for everyone if no one knew. Against his advice, I decided to tell you a little while back, but Cailean stopped me. You heard him trying to talk me out of telling you about werewolves, and everything just started spiraling."

"I know. I'm sorry. I should have trusted you."

"I should have told you," she admitted.

"Yeah," Garrick agreed quietly.

Again, both fell into silence. Garrick was relieved to at least get part of the concern off his chest. At first, he'd been unreasonably angry at her for what she was – as if it were her fault in any way – but he could feel himself moving past that. As for hiding it from him, he was hurt, but she was just trying to protect him. Garrick had long since forgiven her for that, because he was completely unable to hold a grudge.

"On the next full moon, will I be one?" He finally asked the question he had been terrified of.

"Yes," she responded slowly after a brief sigh. She'd seen his scar one day and asked him about it. He'd come up with a weak excuse, but he had known it was completely unconvincing. Garrick just hadn't been ready to talk about it, and he was not sure what it meant. Because their relationship was already strained, if not completely shattered, she hadn't pressed for more information.

"We'll help you. All of us, we've been through it," Hayden empathized.

"Who?"

"Cailean, Brooke, Chase, and Aldric."

"I don't want anything to do with Cailean."

"I know he is rough around the edges. But on the inside, he's slightly less rough. I swear he grows on you. He can be a good guy, and he really cares about... his own."

"About werewolves."

"Yeah."

"I love you, Hayden, and I trust you. I don't trust them, but if you say they can help, I guess I don't have a choice." She took his hands and he turned to look at her.

"It's going to be okay," she comforted. "We'll help you."

"I'm going crazy," Garrick complained. "I can't listen to music; it's always too loud. I feel like I can literally hear your heart beating right now. I can smell everything, and I've never seen more clearly in my life. It feels like I should like it, but I can't handle it. It's driving me insane. I hear every conversation in the hallway; smell every kid that doesn't shower."

He kept rambling as she shifted her position. She wrapped both of her hands around one of his and raised it to her chest, pressing his palm over her heart. As he felt her heartbeat, the rest of the world began to fade away, leaving only that one steady sound. His rambling drew steadily to a close, and his breathing slowed down. Eventually, the sound of her heart faded away, and for the first time in weeks, there was silence.

"It's okay," she consoled. "The first week is always the hardest. It gets easier after the first change."

"I'm sorry," he apologized. "For the past two weeks."

"I'm sorry for everything. But it's in the past – no more secrets. I love you, Garrick."

"I love you too." He leaned his head against her chest. Without the strange new sensations of enhanced hearing, he was still able to hear her heart beat steadily. In that moment, that was the single most comforting sound to Garrick. He closed his eyes and drifted to sleep.

Present
21 Days until the Full Moon

"Okay, Cailean," Garrick began, "my mom gave me an update this morning, and it sounds like the search is really intensifying."

"That's good."

"How?"

"It's their last effort. Any leads will become cold soon, and this will be another unsolved runaway case. It's sad, but that's how this is going to work."

"Okay," Garrick muttered. Understandably, that was helpful to him, but he hated that it was 'good'.

"Don't worry, I still have a few tips for today."

"Right, and what would those be?"

"We've focused a lot on what you do, but what you say can be just as important."

"That seems like a given."

"So, I know you and Hayden were on a break, but I want to hear about this dinner date with the hunter."

"Can we please not do this?"

"Oh, I'm sorry. Should we avoid any topics which make you sad or uncomfortable? Do you not realize what they're going to ask you? They don't care about colors or the beach, Garrick. It's going to hurt."

"I'm sorry. You're right. Let's do it."

"Okay, so when was it?"

"The twentieth of last month. It was a Friday at 6:00 PM. She made pasta."

"That's the first issue. That was far too specific. Not only do you remember the exact day and time, but you started answering questions I didn't even ask. If you give too many details in a lie, you're just leaving yourself open to trip over it later – and you usually don't remember every intricate detail of a true story. Of course, you can't give too little detail, either. Just answer what I ask, and nothing extra."

"Right."

"So why were you with her when you should have been trying to work things out with Hayden?"

"I swear, it wasn't supposed to be anything but a friendly hang-out or whatever. She just took it to mean more than it was. That's why I invited Tyler, to cool the situation down a bit." Garrick felt like everything he'd learned over the past few days had fled his mind in that instant. When the topic actually became something he felt strongly about, he broke down and just tried to defend himself.

"Where to start? Well, saying things like 'I swear' implies guilt. You shouldn't have to constantly assert that you're telling the truth, and it's a way of avoiding a simple and direct answer. Even now, when I'm certain you were telling the truth, it screams to me that you feel guilty about it. Also, you gave me more information than I asked for again, and maybe even more than I knew, so that is simply sloppy. That just opens up more questions, and you don't want the conversation to last any longer than it has to."

"Yeah," Garrick admitted. "I guess I lost my cool a bit there."

"You did," Cailean agreed. "This is when it gets hard – especially for you - but your emotions have to take a back seat."

"So I just pretend I don't feel anything?"

"If that's what it takes," Cailean pondered. "But you don't want to be cold either."

Garrick wasn't convinced he would ever get questioned again, and the entire drill started to feel pointless, but he knew he couldn't give up on being prepared. Things could only get significantly worse if he wasn't ready. He had to be able to convince his mom of his innocence, or, as Cailean explained, far more people would pay the price.

"So, what happened to Chase?"

"I don't know," Garrick said, as calmly as he could.

"You aren't concerned about him?"

"Of course I am."

"Well, it looks like you were the last person he talked to. He said he was camping."

"He never showed up. I assumed his parents just didn't let him go, and we didn't get service out there."

"Has that ever happened before?"

"No. But I didn't have any reason to think he'd run away, so that was just where my mind went."

"Okay, just stop," Cailean groaned. "You sound like a sociopath."

"What?" Garrick asked.

"Your friend is missing. He has been for days. You're scared – you wonder if he's okay."

"You told me to act like I don't have emotions."

"Well, I take that back. This is not at all what I meant. Because that was legitimately terrifying. If you went in talking like that, they'd stop assuming that he ran away and start to assume you murdered him."

As soon as Cailean said that, the air in the room changed. There was an awkward silence that just lingered for a moment, and Garrick's shoulders dropped as his eyes fell to the floor. Cailean got caught up in the moment, and he must have forgotten what they were talking about, and the fact that that was actually what had happened.

"Not that you did."

"I get it," Garrick responded sadly.

"I'm sorry."

"Let's move on. Don't act like a sociopath, point taken."

"We're going to learn a few throws today. It is by far preferable that you don't get close enough to use them, but we must prepare for the worst," Aldric explained to the pack.

"Where did you acquire this array of knowledge?" Tyler inquired. Clearly feeling awkward about asking a question out of turn, he added, "I'm curious because it's apparent you have experience in martial arts, but I can't determine which one."

After the others had arrived, they'd all gathered in the basement for more instruction from their alpha. Aldric had been training Garrick since he became a wolf, but Garrick had never actually questioned where he learned everything that he knew. Since it had never come up in conversation, Garrick had just assumed it was knowledge passed down through the family – but Aldric's family wasn't something he talked much about either.

Garrick should have assumed that Aldric was using some form of martial art, but of course it was Tyler who would look into it. He had probably spent hours reading everything he could or watching old tapes as he tried to find anything similar to the techniques which Aldric used.

The rest of the pack looked around at each other, everyone wondering if any of the others knew – or had even thought to ask. Even Cailean shrugged when Garrick looked at him for an answer.

"Oh," Aldric paused. "I suppose that's never come up. I'm a seventh degree black belt in Tang Soo Do. I also have various degrees of black belts in Shotokan Karate, Judo, Jiu-Jitsu, Taekwondo, and I have experience boxing and kickboxing."

Not for the first time, Garrick pondered just how old Aldric actually was. While he didn't look older than thirty –

which was already impossible – it must have taken years to earn all those belts, and more training than one lifetime could accommodate. Then again, if he were as dedicated to his own learning as the pack was to Aldric's teachings, maybe it wouldn't have taken as long as Garrick assumed.

"From that, you're instructing us on pieces of each in order to adequately prepare for any situation," Tyler surmised.

"Indeed. I have, in a sense, crafted my own fighting style; one which I feel suits the needs of a werewolf."

"That is so awesome," Cailean enthused. Aldric smiled. Garrick knew that his interest wasn't to impress the pack, but any father would be overjoyed to see their son so proud of him.

"So, are we ready?" Aldric asked, pulling himself and the pack back to the task at hand.

"Yes, sir," Garrick quickly responded. The others nodded or verbalized their agreement.

"Okay, pair up," Aldric ordered. "As I mentioned, we're practicing throws today, so I want us to pair up differently. Tyler, you're with me. Brooke, you're with Cailean, and Garrick and Hayden."

Though confused, Garrick opted not to say anything. The last thing he wanted was to give the impression that he didn't want to work with Hayden – even if he didn't. There was a part of him, though, that wanted to express his concern with this idea.

"I want to give everyone experience throwing someone heavier than yourself," Aldric explained. "As for Garrick and Cailean, you two can trade off with Tyler throughout practice."

Although Garrick still wasn't ecstatic about the idea, he knew it was a wise decision. He and Cailean would just naturally weigh more than Brooke and Hayden, and Aldric's sheer muscle mass easily made him outweigh the teenagers.

After Aldric explained the technique and demonstrated a few throws on Cailean, Garrick stood next to Hayden on a mat. Exhaling slowly, he wondered if there was anything he should say to try to ease the tension. Instead, he just focused on training.

"Do you want to go first?" Garrick offered.

"I'd love to," she smiled. Garrick grabbed her wrist firmly, but she quickly turned and threw him over her shoulder, slamming him into the floor. With as much force as she packed into the throw, Garrick was positive he broke something as he landed. He stood up, giving his bones a second to heal.

"That was good," he encouraged, the pain evident in his voice.

"Yeah," she responded with a smile. He turned her around and grabbed her from the back, wrapping both of his arms tightly around her. She slammed her heel down on his foot, breaking his toe, then broke free of his grasp. Again, she threw him over her shoulder and onto the floor. He groaned as he got up, and she laughed at him.

"Is this funny to you?" he asked as he popped his shoulder back into place.

"Not necessarily funny. Cathartic," she smirked. He was happy to see her smiling, even if it was at his expense. If this was the therapy she needed, he was more than glad to take the pain. She grabbed his wrist. Though he was able to break free from the grasp, he hesitated with the throw. He didn't want to hurt her – and he'd get his practice with Aldric anyway.

Hayden took the opportunity presented by his brief pause. She dove forward and locked him in a tight embrace in an attempt to knock him down, but he kept his balance and broke out of her grab. As he broke free, her balance faltered, and she stumbled to the ground. Garrick reached down to help her up, and she pulled his arm, tugging him toward her. He fell toward her, landing on his knees, his face inches from hers.

They both breathed heavily, and he looked longingly into her eyes. He wanted more than anything in that moment to kiss her, but he knew that she wasn't ready for that. It was a hard moment to break – for both of them – but he could see in her eyes that she hadn't forgiven him yet. She let go of his arm and looked away, and he took that as a sign to get up.

"I don't know where he is," Garrick cried. His voice betrayed the pain that he felt, but he tried the best he could to maintain his composure. "I haven't talked to him since he left."

"When did you talk to him last?"

"He was supposed to go camping with us. He never showed up."

"To the best of my understanding, you all camped together a lot. Has he ever not shown up before?"

"No, this was the first time."

"And that didn't seem suspicious?"

"Not really. I just figured his parents changed their minds. It was a school night."

"I suppose."

"I'm sorry," Garrick added, tears welling up in his eyes. "I wish I knew more."

"If he didn't show up, Garrick, why does the last message that he ever sent say that he would?"

"I don't know," Garrick responded, his voice cracking.

"As a matter of fact, it looked like you two were talking about this for a long time."

"We had been."

"But when he didn't go, you weren't at all surprised?"

"I told you, I didn't think anything of it."

"I think you're hiding something from me."

"Why would I?" Garrick questioned, anger starting to take the place of pain in his voice. "Chase was one of my best friends, and he's gone. I don't know where he is. If there was anything, absolutely anything at all that I could do to help you find him, I would. All I want is to get my friend back! There's just nothing more I can tell you. I'm sorry."

A tear dropped from Garrick's eye, and he looked down, unable to maintain eye contact any longer. He closed his eyes, wiping away the tears. His interrogator's response was a single word.

"Was?" Cailean asked.

"Oh, come on!" Garrick groaned.

"It was pretty good," Cailean admitted. "But it wasn't perfect. And it needs to be."

"Yeah, I know."

"I'm serious, Garrick. You think that if I caught it, a cop wouldn't?"

"Honestly, I think you're harder to lie to than the entire justice system combined."

"Probably. But you have to practice harder than you play, right?"

"Okay. I'm going to go home. I'll practice in front of the mirror tonight, and I'll be back at one tomorrow."

"Sounds good," Cailean accepted. "Work on your word choice. You'll get there."

"I know," Garrick replied as he left. For some reason, knowing that he was becoming a good liar wasn't actually a comforting thought.

"Good job in there," Hayden complimented Garrick as he walked outside of Aldric's house. Without turning to look at him, she'd either recognized his footsteps or correctly assumed his identity. Hayden sat on the porch, leaning against the wooden post on the stair next to her. Garrick walked toward her and sat next to her on the stairs, placing a hand gently on her knee.

"Were you waiting for me?" he asked.

"I wanted to talk," she indirectly answered his question.

"Obviously," he laughed. "What's up?"

"You didn't kiss me in there," she started, sounding confused. Rather than once again pointing out the fact that he was well aware of the validity of the sentence, he just let her finish her thought. "I wanted you to. Why didn't you?"

"I've been trying to give you space. And I didn't want to do something that might push you away because it seemed like a good idea in the moment.

"It might have," she acknowledged with a quiet laugh. "I don't know if I am okay with what happened, Garrick. I would never kiss someone else. I couldn't."

"I know," he admitted.

"But I hate being without you."

"It's just…" Garrick started. He fumbled for words, but nothing came to mind. Honesty was the hardest thing he could imagine. He couldn't force himself to say what was on his mind, because he didn't want to make their situation worse. Nonetheless, he was always bad at bottling up his feelings, and he didn't want to start resenting her either. He couldn't pretend he was the only one who'd made mistakes.

"What?"

"I needed you there, Hayden. I needed you with me. I was alone, and you chose to support Aldric."

"I –"

"I know he's your alpha. I know that I wasn't right. You made the smart choice, and I'm terrified to think of what could have happened to you if you'd been with me."

"You think I don't think about it? What might have happened to us? Maybe the three of us would have been enough…"

"No. No, we still wouldn't have been ready," Garrick admitted, beginning to lose track of which side he was supporting. He thought she should have been there, but he was glad she hadn't been in danger.

"You can't know that."

"I do. I do, Hayden. We had never seen hunters before; I had no idea what to look for."

"Garrick," she forced herself to continue talking, although emotion was overwhelming her.

"I know it doesn't make what I did better," he admitted, "but you hurt me. You walked away when I needed you."

"If I had been with you, you wouldn't have fallen for her trap. Your plan would have worked," she finally explained. Garrick felt physically ill – as if all of the air had been ripped from his lungs. He hadn't thought about that. Technically, she wasn't wrong. It didn't by any means make everything that had happened her fault, but that was clearly what was weighing her down. She wasn't having trouble forgiving him, but rather herself.

"Hayden, don't for one-second start blaming yourself for this, do you hear me?"

"You just told me it was my fault," she laughed sadly.

"No. Our relationship had some difficulties. I messed up, but I think we both played a part in that. But what happened to Chase, you can't blame yourself. Anyway, Samantha was already suspicious because she'd seen me in the coffee shop so often. She would have found her chance to pounce. This had nothing to do with you."

She was silent for a moment, processing what he'd said. Garrick could tell that it resonated with her. It wasn't much, but it seemed to be exactly what she needed to hear. Then, her expression shifted, and she fell forward and started sobbing again.

"I'm so sorry," she cried. Garrick hadn't wanted to play the victim, and his intention wasn't to make her cry. It wasn't her fault he'd let things get out of hand, but he was so tired of acting as though he were the only one with any part in their struggles. Loyalty meant more to him than anything, and he acknowledged that he'd broken that loyalty, but so had she. "I don't ever want to hurt you again, Garrick. I want to be with you – by your side. You're the person I chose. I respect you, and I trust you. I'm so sorry I didn't show that. I'm sorry I trusted Aldric more."

"I know. Stand up," he instructed. She clearly didn't want to, but he stood and gently pulled at her arm until she stood with him. Although he attempted to look into her eyes, she diverted them. Somehow, she seemed to be ashamed, convinced she was the only person who'd messed up. He hadn't realized what was going through her head – or that she'd already started blaming herself. Hearing Garrick say he felt betrayed only gave more fuel to that fire.

"I messed up. I know I've said it one hundred times, but I really thought we were friends. Still, I wasn't clear enough. I pushed her away, Hayden, I swear that much to you. But I shouldn't have had to. I should have seen it. And I don't deserve it, but I want a second chance." Tears started to grow in his eyes too as he looked at her. She still refused to look up at him, and he was afraid he'd truly lost her.

"Oh yeah?" she sniffled quietly.

"I'm not really sure which part you're questioning, but yes," Garrick laughed.

"I'm sorry I hurt you."

"I had no idea this has all been on your mind for so long, Hayden. I thought you were just mad at me, so I tried giving you space. I should have been there to help you work through this."

"I guess we're kinda even on that front," she tried to smile, but was still overridden with guilt and sadness.

"Look at me," Garrick commanded. She refused to look up, so he placed a hand on her chin and gently lifted her head. When she saw his eyes, he smiled at her, and even through the tears, she managed to smile back.

"We're going to get through this. We're going to get through everything. But from now on, we have to do it together. No matter what."

"I like that," she responded. Garrick stepped back, holding her hands and admiring her in the dim light from the porch. Clearly embarrassed at the attention, Hayden smiled and looked down.

"If you would allow it," Garrick began. "I would like to take you out for a milkshake."

"Milkshakes?" she asked. Their first date had been going out and getting milkshakes at a local diner. It was the first date Garrick had ever been on, and he hadn't really known what to suggest, so he went with the thing he'd seen in the most movies. That cliché date had become the best night of his life.

"Well of course. They're a dessert similar to ice cream, but blended into a delicious drinkable form. It really is quite ingenious."

"Well that sounds delightful. It would be my pleasure to accompany you to this shaking of milk," she laughed. Her eyes began to light up, and the sorrow drained away.

"The pleasure is all mine," Garrick told her, bringing her hand to his lips and kissing the back of it. She smiled and made an exaggerated gesture, bending one knee and waving her other hand at him. Even in her sweat pants and damp navy blue T-shirt, she looked adorable.

"So it's a date. I'll pick you up tomorrow at 4?"

"I'll make you wait until five," she laughed.

"At least your brother won't be there this time. That was intimidating."

"You could probably take him. Somehow I feel like you have an unfair advantage."

Garrick laughed, glad to see her smiling and joking with him again. Standing on the porch and holding her hands, he wanted nothing more than to kiss her. Garrick leaned forward, and she met him halfway. As she closed her eyes, Garrick kissed her gently on the forehead. Regardless of how much he wanted it, Garrick decided to save that magical moment for the recreation of their first date.

Chapter 19

Thirteen months ago

Confident he wouldn't have been able to handle a full day of mind-numbing classes, Garrick was grateful the full moon fell on a Saturday. That allowed him to sit on his bed all day and just anticipate the night to come.

Over the past week, Hayden and Chase had repeatedly assured him things would get easier after his first change. If they were wrong, he was sure he'd lose his mind. Garrick couldn't handle the sensory overload that came with his new curse.

When night finally came, Garrick met the pack at the edge of the woods. He followed Aldric through the tree line as they hiked to some dark, secluded location where Aldric assured them they wouldn't find campers. Most of the pack stripped, preparing. Knowing Garrick would be uncomfortable, Hayden pulled him to the side and took him somewhere near the others, but not within their line of sight.

"Thanks," he sighed.

"Of course," she smiled. Hayden took her shirt off and placed it in her bag, and Garrick stared at her, mesmerized. A realization pulled his attention away from her, though. They were supposed to bring bags. Even with the frequent reminders the others had given him, Garrick had forgotten his bag at home. Concerned this was an important piece of information, he started to panic.

"Garrick," Hayden comforted, placing her hands on his shoulders. Sensing his very apparent discomfort, she gazed into his eyes. "Calm down." For the first time since he had met her, that didn't work at all.

"I don't think that's going to help," he groaned. His face still facing hers, Garrick glanced at her bag in order to explain the dilemma. She just laughed and turned around.

"Just put your clothes in here," she offered, lifting her bag and waving it through the air. Then she set it back on the ground and took off her shorts, placing them in the bag too. Hesitant, Garrick stood, trying not to appear to be staring at her, but failing miserably. Regardless of how many times he'd seen it, her body still took his breath away. Yet, no matter how many times she'd seen his, he was embarrassed by it. Patient, she just looked back at him.

"Want me to pose?" she joked. Garrick looked down, ashamed that his shameless staring had been detected. With a sigh, he removed his clothes and placed them in the bag as well. Garrick wondered if his internal body temperature skyrocketed near the change, because the freezing air outside had little impact on him.

Trying not to return his gaze to Hayden, Garrick watched as the moon climbed into the sky. Hayden screamed in pain and fell to the ground. Her screams filled him with pain, and he wanted to help in any way he could, but there was nothing he could do. Garrick just watched as she became the wolf he'd seen a month before.

Garrick took a few steps back, but then he himself pitched forward and dropped to the ground. He had never felt such excruciating pain in his life. Agony tore through his body as each bone individually broke, and he felt as though every pain receptor fired as his body changed shape. Within a few seconds, he was unconscious.

Garrick woke up lying on the ground. Unable to remember where he was, he looked around the area, surprised to see trees. As he stirred more, leaving his half-asleep state, he started to remember why he was there. He couldn't recall a single event from the night after Hayden had pulled him away from the others, though. The night had passed as quickly as a sound sleep.

Hayden walked up to him, holding his clothes in her hands. She handed them to him and he groaned as he stood to put them on. He had expected more aching in his muscles, but he didn't actually feel any fatigue whatsoever. Before he could ask Hayden if that was normal, she wrapped her arms around him and kissed him.

"How are you feeling?" she asked.

"I'm okay," he acknowledged, surprised by how amazing he felt. The incessant ringing in his ears which had been there the previous day had vanished. His sense of smell wasn't bombarded with individual components of his surroundings, and his sight had stabilized, so the sunlight all around him wasn't as blinding.

"I can still hear too well," he complained. Garrick wondered if he was the first person to ever experience that problem. If not, it was definitely a rare issue.

"Well," she hesitated. "That is always going to happen. Our senses get better closer to the full moon. It's never going to be as bad as it was before, though."

"Yeah," Garrick accepted. After thinking for a moment, he added, "I think I could actually learn to like this." It was just enough enhancement without the terrible side effects. He could hear Hayden's heart beating if he focused all of his effort on it, but as soon as he stopped trying, it faded away.

"I hope so," she consoled with a sad smile. Hayden's eyes were still downcast and filled with guilt.

"Hey," he told her, holding her face gently in his hands. "This isn't your fault. I remember what happened. You saved me."

"I know," she admitted. "But I wish I had just told you. If I hadn't hidden anything from you, you wouldn't have been out here."

"And I should have trusted you," he responded. "I'm sorry."

"Don't try to turn this around, Garrick Elliott."

"Alright, then how about we compromise. We were both horrible people, and from now on, we don't lie to each other or hide things ever again. And, in return, we both trust each other completely."

"Sounds easy enough," she laughed. He was happy that he brought the smile back to her face. She kissed him and took his hand, pulling him away as she said, "Come on, we should find the others."

Present
20 Days Until the Full Moon

Garrick sat on the couch, his feet up on the coffee table as he thumbed through yet another book. He wasn't fully invested, though, because his conversations with Aldric had convinced him that he was fighting a futile battle. Still, he skimmed through the book, looking for any mention of controlling the wolf. A knock on the door resounded thunderously throughout the house, and Garrick jumped to his feet. His mom had worked a late shift, so he was trying to keep the noise to a minimum. The person at the door clearly had no regard for that wish.

As he opened the door, his heart nearly exploded. Even with all his preparation, he couldn't have possibly been ready for the two uniformed police officers standing on his doorstep. Garrick tried to play off his panic as confusion mixed with a bit of annoyance.

"Hello officers," he whispered. "Are you looking for my mom?"

"No, actually," one of them answered, not matching Garrick's volume level. He had already known that much, but it was best to ask. Though his main goal was to throw off suspicion, it also gave him a moment to hope he was wrong about their intention. "We're here for you."

"Okay," Garrick responded, confusion clear both on his face and in his voice as he elongated the word. "How can I help you?"

"We'd like to ask you a few questions."

"My Mom is sleeping right now, can we step outside?"

"I think this conversation would be better to have at the station."

"I'm sorry," Garrick hesitated. "Have I done something wrong?"

"I'm not sure yet."

Garrick's mom opened her bedroom door and walked toward them, yawning and stretching. When she saw the officers, her demeanor changed completely as she walked up to Garrick and nudged him out of the way. Glaring at the officers, she stood between them and her son.

"Is there a problem officers?"

"No, Detective," the other policeman answered. "We just have a few questions for your son."

"I handled that."

"With all due respect, I'm not sure you're the best for the job. There's a reason we don't interrogate family."

"This isn't an interrogation," she snapped. "He's not a suspect of anything. And there are no grounds for arrest."

"I apologize. You're right. We just have a few questions, and we would like to ask them in a… different environment."

"My son told me what he knows. This is my case, and I want him out of it."

"Actually, Detective Elliott, it isn't. In light of the discovered text messages, the chief decided that you had a conflict of interest." Garrick was surprised to hear that. Those were found days ago – why would they only be bringing it up then? Unless the investigation was taking a turn for the worse.

"You're off the case, and Detective Langston would like to speak with Garrick back at the station."

"Is my son under arrest?"

"No."

"Then I'm going to have to ask you to leave my property, and leave my son alone."

The pieces were falling together in Garrick's mind. She'd been protecting him the whole time. She hadn't shared the fact that she'd found the messages, but somehow someone else got ahold of them. Not only would it look bad for him to resist their questions, he knew it would bring his mother into question as well.

"Mom," Garrick spoke up, putting a hand on her shoulder. "It's okay. I have nothing to hide, and if I can say anything that can help them, I need to do that. I'll follow you guys to the station."

"It's probably better if you ride with us," one of the officers suggested. "So you can leave the car for your mom to come get you."

"You want me to ride in the back of a police car, and yet you're telling me that I'm not under arrest?"

"You're free to do as you like, sir. It was just a suggestion," the officer responded sarcastically.

"Garrick, you don't have to do this," his mom advised him.

"I know, Mom. It's just a few questions."

"Well, then I'll take you myself. I have someone I'd like to speak to at the station anyway." She glared at the officers again as she spoke, and they walked away silently to their car. She looked down at her son and sighed before walking with him to the car. The whole ride, Garrick focused on remembering Cailean's first rule: control your breathing.

"Alright, so first I will ask a few questions to establish a baseline," an officer explained to Garrick. They'd hooked Garrick up to a polygraph. Nothing Cailean had practiced with him had prepared him for that, but he hoped he'd be able to improvise. If he could convince himself he was telling the truth, he could control his heart rate. He'd stayed calm with Cailean, why wouldn't he be able to now?

"What is your name?"

"Garrick Elliott."

"How old are you?"

"Eighteen."

"Great. So when was the last time you talked to Chase?"

"The day he ran away."

"And did he talk about running away?"

"Oddly enough, he didn't mention it," Garrick responded. He could feel his heart rate already increasing, so he decided to feign annoyance as an explanation as he tried to calm himself down.

"Are you aware you were the last person to communicate with him before his disappearance?"

"No."

"You didn't know he texted you?"

"I knew he texted me. That wasn't your question."

"I see. Do you know where he would have gone?"

"No," Garrick groaned. After he'd settled down from the initial fear of the entire process, he didn't have too much difficulty keeping his pulse steady. For the most part, nothing he was saying was inherently a lie, so he didn't have too much difficulty convincing himself it was the truth. They were going down the wrong path, asking the wrong questions, so they weren't likely to get to anything incriminating.

"Do you think there's a possibility this wasn't by choice?"

"What?" Garrick asked, a bit of fear seeping into his voice. By the sound of the machine, it seemed to register a faster heart rate, and that scared him more. He could feel himself losing control, which only served to concern him more.

"It doesn't sound like he'd want to run away. And nothing in your messages mention it. Was there anyone who didn't like Chase?"

"No," Garrick snapped. He was in equal parts concerned that the questioning was changing direction and angry that someone would insinuate that Chase had enemies. "No one. Ever."

"Garrick, I need you to calm down."

"How? I'm sorry, but you're asking me questions that make me think that you don't think you'll find him. Chase is one of my best friends, and it sounds like you've given up! The fact that you brought me here and strapped me into this thing proves to me that you're desperate, and now you're asking me if he had any enemies!"

Garrick felt tears forming in his eyes. They weren't entirely faked, but they added a nice touch to his performance.

"I'm sorry, son," he consoled. "We just have to explore all possibilities."

Garrick refused to look the officer in the eye as he spoke, but a tear fell from his eye onto his lap. He felt the officer gently place his hands on Garrick's shoulder.

"Hey, buddy. Look at me," he comforted. Garrick sighed deeply, forcing himself to turn toward the officer. "He's going to be fine, alright? We'll find him."

"What if you don't?" Garrick asked.

"I can assure you, he's okay. He's seventeen years old, and he ran away from home. He's probably just trying to start life as an adult a bit early. You're bound to hear from him in no time."

Garrick didn't respond. He knew police officers were trained not to give guarantees like that, but he didn't intend to bring that up. Instead, he just followed the officer to the waiting room, but his mother was nowhere to be seen.

"That was unprofessional," he heard her arguing from the other side of the building. "You sent officers to my home to interrogate my son. Never go over my head like that again, do you understand?"

"Yes, of course," another voice responded. Garrick didn't recognize the voice, so he didn't know if it was the chief or the other detective. "I'm sorry, it won't happen again."

Garrick sat and waited for another twenty minutes. He checked his pockets for his phone, but realized he'd left it at home. When his mom finally stormed into the waiting room, he eagerly jumped up and followed her to the car.

"I'm sorry about that, Garrick," she apologized after she'd had a chance to cool down.

"As I said, Mom," Garrick replied. "Anything I can do to help."

Garrick knew it was risky, but he had to ask his mom about the case. He would have been curious if he didn't already know what had happened, and he had to get an idea of just how much the police knew.

"Mom, do they suspect foul play?"

"No," she replied, stopping mid-step to look at him. "Should they?"

"I hope not. Some of the questions they were asking me had me scared. They were asking if Chase had any enemies. It sounds like they think someone hurt him."

"No," she declared adamantly.

"You'd tell me, right?" Garrick pushed. "You can't protect me from everything, Mom."

"I know, Garrick. They were looking at it as a possibility, but there's no evidence. Detective Langston wanted to look into every option, because we're running out of time."

"What do you mean?" Garrick asked.

"Garrick, he's been gone for over a week now. That's given him time to get pretty much anywhere. If he doesn't want us to find him, we probably won't be able to. We're running out of time for this to be considered an active case. If they had reason to suspect foul play, the chief would allot more time, so Langston pushed that. That's what I was talking with them about."

"So they're just going to give up?" Garrick asked. His mom didn't give him an answer for a while. She just looked around, as if she'd find a better response in the air around her.

"Yeah," she said weakly. "Unless you honestly believe that he's hurt, we have to assume that he just doesn't want to be found. Do you think he could be hurt, Garrick?"

He knew his mom. She wasn't asking directly – she was just asking him if he wanted her to say whatever she had to in order to keep the case open. She had already lied for him, and she would do it again.

"No," Garrick sighed. "No one would hurt Chase."

"I know. But that means he's just too far. Unless he chooses to come back, the police are stuck. We just have to hope he's somewhere where he's happier than he was here."

"I know he is."

They continued to the car in silence, but when Garrick sat in the passenger, he noticed the time on the display on the dashboard. Somehow he'd been at the police station for four hours, and it was already five o'clock.

"Mom, I don't assume you brought my phone?" Garrick asked frantically. He was already on thin ice with Hayden; he didn't want to add missing a date to the list of problems.

"I did not," she replied inquisitively.

"Okay, quick question. Do you think it's better if I rush to Hayden's house and apologize or get her flowers and wear something nicer than this?"

"You had a date?"

"An hour ago."

"The flowers. Definitely the flowers. I'll drop you off. You change, I'll get flowers."

"She likes lilies."

"Really?"

"Yeah. Everyone likes lilies. Thanks Mom. I'll just run home from here, because the flower shop is out of the way."

"Garrick, I don't know how much time that will save. Anyway, I don't know if a mile run is a good idea."

"I run every day Mom. A mile won't break a sweat," he assured her. "Really, thank you. I love you. I'll see you at home."

Garrick got out of the car before she could protest and started running. As soon as he knew he was out of sight, he broke into a sprint, taking every back street and shortcut he could think of. If the path were straight, it wouldn't have taken more than two minutes to get home, but he had to navigate through alleys and around buildings. Finally, he approached his street, but he was nearing it from the back, so he'd have to run around the street. Deciding he didn't have time, Garrick jumped over the eight-foot brick wall that surrounded his neighbor's back yard, rolling as he landed. A bulldog rushed at him, barking and snarling.

"Nice dog," he whispered softly. The dog kept growling, so Garrick growled back. The beast cowered and backed away. "Whatever works," he muttered. He ran and took a step up the wall, reaching up to grab the top. Garrick planted his feet on the wall and drove one down, launching himself over the wall and landing in his own yard. Reminding himself not to run too fast into the back door, he slowed himself as he approached it and carefully unlocked it.

By the time he'd changed and applied some extra cologne, his mom was pulling up. Quickly, he grabbed his phone and met her outside, accepting the flowers as she handed them to him.

"Thanks, Mom," he waved as he took off jogging toward Hayden's house.

"Garrick," she stopped after a few steps.

"What?" he asked, hiding his annoyance. He checked his phone to see three missed calls. All he wanted was to get there, explain everything, and grovel for another chance.

"Take the car."

"Right. Thanks Mom," he responded, catching the keys she tossed to him. He kissed her cheek and got in the car, then sped toward Hayden's house. When he pulled up, he parked the car out front and walked up to her door.

Garrick knocked, then hid the flowers behind his back. When she opened the door, Hayden's expression betrayed a mixture of anger and disappointment, and he never wanted to see her look like that again.

"Would it help if I told you I was in jail?"

"No," she answered. "I don't think it would."

"What if I said I was sorry?"

"A little."

"And if I gave you lilies, because I know they're your favorite? Or if I told you that you are the most beautiful sight I've ever had the honor to see? And your dress brings out the natural light in your eyes? Or that your flawless skin is glowing with perfection"

"That might help," she muttered, looking down. "You should do all of those things."

"I brought you lilies." He handed her the flowers.

"Thank you."

"And Hayden," he started. "You're the most beautiful sight…"

"Stop," she laughed.

"If I ever stop complimenting you, it will be too soon, because I won't have described your beauty." He took her hand and stepped closer, looking her in the eyes, "Would you still like to have a milkshake with me?"

"I would like that very much. Ice cream is great for when you get stood up."

Garrick was about to say something to defend himself, but she put a finger to his lips and leaned close.

"I've missed you," she whispered.

Chapter 20

Twelve months ago

Garrick sat on his bed with Hayden leaning her head on his shoulder – his arm wrapped around her as he listened to her breathing. With the first change over, things felt more bearable. It hadn't been as agonizing as he'd been preparing himself for. Of course it was painful, but Hayden had held his hand until she didn't have a hand to hold anymore. After that, Garrick had just tried not to fight the transformation, despite his instinct to try to remain human.

Hayden looked up at him, blinking as her eyes adjusted to the brightness of the light shining from the ceiling. He smiled back at her. Garrick had no perception of time, so he wasn't sure how long they'd been lying there, but her face told him she'd fallen asleep on him. She straightened up, rubbing her eyes and stretching.

As she settled back down, he leaned forward and kissed her. She smiled as he pulled away. This was the first time he'd seen her wake up in a while, because she had decided not to spend a night at his house for the past month. Typically, since Garrick's mom worked most nights, she would stay with him. Garrick assumed that she had decided against it due to his first change. Given that enough time had passed since then, she had finally decided to spend the night at his house. Garrick had felt a bit like she was avoiding him, but he couldn't blame her. He himself was afraid of who he'd become over the past month, with his strength growing faster than he could become accustomed to it and his senses in overdrive. He could easily have hurt someone on accident, and he wouldn't have wanted to be around someone so volatile either.

She pulled him out of his mind with another kiss, but then she quickly retreated and shook her head. Gently, he turned her face back toward his and gazed into her eyes, leaning in for another kiss.

"Wait, Garrick," she stopped him, pushing herself away a bit.

"What is it?"

"We can't do this." Garrick had no idea where that was coming from.

"I... Yeah, okay," he sighed, resigned. There wasn't much more he could say, so he just pulled his arm back and sat further from her. They hadn't slept together since well before he'd been scratched, and he didn't know what the problem was, but it was growing increasingly difficult for him. "Sorry. I didn't mean to pressure you."

"No," she defended. "It isn't that, really."

Garrick bit back any form of response. He couldn't pretend he wasn't frustrated, and the fact that she'd been ignoring any advance without talking to him about the problem was tiring. Still, he was concerned he'd sound annoyed if he tried to reply.

"Look, I have to tell you something."

Suddenly, fear-filled every aspect of his mind. What could she possibly have been hiding? Nothing had happened with Cailean, he had to believe that. Regardless of how much he thought he trusted her, he could still feel himself begin to panic as his heart rate soared.

"Calm down," she consoled softly. The only possible explanation he could think of was that she was about to break up with him.

"Have you ever heard the expression 'wolves mate for life'?" she asked.

"Yeah," he responded cautiously, still unsure of where the conversation was going.

"Well, it's true for us. I can't explain it, but when a werewolf sleeps with someone, they literally give that person their love. You can only love one person in your life, and you choose who it is."

"What?" he wondered aloud. The strange part was that what she was saying made sense to him. A piece of him felt that it was the truth.

"I just want you to think about it before you make a decision like that."

He was dumbstruck, but he continued to stare at her.

"Hayden," he laughed, finally finding his ability to speak. "I love you."

"But if we do this, you'll never be able to love anyone else."

Garrick smiled, pushing a strand of hair behind her ear and gazing into her eyes.

"I never could." Hayden searched Garrick's eyes, looking for any sign of doubt in his statement. He knew she wouldn't find any. When she was satisfied, she wrapped her arms around him and pulled him closer.

Present
17 Days Until the Full Moon

Standing in his front yard, Garrick tossed a ball to Tyler. Having not heard from the police for the past few days, he'd decided he could spend the afternoon catching up with his best friend rather than working with Cailean to hone his lying skills.

"Remember that time we tried to go ice skating?" Tyler asked randomly, returning the ball to Garrick. "We assumed we'd just figure it out naturally, so we stood on the ice in rented skates and failed to balance."

"That's not how I remember it," Garrick laughed as they continued to toss the ball back and forth. "You picked it up like it was second nature, skating off and flirting with all of the girls. When you saw me sliding around like a toddler, you left and held my hand until you led me to more secure ground." It had only been a few years ago, but that night seemed like a past life to Garrick. Nostalgic, he thought of all the nights he'd spent with his friend killing time without a care in the world. After the scratch, though, everything seemed to spiral away.

Recently, any time they spent together seemed to be geared toward lycanthropy. Whether they were researching a cure or learning about werewolves with the rest of the pack, their conversations rarely deviated from the topic. Even if it was an embarrassing memory, Garrick was overjoyed to be able to reminisce with his friend again.

It made sense, that they spent so much time talking about werewolves. Usually they talked about Garrick's dreams to leave town and do something bigger, but since he'd been scratched it felt like there was a part of him that called that town his home, and his impulses to flee had been quelled. Their conversations had always centered around Garrick – not because Garrick was self-centered, at least he hoped not, but because Tyler didn't spend much time talking about his personal life. When he was away from home, he wanted to leave it behind. It had taken five years of friendship for Garrick to even find out that the man married to Tyler's mother was not his birth father, and he still didn't know what had happened to him. He just never pressed his friend for information like that. If he wanted to share, he would.

Tossing the ball back, Garrick considered asking his friend about that situation – and why he didn't seem to get along with Hank. He bit his tongue, though, because Tyler had never responded well to questioning before.

"I was working my way to that part," Tyler smiled, throwing the ball high into the air and watching as Garrick jumped to catch it with one hand. "I used to be the dexterous and athletic one. You were like a little brother fumbling around. When did you grow into someone I admire so much?"

Garrick wasn't sure where any of that conversation was coming from, so he just silently blushed. Throwing the ball he responded, "Maybe I'm just becoming more like you. You've always inspired me, you know. Hey, remember the time we tried to play catch on our bikes."

"You couldn't ride with no handlebars," Tyler laughed, "but you insisted on trying."

"Yeah, the ball hit me in the face and I fell off," Garrick recalled, throwing the ball under his leg in his best attempt at a trick shot. Tyler caught it with a smirk, returning it with a flourish.

Garrick caught the ball and turned to the side, stopping himself before he threw it to the empty air. His hand fell to the side as Tyler's expression betrayed a sense of loss. The two allowed the moment to linger, the silence settling in.

"I'm not mad at you," Tyler finally announced, avoiding addressing what had happened.

"I know," Garrick responded.

"No you don't, Garrick Elliott. I've known you twelve years, I discern the expressions on your face – and I know when you're hiding something. You're perceiving my mood as being upset, and you blame yourself for getting me involved in this world."

Garrick sighed, looking to his friend. "You don't?"

"My only grievance is that I wish you'd told me earlier. I understand why you didn't feel able to, but it's incredible to learn about all of this. For the first time, it feels as though I'm a part of something larger, you know?"

"I just wish I hadn't put you in danger."

"You guys are worth the danger."

"Are you alright, Tyler?" Garrick asked, reading his friend's tone. He'd been melancholy since he'd arrived at Garrick's house, but Garrick had assumed he wouldn't want to talk about it. Still, he at least wanted to offer – to make sure his friend knew he'd be there for him.

"It's just… You know things aren't great at home. I just had to make sure you know how thankful I am to finally feel like I have a family." Tears welled up in Tyler's eyes, but he tried in vain not to let it show.

"You've always had a family. I always have been, and always will be, your brother, Tyler. Where is this coming from?"

"It's nothing," Tyler shrugged, taking a deep breath. "Hank and I just had another disagreement. It just made me realize the difference you make, and I wanted to be sure you knew that."

Garrick wrapped his arm around Tyler's shoulder and pulled his friend in for a hug. He waited almost a full minute before saying, "You're weird, man."

"Yeah," Tyler laughed. "I guess that's why I'm stuck being your friend."

Garrick waited outside Hayden's house for her to change into her training clothes. Tyler had gone straight to Aldric's after telling Garrick he wanted to 'give the lovebirds some alone time.' Garrick wouldn't tell him, but he was appreciative of that idea. He and Hayden had just worked through their issues, and he was excited to be able to talk to her on the walk.

Hayden opened the door and walked outside. Though he hadn't knocked, she was clearly unsurprised to see him; he wondered if she had heard him or if she just knew him that well. Hayden wrapped him in an embrace, and he kissed her cheek gently before pulling away. Staring at her in awe, Garrick couldn't help but think about how thankful he was to have her, and how close he'd come to losing her.

"We're going to be late," he finally spoke up, breaking his own trance. She nodded and released him from her hug, wrapping her arm around his as they started walking.

"What do you think we're doing today?" Hayden inquired.

Aldric's training was practically all-inclusive. So far they'd already gone over multiple types of martial arts, and learned how to disarm enemies. They had even run miles through the forest so they were used to free running with obstacles in the way, just in case they were ever pursued

"I have absolutely no idea," Garrick responded. What else was there to learn? In his mind, the only possibility was more practice, which would definitely help.

The two walked in silence for a few more minutes, just enjoying each other's presence. Garrick had thought he'd be talking non-stop, catching her up on every thought he'd had over the past few weeks, but he was perfectly content to just walk with her. When they reached Aldric's house, there was a note on the door.

I need all of you to report to the woods. Today will be the final day of new training. After today, I will have taught you everything you need to know, and it will just be a matter of honing those skills. For now, it's time for you to take the final.

"Well," Garrick groaned as he finished reading. "That's ominous."

"Yeah. That's just the way Aldric talks, though. Right?"

"I assume he means the same place we usually go," he guessed. She shrugged, so they both just started walking. In only a few more minutes, they were at the tree line. Garrick had never thought about it, but he realized Aldric had probably carefully selected his home specifically because it was so close to the woods. The two of them walked deep into the woods, navigating to the clearing where they normally changed. Garrick pulled himself loose from Hayden's arm and put a hand in front of her, keeping her behind him. With everything Aldric had taught them in the past few weeks, he was fully prepared for an ambush.

The leaves on the nearby tree began rustling, and Garrick froze, turning his attention toward the sound. Hayden noticed his hesitation and stopped next to him, scanning the area.

Cailean and Brooke found their way through foliage, pushing branches of trees aside as they stepped into the clearing. As they approached, both Garrick and Hayden exhaled deeply as they relaxed.

"What's going on?" Cailean inquired. "My father said we had a test out here."

"Yeah," Hayden replied. "We saw the note too."

"Have you two seen him?" Brooke asked. They both shook their heads. As if on cue, Aldric shambled into the clearing on the other side of them. Breathing deeply, he stood tall as he looked at the pack. Garrick noticed an arrow protruding from his bicep.

"Father!" Cailean yelled, running to Aldric's side. Aldric held up a hand, and Cailean stopped in his tracks.

"Run," Aldric told them. "They're here."

For some reason, that seemed like news to Garrick, although he could see that Aldric had been through a fight. His breath caught in his throat as he looked around, as if they would have simply revealed themselves. Garrick stumbled backward, frozen in fear.

"Go," Aldric ordered. He snapped the arrow in half, then pulled it out from the other side, grunting with pain as he did. His attention shifted to Cailean, probably because he knew his son would be the most difficult person to convince. "I'll be fine. Get Brooke and the others out of here."

Cailean nodded, picking up speed as he backed away and turned toward Brooke. Paralyzed, Garrick just watched Aldric. He felt Hayden grab his shoulder, trying to pull him away. What finally snapped him to reality, though, was the distinctive sound of an arrow rushing through the air. Instinctively, he turned, wrapping his arms around Hayden and spinning her out of the way as the arrow dug itself into his shoulder.

He pitched forward, knocking Hayden to the ground with him. Another arrow shot over their heads. Fighting through the pain, Garrick struggled to his knees and moved away from Hayden. Clenching his teeth, Garrick pulled the arrow from his body.

As he tried to find the attacker, Garrick realized that Aldric had vanished. Hayden grabbed his hand and pulled him to his feet. Dizzily, Garrick followed after her, feeling his shoulder heal as they ran. It wasn't quite fast enough, though, because he was still struggling to move as they escaped the clearing.

A man wielding a silver blade stepped in front of them. Garrick couldn't react before he stabbed Hayden, but he was able to catch the hunter off guard with a punch to the face. The hunter stumbled backward, so Garrick turned to Hayden.

"This is going to hurt," Garrick warned, grabbing the handle of the blade and pulling it out of Hayden's stomach. She fell to the ground in pain, so Garrick turned to face the hunter, standing between the two of them. He tried to use the hunter's weapon against him, slashing violently as the hunter easily backed up to dodge. In his flurry of attacks, Garrick didn't recognize the sound of another arrow as it flew toward him, piercing his back.

The hunter in front of him pulled a gun, shooting three bullets at Garrick. Two hit his chest and the third his shoulder. He dropped to his knees, helplessly scrambling to pull the arrow out of his body.

The hunter was about to shoot again, but Aldric came out from behind him and snapped his neck. Another arrow shot out and pierced Aldric's arm. He ran toward the archer, disappearing from Garrick's view once again.

"Garrick," Hayden called, panicked. There was still blood pouring from her wound, but she was able to crawl to Garrick and muster up the strength to dislodge the arrow. He could feel the agony from the bullet wounds, but he knew that he'd heal soon. Garrick tried to stay upright long enough for that to happen, but he collapsed. Due to blood loss, Garrick's brain lost its ability to process thought. He saw someone running at them through the trees, but wasn't able to recognize the person as Tyler until he knelt right next to Garrick.

"What happened?" he asked Hayden.

"They ambushed us," she explained.

"What happened to Garrick?"

"Bullets."

"Exit wounds?"

"I couldn't check."

Tyler pulled up the back of Garrick's shirt. Garrick could barely feel anything, but he noticed himself being turned over. Garrick saw a glint of metal then suddenly felt a rush of agony as Tyler drove the blade into his chest.

Another arrow shot from near them, and Hayden ducked to avoid it. She stood shakily and disappeared into the trees. Tyler moved the blade around in Garrick's open wound, working a bullet out of Garrick's chest, and then proceeded to remove the other. Garrick assumed the bullet had gone completely through his shoulder, because he could already feel that starting to heal. Tyler took his shirt off and wrapped it around Garrick's chest in an attempt to stop the flow of blood.

As Hayden came back, Garrick could see that she had a new wound where an arrow had pierced her leg. Barely struggling to stand, Hayden helped Tyler pull Garrick to his feet, and they supported him as they walked through the forest. Tyler held out his knife as if it would offer any real protection if the hunters found them. His lack of fighting skill and the burden of another person would keep Tyler from doing any damage, but he looked intimidating.

When they broke the tree line and saw a road, Tyler pointed them in the direction of his car. Tyler and Hayden laid Garrick down in the back seat before jumping in the car themselves. Tyler started the vehicle as Hayden climbed into the back seat with Garrick. His head was in her lap and he tried to focus on her face as she whispered encouraging thoughts to him.

She had her hands pressed as hard as she could against his chest. The pain was excruciating, but he knew she had to stop the bleeding. He faded in and out of consciousness more than once during the short drive to Aldric's house. Tyler and Hayden helped Garrick to the door, where the note was no longer hanging. Cailean's mom greeted them, a frantic look on her face

"Hayden, go get some towels," she commanded as she took her place helping Garrick walk. She was clearly expecting them, but Garrick's condition was a surprise. Maybe that meant the others had already made it back safely.

Hayden came back with some towels, and she laid them on the floor. Tyler and Linda helped Garrick lie down on them, and he could feel Tyler using all of his strength pressing another towel against his chest. After another few minutes, the bleeding finally stopped. He could feel his mind start coming back to him, and his double vision started to stabilize. The wounds probably still looked horrible, but they were healing, and his body was quickly producing blood to replace the amount he'd lost.

"Hayden," he finally managed to choke out as a hoarse whisper.

"I'm okay," she replied, clearly anticipating his question.

"Cailean?" he inquired.

"He's here," Linda offered. "Along with Brooke."

There was a worried tone in her voice. That meant Aldric wasn't home yet. Garrick tried to sit up, telling himself he was going to go find him, but the pain was too intense. He just let himself fall back down to give the wounds more time to heal.

The handle on the front door began to shake, so Linda and Tyler rushed toward the door. Hayden stayed with him, holding his hand, but she turned her head with concern. Garrick managed to sit up, dropping the blood-soaked towel from his chest.

"How are you?" he managed. Words came easier to him, but it still hurt to speak. Aware she wouldn't give him an answer, he examined her to see a wound which appeared to still be bleeding on her leg. Lifting her shirt, he saw that the knife wound hadn't begun to close yet. Garrick reached to his side to grab a new towel and gently laid Hayden down. Though she was hesitant, she was clearly too tired to fight.

"I love you," he told her as he pressed the towel against her stomach with as much force as he could muster – which wasn't much.

"I love you too," she responded. She was even weaker than he was because she hadn't quite started healing yet. Though she struggled to stay awake, Hayden drifted off as Garrick continued to hold the towel against her wound. He watched as the first of the cuts on her arms began to mend itself. When he checked her stomach, it appeared that the blood had clotted, at least stopping the bleeding, so Garrick struggled to his feet and walked to the living room.

"Aldric," he greeted, relieved when he saw the man standing just past the entryway.

"Is everyone okay?" Aldric asked.

"Hayden was hurt pretty badly. She was busy taking care of me. She's fine now," he replied, able to formulate the sentences without too much difficulty. Looking around the room, he couldn't notice any severe wounds on the others.

"What were you all doing in the woods?" Aldric inquired angrily.

"What? You left us a note on the door," Cailean replied.

"No," Aldric muttered. Garrick could practically see Aldric's mind working, trying to piece together an answer. Garrick was still slightly disoriented from blood loss, so he decided to leave the thinking to his alpha.

"I didn't leave a note. Darren scheduled a meeting with me, and I attended in hopes it would avoid this battle."

"You were planning on fighting them all alone?" Garrick questioned.

"I'd hoped there wouldn't be a fight. However, I was ready to, yes."

"If you didn't write the note," Tyler spoke up. "They lured you into a trap. The hunters conspired to ambush you. Without you, they'd draw the rest of us out and finish the pack."

"They're getting bold, and probably angry," Aldric continued from Tyler's logic. "They've gone to my home and launched an attack on us."

"Okay, I think it's clear that we'll need a battle plan. I think the first question we should be focusing on, though, is: where will we change?" Cailean contributed.

"For the eclipse," Aldric began, reminding Garrick that there would be a complete solar eclipse in only a few days. "We'll go to the other side of town."

Their town was basically surrounded by trees, but there weren't many areas that were entirely closed off to people – which would be ideal. Since the safest place they could find was compromised, though, they would have to make due.

"There is plenty of cover over there, and we'll only be wolves for about thirty minutes, so we probably can't cause too much harm. After that, I'll figure something out."

Garrick finally understood why he didn't want to change in his basement. If the wolves made too much noise, and somehow the hunters caught on, there would be no mercy. After seeing how ruthlessly they were attacked in the woods – even against people who weren't werewolves – he had no doubt that they'd resort to anything to kill a werewolf. If they knew where Aldric lived, they'd go after his wife, and that last shred of safety had vanished.

"What if they followed us here?" Garrick asked. He realized that he probably looked horrible. His wounds had mostly closed up, but blood soaked his shirt, which had three bullet holes and two from arrows.

"I'm fine," he offered in response to the worried glances. "I've practically healed already."

"Well, they didn't follow us," Aldric replied, "so although it's unlikely, we can at least hope that whichever one knew where I lived died with the information. It seems that the communication in this family is lacking."

"How can you be so confident that they didn't track us?" Tyler questioned.

"They're dead."

A few hours later, everyone's wounds had healed and they were gathered around the living room. Everyone, even Aldric, still seemed on edge, and no one had answers for what the plan was moving forward. The hunters could launch another attack at any point, and they could most likely find any of them at their own homes. Garrick hoped that with the absolute failure of their assault, they would at least have to wait a while before recovering to try again, and that would give Aldric time to formulate a plan.

"What was the plan for training today?" Garrick finally broke the silence.

"Weapons training. My intention was to begin with you, Brooke, and Hayden fighting against me, along with Tyler and Cailean, armed with knives.

"You see, the hunters lose people in their training sessions. During their training, they use real weapons – and death an actual possibility. I won't let us lose anyone, but we need to be training as hard as they do."

"That sounds completely impossible," Garrick laughed – smiling despite everything he'd been through.

"Of course, but you all had to realize you won't be ready. You just have to do the best you can. We'll get into that tomorrow, though. Given what you've all been through tonight, I think you deserve a break."

Garrick thought about that for a minute. He had tried to protect Hayden, but he'd only put her in more danger and slowed her down. She had focused so much on him that she'd ignored her own injuries. Tyler, a human, also got stuck staying behind to help him, getting him involved in a fight which could have very easily meant his death.

Maybe Aldric was right, and they'd never be ready. Maybe some fights were impossible to win. He wasn't ever going to let anyone say, though, that he didn't try.

"What we went through tonight?" Garrick asked passionately, standing up. "What we've been through is proof that we need to train. Who knows what could happen over the next few days? If anything, this only means we have to train harder."

"I don't know what this new fire is, Garrick," Cailean pitched in, "but I like it. I'm in."

"I'll take you both on," Garrick replied, feigning confidence.

Aldric laughed. "No, you two are on a team. Anyone who gets pinned for five seconds sits out of the rest of the fight. Consider it dying."

Cailean and Garrick looked at each other and shook hands. Aldric led them to the basement, and the others followed as well. If nothing else, it was bound to be an interesting fight, so Garrick could understand why they'd want to watch. As they reached the basement, Aldric grabbed a knife. Brooke and Hayden both looked like they were questioning whether they wanted to get involved. Clearly content with the amount of action he'd seen in one night, Tyler sat against the wall.

"Oh, and boys," Aldric paused, turning back to them. "Don't be afraid to stab me. I'll do whatever it takes to win, you should too."

Garrick started to wonder if he'd made a mistake. Even given their circumstances, this training was starting to seem completely insane. As quickly as that thought had presented itself in his mind, he shook it off. This was the only way he'd be able to protect Hayden, or his mother if they showed up at his house.

"Wait," Hayden stopped them. Garrick's heart skipped a beat, and he was filled with concern that she might join them. While he knew she had to be ready just as much as he did, he was scared to hurt her – and he wasn't sure he could go through with that training if she could get hurt. He hoped she'd sit out, at least this once. "I don't like this. What if someone gets hurt?"

"Someone will," Aldric replied earnestly, "but don't worry, the blade isn't actually silver. We'll all be able to heal relatively quickly. Just not in time to avoid getting pinned."

"Oh," Brooke chimed in. "Then I want to play."

Hayden rolled her eyes as she stood to her feet and walked to the middle of the room with Brooke. Tyler groaned and followed them. Garrick sighed. All he had wanted was a one on one because he felt responsible for hurting his friends that night, and he wanted to try to improve his fighting skills so it wouldn't happen again. Instead, his training session had roped everyone else in, and he had practically guaranteed they'd get hurt again.

"Are you all sure?" Aldric inquired. "This is not something I'm requiring, or even suggesting, we do tonight."

When no one left, Aldric shrugged and tossed small pocket knives to Cailean and Tyler as they walked to his side.

"Then we have one last rule: No one stab the human," Aldric instructed. "Begin."

Aldric stood in the middle of his team, and Garrick of his. Hayden stood across from Cailean to his left and Brooke across from Tyler to his right.

A brief lull followed Aldric's instruction, as if everyone was afraid to take the first step. Then, in a blur, Aldric jumped forward and cut deep into Garrick's arm. As he stumbled backward, he regretted pushing for the training, wondering who would be crazy enough to train with real weapons. Given that the hunters were so much better prepared, though, they had to take desperate measures – even if that meant stabbing each other.

Aldric swiped again, but Garrick ducked under the attack, countering with a strong punch to Aldric's ribs. Rising upward, he followed up with an uppercut, but Aldric weaved to the side and landed a jab to Garrick's jaw. Utilizing the opening, Aldric kicked Garrick, pushing him face-down to the floor. Aldric placed his foot on Garrick's back and began counting.

Tyler stabbed at Brooke, but she jumped back, avoiding the knife before catching his hand on the backswing and disarming him. As she moved forward to attack, Tyler backed up, avoiding a punch to his face, then ducked under another blow and rolled forward to grab the knife. Garrick could see Brooke deciding whether to save him or eliminate Tyler. Tyler stood again, holding the knife, but Brooke was already running toward Aldric.

Cailean and Hayden were both moving quickly, but Garrick couldn't see any hits actually landing. She was spending most of her time dodging his attacks, and he was relying too heavily on the knife. Untrained with the weapon, Cailean finally threw an attack sloppy enough for Hayden to intercept and disarm him, giving her an opportunity to land a combination.

Brooke drove her weight into Aldric, knocking him off Garrick. By the time Garrick scrambled to his feet, Tyler was already at her side, and he stabbed her. She rolled off of Aldric, holding her side, clearly unprepared for an actual wound, and Tyler pinned her to the floor. Garrick dove forward, tackling and pinning Tyler, counting as he tried to keep him down.

Brooke pulled the knife from her side and, forcing herself to her feet, blocked the path between Garrick and Aldric. She slashed the knife at him but he easily dodged. With her protecting him, Garrick knew he could hold Tyler down for two more seconds. Aldric, though, threw his knife, which plunged into Garrick's back. Using his experience biting back pain, Garrick clenched his teeth until five seconds had passed, then he collapsed to his side. After giving himself a second to breathe, he stood to see that Brooke and Hayden were both on the floor. Confident he'd miss if he aimed for Cailean, Garrick tossed the knife toward Hayden and it slid within an inch of her hand. Then, he dove toward Aldric.

Aldric, however, anticipated his attack. He held Brooke down with one arm and dropped Garrick over his other shoulder. Garrick slid across the floor until he hit the wall as Aldric counted to five. Brooke walked to sit next to Tyler, removing her bloodied shirt with a groan.

Retrieving Garrick's knife, Hayden slashed deep into Cailean's arm, severing the nerves controlling his bicep, then plunged it into his stomach and pinned him to the ground. Aldric kicked her off Cailean, but Garrick caught Aldric before he could help his son up, throwing him back and locking him in a fist fight, allowing Hayden to pin Cailean again. At five, Cailean angrily grunted and joined Brooke and Tyler. One arm hung limply as he walked, and the other hand pressed over his wound on his stomach, but he still left a trail of blood.

Aldric punched Garrick with enough force to lift him off the ground and propel him into the wall. Hayden tried to defend Garrick, throwing a punch at Aldric, but he easily dodged and knocked her to the ground. Garrick stumbled to his feet and tried to make it to her, but it took him longer than five seconds – so she was already out.

He picked up a knife and tucked it into his back pocket, deciding he was probably better off keeping it hidden. Aldric turned to Garrick, throwing a hook punch, but Garrick weaved backward and countered. Aldric stumbled back, and Garrick ducked his head down and ran into Aldric, pinning him against the wall. Aldric exhaled, trying to prevent the breath from being knocked from his lungs, as Garrick turned and slammed him to the ground. Aldric punched Garrick in the stomach. Even with the limited space to build momentum, he was able to knock Garrick's breath away. He fell to the side, and Aldric pinned him down, pressing an arm against his neck. As quickly as he could, Garrick retrieved the knife from his pocket and plunged it into Aldric's stomach.

With the surprise, Garrick was able to push Aldric down, then climb on him and pin him down. At four, Aldric managed to get a hand under Garrick's rib and slam him into a wall. Aldric lifted Garrick off the ground and dropped him face-first back down. He drove his foot with his full weight into Garrick's back, and the world started to spin.

"One, two, three," he counted slowly. Garrick struggled, reaching his hands behind him, trying to grab Aldric's leg. When that didn't work, he squirmed, trying to find a way out. Finally, he saw a knife barely in his reach and grabbed it.

"Four," Aldric continued. Garrick blindly stabbed behind him, unable to locate a target. When he did, he plunged the knife into Aldric's leg. Aldric collapsed, but maneuvered himself in a way that landed all of his weight on Garrick's back, probably breaking a few bones.

"Five."

Garrick had lost.

"That was a completely terrible idea," Garrick groaned after he and Aldric had returned to the others.

"Are you kidding?" Cailean asked. "That was the single most useful training I've ever experienced."

"It really was eye-opening," Hayden admitted.

"Yeah," Garrick conceded. "I guess you guys are right. It helped, and I know I need to train more. But I never want to do anything like that again."

Chapter 21

Eleven months ago

Garrick sat on his bed, tossing a ball into the air. Over the past month, he'd felt broken, but he also felt a strange sensation – as if he'd spent his whole life looking for a reason he was different only to have one suddenly thrust upon him. Instead of feeling triumphant, though, he was just pensive. With the rush of new information with which he'd been bombarded, he couldn't help but desire more knowledge. He didn't want to be naïve about anything anymore, so he found himself questioning everything.

Over the past few days, Garrick's lack of knowledge about werewolves had been bringing up questions about his father. Though he was well aware he was projecting, and the two were completely disconnected, he couldn't stop himself from asking. It was a similar idea, at the very least. He'd lived his whole life not knowing who the man was, but he'd just been blissfully ignorant. Garrick just didn't want to allow himself to remain in the dark, though. In the same way that his eyes had been opened to a world of werewolves, he wondered if there were any eye-opening truths hearing about his father could tell him. If there was something simple he could do, he owed it to himself not to stay ignorant.

Garrick stood, building up the resolve to walk to his mom's room and knock on her door. This wasn't the first time he'd acknowledged the curiosity, but he'd never had the courage to actually talk to his mother about it. He'd never wanted to bring up painful memories for her. This time, though, he knew he had to ask. Whether the courage came from his inquisitiveness finally overpowering him or his dependence on the fact that there was a beast stronger than himself sharing his body, he didn't know, but he was ready to ask the questions.

"What's up, Garrick?" she questioned as she opened the door.

"Mom, I want to ask you about my father," he blurted out, unsure of how to approach the question other than just forcing it out.

"There's nothing to tell," she muttered, turning away sadly.

"Come on, Mom. I don't know the man. I don't even know his name."

"As I said: there's nothing to tell," she repeated forcefully.

The pain was clear in her voice, and he didn't want to push, but Garrick felt like he needed to know. Was he a hero? A doctor, a firefighter, or maybe a cop like she was. Or was he a criminal? Maybe that's why she left him. Garrick hated not having any idea at all.

"Mom, it's not like I'm going to go find him and start calling him my dad. He's just a person. You're the one who raised me, and you're my mom. I just want to know where I come from, I want to know about him. Maybe there is something important, you know?"

"Like what, Garrick?"

"Like," Garrick started, but he had trouble conjuring an idea. "Okay, like medical records. What if he had a history of cancer in his family?"

"He didn't. He was healthy. Probably the healthiest man I've ever met."

"Well, what did he do?"

"Not much of anything."

"Why did he leave?"

"Garrick, I'm sorry. I just can't. Just trust me, okay. Your life is better without that kind of person in it."

Maybe she was right. As curious as Garrick was, maybe some things were best left alone. If she hated the man so much that she refused to talk about him, he wasn't someone Garrick wanted to know about anyway.

Present
10 days until the Full Moon.

"Garrick," Hayden yawned, stretching her arms. Her head rested on his chest and his arm was wrapped around her shoulders. With his other hand, he traced the single scar she had on her body: three lines across her abdomen.

"Yeah?" he asked. She had one arm wrapped around him, and one knee elevated on his leg. He ran his fingers through her hair as he spoke, but she didn't look up.

"What time is it?"

It had been too long since he'd been able to lie with her like that, and he didn't want it to be ruined. Hesitantly, he glanced at the alarm clock on his nightstand.

"9:15," he answered with a sigh. It was a Saturday morning. His mom hadn't made it home from work until about three o'clock, so she was still asleep. He just wanted to cherish the time alone he had with Hayden.

"We should probably get up soon," she instructed, but she didn't move.

"For what?"

"I don't know," she groaned. "Isn't there something today?"

"Today, there's you."

She smiled as she lifted her head to kiss him. He pulled her closer, feeling as though he didn't have a single care in the world. Outside, he had a plethora of issues to deal with: hunters, werewolves, and school to start. In that moment, though, none of that mattered.

Garrick admired Hayden's perfect, blemish-free body. There were no signs of the battle six days ago. He knew that there were no marks of it on his body either. There were, however, plenty of them in his mind.

He hadn't been able to protect her; she was at risk because of him. He didn't know how he was going to make it right, but he knew he had to do something. Whether that was finding a cure for both of them or just sticking to the training and becoming stronger, he knew he had to act. It only became more important after he had seen what could happen.

"Stay with me," she told him, her eyes gazing deep into his. Her voice pulled him out of his thoughts. She could see when he started to drift into his thoughts. This time, she had pulled him back from it – and he was thankful for that. He wanted to be present.

"What are you thinking about?" she asked him.

"It doesn't matter," he smiled, brushing hair out of her face. "I'd rather be here."

He couldn't explain the emotions that he had for her, but he was fully confident it was a love which humans didn't have the capacity to feel. He'd always cared about her, but it changed when he became a werewolf. The first time they'd slept together after he was scratched, it was like something had changed in him. All of the potential love, any emotional aspect, at least, he could feel for another girl was taken and given to Hayden.

There was a lot he hated about being a werewolf – but that choice was one he would never regret. Being able to feel that way about her almost made all of the other issues of the affliction worthwhile.

He wished he could tell her how he felt; find some way to put his feelings into words for her. No language had created those words, though. He just had to settle with knowing that she already knew exactly how he felt, because she was feeling the same thing.

He kissed her again.

Garrick had reluctantly dropped Hayden off at home an hour later, hoping to avoid her mother getting upset with her. She was already having trouble with how little Hayden was home. Given that Hayden's brother was still off at college, that left her mother in home alone almost constantly – and with no explanation. Unfortunately, there wasn't much they could do to explain that she spent most of her time learning how to defend herself from people who wanted to kill her for being a werewolf.

The eclipse was expected to be at 12:17, so they all had to get to the woods with time to spare. Hayden probably wouldn't have any difficulty convincing her mom to let her "watch the eclipse" but Garrick preferred to be safe. With the two hours he had left, Garrick planned to do some research, but his phone buzzed and interrupted him.

"Garrick Elliott, I think I have some information," Tyler texted with perfect timing. Garrick grabbed the keys from the chain by the door and headed to Tyler's house. As much as he wished he could spend more time with his mom, he couldn't deny that her late work nights and consequently, her sleep schedule, were beneficial.

Garrick checked his phone on his way to Tyler's house. It was only 10:45, so he easily had an hour to listen to Tyler's newest idea. When he pulled up, Tyler was already waiting outside, practically bouncing. Garrick followed him inside, trying not to let Tyler's excitement rub off on him. This wasn't the first time Tyler had found a 'solution' only for them both to be disappointed. As they walked into Tyler's room, Garrick noticed a board set up with pages of notes pinned to it, open books strewn around the floor, and one on the desk surrounded by scribbled comments on pages of paper. There was an organization to it all, knowing Tyler, but Garrick couldn't figure out what it was.

"I have begun to believe everything in these books is fallacious," Tyler opened.

"That's not the best way you could have started this," Garrick joked.

"Acknowledged," Tyler shrugged as he pointed to the book on his desk. Garrick had skimmed through the same book before, but Tyler had copied sections on papers which now surrounded the book. The pages had different colored highlighters marking the top.

"We've already tried that," Garrick groaned as he remembered the book.

"True, but we have yet to organize all of our information. I have green pages for verified information. Red pages are what we've proven false."

"Okay," Garrick responded slowly, trying to follow Tyler as he excitedly explained his new organization method.

"Combining the information we know to be true with that which we can discount, I have reexamined a few sources and accumulated as much information as I could gather."

With that, Tyler pointed to the board, where he had an assortment of green-colored pages with information from other books. Garrick read what he could, but he wasn't sure what conclusion he was supposed to draw.

"It looks to me," Tyler explained, as if reading his friend's thoughts, "that there are commonalities in all of these documents. They all speak of a level of communication. I believe that in order to stop this; you are going to have to see humanity in the wolf."

"And how can I do that?" Garrick asked.

"I haven't figured that out yet, but I assume that would be a link – something which remains the same regardless of the form."

"There is absolutely nothing," Garrick snapped. "Obviously, my body completely changes – even my eyes change color. My mind is altered. We're two completely different beings."

"There has to be something," Tyler sounded unconvinced. "Perhaps somewhere hidden in your personalities, or possibly something physical. Everything points to some connection."

"Okay," Garrick conceded. "Let's assume I find this link. Then what?"

"The other piece appears to be something which you possess uniquely. This will bind you to your humanity, hopefully allowing you to maintain control."

"Pain," Garrick offered.

"My thoughts exactly."

"But, I'm sure the wolf can feel pain," Garrick argued.

"Presumably, but you've used it to impede effects of the transformation before. It's possible that after we find the link, you'll be able to use it to a greater degree."

"That would be amazing," Garrick admitted, allowing himself to become hopeful. Even if Tyler was right, how was he ever going to find something similar between him and the wolf? Garrick wasn't present when the wolf was, and he wasn't willing to risk Tyler getting close enough to find anything.

All of the conflicting thoughts were starting to give him a headache. Still, it was a wonderful idea. It wasn't a cure, but control would at least allow him to avoid causing damage. It wouldn't solve the hunter concern, but it was a start.

"Let's solve this, then," Tyler thought aloud. "Both forms have hair. And skin. And… eyes." He clearly knew he was grasping at straws. Each suggestion he gave was quieter and weaker than the previous one.

"I think it would have to be deeper than that," Garrick sighed, rubbing his temples.

"I'm aware," Tyler agreed. "I'm just brainstorming."

Garrick's headache was getting worse, and his stomach began hurting as well. Unsure of what was causing it, he decided to go home and find some medicine.

"Garrick Elliott, are you alright?" Tyler asked. Suddenly, everything came flooding back to him. How had he been so stupid? He'd completely forgotten. He reached for his phone, but realized he must have forgotten it in the car. Somehow, he hadn't even realized he couldn't get sick, so there had to be another problem. He'd just gotten lost in the hope of a new suggestion.

"What time is it?" Garrick asked.

"It's just after noon, why?" Tyler responded inquisitively. Garrick hadn't thought about the fact that he couldn't get there just in time for the eclipse to start – the change would begin as the moon rose.

"I have to go." He ran to his car, but Tyler followed closely. Garrick clamored into the driver's seat, but he realized he couldn't drive – his inability to focus would cause an accident.

"Garrick Elliott," Tyler demanded. "Tell me what's happening."

"The eclipse," Garrick explained. "I'm changing. I need to run to the woods."

"From here? You'll never make it. Move, I'll drive you."

"No. What if I hurt you?"

"You may, but if I don't, you will without question hurt someone else." Garrick begrudgingly slid to the passenger seat. His phone lit up from the cupholder, the light almost blinding him. He had fifteen texts from Hayden, twelve from Brooke, three from Cailean, and one from Aldric – and double that many missed calls from each. Tyler sped down the streets, and Garrick was thankful that he didn't have to relay any information.

"I'm sorry," Tyler apologized. "I don't know how it slipped my mind."

"No, I should have remembered," Garrick groaned.

Tyler was going fifteen miles over the speed limit. If they got pulled over, there would be no way he could make it to the woods. Still, it was a risk Garrick knew he'd had to take. There wasn't enough time to get there if he didn't. Tyler slammed on the brakes after driving as far into the woods as possible. Garrick could feel his teeth growing as he watched claws grow from his nails.

Tyler got out of the car and opened Garrick's door. He pulled his friend out and wrapped an arm around his shoulder.

"I have to go alone," Garrick argued. "They'll all be changed. And you won't get me there before I kill you."

"I have to try." They were too close to civilization to let him go there, and Garrick knew he didn't have the strength to walk on his own. Still, he couldn't imagine his friend getting hurt because of him. Garrick couldn't live with himself if it happened again.

"Please, Tyler. Go."

"I swear to you, Garrick Elliott, I'll flee as fast as humanly possible the second I leave you somewhere I'm confident you won't harm anyone. First, we have to get you there."

The two continued walking and they crossed the tree line a few seconds later. Tyler kept leading Garrick further into the woods, dragging him along. The pain became unbearable, and Garrick decided they'd gone far enough. Garrick shoved Tyler away, trying to get distance.

He quickly threw his shirt and pants off, leaving them against a tree. He hoped he'd be able to remember what tree it was. Whether or not he did, it was better than letting them get torn to shreds as he changed.

"Are you going to be okay?" Tyler asked.

"Run!" Garrick ordered. He turned back to face Tyler. He knew his face was completely unrecognizable. One by one, more bones shattered and reformed throughout his body. He tried to fight the change, but he knew it was hopeless. At that point, he'd lost hope that he could hold it back until Tyler made it to safety, but he had to give his friend the biggest head start he possibly could, so he kept fighting the agony as his body was torn apart.

Garrick watched hair grow from his arms as the skin stretched to accommodate their new shape. He'd never been conscious this long. He always tried, but he typically gave up long before that point.

He saw that his legs weren't even human anymore. He stood on his toes, which had grown claws of their own. Somehow, he'd maintained consciousness through the transformation, but Garrick felt his ability to process thought fading fast, but he just kept fighting for control.

Though he ran as fast as he could, Tyler hadn't made it far – he was still in Garrick's line of sight. The last thing he saw before he finally succumbed to the pain was his best friend stop and run the other way. Another wolf had blocked his path.

Garrick looked around, taking in the world. He saw a human running toward him. There was a hint of recognition, but he couldn't quite figure out who it was.

"Oh no," the human mumbled. "Garrick Elliott?"

He recognized the sound as the one humans made to get his attention.

"Good boy," the human tried. Tyler. There was fear in his voice as he tried to speak in a comforting tone.

"Garrick Elliott, you know me," Tyler continued. "I know you're in there."

There was no sense in appealing to his humanity. It wasn't there. Still, he didn't want there to be such fear in this human's voice. He liked him. Garrick knew that the human side of him deeply cared for the person who was in front of him.

Cailean strolled out from behind one of the trees. He growled at Tyler, ready to attack. Brooke appeared from behind another tree and Aldric from a third. Cailean was the first to attack, lunging toward Tyler. Garrick jumped too and caught him in the air, driving him to the ground. Garrick slashed Cailean's leg, dropping him to the ground, then clamped his jaw around Cailean's neck.

Brooke jumped at Tyler next, but Hayden dove from the foliage to fight her off. She was always there to defend Garrick and those he loved. Somehow, Garrick knew that Hayden wouldn't hurt Tyler either. The two of them were going to save him.

Cailean broke from Garrick's bite and lunged forward. He scratched Garrick deep across the side, and he fell forward. Angrily, Cailean bit at him, but Garrick managed to scratch Cailean's neck in defense.

Brooke managed to land a few good scratches on Hayden, and she was now on top of her, pinning her down with a vicious bite.

Aldric, larger and more powerful than the rest of them, walked toward Tyler. Tyler was still desperately muttering things like "good boy" in attempt to make them act friendly toward him. Aldric got closer, but he didn't attack. Garrick was torn. That was his alpha. While it may not have been more important than any friendships to his human side, he couldn't defy him. Anyway, he knew there was no hope for victory.

Garrick stood and scratched at Cailean again, but Cailean jumped back. Then, he jumped forward and scratched Garrick, pinning him down again. Garrick felt his power draining away. Cailean wouldn't kill him; but he would beat him until he finally conceded. It was all a power struggle.

Hayden managed to get Brooke off her and scratch her legs up enough to impair her movement. As Brooke limped to a tree to lick her wounds, Hayden dove toward Cailean and pushed him from Garrick. She scratched at him, and then she bit down on his neck until he finally whimpered in surrender.

She let him go and walked back to Garrick, licking the wounds which were still bleeding. Garrick felt a pain in his stomach, and it quickly grew to his paws. All of the others seemed to be reacting to a similar sensation, but he couldn't see the source of the attack.

Aldric, who had walked almost close enough to bite Tyler, fell forward. Garrick watched as his paws shrunk down and human fingers emerged from them. His teeth dulled in his mouth, and his shoulder bones settled down to a human form.

Garrick felt himself losing his form as well. He looked at Tyler as he lost his vision. His friend was alive.

Garrick woke up in the grass. For the first time since he could remember, they all woke up near each other. Groggily, he sat up and walked to retrieve his clothes. Somehow, he had a good recollection of what had happened, and he knew Tyler was alive. Still, he wanted to get dressed and get to his friend as quickly as possible.

"Hey," Tyler muttered with a shaky voice, sitting a few dozen feet from Garrick.

"I'm so glad you're okay," Garrick exclaimed, finishing dressing before running to his friend. Garrick wrapped Tyler in an embrace.

"That was by far the strangest thing I have ever experienced."

"I know," Garrick acknowledged.

"You didn't even attempt to hurt me. You protected me, actually."

"I wasn't sure I would, but I was hopeful. Hayden did the same for me. I think that maybe the wolf knows how good of a friend you are to me."

"That's comforting," he sighed, calming down a bit. Garrick was impressed that he was even able to talk. He himself would probably be speechless after what Tyler had seen.

Hearing rustling in the leaves, Garrick turned back to look at the others. Gently, he told Tyler to wait as he ran to greet Hayden. Removing his shirt, he handed it to her. She thanked him as she slid it over her shoulders. He helped her to her feet, the shirt working as a very short dress for her. It would suffice until she made it back to where she had turned. Before she parted to find where that was, she kissed him and nodded back to Tyler. Garrick nodded and ran back to his friend, falling to his knees near him.

"Sorry," he greeted. Tyler seemed to have settled down a bit, and wasn't shaking as badly. As if trying to force out a sentence, he took a deep breath, but produced no words. His face slowly changed as a smile spread across it. Garrick was confused. What did he possibly have to smile about? Only a few minutes ago he was more than likely going to be torn apart by werewolves. Maybe he was just happy to be alive.

"What?" Garrick asked him.

"Garrick Elliott," Tyler whispered slowly. "This was all worth it. I have it figured out."

"What did you figure out?" Garrick asked, assuming he'd forgotten a piece of a conversation he and Tyler had been having on the way to the woods. Through his foggy mind, he was having trouble processing the current conversation, let alone a past one. It always took him a while for the clouds in his mind to part.

"The link," Tyler explained. "I found the link."

Chapter 22

Eleven months ago

Garrick stared at the ceiling, finding patterns in the texture as Hayden rested her head on his chest. Neither of them had moved in ten minutes, and he didn't want to be the one to break that. Based only on her breathing, Garrick couldn't tell if she was sleeping or not, but he just allowed himself to enjoy her presence.

After a while, though, he stood up, walking over to the mirror. He knew it was a bit self-obsessed, but he couldn't help but look at his reflection. His pecs had already started growing a bit. Mostly, they were just more defined. Without even flexing, the tone in his arms was vaguely visible. When he flexed, Garrick looked like he had been to a gym, which wasn't something he was used to. Silently, Hayden came up behind him, wrapping her arms around him. She kissed his shoulder, then placed her chin on it as she admired the two of them in the mirror.

"We look pretty good together," she flirted.

"You just look good enough for the both of us," Garrick complimented. She smiled.

"I don't think it happened this fast for me," she admitted.

"What?"

"Don't act like you're not noticing," she laughed. "The muscles. I mean, I'm sure everyone is different, and maybe it has to do with your ample supply of testosterone."

"I doubt that's it," Garrick laughed.

"I don't know," she shrugged. "It's easier for guys to put on muscle. I don't see why that would change for a wolf."

Garrick supposed she was right. He wondered when the muscle growth would stop, though. Aldric was a big, intimidating man, and Cailean and Chase looked like they'd worked out every day for their lives, but none of them were built like bodybuilders. Hayden didn't even look incredibly muscular without flexing. Of course, all of them were significantly stronger than Garrick, but at some point, the changes clearly slowed, or at least become less apparent.

"How long did it take for you?"

"Well, after the first change I lost ten pounds," she remembered. "The second one, I could flex and actually see my muscles. I think a few weeks after that is when I stabilized a bit."

"Why does it stop?"

"We don't stop getting stronger. I don't know, I guess our bodies just find a balance."

Garrick didn't say anything for a while. He maneuvered himself behind Hayden, pulling her up against him and kissing her head. She looked so perfect. As they stood there, she subtly moved her hands to cover her stomach.

"Hayden," Garrick whispered, gently placing his hands on hers and moving them to her sides. "You have nothing to be ashamed of. You know that, right? You're beautiful. You're perfect."

"It looks horrible," she complained weakly.

"No, it doesn't. It's one scratch on a perfect girl. And I think it makes you look even better," he smiled at her in the mirror.

"Oh yeah?" she asked shyly, looking down. He never understood why she was so embarrassed by the scar. To him, it was a part of her – one piece in the whole package that was the girl he loved.

"Yeah, it makes you look like a scrapper," he teased.

"You're into that kind of thing, then?"

"I'm into you," he responded. She turned around, wrapped her arms around his shoulders, and kissed him. All Garrick wanted was for Hayden to see herself how he saw her. Admittedly, he could never get his mind off of his own scar either. He always had to make sure to cover it when he was in public, in case a hunter saw him.

Still, thinking about it and being ashamed of it were two different things. If Garrick had any ability to, he would make sure Hayden never felt shame again.

Present
10 days until the full moon

Garrick didn't know how to process the information. Leaning against a tree, he tried to support himself as his head started spinning. Could it really be that easy? Could Tyler actually be sitting right in front of him with the answer he'd been searching for?

No. It couldn't. There was absolutely no way that everyone could be happy. If he was right, and he found whatever the link was, he might think it would be beneficial to hang around Garrick even when he was transformed. Maybe he could find something else that they could use. Garrick couldn't allow that to happen. He wasn't confident that his wolf wouldn't hurt Tyler, and he knew some of the others would.

If he was wrong, they were just getting their hopes up for nothing. Aldric, who seemed to know most everything there was to know about werewolves, claimed that Garrick's attempts were futile. It was probably time to just admit he was right.

Tyler had witnessed all of them turn, and he had witnessed a fight within the pack. The only thing that kept him from getting scratched when Garrick had pushed him away was mere chance. Tyler was getting too close to everything.

"No," Garrick finally muttered, making his decision and shaking his head. Whatever it was that Tyler had to say, he wasn't going to listen. He couldn't. For Tyler's sake, he had to make sure that his friend didn't try to help him anymore. It was just putting him in danger, and it wasn't even worthwhile. Nothing had worked, and Garrick was starting to believe nothing would.

The wolf was its own separate entity, isolated from him, and he couldn't ignore that fact anymore. All he could do was allow it to have its time when the moon was full, and Garrick would be himself for the rest of his life. That was the realization Aldric had come to and tried to share with him, and Garrick finally knew that was the way it had to be.

"What?" Tyler stuttered, clearly shocked.

"We're done with all of this," Garrick replied sadly. "Aldric told me it's impossible, and he's right."

"No, this is too close," Tyler argued, rising to his feet. "I didn't risk my life bringing you out here to watch you throw away your chance at humanity."

Tyler's voice grew louder, gaining conviction as he spoke. Garrick was still crouched to the ground, leaning against the tree. His eyes were downcast; he couldn't bear to look at Tyler. After countless hours of research, trying to help his best friend, he was being told that it was pointless. Garrick knew exactly how that felt, because Aldric had done the same to him.

This, however, was worse. It wasn't coming from someone who was expected to say something so harsh. This was Garrick telling his best friend that everything he'd worked for was completely useless – telling him to give up.

"That's the problem," Garrick replied calmly. "You came out here because I let you get too close to this curse. You almost died because of me."

"This is my choice," Tyler snapped. "I chose to assist you, regardless of consequence."

And I want to help you, Garrick thought. Even more than that – he wanted to save him.

"I don't want your help," he finally responded, fighting back tears in his own eyes. "It isn't worth the price."

Garrick lifted his eyes as he spoke, and he saw the complete shock and betrayal in Tyler's face. He stood and ran his fingers through his hair, trying to collect his thoughts.

"I'm sorry," he explained. "I just can't lose another friend because of my attempts to change what happened to me. It's useless, we both know it. There are no documented cases of someone being in control of the wolf."

"None Aldric knew of," Tyler countered.

"There aren't even rumors in the books. There are all of these different ideas on how, but no one can actually claim that they work."

"To offer personal testimony would be to paint a target on their back," Tyler argued. He was right; no one could silently publish a book, so the hunters would be able to trace them back. Everything had to be intentionally vague.

Garrick didn't say anything for a long time. Though he was desperate to know Tyler's newest idea, he couldn't give his friend that hope. He had to cut off his connection to that part of Garrick's world entirely, or he'd just continue to get put in danger. Already he'd been attacked by hunters, then the other wolves. Garrick couldn't let Tyler keep going through that for him.

"It can't work," Garrick muttered. "The wolf and I are just not the same. It's a monster. You can't control a monster. You just have to contain it the best you can."

"And the best you can –" Tyler started.

"Is to let it out on the full moons," Garrick interrupted. "To give it one night and to not let it rule the rest of my life. I don't want this to be what I think about every minute of every day anymore, and I don't want that for you either. You're my friend, Tyler, you deserve better than that. You have an actual chance to be human. Please, take it."

He turned and started walking.

"Is he okay?" Hayden asked as Garrick walked toward her.

"Now he is," Garrick sighed.

"What happened?" she pressed. "Do you remember?"

"We defended him." The wolves had been more human than Garrick had ever been. Maybe that was what was scaring him so much. The wolf – what Garrick thought of as a monster – was ready to die protecting Tyler – and he wasn't. He let Tyler spend all of his time getting involved in the world of werewolves. It was Garrick's fault that Tyler was in the training sessions and in the woods when the hunters attacked. Garrick decided to take a page from the monster's book. He had to do whatever it took to protect his friend.

Hayden hugged him, wrapping her arms tightly around his waist and burying her face in his chest, relieved to know that Tyler was safe. He'd grown close with everyone in the pack. Even Cailean had started to treat Tyler better. It would have crushed all of them to have lost him, especially with the loss of Chase still weighing on them so heavily.

"I told him that we aren't going to keep trying to control it," Garrick sighed. He was talking mostly to Hayden, but he made sure he spoke loud enough for Aldric to hear.

Aldric nodded and walked over to Garrick. Remaining silent, he placed a hand on Garrick's shoulder. Garrick could see a certain level of sadness in Aldric's eyes, but it was mixed with a sense of understanding. No, not just understanding, but empathy.

"You did the right thing," he offered. "We've pulled him in too far."

"I know."

"Weren't you close to something, though?" Hayden asked.

"Maybe. I thought we'd found a way to stop the change. Tyler explained everything to me right before the eclipse, but I lost track of time, and he had to help me get here. That's why he was stuck out here. I can't keep trying to fight this. I have to stop fighting a losing battle and try to just focus on keeping the people I care about safe."

Even Cailean was solemn. He leaned against a tree, his arm wrapped around Brooke. Garrick hadn't told all of them how hard he and Tyler were looking for a cure, but they all knew it was occupying at least a large portion of his time. Hayden was the only one that knew it took every minute that he didn't devote to her or training.

Garrick knew that there was nothing he could do to fight the beast; it was a waste of his efforts to even try. Instead of wasting his time learning to be a human every single day, he was going to have to focus on being one as often as he could. As he looked around at the people with whom he shared his life, and as he thought about having time to actually spend with Tyler without the concern of wolves, he decided he was okay with that.

After a slightly awkward ride home with Tyler, Garrick sat on his bed. Though he was upset, his friend seemed to accept that Garrick didn't want his help anymore. Soon enough, he'd get over the pain and everything would be back to normal. Still, he completely understood Tyler's frustration. Garrick had forced him to stop what he'd been working on every waking minute for over a month, and there was no resolution.

He still wondered if he had made the right choice. He could have at least tried the one last thing before giving up. It would have made Tyler being put in danger not entirely useless. Instead, by not hearing him out, Garrick had made it exactly that: a useless sacrifice.

Garrick decided he had to go for a walk to clear his mind. In an attempt to find somewhere comforting, he started making his way toward the woods. If the hunters were still waiting, he'd probably be able to outrun them, but he couldn't imagine that they just have people constantly scanning the woods for his face.

When he passed by Hayden's house, he knocked on her door. She always had a way of calming him and putting things into perspective. Maybe she would be wise enough to help him sort through his broken thoughts. Her mom opened the door and called for her. Shortly after, she came downstairs wearing jeans and the same shirt he'd given her a little over an hour ago.

"Want to go for a walk?" he offered.

"Sure," she shrugged. Quickly, she put shoes on and followed him outside. The two of them were silent for quite a while, but when they approached the edge of the woods, he finally spoke up.

"I think we should find somewhere else to go," he told her. The two of them had found a hidden area in the woods covered by enough branches that most people wouldn't try to get through. Hayden, though, had decided she was curious a few months back, wanting to see what was on the other side of the shrubs. She'd climbed through, not without getting a fair share of cuts from the branches and thorns, and then found a small alcove in the trees. Since then, she and Garrick had taken to going there when they wanted to be alone. It was a peaceful place, and the two of them could spend hours sitting and talking, confident no one would find them

"No way," she argued. "The hunters are probably gone. And they aren't keeping me from our place."

Garrick nodded reluctantly. It didn't seem like a good idea to venture into the woods, but he wasn't ready to give it up either. He couldn't help but wonder if he was putting her in danger just so he could walk through the woods and admire the trees though. Was she another victim of his selfishness and carelessness?

Even with all of his doubts, he didn't fight very hard as she pulled him forward. He just followed behind her, almost mindlessly, as she guided him through the trees.

"Do you remember what you told me when you found out about us?" she asked.

"I assume you mean after I threw a fit and called you a monster?" Garrick hadn't taken the news of werewolves very well. For a long time, he'd been afraid of Hayden, even though he knew she had protected him from the other wolves.

"I do," she nodded.

"I told you that I don't care what happens on a full moon. You were you, and that's what I love."

"Right," she approved. She stopped, turning to face him. "And you're you. You're a good man, Garrick Elliott."

"Maybe," he responded. Unsure wasn't really a good word to describe what he was feeling. He was thoroughly convinced that she was wrong.

"Really," she pushed. "You're just trying to make the best of what happened. You want to help people. You can't blame yourself when things go wrong. That's just the world we live in."

She kissed him. He tried to believe that she was right, but how could she be? Was he really spending all of that time trying to find a cure because he didn't want someone to get hurt? Or was it because he didn't want to keep going through the change? Even he didn't have an answer, so how could she be so positive about her own?

Hayden started talking again, but it felt like she was miles away. Her words were becoming distant and jumbled. He tried to focus on her, but she just faded away.

"Hayden!" He called. Somehow, she had just vanished, disappearing into the trees.

He knew what was happening, on some level, but it didn't make it any less terrifying.

He heard that all-too-familiar growl. Garrick turned to run, but the wolf was on the other side. As it walked away from some trees, Garrick backed away, stumbling over his feet. The beast inched its way toward him, but it seemed to approach him with caution, as if it were as scared of him as he was of it.

The wolf was a few inches from Garrick before it stopped moving. Garrick's heart pounded in his chest. In denial, he hoped that it would just go away if he didn't move. Instead, though, it started to smell his hand.

In a futile attempt to get his pulse under control, Garrick took a deep breath. At that point, if the creature wanted to kill him, there was nothing he could do about it. Kneeling down slowly, he lowered himself to be eye-level with the animal. It backed away, but he extended a hand to show he didn't mean it any harm.

The wolf inched closer to him. He looked into the creature's blue eyes. He wanted to call it a monster, but he couldn't think of it like that. It was a beast, yes. An animal – but not a monster.

The wolf stood tall. The animal's paws were about as big as Garrick's own fist. Each had four claws. Two were more to the sides than the others, so each time the wolf scratched it was only likely to connect with three of the claws, depending on the angle – explaining the scar on his arm.

In a way, the wolf was a creature of beauty. It resembled an actual wolf, only much larger, in both size and build. There were clearly defined muscles in the beast's front legs, and Garrick could see the traces of humanity that had been left. It also had significantly less fur, with only a thin layer covering most of its body.

On its left front leg, it had three lines imprinted on its body, and no fur seemed to grow to cover that mark. Instinctively, Garrick rubbed his hand against his own scar, lifting his shirt slightly. As Garrick revealed his scar, the wolf seemed to be put at ease.

That was it.

As the wolf stepped closer, Garrick slowly reached out to touch it. The creature didn't move, but it did tense up slightly. It was ready to attack or run if it had to, so Garrick

moved very cautiously. Slowly, he moved his hand closer –
toward the creature's leg.

The phone ringing scared him awake. He shot up in
his bed, breathing heavily. Garrick looked around his room,
trying to remember exactly when he'd drifted off.

After it rang twice more, Garrick reached out and
grabbed his phone.

"Hayden," he greeted groggily. He hoped his relief to
hear from her didn't show too much in his voice. Though he
knew it had just been a dream, after seeing her disappear in
front of his eyes, it was just good to hear her voice.

"Hey, Garrick," she responded. She sounded unfazed,
so he guessed she didn't catch on to his tone. "What are you
doing?"

"Nothing," he yawned, trying to wake himself up.
"Just taking a nap."

"Oh, sorry."

"No, no, it's fine. What's up?"

"I was wondering if I could come over." It had taken
her a while to start asking that, but Garrick was glad she finally
had. She had always said she didn't want to invite herself
over, but Garrick had insisted enough times that she was always welcome that she'd finally started to just ask to go to his
house, instead of starting with 'hang out' and then having a
conversation about where to go. They almost always ended
up at his house anyway.

"I'd love that," he answered. "I'll see you soon?"

"Yeah," she responded cheerfully. "Love you, bye."

"Love you too," he said. Before he dropped the phone
on the bed, Garrick waited for the beep. Garrick allowed himself a few more minutes to calm down from the rush of adrenaline he'd had when he'd awoken, then walked to the bathroom and tried to make himself more presentable by splashing
water on his face and hair.

He had finally figured it out. It was always there, he'd
just never known it had any significance. It had never been

more to him than proof that he'd been scratched. Maybe, though, it was also the key to him regaining his humanity.

Garrick wished he'd come to the conclusion long before. Why was it, after all, that their healing factor couldn't fix the one scar? Every other wound that they had, even scars from before the turn, disappeared. Those three lines, though, remained.

"How'd you figure it out?" He texted Tyler, excited to have someone to share the information with. As he waited for a response, he heard Hayden knock on the door. When he let her in, she made herself at home, giving him a quick hug before plopping down on the couch. Garrick checked his phone as he followed her.

"I had my suspicion when you turned, but it wasn't confirmed until Hayden jumped over me to fight the other one."

"You could tell who was who?"

"I was able to recognize the two of you. You mentioned a scar on her stomach, if I'm not mistaken."

"Yeah," Garrick confirmed.

"Who are you texting?" Hayden inquired, leaning toward him and nuzzling her way under his arm and in between him and his phone.

"Tyler," he answered before he flipped his phone closed and set it to the side. As she set her head in his lap, he wrapped an arm around her and looked down, beaming.

"What about?" she asked.

"I didn't want to listen to what he thought about controlling the change, but then I had a dream. I saw something odd, and he thinks it is the key to being able to stop the change on the full moon."

"What is it?" Her interest was clearly piqued, but she was as hesitant to accept it as Garrick himself was.

He lifted her shirt slightly, exposing the scar that ran across her stomach. It ran sideways across almost half of her stomach and continued around her side. As he built up the courage to finally say the words, he traced that old wound with his fingers.

"The scar."

Chapter 23

Ten months ago

Garrick walked to the gym, wearing a long sleeve shirt and sweat pants. He hadn't owned a wide selection of clothing to wear to the gym, and his mother didn't have the money to purchase a new wardrobe, so Garrick had to settle for some poorly-fitting clothes Cailean passed down to him. As he walked, he pondered Cailean's advice when he'd thrust the attire upon him.

"A new wolf is a walking target," Cailean had told him. "The sudden changes in physicality are the most obvious warning sign to any hunter."

"So what do you want me to do about it?" Garrick had asked.

"Just cover as much as you can for now. I'll take you to the gym, almost make a scene of it. Everyone with any interest will know that I'm training you, and that way it will at least be believable when you don't look like a scrawny geek anymore."

"Thanks." Given that it was the closest thing to a compliment Garrick had ever received from Cailean, he chose to accept it.

The intense training regimen involved practically every machine in the building, lasted for two hours, and took place seven days of the week. It wasn't the intensity of the workout which bothered Garrick – because that was actually easy to handle. With his newfound strength, it took a lot more to push his limits than he'd thought. Anyway, Cailean had made the point that Garrick had to start off small, so the workout itself was a breeze. Spending two hours of his day on repetitive tasks with Cailean, though, was more difficult.

"You're late, Garrick," Cailean scolded as Garrick entered the gym.

"No, I'm on time."

"On time is late."

"Right," Garrick sighed.

"Early is late."

"Then when is on time?"

"Whenever I say it is."

"But that means you can just always tell me I'm late."

"You're getting it," Cailean smirked, patting Garrick on the shoulder. Realizing that was Cailean's idea of a joke, Garrick laughed and loosened up a bit. He was grateful that Cailean wasn't as completely unbearable as he'd once been. Though he was a jerk to most people, he was very supportive of his pack, and he was willing to spend so much time training Garrick even though it didn't help himself at all. It was possible that it would help protect him from hunters, but that wasn't guaranteed, so it was really for Garrick's benefit.

They walked to the locker room so Cailean could change. Garrick still felt self-conscious changing in front of others, so he always made sure to change at home. That was better because in case hunters were present, they wouldn't see his rapid change. In the mirror at home, Garrick was able to see more definition daily – results far beyond anything a human could achieve.

He hadn't been able to bench the bar, which was fifty pounds, before he was scratched. After two weeks with Cailean, he was already at 180 pounds. He'd also put on twenty pounds of muscle, but he was able to hide it effectively with his clothing options. Thankfully, his build was still similar, and with Cailean's guidance concerning the amount of weight he should be lifting, he was focusing on definition rather than bulking up. Between the light workouts and the rapid healing of the wolf, Garrick was seeing his strength and endurance reach levels he hadn't thought possible. Still, there was always room to improve. As Cailean had put it, Garrick was one of the strongest people he knew; but by far the weakest werewolf.

"You still have to work for it," Cailean explained as he led Garrick to the treadmill. They always started and ended with Cailean's version of light cardio. "Not this hard forever, of course, but you have to exercise just like anyone else. We just happen to be in a bit of a different league."

Cailean started his treadmill and watched as Garrick started his, setting it to the maximum speed and incline. After ten minutes, Garrick could feel his legs protesting – seconds away from simply refusing to work anymore. When he was sure he couldn't push himself anymore, he stopped the treadmill and took about thirty seconds to catch his breath. Unable to convince his body to stand, Garrick sat on the edge of the treadmill, breathing heavily. Within one minute, his legs were completely restored.

"Better," Cailean offered as his own treadmill slowed down. "Not good, but better."

Offering a hand, he helped Garrick to his feet and the pair walked to the next machine.

Present
Morning of the full moon.

The ringing of the bell resounded in Garrick's ears, deafening him regardless of how hard he bit his lip. As the classroom emptied, Garrick allowed himself to heal as he rubbed his temples. Once his equilibrium had been restored, he stood and slung his backpack over his shoulder.

Aldric had reluctantly accepted the only viable solution – changing in his basement – until they discovered a better alternative. Over the past week, Garrick and Cailean had helped Aldric clean anything that could potentially be destroyed from the basement. They'd also installed more locks on the door, but the pack was mostly depending on the stairs to contain the wolves.

Hayden walked by Garrick in the hall, brushing her hand against him and turning to give him a smile. As she continued to walk, he reached out and caught her arm, pulling her back playfully. That earned them a few eye rolls from fellow students who passed them in the halls.

"Hey," he greeted, pulling her close and leaning against the wall, trying to stay out of the way of other students – but not unhappy with the side-effect of being closer to Hayden.

"Hey yourself," she smiled.

"What time were you planning on going over to Aldric's tonight?" he inquired, trying to focus on important matters. He assumed she'd want to go with him, but he wanted to get there early so he could have a few minutes to spar with Aldric. They'd fought every day since training began, but Garrick hadn't won once. He wasn't planning on giving up until he could.

"Well," she teased coquettishly, grazing her finger across his chest, "I was planning on going to your house after school. Thought I'd just go with you."

He smiled but didn't respond – unintentionally hesitating. Though he should have been used to her behavior near the full moon, it still threw him off guard when she was so forward. That type of behavior always instilled a split reaction in him. It was something he liked occasionally, but it was more often than not fueled by her wolf. That was something he tried to fight out of himself every day of his life, and he didn't want to support its blatant command over her emotions.

"If that's alright with you," she added. While he realized it was more than possible he'd waited too long for an answer, Garrick also knew Hayden shouldn't have expected any different response. He decided that he was done fighting the wolf, though. Link or no link, he refused to keep fighting a losing battle – one which put the people he cared about at risk.

"Alright," he accepted, sealing their agreement with a kiss.

The two of them stood in the hall for another few seconds before the bell rang again. Garrick nodded as she mumbled something about getting to class. He watched her hips sway as she walked away before he rushed off himself. Garrick slipped into class a minute late and quietly slid in a seat behind Tyler. He was thankful that the teacher didn't make a big deal about his entry. Tyler was never that subtle, though. As soon as the teacher turned his back, Tyler turned to face Garrick with a cheesy grin.

"It appears the honeymoon is back on, Garrick Elliott," he whispered.

"Yeah," Garrick chuckled quietly. "I guess it is."

For a long while he had been annoyed with Tyler's jokes about their perpetual 'honeymoon phase,' but after losing that closeness with her, he was pleased to have someone else noticing that things seemed right again.

"Moving on then, what is the plan for this evening?" Tyler questioned.

"Is this really the place to discuss that?" Garrick retorted.

Tyler groaned – an exaggerated gesture – as he turned back around. Sinking back into his seat, he pulled out his phone and began very obviously texting under his desk.

"What is the plan for this evening?" Garrick read after pulling out his own phone. All week, Tyler had been pressing for information about Garrick's struggle against the wolf, and Garrick had just dodged the question. Everything he'd said about discontinuing his search for a cure was true. It was dangerous and all-encompassing, and he didn't want himself or Tyler to throw any more time away on that pointless mission. When it was so close, though, with a possible answer within his grasp, it was hard to deny.

On the other hand, he was terrified that it wouldn't work. If he allowed himself one more attempt and it failed him, it would be more crushing than if he simply decided that the endeavor wasn't worth it. It might even make him feel like there should be one more try, and one more – falling into a typical gambler's fallacy. He wasn't sure he would ever be able to stop if he allowed himself one more chance at victory – and if he didn't stop searching for a cure, Tyler wouldn't back off either.

"I'm done," he sent back. *"I'm just going to stop trying to fight it."*

"Just like that, you're going to surrender?"

"I'm not giving up. I'm taking my destiny into my own hands." That was the best way Garrick could summarize his thoughts. He could try to figure out whether or not this new idea would work, but then the answer either way would be another fate forced upon him. Instead, he was making the decision that he would be a werewolf, just like the others. He was deciding to stop fighting it.

"Alright," Tyler sent.

"Are you mad?"

"I think you're making a grievous mistake, and it is painful to watch, but I will support your decision."

"Thanks."

Tyler sat up in his seat and put his phone away, taking out a notepad. Garrick did the same as he tried to convince himself that the decision he had made was the right one.

Garrick rested in his bed with Hayden lying practically on top of him. Before allowing her head to collapse onto the pillow beside him, she showered his face with kisses. When she finally settled down, he silently turned his face toward her and admired her.

She stared intently at him. There was something hidden beneath the loving gaze, and he couldn't figure out what she was thinking. Slowly, she leaned toward his ear, as if she was going to whisper something to him – and she licked him.

"Oh, come on," Garrick groaned, laughing as he wiped her saliva from his cheek.

"You know you like it."

"Oddly enough," he laughed, "I don't."

She gave him a sly smirk before licking him again.

"Okay," he told her as he got out of bed and quickly threw on his old jeans and wrinkled t-shirt. "You have sufficiently ruined the moment."

He wasn't sure if she actually felt compelled to lick him or if she was just messing with him. If it was the latter, it was working. The others started exhibiting some qualities that the wolf would near the full moon. Since they were only hours from changing, she could very well just be acting on her wolf instincts, though her cheery laughing implied otherwise.

By the time he turned back toward her, she was already dressed and tying her hair back in a ponytail. She walked over to him and draped her arms over his shoulders. He wrapped his around her waist and held her for a minute, searching her eyes for anything that made him question her humanity. She leaned forward, her mouth inches from his, and licked his nose.

"Alright," he complained, "you're done."

"Aww, come on," she whined, laughing. He threw his jacket over his shoulder and walked out of the room. Catching up with him, she nuzzled her head against his arm.

"It's just kisses," she defended, solidifying his belief that she was egging him on. Following him to the door, she wrapped her arms around his. If he wanted to arrive at Aldric's house early enough for a fight, Garrick had to be on his way soon, but he decided he still had a few minutes to spend with Hayden.

He paused, pulling her to a stop. In one swift motion, he swept her up and walked a few paces to the couch, dropped her on the cushions, and pinned her down. Holding her arms to her sides, he licked her cheeks a few times as she laughed, trying to dodge him.

Hayden broke free and easily rolled over, tossing Garrick to the floor. She stood and offered him a hand. Laughing, he accepted her help and she pulled him to his feet.

"Truce?" he offered.

"Yeah," she agreed. He held out his hand, and she took it, quickly pulling it up toward her face and licking it. "Sealed with a kiss."

She winked at him.

Maybe she had been right. If he wasn't so scared of the wolf during the entire day of the full moon, it could still be a good day.

Garrick strolled into Aldric's house with Hayden a step behind him. Standing tall and puffing out his chest, he marched forward with as much feigned confidence as he could muster.

"Why are we going so early?" Hayden complained, holding Garrick's arm.

"I'm going to challenge Aldric to another fight."

"Wow," she groaned playfully, shaking her head.

"I'm in the basement." Although he couldn't see him, Garrick recognized Aldric's voice. He had forgotten that Aldric would be able to hear anything they said from anywhere in the house.

"You are going to get beaten so badly," Hayden laughed.

"Thanks for the vote of confidence," he teased. She leaned up and kissed him.

"Better?" she asked with a smile.

"A little."

"Do you intend to flirt until the change or did you come early to challenge me, Elliott?" Aldric inquired from downstairs – though his voice seemed to be coming from close by. Garrick turned red as he walked down the stairs.

Standing in the middle of the wooden floor was Aldric Phoenix. In an attempt to protect as much as possible from damage, they'd removed the mats. The flooring, however, was doomed. As a clear taunt, Aldric stood in the center of the floor, perfectly still, with his eyes closed. Garrick's instinct was to use that to his advantage, but even on nights further from the moon, Garrick hadn't managed to surprise Aldric from that stance.

Cautiously, Garrick circled around Aldric, stepping as lightly as possible. As Aldric had taught them, he remained silent, giving Aldric no indication of his location. Hayden stood off to the side, and the stairs protested as Cailean climbed down them. Cailean had clearly found out what was happening and decided to enjoy watching Garrick get beat up and humiliated. From the corner of his eye, Garrick could see Cailean smirking, fully confident that his father would make a fool of Garrick. He was going to be seriously disappointed.

As the creaking of the stairs faded, Garrick ducked down and faked a punch, pulling it back before it reached Aldric. Sensing the motion, Aldric dropped his hand and drove right through the air where Garrick's hand would have been. Unprepared for the lack of contact, Aldric stumbled forward. Rising into the attack, Garrick landed an uppercut to Aldric's jaw. Since he was fighting someone stronger than himself, Garrick didn't hold anything back, and his punch was enough to launch Aldric off the ground and a few feet away.

If he gave Aldric a second of leeway, he knew the old man would turn the fight around, so Garrick ran and threw a kick to his ribs. Aldric's eyes shot open as he caught Garrick's foot and pulled it to the side, throwing off Garrick's balance. Jumping to his feet as Garrick fell, Aldric threw a scoop kick, narrowly missing Garrick as he rolled over his back shoulder and bounced back to his feet.

Before Garrick could react, Aldric connected a punch to his ribs, shattering at least one. Biting down the pain, Garrick weaved under Aldric's follow-up. He countered with a hook punch, but Aldric moved his head back just enough to avoid contact.

Garrick caught Aldric's next punch with one hand and twisted his wrist, stepping in and putting pressure on Aldric's elbow with the other hand. With minimal reaction to the lock, Aldric used the fact that Garrick dropped his hands to punch him in the face with his free hand. Surprised, Garrick released his opponent, holding his broken nose as he stumbled back.

Aldric tackled Garrick, but he relied too much on the thought that Garrick was stunned, so Garrick was able to surprise him and spin as they fell, landing on top of the larger man. With all his weight, he pinned Aldric as Cailean, who had been silent before, began counting. In an attempt to inhibit Aldric's movement, Garrick pinned both of his arms to the ground. He'd also positioned himself high enough to avoid any kicks, so he seemed to be in a powerful position.

Then, Aldric bucked his hips, knocking Garrick off balance. Caught off guard as Aldric rolled over, Garrick was sent tumbling over, and he slammed his head onto the floor. Aldric was able to pin him easily after that, and it took a few more seconds for Garrick's head to stop swimming.

"You're getting better," Aldric offered, pride clear in his voice.

"I'm not good enough yet," Garrick countered, rising as Aldric released him.

"The day you believe you are, Elliott, is the day your overconfidence kills you."

Hayden paced near the front door, alternating between checking her phone and glancing out the window as she bit her nails. With only about an hour left before the change, there was still no sign of Brooke, and the tension in the room was palpable.

Sitting on the couch, Cailean tried to play calm – but Garrick knew him too well to believe his act. His face betrayed his worry as he too repeatedly checked his phone. Inside, Garrick knew he was reacting the same was Hayden was.

Even Aldric was visibly uneasy as he stood in the corner of the room. He was their leader, and he typically played the role of assuring everyone everything was under control. In that moment, though, he wasn't even making an attempt to hide his own concern.

Garrick walked up behind Hayden and gently placed his hands on her shoulders. Leaning back into his arms, she tried to relax. It was clear that she wasn't able to, though, because she still held her phone in one hand and chewed on the fingernails of the other.

"Where is she?" she asked, as if assuming he actually would have an answer. Knowing the question wasn't actually directed at him, Garrick stayed silent. Admitting that he was clueless had no way of making the situation any better at all.

"Garrick," she cried, trying to contain the tears. "Why isn't she texting back?"

Garrick didn't know what to say. The idea everyone was afraid to verbalize was clearly at the forefront of their minds. What if the hunters had gotten to her?

"Hayden," Garrick offered. "I'm going to go to her house. I'll pick her up and bring her back here. Everything is going to be fine."

"I'm going too," Cailean declared, probably needing anything to distract himself.

"No," Garrick argued. "All of you need to be here…" He wasn't quite sure how to continue, but his point was clear.

"He's right," Aldric conceded. "Elliott is the fastest runner and he has the widest time gap before his transformation – so he is the logical choice. The rest of us will stay here and await news. If anything is amiss, he will call one of us and we'll all be there to help them."

Garrick nodded, both out of agreement and appreciation. He was thankful that Aldric was the one to finally mention the possibility of something having gone wrong, because
he didn't want to have to. Without leaving any more time for
arguments, Garrick opened the front door and sprinted toward
Brooke's house. Thankfully, she didn't live far away. Still,
every second mattered, and each felt like an eternity.

Irrationally, he hoped to burst through her door only to
find her sitting at home, completely oblivious of what night it
was. Maybe she lost track of time, and they'd cross paths on
his way. The logical side of him knew, though, that none of
them could possibly forget a full moon – they counted the
days, the others reminded each other, and the presence of the
wolf was unmistakable. Something had to be wrong.

The other three, of course, were fully aware of that as
well. Aldric had said that they would wait to find out if anything was wrong, but that was clearly a euphemism. Aldric
was waiting for Garrick to tell him if attempting to save her
was worth the risk – or if she was already gone.

Garrick shook those thoughts out of his mind as he approached Brooke's house, ducking quietly behind the bushes
bordering her lawn. Examining the house, Garrick's fears
were confirmed when he saw a van parked outside.

The same vehicle had been outside of Samantha's
home when he had gone to her memorial service. While he
couldn't tell which of the hunters owned the van, he knew it
was a bad sign regardless. Garrick noticed the front door was
slightly ajar, and it appeared that the lock had been broken
from the outside. The door swung open and two men dragged
a blindfolded woman outside. Instantly, Garrick recognized
Brooke, who didn't appear to be struggling. If they'd killed
her, she wouldn't be blindfolded, so he knew she was alive –
but she was clearly hurt.

Sacrificing stealth, Garrick broke from his cover and
jumped over the bushes, determined to protect his friends. He
reached the hunters as they slammed the back of the van
closed, locking Brooke inside. Three more stepped out from

the house, and Garrick realized he was drastically outmatched, but he couldn't give up.

Using his momentum as he approached the group, Garrick punched the nearest one in the stomach, feeling something break under his knuckles. As the man lurched forward and coughed up blood, Garrick grabbed him and threw him aside. One of the others sliced his knife at Garrick, but he managed to dodge the attack, throwing a punch as he stepped back. The hunter was quick, though, and he weaved under Garrick's attack.

Pain shot through Garrick's body as an arrow pierced his leg, probably from one of the hunters still near the doorway. Another arrow lodged itself in his shoulder. He stumbled back, right into the blade of another hunter.

"Great," one of them muttered. "This one isn't going to tell us anything."

Garrick dropped to his knees. Blood poured from each of his wounds, and not a single one was healing. Any semblance of strength was draining from his body.

"Just let him go, he'll be dead in a minute," one hunter spat. Garrick collapsed, dropping face-forward onto the pavement. Weakly, he tried to pull the silver blade out of his back, but was unable to reach it.

"We have to get this one back before they change, anyway," another agreed.

"Hold on," a third one hesitated. Garrick recognized this one as their leader, Darren. Darren squatted down, lowering himself to Garrick's level. "Hello there, Garrick Elliott. You, my friend, don't have much time to live, clearly, so let's make your miserable life mean something. Why don't you tell me where your friends are hiding out tonight? We're going to find them either way, but if you just tell us, it will save this one quite a lot of pain in the process."

Garrick tried to force out an angry and sarcastic retort, but his mouth wouldn't move. Despite his best efforts, the best he could force out was a weak growl.

"Alright, I get it. It's hard to talk. Maybe you can't even process what I'm saying," Darren taunted with a smirk. "Well, let's try this to spark you into action. If you tell me where they are, this all ends. If not, I'll have to ask until someone finally answers my questions. Maybe Brooke won't, but I'm sure your buddy Tyler can be broken. Or your lovely mother."

Although there was nothing they could do to convince Garrick to divulge the location of his friends, he wished he could at least find the strength to warn the people he loved. He couldn't. All he could do was watch as Darren stood, groaning overdramatically, and stretched. His pants slid up, revealing one of the probably many scars which coated his body from the training that prepared him so adequately to handle Garrick and his kind. As the hunters drove off, Garrick finally found the hilt of the dagger in his back. They had just left him there without verifying that he was dead. Maybe they were just overly confident they'd damaged his body beyond repair, assuming he was closer to the change than he truly was. It seemed like a terrible strategic move, but Garrick couldn't help but wonder if Darren had allowed him to live. Maybe it was all just another part of his sick game, or maybe he thought Garrick would find him and give him the answers he wanted in order to protect the people he loved.

More blood poured out from his back as Garrick removed the blade. He grabbed one of the arrows, but there was no more strength in his arms. Garrick tried to retrieve his phone, but he couldn't move his arms. The more he exerted himself, the more blood drained from his open wounds. He could feel any will to fight draining out of his body. Finally, he realized that the struggle to keep his eyes open was futile. The world faded around him.

When Garrick woke up, he was still lying on the ground, but it wasn't the pavement he remembered falling on. Instead, he was on a bed of grass and fallen leaves, surrounded by trees. The setting sun painted the canopy above him hues of orange and red, but it didn't allow for much light to reach the ground around him.

Completely paralyzed, Garrick struggled to move. The pain from the holes in his body was dulled, but he could feel the strange sensation of blood seeping from them. A figure started to move in front of him, barely coated in the shadows. Though he couldn't determine what exactly the shape was, Garrick had a suspicion that he knew. Unable to escape, Garrick just waited for the beast to show itself.

Garrick tried to move his hand, and he could feel his finger twitch slightly. Slowly, the pieces fell together in his mind. The knife pierced his spinal cord. In removing the blade, he'd probably severed a nerve, paralyzing himself below that point. Though his body was beginning to heal, it couldn't keep pace with the blood he was still losing from all three wounds.

From the edge of the trees, the wolf examined Garrick with what appeared to be concern in its gaze. Maybe it was instinctually aware that if Garrick died, it would too. Cautiously, it inched toward him. Garrick was able to lift his hand a few inches off the ground, but it required too much effort for him to hold it up, and it simply fell back down.

The wolf leaned forward, bending its front legs to get closer to Garrick. Its face couldn't have been more than a few inches away from his own.

The animal whimpered. It seemed like it could understand the pain Garrick was feeling. Maybe it could feel what was happening to his body when it was so close to taking control of it.

Garrick reached out for the creature. It brought him a strange sense of comfort. On edge, the wolf backed away, hesitantly sniffing him. Garrick let his hand fall back down again, losing focus. This world too was starting to grow dim.

The wolf lifted its head toward the sky and howled.

Garrick's eyes shot open. All of the pain which had been faint a minute ago flooded back into his body – but so did his control. He struggled to his feet and limped into Brooke's house. With no clear direction, Garrick just searched relentlessly for a clue.

What he found, though, was a corpse. Brooke's father was lying on the floor, blood pooling around him. He had probably resisted telling the hunters where his daughter was. Maybe he had even put up a valiant fight against the intruders. In the end, though, he hadn't had a chance. Reluctant to accept the scene in front of him, Garrick turned away, but he only found something worse. Brooke's mother appeared to have been running to Brooke's room upstairs when she was shot in the back, collapsing near the top of the staircase, blood running down them.

The hunters were ruthless – willing to do whatever it took to get to the beasts. Garrick had already known that was their attitude, but he hadn't known how all-encompassing their hatred was. They would even kill a human if they suspected to be guarding a wolf.

Garrick stumbled backward, tripping over the threshold and collapsing to the ground. His phone vibrated in his pocket, and he fished it out. Across the top of the display, he could see that thirty minutes had already passed, and Hayden was calling him.

"Hayden," Garrick croaked as he answered the phone.

"Garrick, what happened?" she asked frantically.

"I'm okay," he coughed. He tried to clear his throat and make it sound convincing, but it only made matters worse.

"No, you aren't," she argued. "We're coming to get you."

He wanted to send her to chase after the van instead. The three of them could possibly catch up to the hunters and save Brooke. There was nothing they could do for Garrick – he was either going to heal or die, but that wouldn't change just because they found him.

Despite his efforts, though, he couldn't force any more words out. Losing the strength to keep holding the phone up, Garrick dropped it and fainted again.

Garrick woke up in Aldric's basement. There was no more pain in his back, and the arrow wound in his shoulder had begun to heal. Sitting up and examining the room, Garrick tried to convince himself everything that had happened had been a terrible dream.

"Hayden," he groaned, turning to face her. Both of her hands were clasped around one of his, and tears streamed down his face. Garrick knew they weren't just for him, because Brooke was still nowhere to be seen.

Cailean was standing against the wall, occasionally punching it. He turned to face them, preparing to say something, but then turned back and slammed his fist into the wall again.

"Yes?" she inquired through the tears. In her voice, relief at his awakening was mixed with the grief of Brooke's absence.

"How much longer do we have?"

"Ten minutes," she answered.

He struggled to his feet, leaning against a wall. Hayden helped him up, keeping a hand on his back to help him stand up steadily. Soon, he was able to stand on his own. The last remnants of pain from his wounds faded away. Due to the sheer amount of blood he'd lost, he still felt nauseous. The blood would replace itself in a few minutes and he'd be fully healed, but he didn't have time to wait.

"Aldric," he muttered. His alpha wasn't in the room, but Garrick knew that he'd hear him. They had to find a way to save Brooke – along with anyone with a connection to the pack.

"Yes, Elliott?" Aldric asked, already at the top of the stairs. Closing the door behind him, he descended toward them. His voice was stone cold, and his eyes steely.

"I know where they are," Garrick offered.

"It doesn't matter," Aldric replied. "It's too late to take any action. I should never have sent you out there alone."

"Don't say that," Garrick muttered under his breath. If Aldric already regretted his decision, it would take a lot more convincing to get him on board with Garrick going out again, and he didn't have time to convince him.

"It's the truth. You weren't ready. None of you would have been."

"I'm going to go help her," Garrick declared, ignoring Aldric's explanation. "You all have ten minutes before you change; the house is at least five away. There's no way you could make it – but I can. I can hold the change back for another twenty, maybe twenty-five minutes. I can get her out and to the woods. It's her best shot."

"What makes you think you could get her out of there?"

"I'm just going to have to trust that you trained me well."

"No," Aldric commanded. "This pack won't lose both of you tonight."

Shaking his head, Garrick chose to ignore his alpha's order. There wasn't enough time to defend his position. Instead, he ran up the stairs and opened the door. Glancing back before he closed the door, he saw Hayden running after him, but Aldric held her back, placing a hand in front of her. Garrick couldn't understand the look in Aldric's eyes. It was clear he was angry to be disobeyed, but he also appeared proud. Cailean stood by his father's side, pained that he couldn't go with Garrick, but gratitude displayed on his face.

"He'll die," Hayden cried, struggling as Garrick closed the door.

"We could kill people," Aldric told her.

"We have to do whatever it takes."

"You think I don't want to be out there?" Cailean pitched in. "Right now, all we can do is trust Garrick."

Chapter 24

Nine months ago

Garrick sat in the coffee shop with Tyler and Chase, his jacket resting on the chair behind him. For the most part, he still tried to cover his arms in public, but his short sleeve t-shirt exposed his arms. Cailean had only suggested that attire for a month, though, and Garrick was well beyond that. Anyway, there weren't many people around, so he felt relatively safe.

"I have a hypothetical scenario," Tyler suggested. "Imagine you are born with the superpower to absorb supernatural abilities of those around you – however in this world, you are the only person with any such ability. Essentially, it's completely useless. Would you rather know about it or be ignorant?"

Garrick laughed, and Chase inhaled deeply. They had been playing would you rather since they got there twenty minutes ago, and, as with most of their conversations, it was growing increasingly nerdy.

"Definitely not know," Garrick answered. "What's the point? I'd just be tortured by it."

"No way," Chase argued. "At least I'd know I was special."

"Who would believe you?" Tyler questioned.

"Me!" Chase laughed. Garrick stood and walked to the counter to get another coffee. Since he'd been young, he had liked black coffee, probably because his mom constantly drank it. However, after he got scratched, the caffeine had absolutely no effect on him, so he'd spent a long time drinking it waiting for it to work. Finally, he gave up and started drinking it for the taste. At least there wouldn't be negative effects from it either.

As horrible as the curse was, the healing effects were positive – so there was a silver lining. Being a werewolf provided him immunity from practically every known disease. As a matter of fact, it worked on mostly anything health-related – even something which didn't qualify as a disease.

"Hey, Garrick," Samantha, the waitress, greeted. Every time she greeted him by name, it only reinforced to him that he spent far too much time there. Garrick noticed her staring at his biceps, and her eyes quickly darted away. Torn between feeling awkward or flattered, Garrick just stood at the register. Garrick was in love with Hayden, so he knew nothing would ever come of it – and he didn't want it to – but it still felt nice to be noticed. "Have you been working out?"

"That is the oldest line in the book," he laughed.

"Sorry," she responded shyly. It was amazing what a few muscles could do. She'd never given him a second look before, and suddenly she was barely able to formulate a sentence. "It's impressive. You look good."

"Thanks," he accepted the compliment, then casually tried to explain it away. "My friend is a personal trainer."

"But he lets you drink unlimited coffee drinks?"

"What he doesn't know won't hurt him."

Having spent his entire life dealing with the side-effects of being a werewolf, Cailean had probably dismissed plenty of compliments. According to him, there were three important steps: joking about the compliment given to change the mood, accepting it, and then reasoning it away. That was the most natural way to avoid appearing awkward when given a compliment, but also to avoid further conversation. Since Garrick had no faith in his improvisation skills, he and Cailean had rehearsed that exact conversation so many times it just flowed off Garrick's tongue. It worked, and she smiled at him as she handed him his drink without another word.

"Wow," Chase joked as Garrick sat down.

"What?" Garrick asked.

"Smooth, Garrick Elliott," Tyler finished Chase's thought.

"Oh," Garrick laughed, then shrugged it off. Then he whispered, "It's easy when you aren't interested."

Present
Night of the full moon

Faster than humanly possible, Garrick's legs propelled him forward. As Garrick approached Darren's door, he felt the first twinge of the wolf pressing against him, trying to break free of its cage. The van was parked sloppily in the driveway, and Garrick wondered if Brooke had started changing in the car, because it seemed like they rushed her inside. A howl from the inside of the building in front of him gave him an even greater sense of urgency.

Without hesitation, Garrick pushed through the gate, then kicked the front door down. By the time a hunter stood in his way, his claws were already fully grown, and he was aware he was running out of time. The adrenaline only served to speed up the transformation. Using the enhanced reflexes to his advantage, Garrick sidestepped as the hunter slashed at him with the knife, then he drew his claws across the hunter's neck, and the man dropped to the ground, hands pressed over the wound.

Three more stepped into the room, and Garrick's arms twitched. He caught an arrow flying toward his head and snapped it in half. Another arrow soared to him, and he ducked, so it hit one fellow hunter. That left two more of them, standing directly in front of him.

He ran at them and drove his fist into one of their chests, holding nothing back. The man flew across the room and shattered his skull as it collided with the wall. The other drew a gun and shot Garrick's arm. He howled in pain, but the bullet was quick to force itself out of his skin.

Anger burning in his eyes, Garrick stepped toward the hunter. He grabbed the man's arm and hit the back of his elbow, snapping the bone and forcing him to drop the gun to the floor. Moving his hands to the hunter's head, Garrick quickly broke his neck. The third hunter, still bleeding with an arrow in his chest, was simply watching the spectacle with wide, fearful eyes. Garrick froze for a second, torn. Part of him wanted to kill the hunter, but he was a defeated foe, and anger would help no one. Garrick scowled as he turned away and moved toward the basement, kicking open the door and dashing down the stairs. Brooke was chained to a post cemented into the ground, and a man was leaning against the wall near her, holding a large silver sword.

"Glad one of you could make it," the man taunted. By the way this hunter held himself, Garrick assumed he was higher up the chain of command than Darren himself. "Now we will have one fewer to hunt over the next month."

Unable to hear any other sounds in the house, Garrick assumed Darren and the others he saw earlier had taken back to the streets – searching for other wolves or other people to torture for information. It was clear he wasn't going to be able to protect everyone just by showing up at that house. Garrick had never been more thankful that his mom worked nights, because they wouldn't attack her at the station, but he'd still have to find a way to warn Tyler.

Garrick couldn't force out any words. He just snarled, and the man laughed as he raised the sword to cut through

Brook's waist. Brooke didn't have any wolf-like characteris-
tics, which confirmed the hunter was using a silver blade. Silver would halt her transformation temporarily, and this hunter
seemed to know exactly how long he had to wait between cuts.
This wasn't the first time he'd tortured a wolf for answers, but
Garrick was going to ensure it would be the last. Sickened by
his very existence, Garrick dove straight at the hunter. The
hunter stepped back, easily dodging the blow, and then swung
the sword in one fluid motion, leaving a deep cut in Garrick's
arm.

Blood poured out of his arm, and, based on his experience with silver, it wasn't going to go away too soon. He felt
his strength slowly fade – but it didn't disappear. Instead of
rushing in again, Garrick breathed, realizing he had to be calm.
It was just another fight, he couldn't think about what was happening to Brooke. If he let the anger rule him, he'd make more
stupid decisions. The hunter stepped in with another swipe,
and Garrick dodged. Using the recoil as an opening, he dove
forward, slamming his fist into the man's gut and knocking
him backward.

Garrick stepped forward but carefully stayed out of the
reach of the sword as the hunter stood. Though blood still
poured from his wound, he could feel his healing process start
as his fangs grew, and his strength began to return.

The hunter attacked again, but Garrick was able to
counter the strike. He ducked under the sword and caught the
man's arm. Bringing his shoulder up into his elbow, Garrick
broke the hunter's arm and the sword clattered to the floor.
Preparing to finish off the hunter, Garrick raised his claws, but
an arrow penetrated his back before he had time to react. Two
more arrows within another second hit the back of his knees,
dropping him. Turning his head, he saw one more hunter he
didn't recognize from the group he'd seen earlier. It was becoming clear that they'd reached out for help outside the family.

The scraping of metal filled the room as the other
hunter struggled to his feet and lifted the sword in his non-

dominant arm. Garrick turned his head back and saw that the hunter had already gotten to his feet, and he had the sword raised above Garrick's head.

A growl caught all of their attention and a wolf with golden eyes stood in the doorway. Cailean dove at the hunter wielding the crossbow, tearing him apart within a second. Hayden, also a wolf, of course, was next to bound down the stairs. She rammed into the hunter, knocking off his balance and forcing him to drop the sword again. Then, she stood between him and Garrick, growling.

Aldric, still a man, strode down the stairs next. Much like Garrick, he was half transformed, but he still had some sense of humanity. Other than a slight limp, Aldric didn't seem to be experiencing much pain as he fought the transformation. Given that he knew Aldric's wolf had been pushing for freedom since before any of the others, Garrick was impressed once again at his alpha's strength. Confidently, Aldric walked up to the hunter on the ground and stepped on his temple, crushing the bone and killing him instantly.

Hayden licked Garrick's wounded arm as he pulled the arrows out of his back with the other one. The silver was wearing off, so his arm was healing, and the wounds on his back closed almost instantaneously. Focused on the task at hand, Garrick forced himself to fight the change, but it was getting increasingly difficult. Touching Brooke's shackles was agonizing, so he pulled back, defeated. Aldric used every ounce of strength he had to break one, so Garrick followed his lead and tugged at the other – and Brooke dropped to the ground. Within a minute of being freed from the silver, she was fully transformed. Garrick wobbled to the stairs, painfully fighting the change. Planning to lock the door, he slowly ascended. Locking themselves in a hunter's house was risky, but he couldn't allow all of them, himself included, to escape into the town.

As he climbed, he dug his fingernails into his flesh. The pain from the fight hadn't stopped his change, but he hadn't wanted it to. Staggering up the stairs, he caressed the scar on his arm. This would be the perfect time for Tyler's idea to work.

When he arrived at the door, he reached out to close it – but he was too late. Cailean bolted past him, knocking him onto his knees. Brooke shot out next, and even Hayden raced to the streets. Hoping for advice, Garrick looked back at Aldric, but could barely talk. The two of them chased after the others. They all stood on the street, and Garrick fumbled after them, hoping to get them to go somewhere safe.

"Elliott," Aldric managed to say. He was on all fours, unable to look up, and Garrick could see that he was losing to the beast. Garrick knew he himself couldn't fight the transformation much longer either. "I was wrong. I told you it was pointless, that isn't true. I thought you were weak, but you aren't."

Garrick didn't know where he was going, but he hoped he had time to get there. Hearing Aldric admit that he was wrong was nice, but it didn't seem urgent at that moment. He just wanted his alpha to tell him what their solution was going to be.

The other three wolves circled around them, waiting for them to finish their transformation. They all looked impatient as Garrick and Aldric struggled to remain human. It had been at least ten minutes since Hayden and Cailean had changed, and the wolves clearly wanted to run with their pack.

"You're stronger than I am," Aldric told Garrick. "You can hold this off longer than any of us. I can't keep doing this, but you can. You need to run – get to the woods. They'll follow you."

"Can't I lead them back to the basement?" Garrick asked. While he appreciated Aldric's confidence, he was already succumbing to the beast, and there was no way he could make it through multiple blocks of the city without losing himself. Aldric's basement was much closer, and there was at least a slight chance Garrick could make it that far.

"No, they won't follow you to a cage. They'll follow you to somewhere familiar." He paused for a moment. "We all will. You're the only hope to protect this town, Elliott."

Garrick wanted to ask more questions, but the wolf finally overpowered Aldric. Within a few seconds, he was fully in his wolf form. Garrick turned and started running, but he collapsed after two steps.

He clenched his teeth and balled his hands – his claws drawing blood from his palms. Intending to harm himself enough to fight the change, Garrick bit his lip as well. He felt the pain, but it was diminished – a fraction of what he'd expect – and he could feel himself healing even as the wounds were being inflicted. The pain wasn't strong enough to fight the wolf.

When he closed his eyes, images of the little girl the wolf had seen in town flashed through his mind. Had he not been scared away, he may have hurt her. Now, if he didn't stop it, there would be five of them running free. Reminding himself of the importance that he prevent that, Garrick tried to think of a way for him to guide them away. All he had to do was control himself for long enough to get them all into the woods.

He tried picturing the wolf in his mind. He imagined himself reaching out for the scar on the creature's leg – a scar which exactly matched his own. Nothing was working, though. The wolf tore him apart from the inside, and he couldn't fight it any longer.

"I'm sorry, Aldric," he cried. "I'm sorry."

The second apology wasn't for Aldric. It was for whoever got hurt that night because of him. Anyone that the hunters got to along with anyone that he and the other wolves got to.

He let go, feeling the tidal wave of the wolf's power rush over him.

Garrick heard a scream. At first, he thought it was coming from his head – from the night only one month ago that had haunted every dream since. As the scream drew on, though, he realized that it was different. It was the material for a new nightmare – another child, scared and alone, screaming for help.

That gave Garrick the last burst of adrenaline that he needed to continue his fight against the wolf for a bit longer. Shoving the beast back down he stood and ran, but he collapsed only a few feet away. It was too late. Even as he fought it with all of his strength, he could feel the wolf overpowering him. Garrick watched as the four others circled around the child, devoid of hope for escape. The last shred of his humanity was slipping from his grasp, and he could feel the peculiar sensation of his eyes shifting, taking on a blue hue. If he gave up, he was going to help his pack murder that innocent child.

"No!" He grunted, more to himself than anyone else. Screaming on the inside, he willed himself not to change. On the outside, all he could muster were a few weak, barely audible words. "No!"

But he knew it wouldn't help.

Although he knew there was nothing left for him to do, he stumbled to the others. The animalistic side of him was too powerful, and the world darkened as his human side lost its vision. When he blacked out, he had no idea where he'd go, but he knew that child would die.

He felt the bone in his arms shatter. Brooke prepared to take the first leap and pounce at the child, and all Garrick could do was watch in horror. Garrick bit down and summoned every ounce of strength he had left, and then a bit more. He struggled to his feet.

Garrick's arms were healing already, but they didn't look how he thought they would. They had healed to human arms, not those of a wolf. Brooke pounced, and Garrick grabbed her hind leg, turned, and slammed her to the ground. Panting, he stood tall as his ribs cracked.

"Stop!" He tried to yell, but it was a broken plea. Suddenly, he was overwhelmed with emotions. It wasn't just the self-pity and guilt anymore, there was also rage. Mostly, it was fear of what was to come. Channeling everything he had, as if he truly believed it would make any difference in what was happening, he forced the word out again.

"Stop," he growled; his voice guttural and barely able to be described as human, but audible. It was a shout. His arms finally started to change shape slightly, as his shoulders expanded to accommodate the new form he was taking. At maximum, he had a minute before he lost control entirely, but he had to use it for what he could. Stepping into the center of the circle, he stood between the child and Aldric.

Hayden and Cailean traced the circle until they were back at Aldric's side. All of them seemed angry at Garrick for standing in the way of their hunt. Brooke lay on the ground a few feet behind her pack, giving her wounds time to heal before she got up. Garrick turned to face the child, who screamed in fear upon the sight of Garrick's half-human face.

"Go," he instructed, attempting to sound as friendly as possible but only succeeding in producing a scratchy and unrecognizable sound. The kid turned and sprinted toward his front door. The other wolves moved forward to pursue him, but Garrick growled deep within his throat, and they backed down.

Garrick held his ground, staring directly into the eyes of Aldric. Staring down his alpha.

Brooke got up, limping with the first step, but walking normally quickly after, and stood next to Cailean. Glaring at Garrick, she growled. Garrick tried to speak, he tried to reason, but he could feel the other side vying for control, and he was losing his ability to produce words. He was already too close to being lost to the beast. Instead, he just growled again.

He growled more forcefully than he knew possible, not just for him, but for any creature. The ground underneath him shook. Cailean stared angrily for a moment, but he backed down. Brooke whimpered and shifted backward with him. Hayden was unusually quiet. She didn't growl back, but she didn't back down either. Instead, she cautiously stepped forward, and he closely watched her graceful walk.

A mixture of terror and agony caused his heart to race as Hayden reached his leg. If she fought to defend her alpha, either he'd have to hurt her, or she'd hurt him and destroy any hope he had of stopping the wolves. He just stood tall, fighting through the pain as he forced himself to appear powerful.

Hayden turned, standing at Garrick's side. Facing the other wolves, she snarled.

Garrick allowed himself a glance to make sure that the kid was alright. He was already on his porch, opening the doors, tears streaming down his face. Garrick could feel the stares of the people watching through the windows and hear the faint noises as some of them called the police – and others animal control. Their conversations, the hushed whispers through closed doors down the street, were all audible to him. Not only could he hear them – but he could also understand them. Not well, but he could process them much better than he would be able to when fully changed.

Matching Aldric's glare, Garrick growled again. Finally, to assert his dominance, Aldric pounced. Garrick stepped to the side and used Aldric's momentum to toss him aside. With each passing minute, Garrick's strength depleted, and he couldn't use as much of it to fight himself. Mid-transformation, he stood a foot taller than usual, and every muscle in his body bulged out. Though he stood like a man, he had the claws, fangs, and eyes of a wolf.

Garrick couldn't help but wonder if this was what everyone meant to be in control of the wolf. As if two brains were attempting to crowd themselves in one skull, Garrick's head pounded painfully. If this was what he'd been trying to learn to do, he simply wanted to forget it after that night. After he made sure they were safe.

Aldric took a swipe at Garrick, digging his claws into Garrick's leg. Garrick dropped to his knees. Hayden bit at Aldric, but he was quick. In a flash, he dug his claws deep into her side, and she dropped to the ground with a whimper. Although everything in him wanted to help, Garrick had trouble

standing; not solely due to the wound, which was already closing, but because wolves didn't stand on two legs, and that was
by far the dominant side of him. Wavering on his feet, he
managed to rise, but Aldric was swift to jump at him, ready to
bite. Garrick kicked the wolf in the stomach, sending him flying down the street. Climbing to his feet, he charged at Garrick again, but Garrick ducked down and cut deep into Aldric's
front leg.

The wolf slid a few feet past Garrick. As he skidded
to a stop and turned, he left claw marks in the asphalt. Hayden
stood, but she collapsed again. Determined, she rose to her
feet and stepped toward Garrick. He didn't know how much
human was left in her, if any, or if she'd understand any communication he attempted with her, but he had to try. Trying to
tell her to stand down, he held his hand out, palm facing her.
In response to either him or the pain, she backed away and
dropped to the ground again.

Garrick dodged another attack, realizing that he was a
much more effective fighter when he had at least a small part
of his human mind left to work with. He dove to the side and
rolled, again avoiding Aldric's blows. Garrick didn't want this
fight for supremacy; he just wanted to make sure the boy and
the other citizens of his hometown were safe. If the only way
to do that was to fight Aldric, then that's what he would do.

The pain was starting to fade as if the wolf had stopped
fighting him and turned its attention to Aldric. Without it distracting him, his thoughts became less foggy, and his mind
raced with plans on how to lead the other wolves somewhere
they couldn't cause harm.

Garrick sidestepped a bite from Aldric, and he kicked
the wolf in the nose, pushing it to the ground. While the wolf
was on its side, Garrick scratched its stomach, drawing blood
from a deep wound. In retaliation, Aldric bit Garrick's leg and
pulled his head back, dragging Garrick to the floor. He kicked
frantically with his other foot until one kick connected with
Aldric's nose, causing the wolf to release its grip on him. With
every attack that Aldric landed, Garrick could feel his own

wolf pushing itself to the surface. It wanted to be free – to fight back. The feeling, though, was unlike anything he'd felt. It was almost as if it were asking Garrick for more control, rather than taking it from him. The only thing left giving Garrick strength was the knowledge of what would happen when he gave the wolf what it wanted. Despite his body's protesting, he stood and kicked Aldric again.

Aldric flew backward, lying on the floor for so long that Garrick began to worry for him. When he stood again, the snarl was gone, as if Garrick had finally proven himself as a member of the pack. Garrick didn't want to keep fighting, especially not to try to prove anything to Aldric. Despite what Aldric's wolf though, Garrick wasn't interested in fighting for the role of alpha – he just wanted to protect the innocent people around them.

Once more, Garrick checked over his shoulder to make sure the child had made it inside. There was no sign of the boy, and the door was shut. Listening closely, though, he could hear the boy's cries and his mother's attempts to comfort him.

Aldric's wounds had closed, and he looked back at Garrick, ready to charge again. As much as he'd wanted the fight to be over, Garrick stood his ground. Still, he didn't know how much longer he could keep going. It was becoming impossible to fight Aldric while still holding off the beast which was tearing at him from inside, pleading for the chance to protect itself. Garrick could feel himself fading, and soon he'd lose both battles.

Garrick stood shakily on two legs, barely able to hold himself up. Aldric had yet to charge again, and Garrick hoped he could just win by staring down his opponent. The wolf seemed to be taking another chance to size him up. Although he hoped it wasn't the case, it almost seemed to Garrick as if the wolf was planning an attack – consciously thinking. With the two current opponents, Garrick was already struggling, so he didn't need Aldric's human side offering strategy to the wolf.

BRENT MILLER

The wolf looked like it was about to charge again, and Garrick could feel his hope slipping away. Garrick felt his knees collapsing under him, but he fought to stay standing, giving everything he had to appear powerful. Calling his bluff, Aldric rushed forward, and Garrick knew he had nothing left to give. Then, he saw a flash of brown fur as another wolf intercepted Aldric, tackling him to the ground. Hayden had come to his rescue again. Using all the energy left in his muscles, Garrick maintained his posture, refusing to give Aldric a reason to think he was weak. His shoulders rolled forward and his breathing was labored, but he refused to fall.

Garrick could hear the growling and scratching in front of him as Hayden defended him. He wanted to help, but he knew there was nothing he could do. The fight in front of him broke up, and the two wolves stared at each other. Though his head was downcast, Garrick kept his eyes forward.

Aldric growled at Hayden, warning her to back down. By choosing to protect Garrick, Hayden only served to make Aldric angrier – and he probably took it as another threat. In this animalistic state, she should have sided with the stronger wolf, so Garrick wasn't sure why she was defending him.

Maybe it was like the day she saved him from Cailean. Somewhere, deep down, this wolf was still Hayden, and she wasn't going to let anything happen to Garrick. Standing between them, she made it clear that Aldric was going to have to go through her to get to Garrick. Maybe her love for him was giving her the strength to stand against her alpha.

Aldric charged forward, and the other wolf rushed in to meet him. The two of them viciously bit and scratched at each other again, locked in close combat.

"Hayden!" Garrick coughed. He didn't know what he wanted her to do, but he couldn't let her get killed for him. A soft brush of fur rubbed against his right leg, and he looked down to see another wolf standing by his side. Blue eyes looked up at him with nothing but love.

"Hayden?" he asked. As he looked back up, he saw Brooke walk toward him, standing at his left side. The wolf fighting Aldric bit his neck, spinning him around and throwing him to the ground. Garrick saw Cailean's golden eyes flash as he pinned his father down, clamping his jaw around his throat in an attempt to force him to surrender. No words managed to force their way through Garrick's lips, but he tried to express his gratitude as he sighed with relief.

Aldric broke free by scratching Cailean's leg. Cailean fell to the ground and Aldric climbed back up, biting Cailean's neck. He threw Cailean, who landed a few feet away with a whimper. Turning his attention back to Garrick, Aldric growled angrily. Hayden and Brooke inched closer. Placing a hand on Hayden's head for support, Garrick was still able to stand.

Cailean, still limping as blood seeped and covered the fur on his leg and throat, closed the distance and stood directly in front of Garrick, blocking his father's advance. He growled, shaking the earth beneath him.

Garrick still felt the wolf clawing at him – tearing him apart inside. Though it had subsided somewhat during the fight, it was back in full force, and with a vengeance. The beast was infuriated that Garrick wouldn't let it fight its own battles. The internal struggle was becoming so painful that it was nearing a physical feeling of being ripped to shreds. Although he did everything he could to muster the strength to fight through it, he could feel himself wavering.

Finally, Aldric looked down. Garrick started to back away, and the four wolves walked closer to him. In his breaking mind, he formulated the closest thing to a plan that he could. Garrick mustered the last of his strength to move, limping as he inched his way back to Aldric's house. Hayden stood at his side, supporting him as they walked. Along the way, he carefully listened for the footsteps of the others as they kept at his heels. Aldric had warned him that they wouldn't follow him to a basement, but he didn't have many options. They followed him all the way up to the door. Garrick didn't know if it was loyalty that kept them following him – because they were willing to protect their own and they could see his pain –

or respect – because even in their animalistic states, they recognized the strength it took to fight. However, none of the
wolves, even Hayden, followed him as he crossed the threshold. Aldric had been right; none of them wanted to enter the
small space. It felt like a cage.

"Linda! Hide upstairs!" Garrick yelled as he collapsed
forward, pushing the door open. He saw her looking over the
banister at him, probably in complete disbelief of what she was
seeing and hearing. Garrick couldn't tell anymore, but his
voice was probably monstrous enough to induce fear into the
bravest of people. It had been at least twenty minutes since he
was supposed to change, and any semblance of humanity was
quickly fading.

She didn't argue, though; she just watched as Garrick
limped to the basement stairs. Unable to muster the strength
to walk down them, he reluctantly accepted the only alternative. The fall couldn't cause more pain than he was already in,
anyway. With a sigh, he closed his eyes, covered his face, and
threw himself down the stairs and into the basement. Upon
landing at the bottom, he struggled to all fours. Taking a deep
breath, Garrick tried to control the wolf for one more minute.
He opened his mouth and tried to let out a powerful howl.

He didn't. It was a very human sound; weak and full
of pain. His howl sounded more like a sick child pretending
to be a dog. On his second attempt, he could feel the wolf
lending its strength. The sound radiated around him, pushing
its way through the air, and it was enough to entice the other
wolves to run down to meet him. With the last bit of energy
he could muster, he forced himself to his feet.

"Please," he begged, "just let me do this."

He didn't know if the wolf could understand him. He
didn't know if it was really a separate being. He didn't know
anything. The only thing he did know was that he didn't have
another choice. Everything was blurry and his thoughts were
covered in a haze, and he couldn't think straight, so he just
spoke.

"You can have control," he tried to offer. The words may not have even made it past his lips – he couldn't tell past the deafening ringing in his ears – but the wolf was in his mind anyway. "Just let me do this."

The pain didn't subside, but he felt determination and strength coursing through his veins. Refusing to surrender or to put anyone else at risk, Garrick crawled up the stairs and slammed himself into the door, thrusting it closed. Using the frame as support, he inched his way up until he could reach the doorknob. Then, pulling himself up the last stretch, he locked the deadbolt and chain, locking himself in the basement with them. Satisfied that he'd done all he could, he finally stopped fighting; giving in to the completely unbearable agony. Breathing out a sigh of relief, he fell backward and tumbled down the stairs. Compared to what he was already feeling, the pain of tumbling down the stairs was almost a comfort.

Resting on his back, all of the pain subsided. The wolf was content, and Garrick was no longer fighting. Garrick climbed on to his hands and knees as he prepared to feel the bones in his legs shatter as they reformed to those that would help him run as a wolf. He prepared himself for the muscles in his arms to rip and tear, allowing the form to change. He was even ready for what always hurt him the most, the expansion and reforming of his spinal cord, which would allow his movement as a werewolf.

But what he got was peace. The pain waned until it just faded out completely. Garrick waited a few minutes, allowing time for the rush of the transformation to bring him into his wolf state. When nothing happened, he stood and took a few deep breaths. His arms were twice their size and he towered over his normal height, but he was not a wolf.

Garrick tried to steady his heartbeat – which wasn't a simple task given the current events, but he closed his eyes and focused on his breathing. Muscles in his arms tore and reformed, but they took a smaller, more compact form as they wrapped tightly around his arm, returning to their normal size.

Garrick felt a sickening movement in his eyes as they shifted in color.

He could feel his ribs reforming, creating a barrier around his human heart, which was beating at an almost reasonable pace. He felt his elbows pop back into place, allowing for their standard range of motion. His legs twitched as the bones changed back to their normal shape and size, allowing him to climb to his feet and stand normally.

His fangs shrank back as he opened his eyes. Garrick held his breath for a moment, unsure of whether or not to believe what he was feeling. Looking down at his hands, he watched the claws condense into fingernails.

Breathing deeply, he saw the confusion on the faces of the other wolves. While they couldn't have had the processing ability of a human being, they were cognizant of what was supposed to be happening, and they knew that Garrick had defied all possibility.

Still, he tried not to let himself get his hopes up. It could still happen at any moment; he tried to convince himself it was a fluke. Garrick climbed the stairs and leaned against the door, resting his head on it. After an hour, he still didn't feel any pain. There was nothing – as if the moon weren't full outside. Slowly, he began to let himself hope. Another half hour later, he stood on legs shaking not with pain, but with excitement.

Garrick faced the door, exhaling deeply as he placed his hand on the knob. Stepping outside, he locked it behind him and left the house in a trance. For the first time in over a year, he looked up at a full moon and thought. Overwhelmed with emotions, he fell to his knees, beaming. Tears welled up in his eyes as he started laughing.

It was eleven o'clock at night, and the full moon illuminated the sky.

Garrick's pack – Aldric, Cailean, Brooke, and Hayden – were monsters, unable to control themselves, locked up in the basement of their alpha.

They were werewolves. And Garrick Elliott was a human.

Chapter 25

Eight months ago

Garrick ducked, avoiding Cailean's fist. He swung his elbow into Cailean's ribs, and then landed an uppercut on Cailean's jaw. Cailean took a few steps back, and Garrick tracked him, falling into his trap. Always one for theatrics, Cailean turned and ran a few steps up the wall, flipped and spun around to kick Garrick in the face.

Using his dramatic move against him, Garrick caught his leg and slammed him to the floor. Staying low, Cailean swept Garrick's legs out from under him, and Garrick plunged to the floor. Standing up, Cailean kicked Garrick in the ribs – sending him flying across the room and slamming into the wall on the other side.

Garrick struggled to regain the breath which had been knocked from him as Cailean closed the distance. Leaning against the wall, Garrick weaved as he dodged a few punches and countered with a side kick to Cailean's gut. As Cailean lurched forward, Garrick slammed his elbow down on the back of his head. Collapsing to the ground, Cailean landed on his forearms to protect his face. He rolled onto his back to prepare to stand, but Garrick fell on top of him, pinning him to the ground.

Cailean was able to get a leg free, and he placed the foot squarely on Garrick's chest. Before Garrick could respond, he was sent flying into the ceiling. On his way back down, Cailean punched up, landing a rising uppercut to his stomach.

Garrick stood, dizzily shaking off the attack. Catching his breath, he staggered back a few feet. Once he'd recovered, he stepped in and punched at Cailean's face. Cailean easily parried the blow and countered with a hit to Garrick's stomach. Garrick stepped back, covering as Cailean threw a flurry of attacks.

The second an opening appeared, Garrick kneed Cailean in the stomach, threw a hook punch at his jaw, and then launched him backward with a kick. Cailean stumbled, losing his balance, but didn't fall. Wiping a drop of blood from his nose, Cailean smiled.

Garrick ran forward to attack again, but Cailean deflected blow after blow. He finally caught one of Garrick's arms and spun him around, slamming him against the wall. Garrick tried to struggle, so Cailean turned and dropped Garrick to the ground, landing on him with his full weight. As Cailean landed, he drove a knee into Garrick's spine

Knowing he'd lost, Garrick tapped the ground.

Returning to his feet, Cailean reached down and offered Garrick a hand. As he accepted Cailean's help, he pondered the reasoning behind combat training. Maybe it was just because Cailean liked fighting. It didn't matter, though, because he was having fun – and if it ever came in handy, he'd be grateful.

"I'm impressed," Cailean offered. "You had me going for a minute there."

"Yeah, right," Garrick sighed. "Thanks for the confidence boost, though."

"Well, I figured you needed it after I beat you down so badly."

Garrick leaned back against the wall to recuperate as Cailean walked back to the center of the room to fight Chase. Chase would be able to hold his own much better than Garrick could, so at the very least, Garrick was going to watch an interesting fight.

"My turn?" Chase smirked.

"If you're desperate for a beating," Cailean taunted.

"It has been a while since I've given one of those," Chase replied, jokingly pensive. "I guess now's a good place to start."

"Keep that confidence," Cailean laughed before rushing in and landing a quick combination, catching Chase off guard. Garrick didn't want to admit it, but Cailean's arrogance was well- deserved. Even in their human forms, Cailean was a very skilled fighter. Since Aldric didn't train with them much, Cailean typically led their practices, and he hadn't lost a match to any of them yet. When Aldric did join them, though, he always won. No one beat Aldric.

Present
Night of the full moon

Garrick walked. Not away from, and not toward, anything at all. Entranced by the full moon, he just walked and admired the scenery. For the fifth time, he pinched himself, still trying to convince himself that he wasn't in the middle of a dream.

Although he was getting tired, Garrick didn't want to let the night end, so he avoided returning home and sleeping. The only negative thought he could conjure about that night was that he couldn't share it with Hayden. No one would understand what this meant to him more than her, so he couldn't wait to talk to her about it.

Absentmindedly, he pulled out his phone to call her. Of course, she was otherwise occupied at the moment. Shaking his head, he dropped his arms and held his phone at his side.

When he looked up, he realized he had wandered to the front lawn of a house he recognized. The house was two stories high, with a well-tended garden that he had somehow avoided trampling. The driveway was occupied by two cars, and the path to the door was decorated with colorful stones and plants. Garrick stood on the edge of the lush green grass of the lawn, directly beneath a window on the second story.

His subconscious had led him to his best friend's lawn. Without processing the time of night, or the fact that most people would be asleep – given the fact that there was school the next day – Garrick lifted his phone back up and called Tyler.

The full moon was the biggest hassle on a school night, because they typically had to wake up and rush to change and get to school, trying their best to look presentable. Especially on those days, though, they had to go in order to keep up appearances. There was no more obvious sign than all four of them missing school every morning after a full moon.

The phone rang a few times, and Garrick waited impatiently. The ringer was loud enough to awaken Tyler, and Garrick heard shuffling as his friend tried to grab the phone. There was a clattering as it fell to the ground, and he muttered something under his breath. Finally, Tyler opened the phone and stopped the ringing.

"Garrick Elliott," a voice answered groggily on the phone. Garrick tried to respond, but his voice caught in his throat. What was he going to say?

"Do you have any idea what time it is?" Tyler asked, whispering into his phone. The concern in his voice was so strong Garrick would almost call it fear. "Are you okay?"

"Yeah," Garrick managed to say. He kept his excitement buried as well as he could, but he was sure there was a twinge of it detectable in his response. "Yeah I'm fine."

"Then what's going on?" Tyler asked, keeping his voice low. "It's after midnight. Hank is asleep, and I... I don't want to wake him." Garrick had forgotten that Tyler's step-father worked early in the morning.

"Yeah, sorry," Garrick responded, shaking his head.

"Are you sure you're okay? You sound out of it."

"Look outside."

"Why?"

"Do it."

Garrick looked up, beaming, his eyes shining with the tears which were brewing. When the curtains opened, Tyler's expression by no means mirrored his own. Annoyed and tired, Tyler glared at Garrick, clearly upset that Garrick was causing such a commotion.

"Why is it that you have situated yourself upon my lawn? Do you intend to throw pebbles at my window now?" Tyler asked. Based on his verbiage, Garrick hoped that his friend's playful demeanor had returned. Sometimes, though, that was just the way Tyler spoke, and he did still sound annoyed.

"That could have worked," Garrick thought absently, unintentionally saying the words out loud. Tyler's lack of enthusiasm wasn't going to ruin his great mood. "Look up."

"I have no desire to continue watching you positioned outside of my window like a serial killer. Or a clown. You're like a creepy, serial killing clown right now, Garrick Elliott."

Garrick saw Tyler's curtains move to the sides again, and as soon as he saw Tyler's head, he pointed into the sky. Confused, Tyler looked at him questioningly, but Garrick could practically see gears turning behind his tired eyes. Following Garrick's pointing, Tyler finally looked up.

"I'm tired, I can't adequately process subtlety. What are you trying to say?" he sighed, still exasperated. "Wait, wait, wait!" His tone shifted to mere excitement. The first time he said the words, his voice raised, so he quickly compensated and whispered the subsequent words. Closed the curtains, he apparently changed in a matter of seconds – because he was wearing jeans, a T-shirt, and a hoodie by the time he opened his window and stepped out onto the ledge. In a smooth motion, Tyler reached for the branch outside his window and jumped to it, using it to swing himself down to the ground gracefully. There was not a doubt in Garrick's mind that it wasn't the first time Tyler had snuck out that way.

Garrick wasn't sure if he would have done that before Aldric's training, but he definitely would have hesitated if he'd tried – and there was no chance he would have been able to pull it off with as much finesse as his friend.

Tyler didn't say another word, he just stared at Garrick. After a moment, his gaze shifted to the full moon that hung in the sky above them, and back to Garrick. The two of them stood in silence for at least two minutes before Tyler finally asked a question.

"How?"

"I don't know," Garrick laughed, unable to contain his joy anymore.

"It worked? It worked!" Tyler gleefully exclaimed. Garrick wasn't sure it was actually Tyler's plan that had worked. It had probably helped, but he'd tried thinking of the scar, and that didn't feel like it was working – he almost changed anyway.

Even if it played a role, that couldn't be the only piece of the puzzle. It was something else, but he couldn't even begin to speculate what that was. It wasn't until he'd given up that the transformation had reversed. He decided just not to respond, letting Tyler think that he had found the cure for Garrick. What he didn't know wouldn't hurt him. Anyway, Garrick hadn't seen that expression of proud joy on his friend's face in a long time, and he didn't want to pointlessly take it away.

"In what state are the others?"

"They turned, they're back at home," Garrick answered. He knew Tyler would know what he meant, but on the off chance someone was listening, Garrick was trying to train himself to be careful with his word choice.

"Yet here you stand. You're human!"

"Yes, that I am."

"Incredible!" Tyler exclaimed, raising his voice. Nervously, he looked behind him, probably to verify that he hadn't awoken his parents. He turned back to Garrick and repeated himself, in a quieter tone.

"I just... I don't know. I didn't change."

"So, do you think this is indicative of a complete cure?"

"Yeah, I guess. I can't be positive until the next full moon. Maybe it was a fluke," he shrugged. Logically, it was a possibility that his level of control was only due to the extenuating circumstances, and it wouldn't repeat itself. Every cure so far had failed, and it was a dramatic evening, so he tried not to let himself hope the curse was gone. That was difficult, though, as he looked up at the moon, triumphant.

"Let's go," Tyler urged, pulling Garrick out of his depressing thoughts.

"Go where, exactly?" Garrick inquired.

"My best friend is human during a full moon for the first time in ages. I do not want to spend this momentous night cooped up inside like –"

"A human?" Garrick teased.

"Shut up. Let's go crash a party, I'm sure we can find one and I doubt a bouncer would be capable restraining you."

"In the middle of the week, we're going to go crash a party?"

"Point taken. To the arcade, then."

"They close at like eight."

"In that case, we will traipse around in the middle of the street and pretend we're enjoying ourselves! I will not allow you to kill the mood, Garrick Elliott."

"You're right," Garrick laughed, grateful to have such a persistent friend. Aimlessly, the two of them started walking into the night. For the first time since he'd been scratched, Garrick felt like everything was right again. Tomorrow, he could explain everything to the others and together, they may find a way to beat the curse. Despite the tragic events of that night, Garrick allowed himself to believe there was hope for his situation to improve.

Garrick felt like nothing in the world could go wrong.

Chapter 26

Six months ago

Holding Hayden's hand as they walked through the forest, Garrick admired the scenery. Since his childhood, he'd been drawn to nature – but he had fallen even more in love with it after the scratch. A part of him felt at home and at peace.

It had taken him time to overcome the anxiety he'd felt initially after the scratch, but when he did he began to appreciate the almost mystical calmness of the woods. He and Hayden spent a lot of their time walking around together, talking about everything and nothing at the same time. It had been their goal to never take the same path twice, but that was growing difficult due to the amount of time they spent perusing the area. Between the two of them, one could always recognize their surroundings.

Even so, there were always more secrets to be discovered within the foliage. That sense of exploration was another thing that made their walks one of Garrick's favorite ways to spend time with her. Regardless of how much he thought he knew, he could still be surprised.

"What's that?" Hayden asked, pointing to a couple of trees. Some of the low-hanging branches were coated in a thick layer of leaves, rendering everything behind them invisible. Beneath them, shrubs were clearly visible, so Garrick could only assume the branches only hid a mass of tangled brambles.

"It looks far too dense to get through," Garrick noted. Unintentionally, with that statement, he'd guaranteed that Hayden would find her way through the smallest opening to get behind the trees.

Garrick sighed as Hayden let go of his hand and tried pushing some of the branches to the sides. She stood still for a few minutes, assessing the situation and discerning the best plan of attack. Suddenly, she dropped to her knees and crawled through the shrubbery, disappearing from his sight.

"Garrick!" She called from the other side. "This is really beautiful."

"I'm sure it's more trees," Garrick called back, unwilling to crawl after her.

"Oh, come on, come check it out."

"Fine," he groaned with exaggerated annoyance.

"Careful," she warned. "I got cut up pretty bad by a couple of those branches."

During her journey through the brush, she hadn't made a single sound to indicate that she was hurt. Either she was just teasing Garrick or she had simply silently taken the pain. The latter wouldn't have surprised him, because her pain tolerance was impressive.

Dropping to his hands and knees, he crawled after Hayden. As he forced his way through the thorns and branches, Garrick was grateful that he'd worn a short-sleeve shirt. Only a few months ago, the opposite would have made sense. Now, though, it was easier for his arms to get cut up than his clothes, because his arms were much easier to repair.

Garrick had to push branches out of his way as he crawled, most of them leaving small scratches on his forearms.

Embarrassed by the fact that Hayden had made it through silently, Garrick tried to fight back any expression of pain – aside from one quick yelp when a branch he'd thought he'd passed swung back and cut his cheek.

Finally, he emerged on the other side of the thicket to find Hayden sitting on the ground, leaning her back against a small slope made by a dirt mound. As he sat next to her, she ducked her head under his arm and nuzzled her way into the small gap.

He smiled. When she did that, Garrick would keep his arm still rather than wrapping it around her, until she'd managed to move it enough to make room for herself. It wasn't that he didn't like holding her; it was just that he found it adorable to watch.

"This is amazing," Garrick admitted. They were surrounded by trees that were much closer than most of the others in the woods. There were dense bushes and shrubs encircling them on the ground, and the only entrance seemed to be the one they'd forged. Dense foliage surrounded them, blocking any light from the surrounding area. Minimal sunlight found its way through the canopy, leaving them with only a few scattered rays to appreciate their small discovery.

"Yeah," Hayden agreed. "And it's ours."

Present
One day after the full moon

"What time do you expect the others to awaken?" Tyler asked. Garrick had made it clear throughout the night that he'd wanted to be back by the time they woke up – mostly because he didn't want anyone worrying about him. After a full moon, though, they often just rose naturally, and they didn't have clocks around.

"I don't know," Garrick realized. Watching the sun rise, he added, "Probably soon."

"We should probably make our way to Aldric's house, then."

"I will," Garrick countered. "You should get home. Maybe you can get another hour of sleep before school, since I stole that from you."

"Nice try," Tyler laughed.

"No. No more involvement with werewolves, Tyler. The hunters already threatened to use you against me. You're putting yourself in danger every second you spend with the pack."

Darren's threat squirmed its way back into the front of Garrick's mind. Remembering Brooke's parents on the floor in her house – he had no doubt that they were capable of harming the people he loved. They hadn't even known about werewolves, they just got in the way when the hunters tried to kill their daughter. The hunters were monsters, and there would be no hesitation to use people as a means to get what they wanted.

Darren had threatened Garrick, claiming that he would go for his mother or Tyler if they couldn't get information out of him, and he hadn't provided information. After his mother had returned home from work, Garrick and Tyler had wandered by the house so he could listen for her heartbeat. At least for the night, she was safe. Tyler was obviously safe as well, but that wouldn't last long if he kept trying to get involved in a fight that was too far over his head.

"Seriously?" Tyler groaned. "After everything we've been through, you actually expect severing my ties with your world to provide an adequate form of protection? Let me ask you this: If I am already a target, am I safer fighting hunters alone or with the assistance of five werewolves?"

He was right. They were ready to go after Tyler, and as long as he was with the others, maybe he had a fighting chance. At least with Garrick, he'd have back-up, so he wasn't likely to be ambushed when he was alone. Still, Garrick couldn't decide the best course of action.

As he tried to think it through, Garrick realized that it wasn't his decision. Tyler was going to help him, no matter the cost. His best friend wouldn't give up on him just because Garrick told him he didn't want the help. Silently, he started walking toward Aldric's house, allowing Tyler to make his choice. Unsurprisingly, he followed.

"What do I tell them?" Garrick asked after a few seconds of silence.

"I'm sure you'll figure it out."

The sun rose over them as the pair walked toward the rest of Garrick's pack. Nerves were starting to force their way into Garrick's heart, and his ability to stay calm faded quickly. The closer he got to the house, the more his instincts screamed that something was wrong.

Hopeful, Garrick knocked on the door, hoping Linda would answer with a smile. She could lead him to the basement and he would see the other four as they woke up from the change, and his unsubstantiated fears would be quelled.

Instead, as he tapped on the door, it creaked open. Through the slight gap, a disconcerting metallic smell wafted toward Garrick's nose. The lock was broken, and the wood around it was splintered. Glancing back at Tyler, he held one hand toward him, warning him to stay back, while pushing the door open with the other.

There was blood – a lot of it. Judging by the sheer amount, there had clearly been more than one victim. There were a few bodies lying on the floor, and he recognized one from his altercation the night before. Fear both driving him forward and pulling him back, Garrick stepped into the house.

The basement door appeared intact, so Garrick pushed it open and climbed down the stairs. Hundreds of scenarios raced through his mind during the brief descent, and he didn't know what he hoped to find. Tyler was close at his heels, surveying the room.

At the bottom of the stairs, Garrick found absolutely nothing, but the blood smelled fresher. Examining the room, he finally saw a figure leaning against a wall in the corner. Linda had her hand pressed against a bleeding wound caused by an arrow in her shoulder. Garrick ran to her, dropping to his knees beside her. Listening intently, he heard a faint pulse.

"Tyler, call an ambulance," he called to his friend, who was still descending.

Garrick didn't hear any hesitation as his friend stopped walking and retrieved his phone, pressing a few buttons. Garrick carefully lifted Linda, cradling her as he walked outside. Though it was probably best not to move her, he also couldn't answer questions about the men in the living room.

They would have to find some explanation for an arrow in the woman's shoulder, but he hoped they wouldn't ask for too much detail. Aldric would know what to do – and he could provide a better explanation after everyone was safe. For now, Garrick just had to make sure Linda received the help she needed, then he had to find the others.

"Garrick," she coughed, her eyes fluttering open as she stared at nothing.

"What?" he asked, surprised to hear her voice.

"You have to run," she warned. "They'll come for you."

"No," he told her. "I'm going to get you help."

Straining to place her hand over his, she smiled sadly. As he set her in a seated position against the wall on the front porch, Tyler stepped out with the phone pressed against his ear, closing the door behind them. Without divulging information about hunters or werewolves, Tyler was trying to provide the best details he could as he walked toward the street.

"You can't," Linda forced the words out, barely audible over Tyler's conversation.

"Yes," Garrick argued. "I can. I don't care what happens; you are not going to die for our secret." The secret wasn't even her burden to bear. She was a human, even though she'd married a werewolf. Garrick wasn't going to let another human pay for loving someone that the hunters didn't think should exist.

As she faded out of consciousness once again, her eyes fell shut. In the distance, Garrick could hear the sirens, but he had no way of knowing how close they were. He glanced at Tyler, about to ask if the sirens were close enough for his friend to hear. Suddenly, a scream resonated above the other sounds, surprising Garrick. His head jolted up as his eyes darted around the street, trying to find the source of the noise.

"Did you hear that?" He asked Tyler when he noticed that his friend wasn't reacting.

"Yeah, it's the ambulance. It's getting close," he answered.

He hadn't heard it. Suddenly, it clicked in Garrick's head. It wasn't a scream – it was a call for help. It was a howl. Hoping to pinpoint the source of the sound, Garrick listened again, but no other sound came. The voice had been masculine, but it also sounded filled with a thinly concealed sense of fear. Knowing Aldric had too much pride to show any type of fear, that only left one possibility.

"Cailean," Garrick muttered. His head was spinning, searching for the best course of action. There was no way he could make it to Cailean. Even if he started running at that moment, it would be too late – let alone if he waited for the ambulance.

"What?" Tyler questioned.

"You stay here," he ignored his friend's question. He'd forgotten that he had help, but when Tyler reminded him, the solution seemed apparent. "Wait for the ambulance. I have to go find the others."

Tyler looked torn for a minute, as if he wanted to argue. Obviously, he wanted to help Garrick, and it was clear that the idea of his friend handling the search alone didn't sit well with him. Admittedly, it was a huge risk to be alone at that point, but there wasn't any other option – so Tyler nodded in agreement.

As he stood, Garrick sprinted in the direction of the scream. Instead of sticking to the streets, he tore through bushes and jumped fences in his way. He wasn't sure how he was so confident that he was going the right way – it was almost as if he were supernaturally drawn to his friend – as if the wolf could remember exactly where the scream had come from.

Garrick jumped into someone's backyard then quickly scaled the wall on the other side that separated them from the street. When he dropped to the ground, he unconsciously skidded to a halt. When he looked to his left, he saw Cailean lying on the ground – a hunter with his sword raised standing over him. By his elevated breathing and increased heart rate, along with the apparent wounds on his body, Garrick could clearly see that Cailean was losing the fight.

Covered in cuts and with blood pouring from a few stab wounds, it was a wonder Cailean had been able to produce such a powerful call. He looked like he had already given up as the man brought the sword down toward him. Garrick was on the hunter tackling him to the ground with the sword only about an inch from Cailean's skull. The momentum sent the sword flying, clattering to the ground about a foot from the altercation.

Pinning the hunter to the ground, Garrick threw two punches to his face. Blocking his face with one hand, the hunter used the other to punch Garrick's ribs. There wasn't enough momentum to do any real damage, but it was enough to surprise Garrick – and the hunter used that to buck Garrick off of him, rolling over. Garrick fell to the floor and the hunter pushed away, retrieving his sword. Quickly, he brought the blade down toward Garrick. Following his first instinct, Garrick raised his arm to block his face instead of rolling away.

The sword cut deep into Garrick's arm, and when the hunter pulled the blade away, Garrick could see his ulna through the deep gash. Adrenaline helped to dull the pain, but it didn't eradicate it, and Garrick gritted his teeth, trying to remain focused.

Cailean stood shakily and closed the small distance between himself and the hunter. Placing his foot on the hunter's back, Cailean knocked the man to the ground and Garrick rolled on top of the man. He punched the hunter anywhere he could find an opening. He tried to reposition the sword in his hand so he could stab Garrick, but it was large and awkward to maneuver in the tight space.

Garrick grabbed his arm, snapping the bone with ease and dropping the blade to the ground. Garrick tried to follow up with a flurry of punches, but the man kicked him off. Rolling over his back shoulder, he jumped to his feet. Garrick stood as well, lifting his hands to cover his face and backing away.

Cailean stood a few feet away. There didn't appear to be new blood coming from the stab wounds, and the cuts were slowly closing. Garrick could hear his breathing slowly settling back into a normal rhythm.

Garrick ducked as the man swung the sword with his good arm, countering with a hook to the ribs. Stumbling backward, the man fell into another kick from Cailean that knocked him to the ground. The sword dropped, and Cailean quickly picked it up.

The man stood and threw a punch at Garrick, but he weaved backward. He avoided a few more punches from the only operable arm and blocked a kick. The hunter threw another punch, and Garrick dodged to the side, throwing a hook to the hunter's exposed jaw. The impact spun the hunter toward Cailean, who drove the sword forward and stabbed the man's heart. Cailean released the sword as the man fell dead between them.

"What's going on?" Garrick asked, fighting through the agony that seared in waves through his arm. As the adrenaline faded from his bloodstream, it was replaced by pain. He bit his teeth down, willing the effects of the silver to end quickly.

"I don't know," Cailean replied pensively. "For the first time, I remember changing back. We didn't sleep – we just changed back knowing we had to run. Finally, we found somewhere we thought was safe. We found some of our old suitcases and put on some dirty clothes.

"But the hunters were after us. They chased us into the woods. Dad told us all to run. I tried to get away, but this one caught me by surprise."

"What about the others? Did they make it out?"

"I don't know! Honestly, Garrick, I panicked. I thought they all ran."

"Aldric would never run."

"I know," Cailean agreed, looking down at the ground. "I should have fought, I know. But it's hopeless, Garrick. There are just so many of them."

Cailean's eyes welled up with tears. Garrick had never seen him cry before, but he could relate to what was going on in his head. Terrified and guilty, Cailean was trapped in a cycle of questioning his own actions. Garrick himself felt that terrible mixture of emotions on more than one occasion. Being the best fighter and the only one always ready to spar, Cailean seemed like he'd be the most prepared for a fight, but even he wasn't. As soon as the hunters actually showed up, he had run. He was probably imagining the worst and blaming himself, even though any rational person would have been afraid.

"Nothing is hopeless. Let's find them. Just smell for them, your senses are still stronger, from the change."

"Aren't yours, too?"

"I'm not sure. Just do it, we have to find them."

Garrick knew that on some level, his senses were stronger as well, but he didn't want to try to test the limits of it. It was a fine line which he wasn't sure how to maneuver yet, so it was easier just to assign the task to Cailean. Garrick also knew that if Cailean were similar to him in any way, it would be better to have a task.

Cailean choked the tears down, looking up and smelling the air, trying to lock onto a scent. Garrick could tell from the look in his eyes that he wasn't able to find a trace. Given their distance from the woods, it made sense if none of them had gone the same direction.

"Alright," Garrick thought aloud. "We'll start heading to the woods. Maybe we'll find them as we get closer."

Cailean looked hesitant to go back in that direction, but he nodded. Garrick started running toward the woods. After a brief second of uncertainty, Cailean followed.

Garrick was the first to break the tree line. It was clear that the others were close when they got near. The clashing of fists and grunts exchanged during a fight were audible, even from their distance. Instinctively, Garrick wanted to call for Hayden, but he couldn't risk any small element of surprise he had.

When they crossed into the woods, he slowed to a walk, realizing that they shouldn't be rushing into the fight. The woods were probably teeming with hunters, and they didn't want to alert any more of them, so stealth was their best option.

He held his hand back, signaling to Cailean that he should slow down. Both of them ducked down behind a nearby tree. Garrick focused on listening for any movement in the trees around them.

One of the hunters was walking slowly, quietly searching the area with nearly silent footsteps. Garrick could hear his heart pounding, though, and the displacement of the air as he swept his bow left to right. On Garrick's signal, Cailean circled around him.

Garrick snuck up to one side of the hunter, and Cailean on the other. As a distraction, Garrick threw a rock against a tree. It worked like a charm, and the hunter aimed his bow at the sound. Cailean snuck out of the trees behind him and snapped his neck.

Garrick and Cailean progressed slowly, trying to sneak their way toward the others. Garrick was the first to see the battle, but Cailean wasn't far behind him. There were hunters in the trees all around them, shooting arrows for support as the hunters in closer range fought with swords.

Without discussing the plan, Garrick and Cailean silently ran in opposite directions. Each of them killed one of the hunters before they were caught. Garrick was ambushed, though, by two hunters with silver knives, and he stumbled back into the clearing with the others. Cailean was next to join them, along with five hunters aiming crossbows at him.

They all shot at once, and Aldric pushed Garrick and Cailean to the ground with one hand each. He covered Hayden and Brooke with his own body. One of the bolts from the crossbows plunged into each leg and three hit his chest.

Shouting out a battle cry, he ran forward as they reloaded, pulling the weapons out of his chest. Garrick ran after him as soon as he'd regained his footing, but Aldric had a big head-start. Trying to protect his father, Cailean ran alongside Garrick.

Using the momentum he'd gathered, Aldric stabbed one of the quarrels from his chest into the heart of one of the hunters. Three of the others started running backward, trying to reload their weapons simultaneously. The fourth drove a silver dagger into Aldric's stomach. Despite the wound, Aldric lifted the man and threw him against a tree, breaking his back.

The other three hunters shot their weapons. One arrow hit Aldric in the shoulder. The other hit him as he tried to maintain balance, refusing to fall. The third arrow missed entirely, and Garrick had to dodge past it as he ran toward the brawl. Aldric fell to the ground, and Garrick couldn't hear him breathing.

"Father!" Cailean screamed. He dropped to his knees beside him, apparently too focused to even consider the hunters anymore. Hayden and Brooke, who had been stunned into paralysis at first, were moving to help Garrick.

As he reached the first hunter, Garrick kicked and shattered his ribs. Before he even hit the ground, Garrick had ripped the weapon from the hands of another. He threw the weapon into the trees, but the hunter retrieved a silver blade from a holster on his side and drove it into Garrick's stomach.

Garrick punched his jaw, shattering the bone. The hunter collapsed, hitting his head on a rock with enough force to end his life. Blood pouring from his stomach, Garrick stumbled forward, trying to keep fighting, but the other hunter kicked his chest, knocking him to the ground as he aimed a crossbow at his head. Before he could pull the trigger, he inexplicably dropped to the ground. Tyler stood behind him, pulling his own knife out of the man's back. If he hadn't killed the hunter, with the placement of the blade he'd permanently paralyzed him. Tyler offered Garrick a hand and pulled him to his feet.

"Why are you here?" Garrick choked.

"I had a feeling you might need me."

"It's dangerous," Garrick coughed. He wanted to be upset, but his friend had just saved his life, so he couldn't keep a harsh tone. "Thanks."

Tyler nodded, but his expression suddenly went dark. Catching his eye, Garrick knew exactly where he was staring. He himself turned and saw Hayden running toward him. Beyond that, Cailean and Brooke were kneeling near Aldric.

Hayden grabbed Garrick and pulled him in for a hug, pressing his body tightly against hers. He avoided making a joke about how she was hurting him due to the situation, so he just ignored the pain as she compressed his wound.

"I'm so glad you're okay," she cried, pulling back to look at him.

"Yeah, it's good to see you too," he replied, distracted.

"What happened to you?" she inquired.

"That doesn't matter right now," he dismissed. "We have to get Aldric out of here."

"Garrick," she stopped him as he tried to walk away, tears filling her eyes as she shook her head.

"No," Garrick refused to accept her implication. She placed a hand on his shoulder, but he shrugged it off and ran to Aldric, falling to his knees at his alpha's side. Hayden and Tyler walked melancholically to join them.

"I'm sorry," Aldric managed to say. Garrick could hear his heartbeat, but it was the faintest he'd ever heard. He honestly couldn't believe that Aldric was still alive with such a slow beat. Between the silver halting his healing and the sheer number of mortal wounds hemorrhaging blood, Aldric was fading fast.

"Don't," Garrick interrupted. "We're going to help you. The silver will wear off, and you'll heal. We'll get you home and we'll figure this all out."

"No," Aldric argued. Garrick knew that it was hopeless to make those promises. Transported mentally to what happened with Chase, Garrick found himself in an all-too-familiar situation. He had tried to lie to him – to tell him it was going to be okay. He caught himself making the same empty promises to his alpha as he lay dying in front of them.

Cailean tried to say something, but his chest heaved, and tears flowed from his eyes, limiting any speech. He held his father's hand as he looked down at the man who for years had been their symbol of strength and power.

"You all have to run," Aldric pressed.

"No," Cailean cried. "This is my fault. If I'd been here... If I hadn't run..."

"You can't blame yourself," Aldric cut him off. "It was my call – I wanted you to escape to safety. I still do."

Each of Aldric's words was becoming more labored and more difficult to understand. Garrick knew he didn't have much time left. He was only hanging on to deliver whatever message it was that he had for them.

"They sent everything they have. In this town and any of the neighboring ones. I don't know why, but Darren, their interim leader, decided that this is an all or nothing attack. There are too many of them, and they won't stop until you're all dead. You have to leave town."

"I'm so sorry," Garrick whispered, unable to ignore the same thoughts Cailean had expressed. If only he'd been there, maybe it would have been different. Taking a deep breath, he stood, placing a hand on Brooke's shoulder to indicate that she should follow. Aldric was an alpha to all of them, but he was only a father to one, and his final moments should be spent with his son.

The others seemed to catch on to what he was thinking, and they all stepped away to join him one by one. Brooke ran a hand along Cailean's shoulder as she left; attempting to comfort him, even though everyone knew it was futile.

"Father," Cailean cried, tears apparent in his shaky voice. Garrick walked to the other side of the clearing, trying to avoid eavesdropping and give them their space – although it was difficult with his hearing.

"Son, listen to me," Aldric said. "I know it's hard, but you have to leave."

"No. This is only because I ran. I swear to you, Dad, I will never run away again. I won't abandon my pack."

"What happened isn't your fault. But if you stay, what happens next will be. Go."

Aldric's hand moved slowly, closing around his son's, handing him something. He struggled to move his head closer to his son, whispering under his breath. Garrick couldn't make out the words he whispered, which was probably for the best.

"Please, Cailean," Aldric continued, loud enough to be heard by them all. "Don't let this be a waste. I need you to be safe."

Cailean didn't respond – he couldn't. His head fell forward as he sobbed, one hand tightly clasped around his father's and the other holding onto whatever Aldric had given him. Once again, Aldric leaned his head up, using the last of his strength to be closer to his son.

"They'll all be here. They'll surround you. Run," Aldric ordered. Nothing was said for almost a full minute, but he finally forced his last words out of his mouth.

"I love you, Cailean. You're the best son I could have asked for."

The last labored breath passed Aldric Phoenix's lips.

Garrick stood with the others. He knew they couldn't wait long before they all had to leave, but he wanted to give Cailean as much time as he could possibly could to grieve. After waiting a while, though, it was getting too long, and they had to go before more hunters found them.

He walked back to Cailean, trying to be supportive. Squatting down next to his friend, he placed a hand on Cailean's shoulder. Cailean tried to shake him off, but he couldn't muster enough force to actually make Garrick let go. He gave up and just accepted it.

"We have to go, Cailean," Garrick whispered apologetically.

"I can't leave him."

"We don't have a choice."

Cailean didn't say anything. Garrick could relate, at least on some level, to how he felt. Garrick felt similarly about Aldric. Garrick's father had left when he was a child. He grew up with just a mother, and he'd never had a problem with that. When he was scratched, though, and taken into this new family, Aldric had filled that role. He was the closest thing Garrick had ever had to a father. Now, he lay lifeless in front of them. Still, he wasn't going to try to relate to Cailean or compare. There was no way he could possibly comprehend what his friend was going through. All he could do was be there for him.

Cailean nodded, slowly bringing his head up and opening his eyes to look at his father one last time. He released his hand, setting it on the ground next to him. Cailean breathed a shaky breath as he lifted his hand and closed his father's eyes for the last time.

Chapter 27

Four months ago

Garrick opened the door to his house. All of the lights were off. To the best of his knowledge, his mom didn't have work, but it was possible she'd been called in at the last minute. He flipped on the light to the living room.

Part of him expected people to jump out at him, but he was also slightly relieved when no one did. Closing and locking the door, he wandered over to the couch and sat down.

"Surprise," he heard as Hayden hopped over the couch and sat next to him. Startled, Garrick jumped and turned to face her. He hated being startled, but he assumed that hadn't been her intention, so he tried to let it go. It was a few seconds before he'd relaxed to speak.

"Hey," he greeted. "I thought you were busy tonight."

"I have been very busy, thank you," she said, feigning offense. "How else could I have set this up?" As she asked the question, all of the lights in the halls and the kitchen flipped on simultaneously. People jumped out from every opening and shouted 'surprise.' If he had done anything at all besides go straight to the couch, he would have seen someone and ruined her surprise. He wasn't sure if he was that predictable or if she just knew him too well.

"Happy birthday, babe," Hayden smiled, giving him a quick kiss. There were decorations all over the kitchen, but the living room was completely bare. Everyone walked into the living room, talking over each other. Tyler found him first, pulling him in for a hug. Chase pulled him away from Tyler and hugged him next. Finally, Brooke and then his mother, and Garrick almost got dizzy from all of the spinning around to hug new people. Aldric and Cailean were there too, but they settled for handshakes. Mrs. Phoenix was also there, and she wrapped Garrick in an embrace. Garrick was glad Hayden had invited her – it would have felt wrong for the rest of her family to be there without her. Hayden knew that Garrick wasn't a fan of parties, but this was perfect. A small gathering of everyone important to him was all he could have asked for.

After embarrassingly forcing everyone to sing "Happy Birthday," Garrick's mom cut a cake. Though he felt that eighteen was a little old for the tradition, he wasn't about to turn down cake.

His phone vibrated, and he pulled it out to check it. Everyone he talked to was already in that room, so he had no idea who would be texting him.

"We didn't do presents. I know they make you feel awkward. But I did get you something." Hayden. When he looked up at her, she gave him a flirty wink.

She walked around and wrapped her arm around him as Garrick's mother handed people cake. Most of them were werewolves, so they didn't have to be concerned about their bodies, making sugary deserts an easy sell. The party wasn't very eventful – everyone just talked and visited. Listening to the pack try to tiptoe around the topic of lycanthropy was both hilarious and painful, though.

Tyler started digging through the cabinets. Having spent enough time at Garrick's house, he quickly found a glass and a spoon and started exaggeratedly tapping them together.

He started chanting "Speech," until most of the others joined in.

"Ugh, really?" Garrick asked.

With that, the chanting just grew louder. Cailean, who hadn't participated in the chant at first, joined in when he saw that it made Garrick uncomfortable.

"Alright, Alright. I guess I just want to say thanks to everyone here. Mom, you're always there for me, of course. Since Dad left, you've never stopped working, and you've managed to provide for me and still have time to raise me – and you've done an amazing job. I mean, look how great I turned out. I love you.

"Tyler, Chase, you guys are my best friends. I feel like I can share anything with you, and you've been there for me through everything – all the ups and downs – especially over this past year. It's been crazy, but thanks to you, there wasn't one thing I had to face alone.

"Brooke, you deserve a special thanks. Aside from being there for me, you're there for Hayden. Any time she has to rant about the latest stupid thing I've done, there you are. You're the queen of damage control, and I have no doubt you've saved my relationship.

"Cailean, you're like a brother to me. You've been the strangest person for me to get to know. I don't like you most of the time, but I love you. I know that you'll always have my back, no matter what comes our way.

"Aldric and Linda, you two are like parents to me. I went from only having one for most of my life to having three, and it's absolutely amazing. I know Aldric will always have some fatherly advice for anything I'm going through that I feel awkward mentioning to my mom.

"And my beautiful girlfriend, Hayden Faye. I know this whole thing came out of that perfect mind of yours, so thank you. I know that you have had to put up with a lot from me. I've changed more than I can explain over the time that I've known you, and you've stuck by me and helped me through all of it. Even when I wasn't understanding toward you, you never gave up. I love you. And I don't deserve you.

"Honestly, I don't deserve any of you. But you've become a family to me – and you're the best one I could have asked for. I don't know what I'd do without each and every one of you in my life. I love you guys."

Present
One day after the full moon

Garrick walked back to the others with Cailean. Cailean had his head downcast, staring at the herb his father had placed in his hand. When he got close, Brooke wrapped him in an embrace and he weakly hugged her back.

It was a tough moment for all of them, and Garrick didn't want to rush it, but they were quickly running out of time – and they had to get as far away as possible, and fast. Footsteps were already resonating through the woods. He led the others to the cover of some trees, where they at least weren't out in the open in case arrows started to fly in their general direction.

"We have to go," he commanded.

They were too late. An arrow flew past him, and he assumed it had missed intentionally. All five of them dropped to the ground, covering their heads.

"You all need to run," Garrick ordered, looking up at them.

"No way," Cailean argued, "I am not running again. My father gave me wolfsbane. I can use it to buy you all some time to escape."

"The pack needs you," Garrick countered. "You're the new alpha."

"Garrick Elliott," a familiar voice taunted melodically, "let's have a chat."

Garrick crawled into view, giving the others time to protest or point out that it was a horrible idea. Although he knew they wouldn't, he hoped they'd take that opportunity to run.

"I'm here," Garrick replied as he rose to his feet. "I know what this is about. I'm the one that killed your sister. Leave the others out of your vendetta."

"Oh, it's quite the opposite," Darren patronized, waving his hand in a performative gesture. "I'm actually going to let you live as a show of good faith. You see, we hunt werewolves because they are monsters."

"Who decides who the monsters are? It seems to me like it takes a heinous brute to kill innocent people just because they won't tell you where their children are hiding."

"No!" Darren screamed, inexplicably passionate in proving himself. Nothing he said could justify his deeds. "Monsters kill for revenge. For anger. For fun. We hunt those monsters, and we kill only because it is our duty. We kill only when we must."

"You're sick," Garrick muttered.

"And you're not!" Darren replied with a short laugh. "My men saw you last night. You were a human. I don't know how you did it, but you found a cure. You don't have to die for them. You aren't one of them anymore. For Samantha's memory, because I know how much she liked you, and because I am not bound by duty, I have chosen to grant you your life. Walk away, Garrick."

"And leave my friends – my *family* – behind? No. See, you don't understand, Darren. Whatever you think happened, you're wrong. I am one of them. And if you want to get to my pack, you're going to have to get through me."

Garrick could hear the others standing and moving behind him. He motioned for them all to run, but not a single one heeded his advice. Instead, they all walked and stood by his side.

"Okay," Darren shrugged dramatically. "You had your chance."

Moving faster than Garrick could have expected, he drew his bow and shot an arrow toward Garrick's nose.

Garrick blinked his eyes and suddenly he was back in the most brightly lit world he'd ever seen. All of the colors just seemed purer and more vibrant – the green of the leaves and the brown of the trunk, the blue of the sky and the dark soil beneath him.

All of the hunters had vanished, and even his friends were gone, leaving him alone in the silence. He recognized the woods around him, but not from the waking world. This was the distorted version of the woods he'd seen in his dreams.

However, nothing had ever seemed so refined. It was as if the fog that clouded his mind whenever he thought of that place had been lifted, and he was finally seeing it in its perfection. The thought crossed his mind that he had already died. Maybe the arrow had hit its mark, and his death had been quick and painless.

Unsure of what to expect, Garrick glanced around the woods. Part of him expected to find the wolf come strolling through the trees, but another part was expecting to see an angel or a white light to lead him away from that world.

Garrick heard a low panting from behind a tree to his left. At first, he took a step back when he saw the wolf. He had come to accept that what he saw was his wolf form, but it still startled him when he saw it. It stayed a few feet back, but Garrick slowly inched toward it. Even though Garrick had been much closer to it before, he had never felt so scared.

Maybe he was just afraid of the animal because the dark colors of its fur appeared even more menacing in contrast to the purity of the world that surrounded him. Maybe it was just the feelings that he'd felt from the arrow were lingering. He couldn't tell how long ago that had been. The concept of time didn't exist where he was. It could have been hours, or maybe years, since he'd stood against those hunters with his friends.

The wolf cowered near some of the trees, but Garrick reached his hand out to it and dropped to one knee, opening both of his palms, careful not to look into the animal's eyes. It hesitantly walked toward him.

"It's okay," he soothed. "It's okay."

Finally, the wolf was close enough to cautiously sniff his hand. A sense of recognition seemed to wash over the animal. The wolf stood, lifting its head so it was eye level with Garrick. He stared, just for a moment, into those eyes. How could something so graceful, with such pure and innocent eyes, be so evil?

But it wasn't evil. It just wanted to survive. He could see that now. It was a large, powerful creature, but it was still a scared animal on the inside. There was just as much fear in the wolf's eyes as there was in Garrick's heart. Returning his gaze, the wolf settled down. Its ears fell back as it relaxed. Garrick's pulse quickened as the wolf lifted its front paw, bringing it toward him. As gently as a three-hundred-pound wolf could, it placed its paw on his knee.

"I don't know what to do," Garrick said. Whether or not the wolf could understand him, he was aware that he was technically talking to himself. "Aldric is dead. Am I just supposed to run? I mean, that's what he gave his life for – but then I would be letting the people who murdered him get away. I may not be strong enough to do anything, but I have to try, right?"

The wolf barked. Not angrily, and not even loud enough to scare Garrick. It seemed like it was simply telling him to stop babbling. It was answering him. It growled, and Garrick knew the anger was directed not at him, but at the hunters.

"You're right."

He knew he was probably crazy. Seeing things, first off, but then talking to them. That didn't stop him, though. This was the first time that he and the wolf were fighting for the same cause; the first time he sincerely believed they were one.

"I need your help. I can't do this alone. I know that I've pushed you down and locked you away. I thought you were a monster." That earned a whimper from his companion. "But you're not. No more than I am. I know now that I need you."

Slowly and cautiously, Garrick raised his trembling hand. The wolf tensed up for a moment, but it didn't move away. Garrick brought the hand over to his shirt and lifted the sleeve, revealing his scar. The wolf looked more at ease, just like it had last time he'd seen the scar. As he reached for the wolf, it didn't flinch. He gently caressed the three lines on the wolf's front leg softly. Garrick brought his hand up, resting it on the back of the wolf's head as it leaned toward him, grazing its snout against his nose.

Pulling his head back, Garrick stood to his feet. The creature lowered its head a bit, allowing Garrick to rest his hand comfortably atop its head. The wolf inched itself closer to him and nuzzled up to his leg. It looked up at him and its eyes were the beautiful color of the sky and licked his hand.

Redirecting its gaze to look ahead, the wolf growled. Garrick wasn't sure what it was seeing at first, but it quickly dawned on him; the wolf wasn't looking at anything that was in front of it. It was thinking about the same thing he was.

"I need you," he told his counterpart. "Together, we can do this."

On pure instinct, Garrick's hand shot up and caught the arrow that was only a few inches from his face. Without taking time to process what was happening, he snapped it in half and dropped it to the ground.

"Tyler," he directed without turning from the stunned hunters. "Get them out of here. You're the only one with a weapon; I need you to make sure all of you get somewhere safe. Hayden, Brooke, Cailean, defend him. He's still human. Protect each other."

"I am going to change," Cailean argued. "I'll fight them off. You run too, Garrick. They killed my father. I won't let them get away with that."

"Don't be stupid," Brooke challenged. "Not even a wolf can take down twenty men."

She was right. There had to be at least twenty of them now, coming out of all of the trees in front of them. Each of them aimed their bows, waiting for one of the wolves to make the first move. Garrick's display had caught them all off guard enough to buy them time for their conversation, but he knew it wouldn't be long before the hunters launched an all-out attack. He couldn't catch twenty arrows.

"Aldric died for us. His sacrifice is worthless if we don't just run," she continued.

"They'll catch us if we all run," Garrick replied. "I'm going to buy you all time."

"If you fight," Hayden told him, "Then I fight. I'm going to be right by your side."

They all started to speak at once, arguing over whether or not they should run. Some of the hunters looked almost amused, but a few others looked scared as they trained their bows on the pack, waiting for any of them to make a slight move.

They were all only a few inches from the trees, so in one coordinated moment, they could avoid all of the arrows. The time that it took them to reload would give Cailean enough time to change and the others enough time to get a head start.

"That's enough!" Garrick growled. There was more power and conviction in his voice than ever before, and he could feel something within himself changing. "You all need to go, now. I'm going to stay and fight."

"Garrick, please, don't. You'll die," Hayden cried.

"You won't. I won't let that happen."

"I won't run away from you."

"I wasn't asking."

"We'll be fine," Cailean added. "I have this." Gripping it tightly in his hand, he lifted the wolfsbane so that the others could see it. "Garrick and I will each use half."

They were all still hesitant, but Garrick, feeling a power surge through his body, locked eyes with Hayden for a moment, and any defiance she showed in them slowly melted away. She knew that she couldn't argue with him. Brooke, tears streaming down her face, grabbed Hayden's arm and dragged her away. It wasn't long before Hayden's feet started to move with Brooke's and they were both running. Tyler was the last to leave, breaking his gaze into Garrick's blue eyes as he ran to defend Hayden and Brooke.

"Well," Darren commanded, waving his arm at the hunters, "kill them."

A barrage of arrows flew toward the fleeing trio, but Aldric had taught them to use the trees as cover. Brooke was shot in her shoulder and Hayden reached out her arm to block an arrow flying toward Tyler's back, so it lodged into her arm instead.

Those wounds didn't slow either of them down, though, and they ran full speed into the forest. Garrick and Cailean, who'd ducked just in case some of the arrows had come their way, stood back to their feet and turned away from the others, facing the hunters.

"Cailean, this is your last chance to run." Garrick warned him.

"I can't. Not anymore."

"Fine. Then we fight together. Let's finish this."

"My father told me not to use this unless we really had to. He said that if I had to, I would be able to control myself and fight for us. If any of us could, I would be able to. I think he was wrong," Cailean explained, looking down at the wolfsbane

"No, he wasn't," Garrick retorted, placing his hands on Cailean's shoulders and looking him in the eyes. "You can do this."

"If any of us can control this long enough to hold them off, Garrick, it's you. You need to use this. I'll keep them back long enough for you to change, and you finish this. Avenge my father and protect our friends. Our family."

Cailean held his hand out and opened his palm. Garrick placed his own hand on Cailean's fingers and pushed them closed.

"That isn't how this is going to happen. We aren't losing anyone else today. You use this. I don't need it."

"Garrick," Cailean started to argue, but Garrick cut him off.

"We don't have time. Hurry up and change. I'll stand in front of you. I need you to trust me."

Cailean placed the wolfsbane in his mouth and fell to the ground. It didn't take long to reload a bow, so the hunters were ready to shoot, but Garrick stood in front of his friend to make sure none of them got a good shot. Cailean's bones shattered and reformed, his body changing shape rapidly

"Oh, so we're already employing our trump card?" Darren teased. "Okay, I can play dirty too."

"Playing dirty was when you chased my unarmed friends out here with weapons. No, this is evening the playing field," Garrick growled, surprising even himself. As he spoke, fangs grew in his mouth. He watched his nails grow as he took on the claws of the wolf.

Every hunter's bow lowered, along with their jaws, as they watched Garrick's muscles tense and relax, growing until his shirt tore. They watched in horror as the fur coated his arms, and as his legs started to stretch. His jeans tore, first at the knees, and then at a few various places along his lower legs, but they weren't torn to shreds. Garrick howled, preparing for a battle. Regaining strength and completely transformed, Cailean strode to Garrick's side.

Darren's eyes briefly widened, but he shrugged off Garrick's new transformation. Even as Garrick towered over him, standing on two feet, a mixture of human and werewolf that he hadn't thought possible, Darren was calm. At least, he was able to act calm.

"You want to hear something funny, Garrick? Did you wonder where I went after I helped take your friend? You see, there was another werewolf yesterday. When you boldly waltzed to my sister's wake, Aldric came to save you. Well, it turns out I'm not as fast as I'd thought," he grimaced, almost amused, as he lifted the leg of his pants to reveal a scar. "No, I was scratched. So, I had to come up with a plan. I had to kill all of you, because you'd already killed me."

With a flourish, Darren pulled a syringe out of his back pocket, holding it on display for them. "So last night I prepared this – a solution of my own blood mixed with wolfsbane."

"That will kill you," Garrick assessed, his voice a guttural mixture of man and beast. The shock in his voice was still evident, though. The wolfsbane flowing through his bloodstream would cause a rapid and powerful transformation, but as it circulated, it was bound to have a detrimental effect on the body.

"Yes, that is true," he replied, laughing as he pointed at Garrick. "But not until I kill each and every one of you. I'll kill six werewolves today."

"You're insane."

"Maybe," he accepted as he injected himself with the tainted blood. "But I'm also going to be more powerful than you could dream of."

He finished his transformation within seconds, and Garrick knew he wouldn't have a chance to rush forward and stop him. If he tried, the hunters – who had recovered their composure and aimed their bows at him and Cailean – would attack, hindering him enough to allow Darren to transform. They'd turned his own plan against him. As Darren started circling them, Cailean growled at him, trying to block him from Garrick.

Garrick nodded, motioning for Cailean to attack Darren. Every arrow was released, but Garrick deflected them with his arms and his tail. Garrick jumped forward, tearing the nearest hunter apart before the others could react. Two drew swords, running at him, and he stepped to the side as they both swung. He kicked one forward, pushing him onto the other's sword, and then threw them both against a tree, audibly cracking the skull of the one in the back.

Cailean dove at Darren, but he missed. Darren swiped his claws and cut into Cailean's side, but he just retaliated by slashing at Darren's gut. Darren jumped back, both of them bleeding slightly before their wounds healed up. Darren seemed to heal slightly faster.

Garrick retrieved a sword which one of the hunters had dropped and threw it at another, who had an arrow aimed at him. As he fell to the ground, he accidentally released the arrow and it embedded itself in another hunter's chest. Garrick barreled toward another and bit down on his stomach. Ripping his head away, he spit out the flesh and muscle he tore off.

Cailean jumped on Darren and they rolled to the floor. Cailean bit into Darren's neck, refusing to let go. Darren scratched at Cailean, but his attacks didn't hit. Finally, he scratched across Cailean's eye. With a yelp, Cailean released Darren, turning his face away. By the time his face had healed, Darren had rammed his head into Cailean's side, knocking him down.

Garrick growled again, and the remaining twelve hunters were visibly terrified, but they didn't back down. Three drew silver daggers and the others were drawing their bows back again. Distracted by dodging a swipe of a dagger, Garrick wasn't able to dodge the two arrows that landed in his back. The arrows didn't pierce through his entire body, but they were embedded so deep that they didn't leave room for him to grab and pull them back out.

Cailean squirmed out of Darren's hold and he jumped back to his feet. The two wolves glared at each other, circling around for a few moments. Darren lunged forward, but Cailean dodged to the side, then lunged in and bit Darren's neck again.

Garrick turned on the closest hunter behind him, hefted him into the air, and slammed him back to the ground. A silver dagger slashed across his arm, but the pain was minimal. He wondered if, since silver was the wolf's weakness, it didn't affect him now that they had truly become one being – or if it was just the adrenaline.

Darren swung his entire body, and Cailean went flying away, into a tree, pulling off a piece of flesh with him. The wound was substantial, but by the time Cailean was back up and running at Darren, it had healed. Cailean barked at Darren, who quickly stepped forward and bit down on Cailean's neck. Cailean tried to break out, yelping in pain. Darren used his full strength to shove Cailean, while still biting onto his neck, and drive him to the ground.

Garrick slashed his claws at one hunter's throat, and he dropped to the ground, holding his neck in a futile attempt to stop the bleeding. Kicking another one, he launched him into another hunter. The force sent them both tumbling into a tree hitting their heads as they rolled on the ground. The pain from the arrows was getting worse, and he knew that he had to remove them. He rammed his back into a tree, driving the arrows further into his body. They pierced through his chest, so he just pulled them forward. The wounds healed in seconds.

Cailean's whimpering slowly died down, but he managed to land a great swipe on Darren's face in a last desperate attempt to break free. As Darren let go, Cailean swiped at him again, leaving deep gashes on Darren's face, and a third slash wounded the wolf's front leg. Cailean stepped back, allowing himself to heal before he dove forward, pinning Darren.

Two of the hunters tried to run, but Garrick couldn't risk them hurting the others so he caught them, dragged them back by their feet, and slit their throats. He heard the distortion of air behind him, so he turned quickly to see an arrow. In one smooth motion, he caught it and redirected it, stabbing behind him into the heart of a hunter charging at him with a sword.

Darren scratched at Cailean with his back paws, cutting into both of Cailean's hind legs. He collapsed on top of Darren, who was able to reverse the position to pin Cailean.

Garrick pounced at another hunter, killing him before he had a moment to react. Then he stabbed another close hunter in the back with his claws. He lifted the man before dropping him to the ground, dead. Scared, one of them tried to escape, so Garrick slashed his ribs. If he'd survived, he may have become a wolf, but the wound was too deep, and he bled out.

Cailean managed to wiggle free and climb to his feet. He and Darren circled around each other for a moment, once again allowing their wounds to fully heal. The only evidence of them was the blood that matted their fur. Cailean and Darren simultaneously stood on their hind legs, throwing their front paws on the other. Cailean was able to bite down on Darren's neck, but Darren was the one to throw Cailean down, forcing him to let go. In turn, Darren clenched his jaw around Cailean's neck.

The last two hunters managed to break the tree line, but Garrick tracked them down by scent. The first hadn't gone more than twenty feet before Garrick tackled him. Prone on the ground, Garrick slashed the back of his neck. The other was further into the woods, so Garrick had to run at full speed for a few seconds before catching him. When he did, he slashed the man's legs. The man tried to crawl away, but Garrick drove his foot down on the man's back, fragmenting his spine. That just left Darren. He bolted back to the clearing.

Garrick never even questioned whether he was doing the right thing. He hated the violence, but he couldn't let any of them escape. They would just come back with help. Or worse, they'd run into the others and catch them off guard. No, the only way that Garrick could be sure that his friends were safe was to dispose of them all. As horrible of an option as that was, it was the best one.

After Darren was sufficiently sure that most of the life had drained out of Cailean, he threw the wolf against a tree.

Preparing to cut into Cailean's throat for the killing blow, Darren strode toward the defeated wolf. Cailean was already all but dead, but Darren hadn't been happy to just let the life drain out of his opponent as he bit down on his neck. Even in his wolf form, he wanted the last attack to be something more theatrical. He dove at Cailean, his claws ready to cut through Cailean's throat.

Garrick grabbed Darren's hind leg, stopping him in mid-air and slamming him into the ground. With a kick to the side, Garrick sent Darren flying into a tree. Garrick and Cailean stood side by side, prepared to finish the fight. Cailean was barely able to stand, but he was gaining strength by the second.

Suddenly, a scream erupted through the trees.

"Brooke!" Garrick, the only one who could speak, or even understand English, said. He locked eyes with Cailean, giving him his command through their unspoken language. He nodded in the direction of the scream, and Cailean darted off after it. Garrick had to trust Cailean to defend the others while he dealt with Darren.

Darren, fully healed, started to circle around Garrick, sizing him up. Darren dove, but Garrick kicked his chin, flipping the wolf backward. Darren stood shakily, and Garrick closed the distance before he'd fully recovered. Swiping his claws, Garrick left deep wounds in Darren's side. Darren clamped his jaw on Garrick's arm and refused to let go.

Garrick slammed his arm against a tree, and Darren's jaw opened as he dropped to the ground. Garrick kicked the fallen werewolf, which slammed him against the tree once again, even harder this time. As the tree cracked, Garrick watched it to determine if it would collapse.

His brief moment of distraction was enough for Darren to pounce, knocking him to the ground. Darren bit down on Garrick's neck. Fighting the pain, Garrick punched the wolf in the nose, causing it to yelp loudly and stumble backward.

Lifting the wolf, he threw it into that same tree, finally breaking through the trunk. The trunk split unevenly, cutting Darren as he fell with the tree.

Darren stumbled up, charging at Garrick again. Dodging a swipe, Garrick stepped to the side, but the wolf had used it as a distraction. It clamped its jaw around Garrick's ankle. Garrick fell to the ground, and the wolf tore at his other ankle, rendering him unable to walk.

The wolf tried to bite Garrick, but he grabbed either side of its head and held it back. Digging his thumbs into its eyes, Garrick was able to throw the wolf back. It yelped in pain, stumbling backward, temporarily blinded. In the time that he'd taken to get the wolf off him, he'd healed a bit and his ankles were strong enough to stand on. Darren stood again and dove at Garrick, but he stepped to the side and kicked the wolf in the gut, knocking it back.

Garrick got on his knees and pinned the wolf down on its side. He raised his claws high and brought them down on the wolf's neck. That was a blow which would have killed anything, even a werewolf, but the wolfsbane running through Darren's blood, the very poison which would kill him soon, was better than any adrenaline. The wound was gone in seconds, and he was able to escape Garrick's hold, fully recovered.

Darren swiped at Garrick's leg, dropping him to his knees. It bit down on his neck again, and Garrick was unable to escape it this time. He reached his arms around the wolf's neck, holding it as tightly as he could, cutting off the air flow. He felt himself getting weaker, but he twisted his arms with all the strength he could muster.

He heard the bones break, and Darren's head went limp.

Garrick let him go, and the body fell to the floor. Breathing heavily, he watched as the bones repaired themselves, and the wolf started to twitch again. Darren managed to return to his feet after being dealt two blows which should have ended his life.

He lunged at Garrick once again, and Garrick jumped backward. Footsteps were approaching him from behind. Whatever had scared Hayden and Brooke, it must have made them turn around, losing their sense of direction. They were running right back to him – and right back to Darren. He had to end it quickly.

He raised his knee, which slammed into Darren's jaw, and knocked the wolf to the floor. He grabbed its neck in his massive hands once again and broke the bones, hoping to buy a few seconds. Frantically, he searched for one of the hunters silver swords as he listened to the bones once again reform themselves.

As Garrick walked to Darren's body, he retracted his claws and fangs. The eyes of the others were fixed on him. He felt his body returning to its normal size as he walked toward the fast-healing werewolf. His jeans were torn and ragged, and his shirt was completely decimated.

Garrick stood over the wolf's body, watching it twitch once again. He raised the sword high and plunged it into Darren's neck. The sounds of his healing were brought to a halt. Garrick stood over the corpse, breathing heavily for a few seconds, before the body started to spasm. Sighing deeply, Garrick stepped back and opened his hands, his claws growing again.

Garrick could only assume the wolfsbane and silver were counteracting, but he had to be cautious. Darren's face slowly fell back to normal, but not entirely. It was still somewhat inhuman, and the fangs were there. One arm started to look human, but never completed the transformation, and pieces of his stomach were the lighter color of his human skin.

Garrick stood, arms hanging at his side, his left foot closer to Darren's corpse than his right, as if he wasn't sure whether he should approach it. Cailean walked up, still in his wolf form, and wrapped his tail around Garrick as they stood in front of what could only be described as the corpse of a half-human monster.

Hayden stepped up, slowly and cautiously, standing on the left side of Garrick. She stood close to him for a few moments until he reached for her hand, locked it in his, and then she took one step closer. Brooke stood on the right side of Cailean, her hand on his head. Tyler came up behind Garrick and placed his hand on his shoulder.

Hayden leaned against Garrick as he wrapped his arm around her and pulled her closer. Garrick knew he could never turn his back on these people. He could never leave them. This was his pack.

Garrick sat in the hospital room with the rest of his pack. Linda was in the bed, the heart monitor beeping slowly. The doctors had removed any remnants of the arrows and stitched the wound, and they had said she'd be fine. However they, along with the police, had plenty of questions about what had happened.

Garrick was wearing his jacket, which had been in the car, over his torn shirt. His jeans were still torn and ragged, but, oddly enough, he looked the most presentable. The others were wearing clothes that were coated in dirt and blood, even though they'd brushed as much of it off as possible. They'd rushed to the hospital so fast that Cailean had almost forgotten to put his clothes back on after changing back – no one wanted to lose another family member.

"I don't know," Garrick answered again. "I found her in the house like that."

"With three dead men," the police officer retorted, unconvinced.

"Sir, it's been a long day," Garrick complained.

"I'm sure it has, but I need some answers here."

"Here are your answers," Cailean spat. He had been sitting silently next to his mother, but he looked up and glared at the police officer. "Some men broke into my house and they shot my mother. My father defended our family. They took him and murdered him. I don't know anything more. Now get out of here."

"I'm sorry, son, I know this is tough," the officer defended.

"I am not your son," Cailean growled, a passionate flame burning in his eyes. "I want you to leave this room now and give my mother some peace."

The officer was silent for a moment, but he folded up his notepad, nodded, and walked out of the room. No one else said anything for a few more minutes.

"You guys can stay at my place," Garrick offered. "Until something else works out."

Both of their houses were crime scenes, and Brooke was technically an orphan. She would be 18 in a week, though, and she and Cailean had discussed asking Linda when she awoke if Brooke could move in with them. Cailean's mother was a very understanding woman, and Garrick knew everything would work out. He was just grateful that she was going to make a full recovery.

"Thanks," Brooke acknowledged. Cailean didn't respond verbally, but he nodded in appreciation. Garrick stood and headed to the door. It was as good a time as any to get home and explain to her where he'd been. The school had notified her that he'd been absent, and she had left texts wondering where he was. Hayden and Tyler left with them, each having some answers of their own to give their parents. Garrick couldn't complain, though. He hadn't been the one to lose the most over the past few days, and he still had a mother to whom he had to answer.

"I appreciate the ride," Tyler solemnly thanked Garrick as he climbed out of the car. Hayden and Garrick lived closer to the hospital, so they were just able to walk. Tyler didn't live as close, though, so they'd gone to Garrick's house to pick up his car and drive Tyler home.

"No problem," Garrick replied, equally somber. Garrick tried to find a way to phrase all of the words that he wanted to say. Tyler was the best friend anyone could ask for, and Garrick couldn't be more thankful for him, but he also felt terrible for bringing him into that situation.

"Thanks," he finally said as Tyler was about to close the door. "For everything. You really saved us back there."

"What are friends for?"

"I wish I'd never involved you in all of this, Tyler. I really do. But I can't think of a better person to have gone through it with. You were there for us when we needed you."

"Really," Tyler smiled, "don't mention it."

Garrick nodded. He would let it rest, though he felt he should be thanking Tyler every day for the rest of his life. Without him, he didn't know if he'd have made it, and Hayden and Brooke would have had a much harder time too. Tyler smiled as he turned but hesitated before closing the door. Spinning back, he peeked his head into the car again.

"So, tangent," Tyler started awkwardly.

"What's up?" Garrick questioned.

"Last night I was so excited about your news that I forgot to mention something. Kayla came by my house yesterday. We had an extensive conversation which culminated in her kissing me."

Garrick sighed. He wanted to be happy for his friend, but they'd been broken up for a while, and he had thought it would stick that time. All she ever brought him was more pain. Still, he pasted on a fake smile and tried to congratulate Tyler.

"Although I am aware of the fraudulence, I am grateful for your feigned gaiety."

"I don't know those words," Garrick joked. Tyler laughed before continuing his monologue.

"I know you aren't fond of her, and I can't deny that I struggled with the frequency that she pointed out cute guys, but I realized how fleeting life can be, and how much it means to spend it with the people you love."

"You love her?"

"Yeah, I think I do."

"Say no more. If she's important to you, I can be civil." He smiled. The two of them had had plenty of deep and emotional conversations; that wasn't uncomfortable for them. What was always weird, though, was finding a way to end them.

"Yeah, okay," Tyler accepted, "thanks."

They both laughed as Tyler closed the door and walked back inside.

"Mom," Garrick called as he walked into the house. She ran up and hugged him, squeezing him tightly enough to restrict his breathing. A mixture of anger, relief, and worry was painted on her face as she pulled away and looked at him, but the expression settled into sadness.

"I'm so sorry," she told him, but he had no idea for what. There was no trace of the anger he'd expected. "Why didn't you answer my calls? I was so worried, Garrick."

"I'm sorry," he choked. He wanted to tell her the entire truth, but he knew that wasn't a possibility. The hunters were gone, at least for a while, so it was probably safe to tell her everything, but he wasn't willing to take the risk. Instead, he just decided to tell her as much as he could without putting her in danger or revealing the truth about werewolves to her.

"Something bad happened," he told her. "Last night."

"What's wrong, Garrick? Are you okay?"

"Yeah, Mom, I'm fine."

"What happened last night?"

"Mom, please. Let me talk. Okay?"

"Sorry," she responded with a nod. She still had her hands on his arms, and he gently moved them. His eyes already filling with tears, he led her to the living room and sat on the couch.

"Some men broke into Brooke's house. I don't know what they wanted, but her dad tried to fight them off. They killed him. Her mom, too, as she ran away."

His mom's eyes fell with a knowing sadness. It was no surprise she'd already heard of the attack – which probably accounted for her being so scared about his location.

"They didn't find whatever they wanted," he continued. "I don't know who they were, or what they wanted, but they knew them, because they went to Cailean's house next. They shot Mrs. Phoenix. Aldric fought them off, but... He was shot. He's dead. Mrs. Phoenix is in the hospital. She's going to be fine, but she'll be in there for a while. I was there with Cailean this morning."

"I'm so sorry, Garrick," she sympathized, placing a hand on his shoulder.

Finally, the bottled-up tears poured down his face, and he couldn't respond. He'd tried to be the strong one for the others, and he'd managed to keep his emotions hidden, but he had no more reason to. His mom wrapped her arms around him as he cried.

Garrick lay in his bed with Hayden. Wanting to spend the night with him after everything they'd been through, she'd snuck out of her house for the night. Even in the darkness and complete silence, having her next to him was comforting, and it was possibly the only thing that was keeping him sane.

Cailean and Brooke were sleeping in the living room. When Garrick had tried to bring the idea up to his mother, she'd suggested taking them in.

"Garrick," Hayden whispered. He didn't respond for a moment, just letting the beauty of her voice resonate in his head.

"Yeah," he finally replied.

"I love you."

He pulled her closer to him, relieved to have her in his arms. More than once that day he'd thought he could lose her. When she and Brooke had run, there had been other hunters stationed in the woods. Garrick had taken out the main force, but there were four more wandering around in case they ran.

They had ambushed them and stabbed both Hayden and Brooke with silver.

Tyler had taken two of them out, but the third one had cut his arm. They'd knocked him down. Cailean was barely able to get there in time. If he'd been a few seconds later, or if Tyler hadn't been there, things would have ended differently. She'd told him the story on the walk home from the hospital and he'd panicked as if it were happening in the present.

Wishing it were possible for her to get closer than she already was, he held her in a tight embrace. He turned and kissed her.

"I love you too," he told her.

They'd been through a lot, but looking at her in the faint light shining in through his window, he knew that he could take on the world. Even with all the pain he'd been through, he wouldn't change a thing about his life.

He was Garrick Elliott. He had the best friends in the world; a group who would support him through anything. He had a girlfriend that he couldn't possibly adore any more.

For the first time in a long time, he was proud of who he was. As he lay in that bed with Hayden, he was thankful for the scratch which had changed his life. He was Garrick Elliott, and he was a werewolf.

Epilogue

Garrick watched with renewed hope as the moon rose into the sky. Though he'd controlled it once, Garrick wasn't completely sure he wouldn't become a wolf – and he knew his friends would. Inside, though, he knew that he had won the fight, and the wolf was no longer vying for supremacy. Garrick believed that he'd be able to teach his pack to control it as well, but there hadn't been time yet. So as he led his friends to the woods, all of them walking in a group. Though Aldric wasn't there, his guidance still resonated in him as Garrick scanned the area, carefully looking and listening for any sign of humanity.

"Here," Garrick directed. The pack spread out, preparing for the moon to reach its zenith. Preparing to, for the first time, fight the change. Garrick watched the silvery orb crawl through the sky with a sense of mysticism, admiring its shine.

Cailean was the first to transform. Based on his own method for regaining control from the wolf, Garrick assumed being a purebred would only make it more difficult for his friend. Cailean fell to the ground, gasping as his bones, slowly and audibly, fractured. His teeth grew to twice their normal size as his mouth, along with the rest of his face, elongated to accommodate them. His claws broke from his nails, and his palms grew, encompassing his fingers until his hands had become paws.

"There has to be an easier way to do this," Brooke choked through clenched teeth. The words were obviously agonizing to force out. Garrick searched his mind for advice to give them. How was he supposed to teach them how to do something that he wasn't sure how he did himself? Garrick turned his gaze toward her, preparing words of encouragement, but Brooke was already on all fours – and twice her normal size – by the time he could even begin to speak.

What was he supposed to tell them? That he had mystical conversations with the animal side of himself? When he zoned out, he went to a magical forest where he saw his canine counterpart and conversed with it, and that they somehow understood each other?

Hayden fumbled to him, placing her hand on his shoulder. He hugged her close, and she fell into his arms. Her ears grew to a point, and her nails sharpened into claws.

"It's okay," Garrick comforted.

"No, I have to try," she argued through the tears that streamed down her face. Garrick squatted down, bringing her with him. Gently, he lifted her hand from his shoulder and placed it on the ground.

"Let go, Hayden. I'll think of a better way to help all of you. This won't work."

"I'm sorry," she cried. He lifted her face and kissed her. Weakly, she kissed him back. When he stepped away, he saw her left shoulder expand, and the other one quickly followed. Her knees changed to support her new legs as her appendages became those of a wolf. Garrick affectionately pet her head as the others walked up to him, a sense of confusion in his eyes. Maybe the wolf versions of his friends were unsure of what he was – or at least wondering why he didn't look like they did.

"Alright," he muttered to himself, "it looks like I'm spending the night keeping them at bay." Garrick took a deep breath as he took his shirt off, tossing it to the ground. For the first time, he actually didn't mind allowing himself to change because he knew that he was in control.

Not willing to ruin every pair he had, he'd also removed his jeans. He'd learned from his last transformation that they wouldn't be destroyed, like any clothes the others wore, but he didn't want to tear holes into every article of clothing that he owned.

He watched as his nails grew and sharpened. Still human in shape, his hands grew slightly larger than normal and became coated in fur. He watched as the muscles in his arms began to bulge out, just before his arms themselves grew to accommodate them. Hairs started to grow, coating his arms in a thick layer of fur. His chest expanded. His stomach, the first part of his body which wasn't completely coated in fur, was also the part which showed that his skin itself darkened and stretched with the change. His feet maintained their shape, mostly, but their size did change to support his new, bulkier form. In the same fashion as his arms, his legs grew, muscles and tendons showing themselves clearly before the entirety of the leg was coated in fur. His canines grew in his mouth and his ears came to a point.

"That was my favorite pair of boxers," he muttered under his breath, looking at the scraps around him. He kicked his jeans toward the suitcases the others had brought.

His pack gathered around him, waiting for him to move again. Garrick raised his head, facing the sky, and howled.

Made in the USA
Middletown, DE
08 June 2019